COMING HOME

The Route Home: Book 1

JENNIFER CROSSWHITE

Praise for Jennifer Crosswhite

What Readers Are Saying…

"Definitely on my to-buy list now. I can't wait for more!" Hawaiibooklover, Amazon reviewer

"I look forward to reading more of [her] books." Amazon reviewer

"If you enjoy a good, clean love story then give this novella a try. You will not be disappointed." Danielle, Amazon reviewer

Other books by Jennifer Crosswhite

The Route Home series

Be Mine, prequel novella
Coming Home, book 1
The Road Home, book 2
Finally Home, book 3

Contemporary romance

The Inn at Cherry Blossom Lane

Hometown Heroes series, writing as JL Crosswhite

Promise Me, prequel novella
Protective Custody, book 1
Flash Point, book 2
Special Assignment, book 3

In the Shadow series, writing as JL Crosswhite

Off the Map, book 1
Out of Range, book 2
Over Her Head, book 3

Eat the Elephant: How to Write (and Finish!) Your Book One Bite at a Time, writing as Jen Crosswhite

Devotional

Worthy to Write: Blank pages tying your stomach in knots? 30 prayers to tackle that fear!

Published by Tandem Services Press

Post Office Box 220

Yucaipa, California 92399

www.TandemServicesInk.com

Ebook ISBN 978-0-9978802-1-2

Print ISBN 978-0-9978802-0-5

Cover photo credit: Lightstock and Depositphoto

To my grandma, Marian Crosswhite, who read this from the beginning.
And to English teachers everywhere who inspire the love to write, like my high school teacher, Mrs. Strickland, did for me.

Prologue

R*eedsville, Oregon ~ 1881*

"Watch out!"

Furious, Thomas Wilson hauled the careless man back. He'd come within an inch of being whacked by a whip saw. Thomas released him with a glare.

The man's gaze drifted to the saw. A near miss. Eyes round, he stumbled away across the uneven ground.

Thomas inwardly groaned and ran his hand through his hair. This new man was particularly careless. Maybe he should fire him before he got himself killed. The safety of their men had always been a priority for Thomas and his partner Seth, which made them different from other outfits. He held his beliefs private, but he reckoned men were more productive when you treated them like men instead of animals. Of course with some outfits using steam engines and locomotives for logging, there might not be logging much longer--for men or beasts.

Normally being out among the trees was the best part of Thomas's day. The scent of pine and fresh wood chips with the forest floor crisp under his boots beat doing paperwork at his desk any day. Seth caught that chore today. Though now he wondered who had the better deal.

Thomas figured he and Seth wouldn't have to try to make a success at this business much longer. In fact, what might be the perfect opportunity to get out of logging all together lay in a letter on his desk. On top of that, once his little sister, Becca, graduated from the University down in Salem and got herself married off, Thomas wouldn't have her to worry about. Then whatever he turned his hand to wouldn't matter so much.

It'd just been him and Becca for the past ten years, and he'd done a fair job of caring for her. Hopefully, that time was drawing to a close. She could be a handful at times, and he'd be more than happy to turn her over to the right man who could handle her.

Raised voices carried through the air, yanking him out of his thoughts. He jerked his head up, and he listened to the commotion that brewed between his men. He jogged over.

"This has conk rot," a logger yelled from the top of a tree. "It's no good. Check the others."

Thomas groaned again. This day was souring fast, like left-out milk. Seth definitely had the better draw today.

"Look out!"

He spun just in time to see a log break free of its chains and barrel downhill. The new man stood dead center in the path of the runaway log, back turned.

Sprinting at full speed, Thomas plowed into him, tumbling him out of the way. Sprawled on the ground. Tried to scramble to his feet. Something grabbed at him. He looked down to see his leg tangled in tree branches the men hadn't yet cleared.

Panic shot through him. He kicked. And kicked again. The branches cinched around his legs like a noose. He'd need to be cut out.

But there wasn't time.

The roar in his ears told him it was too late.

Dear God, Becca . . . was his last thought before all went black.

Chapter One

BECCA WILSON RISKED A PEEK out the stagecoach window. Mere inches of rocky dirt road separated them from the gorge below. Rocks kicked up by the horses' hooves ricocheted down the precipice and banged into the brush and few scraggly trees that clung to the cliffs. Her heart pounded at the sight. Exhilaration mingled with fear, bringing back memories.

Their stagecoach driver, Josh, did have a taste for adventure. With the breakneck way he drove down the mountain, she had always suspected he enjoyed scaring the passengers. That hadn't changed in four years.

Another jostle and a gasp escaped from her white-knuckled seat mate. "This is the worst part," the woman whispered, eyes squeezed shut.

Becca kept her face composed, thinking if Josh knew, he would be amused.

"It'll get better in a few minutes and then we're there."

Becca wasn't sure if the woman was saying that to reassure herself or Becca.

The woman's eyes widened, and she turned to Becca. "Ever been to Reedsville?"

"Yes. It's my hometown."

The woman narrowed her eyes and leaned even closer, if that were possible. Her hat poked Becca's, creating a bit of a barrier, but not for her scent. Her lilac *eau de toilette* competed with the dust as to which could be more overpowering. Becca stifled a cough, and reached into her reticule for her handkerchief.

The woman's pale gray eyes seemed to search Becca's face, their harrowing trip down the mountain apparently forgotten. "I don't believe I've seen you before. My daughter and grandchildren live here. She followed her man out here for the logging." She gestured out the window then quickly grasped the seat again.

Most likely the woman hadn't seen Becca because Becca hadn't been back. Until now. When Thomas was—she couldn't even think the word. *Gone.* Guilt rose from the pit of her stomach. She held her handkerchief to her lips briefly.

"I've been away at school for some time." She glanced out the window. *Thomas.* It wasn't like she hadn't seen him in four years. When the logging business slowed in the winter, he'd often come to spend several weeks with her.

But she hadn't come home once.

Instead Thomas had come to her, taking care of her like he always had. A memory flashed like heat lightning. They were in the kitchen. He held a wet cloth stinging against the wounded skin of her knee. She was ten, too old to need him to tend to her scrapes. Too old to be getting scrapes. Or crying over them.

But Ma wasn't around anymore to remind her to be a lady. Which hurt more than the scrape did. The tears had started that day and wouldn't stop. He didn't scold her or tell her she was too old to cry. He just held her until the tears were gone.

Becca blinked away the moisture in her eyes. Too much dust. The jarring ride smoothed out, and she eased her death grip on the leather seat that she hadn't even been aware of. If Josh saw her holding on for dear life like the other passengers she'd never hear the end of it.

The stage slowed as it emerged from its downward plunge to a flat road.

"What'd I tell you?"

Becca turned. "Beg your pardon?"

Smiling, the lady reached over and patted Becca's knee. This time the lilacs were victorious. Surely that's what was making her eyes water. "See? We're nearly there." She extended her hand to Becca. "I'm Margaret Poole."

"Rebecca Wilson." She shook Mrs. Poole's hand then looked past her. They had rounded the final bend, and the town of Reedsville, Oregon came into view. Main Street dashed by in a blur then the stagecoach was pulling up in front of a white, two-story, clapboard building. Straining to stop, leather and wood groaned as the motion pitched the passengers forward one final time.

The sensation she was still moving kept Becca pressed into her seat. The dust settled around them. And on them. The jacket on her blue traveling suit wore a layer of dust. She brushed at it, but only succeeded in dirtying her gloves and handkerchief. Her first trip home in four years and heaven only knew how she looked. She'd hoped to make a better impression. The university should have given her an air of culture and refinement, but inside she didn't feel much different than the girl who'd left here a lifetime ago.

Sighing, she tucked her handkerchief away and leaned forward to look outside. Most way stations were run-down shacks, but Becca knew Maggie Kincaid prided herself on keeping her boardinghouse and way station looking like a home. While it had never actually been Becca's home, it was the closest thing she had left.

Dratted dust! Becca blinked rapidly to clear her eyes.

The boardinghouse hadn't changed much. A porch, with a swing at one end wrapped itself around the front of the house. Riotous wildflowers bloomed in stark contrast to the white-washed building.

For a moment, the past overlaid the present, and Becca stood on those very steps, leaving instead of arriving. Her cheeks burned even now with the memory of what she had done. She could only hope Seth had long forgotten her foolishness, chalking it up to childishness.

She leaned forward in her seat to see who was waiting for the stage. She hoped Seth wasn't there.

Mrs. Poole pulled on Becca's shoulder. "That's my Sue Ann with the two little ones. They live in town and her husband comes home from the camp on weekends. He doesn't want his family around those rough men."

She followed Mrs. Poole's gaze to a young woman about Becca's age, one tow-headed baby on her hip and one held by the hand. And by the straining of her shirtwaist, it appeared as if another was on the way. The young mother looked as worn out as Becca felt. Having her mother come help out must be a relief. Becca watched the tableau a moment more before shifting her eyes.

Next to Mrs. Poole's Sue Ann stood Maggie, her coppery hair as nearly as bright as the wildflowers besieging the house. Her kind smile, open and sweet like the little Johnny jump-ups along the walkway, enhanced her motherly appearance. Of course Maggie would be here to meet her.

Becca's heart felt like warm candle wax, and she struggled to keep tears in check when all she wanted to do was throw herself in Maggie's arms and sob. But she couldn't, so she settled for recalling the books she still needed to read for this semester. Logic was always a good antidote to tears.

The stagecoach door opened. Josh helped the other passengers disembark then nodded to Becca and smiled. He was about her brother's age, but he'd always appeared younger.

Becca half stood, her stiff muscles threatening to drop her back in her seat. Her bustled skirt, while not as full as some, still didn't allow much freedom of movement. Hiding her grimace, she edged forward and climbed down. Josh held her steady for a moment until she balanced herself—which was embarrassing—then he gave her hand a quick squeeze before releasing her. She smiled at him, astonished at how good it felt to be home.

Mrs. Poole said something about coming to call and hurried over to her daughter.

Before Becca could respond, Maggie flew over and pulled her into her arms. "Oh, my girl! We've missed you so much!"

Emotion filled Becca's heart and spilled out her eyes—no logic could stop them—as Maggie's plump, motherly body pressed against her own, the smell of Maggie's homemade soap surrounding her. Home. Maggie felt like home. She didn't want to leave Maggie's embrace.

She gave Maggie one last squeeze and straightened. Between the dust and the traveling and her brother's death . . . well, it was no wonder she wasn't quite herself. Still it wouldn't do for them to see her fall apart. She was a modern, educated woman, able to handle any circumstance with aplomb. A good self-talking-to always worked.

Maggie held Becca back from her, inspecting her from head to toe. "Well you're not a girl anymore, that's certain. Such a stylish young lady!" She rested her arm around Becca's shoulders and led her up the porch steps. "I'm truly glad you're back, although I wish it were under better circumstances. How long can you stay? Are you back for good?"

Becca looked up as she climbed the last step, listening to the questions pummeling her like the dust on the stagecoach. But the front door opening caught her attention. There, coming out, was Seth. His face, bronzed by the sun, had more prominent cheekbones and a stronger jaw line than she remembered. But he still had those bright blue eyes and dark brown hair that fell boyishly across his forehead.

As if he could read her thoughts, he pushed the hair back from his brow.

"Well, I'm—" What had Maggie asked? She froze; every thought flew out her brain.

Maggie glanced up. “Oh, Seth, you made it.”

“I got away from the logging camp for awhile.” Uncertainty, confusion, and then surprise progressed across his face while he glanced between the women. “Becca, it’s good to see you again. How are you?”

His deep voice washed over her, unburying old memories. She almost gasped with the intensity. She closed her eyes for a moment, recalling her own talking to. Forcing herself to look at Seth, she willed away the uncomfortable warmth flooding her cheeks and gave him a polite smile.

“I’m well. It’s good to be back.” As she said the words, she realized it was true. The dread at returning to her hometown still remained—certainly she had reason for that—but it did feel like —well, home. There was some comfort in that. But mostly the comfort came from knowing she wouldn’t be here long. She could manage for a short period of time.

“You’re staying for supper, Seth.” Maggie clearly made a statement, not a request. She shot a look over her shoulder to where Josh had just finished unloading the luggage. “You, too, Josh.”

“Soon as I get the horses and stage put away,” Josh replied, climbing back in the driver’s seat.

Seth backed through the door, holding it open as Maggie ushered Becca inside.

Please say no. She’d forgotten how blue his eyes were. Sitting across the supper table from him was going to strain every bit of her manners, given the way she’d left him.

“I’d love to. Never miss a chance to have one of your meals, Maggie.”

Becca stifled a sigh. This day was going to be longer than she thought.

SETH SPLASHED water on his face. Was he dreaming? The beautiful young woman Maggie brought into her house bore very little resemblance to the awkward, gangly girl who'd left.

When Becca stepped off the stage, her clothes were dusty and wrinkled, and there was a hardness to the light in her green eyes. But the sunlight hit her hair, making it gleam like polished gold. Fascinated by her smooth skin and full lips, he hadn't even recognized her! The old tintype photograph on Thomas's desk at the logging camp didn't do her justice. What happened to the girl he'd once called his Li'l Sis?

When they were much younger, she'd beg to go on adventures with Thomas and him, and usually he was the one to give in. Without siblings or a mother, Seth found Becca to be somewhere between a curiosity and a nuisance when he wanted to go fish with Thomas. Braids flying, freckles dotting her nose and cheeks, all elbows and knees, determined to keep up with the boys.

Running the linen cloth over his face, he grinned remembering Becca throwing herself in his arms, whispering she loved him. She'd spun around and jumped on the stage without hearing his reply. He'd repeated that scene many times in his mind since she left, touched she'd thought of him as another big brother.

He sobered at the thought. It was his fault her real brother was dead. Up until he left the logging camp to meet her stage he'd thought Thomas's death was an accident. But Owen Taylor had stopped him, coming out of the logging camp office carrying a pile of chains.

"Hey, Seth, I've been thinking about… well, you know, the accident. And I remembered one fellow saying how eerie it was the way the chain broke. I didn't think much of it at the time—you know how riled up about ghosts and such some men can be—but I went to the tool barn to see if I could find the chain.

Sure enough, it was sittin' there in a pile." He held out a rust-flecked chain and pointed to a link. "Look at this."

Seth lifted his hat and resettled it on his head. He didn't have time for this if he was going to meet Becca's stage. He should have left before now. The chain in Taylor's hands looked like one of many. He eyed the links. What made this one so special?

Then he spotted it. The one link, pulled open like an ugly mouth.

His stomach dropped, his head spun, and bile rose in his throat. He swallowed hard. It was his fault. He'd made the mistake and that chain, that link, proved it.

Grabbing Owen by the shoulder, he shoved him back into the office. "Leave that here. Don't put it back in the barn, you hear me? And make sure nothing happens to it."

Owen nodded slowly, his eyes round with surprise. "Sure, Boss. Anything you want." He tossed the chain into the corner behind Seth's desk, the clanking links sounding oddly like a death rattle.

Seth gave him a terse nod and strode out the door, rounding the building and heading for the outhouse. He stared at it for a moment before hauling back and slamming his fist into the door. The door bounced front and back a few times before giving a groan and swinging lazily from one hinge. He'd have to fix that tomorrow.

His fist stung at the memory. He glanced at the red scraped knuckles. Though injuries weren't uncommon to him, he'd keep his hand out of Maggie's sight or she'd want to doctor it. And he didn't want to explain how he got it.

He tossed the towel on the hook. Her brother was dead, and he was responsible. He had to look after her; Thomas would have expected it.

Seth headed into the dining room—to a woman he didn't know and a responsibility he didn't know how to fulfill.

Chapter Two

I *can't do this!* Becca clenched her black bombazine skirt into her fists. The image of her brother's coffin being lowered into the ground played over and over in her mind. Her chest heaved as she struggled against her corset to breathe. She should have left it looser this morning. *Lord, please, help me.* She rushed to the porch railing, certain she was going to be sick. Leaning on it, she took more deep breaths. Slowly, the heat drained from her face, and she felt a bit steadier.

She had to pull herself together. The whole town was inside Maggie's boardinghouse. Her eyes roamed trying to find something to distract her long enough to get her emotions under control. Her gaze settled on the deep woods behind Maggie's, her favorite place to run off to as a child. What would happen if she did that today? What would the townspeople think if she never came back inside? Most likely that she was addled from all that schooling, which would support their belief that schooling put unnatural notions in women's heads.

At the sound of footsteps thudding over the wooden floor, Becca suppressed a sigh. Someone had found her. She dashed the tears from her face with the back of her hands and drug them across her skirt. With a deep breath, preparing herself to receive more condolences, she turned around.

And there he stood. Seth Blake.

Her heart skipped in her chest, betraying her. She'd tried hard not to be alone with him, certain he could recall that mortifying memory of her kiss as well as she could.

He took a step toward her. "Are you all right?"

"Yes. I'm fine." *Physically, that's true.* She looked past him into the house. "It seems like the whole town's here. I needed to get a bit of air." *And a moment alone from all these well-wishers before I scream.* She pulled at her skirt. She'd forgotten the closeness of small-town life. Everyone involved in everyone else's business. After the anonymity of a big city like Salem, the interest felt cloying.

"I haven't really had a chance to talk to you yet."

Her cheeks smarted. He didn't want to talk about what she *thought* he did, did he? *We are* not *having this conversation now.* A few more days and she'd be gone. Surely she could put him off until then.

If she hadn't been such an emotional child, bent on living out her silly daydreams, none of this would have happened. Yes, Thomas might still have been killed, but she would have been back home before now, before . . . everything.

It had started on this very porch, almost a reverse of yesterday. She was waiting to board the stagecoach that would take her away from Reedsville and on to her new life. Her new tailored dress was pink with black piping, made especially for this occasion. No more tomboyishness. She was a lady. Or going to be one.

Just before she reached the stagecoach door, she turned, hitched up her skirts, and threw herself into Seth's arms. She stood on tiptoe and whispered in his ear, "I love you. I couldn't leave without telling you." Then, just as quickly, she climbed on the stage and left, never looking back to gauge his reaction.

And she certainly didn't want it now. She hoped desperately

her face wouldn't reveal her thoughts. Her mind scrambled for a change of subject.

The funeral. She seized it. "Um, thank you for what you said about Thomas today. It meant a lot to me when you and Josh shared about looking forward to seeing him again. And you encouraged others to share the love of Jesus with someone because we never know what tomorrow holds." She glanced at Seth, her apprehension receding a bit. "Thomas would have wanted that. He would have wanted his… wanted to make a difference in someone's life."

Lines of pain crossed Seth's face, settling in around his mouth.

Perhaps that wasn't the best subject to move to. Dropping her gaze she realized she had twisted her gloved hands into knots around each other. She tucked them behind her back. She'd known Seth too long. She couldn't pretend to make polite, appropriate conversation.

"I should have come home sooner. He was always asking. Why didn't I listen? Now it's too late." She wrapped her arms around herself, shaking her head.

His boots scuffed on the worn boards as he took a step forward.

A thousand thoughts flooded her brain. Images and emotions swirled in a tornado of confusion. She tried to say something, anything, but the words wouldn't come. She couldn't even form a coherent thought. All she could see was the image of the wagon carrying her brother's casket as they headed to his gravesite. The rhythm of the wheels beat an accusation. *You missed your chance. He's dead. He's dead. He's dead.*

She shook her head and took a step back, reaching for the railing behind her, but a moment later found herself pulled into his arms, her face pressed into his Sunday suit. The smell of laundry soap, the same kind Maggie used—she must still be doing his laundry—made her homesick. The security of his arms broke down the last barrier, and she couldn't stop the tears from spilling over, despite her best efforts at decorum. Once again she was making a fool of herself in the arms of Seth. And she didn't care.

At some point it registered that someone had joined them on the porch. As Seth released his hold on Becca, Maggie put a motherly arm around her shoulders and led her inside and up the stairs. If the townspeople were watching this spectacle, she didn't want to know. She kept her eyes focused on the floor. She wanted to lie down. If she went to sleep and woke up again, then maybe, just maybe, this horrible nightmare would end.

Chapter Three

Seth caught himself for the third time this morning looking out of the barn toward the boardinghouse. He finally admitted to himself he was hoping to catch a glimpse of Becca. How was she holding up after yesterday? He didn't really need to worry; Maggie was there, and mothering people was what she lived for. Not that Becca ever needed much mothering. Still his new sense of responsibility weighed on him.

He pulled a harness down and methodically ran his hands over it, checking for cuts and tears in the leather. Though he'd been in logging for years, he helped Josh out with the stage when needed. Plus, Owen Taylor ran things just fine when Seth was gone. Maybe too fine considering he'd discovered the faulty chain. Seth shoved those thoughts away. Today the solitude of animals and the quiet, familiar barn work made a nice change from the noisy camp.

He didn't think he'd have too much peace and quiet once Becca rejoined Reedsville society, such as it was. She was sure to catch a few eyes; that seemed certain. A scant handful of eligible women resided in Reedsville. Some of them had even set their caps for him. It seemed that Parsons's wife never missed an opportunity to push their daughter, Cassandra, into Seth's path —figuratively, if not literally.

But Becca would be a standout. She'd have men following her everywhere and would surely have her pick of beaus, though Seth couldn't think of one man offhand he'd consider worthy of Becca's attentions. Guess he'd get to play big brother after all.

He scowled. His stomach didn't feel too well. Funny, Maggie's breakfasts were usually a treat, but this one rested heavy.

Seth hung up the last harness and walked down the aisle, checking each horse in its stall, then headed out of the barn and to the woods. He needed to spend some time in prayer. This was too much for him to handle, a rare thing for him to admit. He wasn't prepared to run the logging company by himself, let alone be Becca's big brother. Feeling overwhelmed and uncertain—a feeling he didn't like at all—he again wondered why God allowed Thomas to die.

And why God allowed his carelessness to play a part in it.

Embarrassing situations seemed her specialty around Seth, Becca decided, not wanting to get out of bed. Sobbing all over his Sunday suit yesterday did nothing to help him see her as a grown woman instead of Thomas's little sister. She proved again how weak and emotional she was. Yes, she'd had good cause, but a lady never gave into displays of emotion.

Maybe if he saw her as a woman, he'd forget about that incident when she left Reedsville. Or if he did think of it, he'd chalk it up to a young girl's impetuousness. That was it: She must replace his old impression with a new one.

She shook her head, instantly regretting it when pain shot behind her eyes from her night of tears. What Seth thought of her should be the least of her concerns. If she hadn't been so foolish to begin with, or so concerned with what Seth thought afterwards, she would have come home sooner. Before her brother died. That was all he'd asked of her.

She desperately wanted to crawl under the sheets and forget about getting up today.

Instead, she eased out of bed. Her eyes had swollen nearly shut. They scratched and burned; even her eyelashes hurt. It felt like mattress ticking stuffed her head. With rubbery arms she dressed and ran the brush through her hair, doing the bare minimum to make her fit to be seen.

The memory of her cheek against his solid chest and his gentle arms around her played through her mind. She pushed it away. She needed to leave Reedsville and Seth. She would be here one week, and that would be more than long enough. Time away did nothing to diminish Seth's appeal. She'd only do something foolish again and get her heart hurt. She tossed the brush on the dresser.

At least she was presentable. She gave a half-laugh as she looked in the mirror over the dresser at her swollen eyes. She flicked her hair over her shoulder, letting it hang in soft curls at the middle of her back. She would just leave it down. She wasn't going any place. Brushing her hands over her skirt, a simpler one than she usually wore in deference to getting around the more rural Reedsville, she took a shuddering breath and started down the stairs.

As she suspected, she found Maggie in the kitchen. That much hadn't changed.

"Good morning," Maggie said, turning from the stove. "I wasn't sure you'd feel like getting up today. Are you hungry?"

Becca couldn't remember the last time she'd eaten, and the smell of bread baking made her stomach rumble. But her mouth felt dry. She wasn't sure she could choke down a bite.

Maggie pulled out a chair for her at the kitchen table. "I have some biscuits from breakfast and some of last year's strawberry preserves left still. There's coffee, or I could make you tea if that'd sit better."

Becca lowered herself into the chair. She'd missed Maggie's mothering. She didn't need to be mothered—she was a grown woman—but it was nice. She could enjoy it the few days she'd be here.

Before she knew it, a plate of warm biscuits, butter, and bowl of preserves appeared on the table in front of her. Maggie poured Becca a cup of tea in one of her good china cups reserved for special occasions. She took that as a sign Maggie was glad she was back and didn't hold a grudge over her absence.

She took a sip of the steaming liquid.

Maggie finished bustling about the kitchen and sat down next to her. "I think we had nearly the whole town in here yesterday. Even those who didn't know you stopped by. I won't have to bake a pie for a month."

She should have known she'd be the biggest news in this town. If they had a town newspaper, *Becca Wilson Returns Home* would have been today's headline.

"Josh asked about you before he left on the stage run, and Seth even came into town to see how you were doing."

Maggie continued talking, but Becca's mind had stopped listening at the mention of Seth. Probably to see how the weepy girl was doing. In his mind she was still Thomas's little sister, not a grown woman who'd lived on her own in a big city. Did he feel a duty to look after her now? She supposed she could put up with Seth's pity for a couple of days. With great effort, she pulled her mind back to what Maggie was saying.

"Just because you've been gone doesn't mean we don't still think of you as one of our own. It's hard for us, too, having him gone. We've seen a lot of good men die."

Maggie patted Becca's hand as she got up and checked on the bread in the oven. Satisfied, she pulled it out. "You know, for all of the harshness of this land and the pain it causes, there is a beauty here that's nowhere else. Though I wouldn't blame you if you find city life more to your liking. More modern conveniences there, that's for certain."

Becca sipped her tea. Salem was a modern, fascinating city, but until she'd returned to Reedsville, she hadn't realized how much she'd missed having the mountains up close and the scent of pine heavy in the air.

"I know Thomas felt that way," she said. "He didn't like to stay too long in Salem. Now that I've been back, I know I'll miss Reedsville even more when I leave."

"Are you sure you want to? You've just got here. Stay and rest a spell."

She shook her head. "I've got to finish out the term and graduate. Then I need to find work." *And to avoid Seth.*

The kitchen door banged against the wall, and Maggie's almost-grown son stepped inside in stocking feet.

"Coffee, James?" Maggie filled a mug without waiting for his answer. "I thought you were taking this run with Josh." She handed it to him.

He nodded at Becca. "Morning, Becca." He turned back to his mother. "I was, but one of the mares is looking poorly so we thought it best I stay close."

Becca's head ached. She rubbed her temples.

Maggie laid a hand on her shoulder. "Perhaps you should go lay down. A wet cloth on your forehead might help."

"I think I'll take a short walk out back." She wanted to revisit her old haunts while avoiding the nosy townspeople.

Maggie nodded. "The fresh air might help."

Becca left the kitchen the way James had just come in, carefully avoiding his boots on the back porch. Thinking about all she should do before returning to Salem made her headache worse. She needed to go through Thomas's things, find his will, and take care of his final wishes. But today, she was reliving memories. Good memories.

As far as she could tell, nothing had changed since she left. The wash line remained strung up several feet from the house, next to Maggie's large vegetable and herb garden, with the barn and corral farther back.

But beyond that, the land looked untouched, turning into a forest that climbed mountains still capped with snow. She knew better. The people of Reedsville had made their mark on this land, whether it was visible from here or not.

She had whiled away many an hour amid the grass and trees, as she was certain other children did now. She would never tire of this view. Until this moment, she hadn't realized how much she'd missed it. It was just one more thing Salem didn't have.

She followed the meandering stream behind the garden and barn, the scent of grass wafting up as she walked along the riverbank packed with wildflowers until she reached a large rock jutting out into the stream. Gathering up her skirts, she sat and scooted across the rock's sun-warmed surface.

When she was younger she used to remove her shoes and stockings and dangle her feet in the icy water. Thomas had tried to teach her to fish from this rock. She giggled at the memory. She had been bugging him for days, and he finally gave in. They'd come to this stream and settled on this rock. He'd been annoyed with her when she wouldn't bait her own hook. But he did it for her anyway. A shiver ran up her spine at the memory of the fat, slimy worm being punctured by a hook.

She didn't know how long they'd sat there, her trying to cast and catching the grass, bushes, even Thomas's shirt—anything but a fish. Of course, Seth had told her later there was nothing in that stream but tadpoles and pollywogs. She'd been outraged that Thomas had so underestimated her fishing skills.

The sound of her own laughter surprised her and she stopped, only to softly chuckle a minute later. Then guilt seeped up. How could she be laughing when she just buried her brother?

She frowned and shook her head. Right now, all she wanted to do was return to Salem and pretend none of this ever happened. But her old hometown comforted her, like a well-worn blanket. Sometimes musty and smothering, but familiar. She felt close to her brother. She almost regretted having only a few days. Could she stay a few more days? How much school could she afford to miss?

No! She shook her head. She wasn't staying in Reedsville any longer than necessary.

Hearing footsteps in the grass, she turned around. Seth stood just behind her, his eyes shaded by his Stetson.

Had he been watching her? Remembering what happened the last time they spoke, she chose her words with care. "Why aren't you at the logging camp?"

He hesitated a moment, rocking back on his heels. "Josh asked me to keep an eye on one of his ailing mares. James does a good job with the horses, but he's still young." He paused. "How are you feeling?"

So he did remember. Time to leave a different impression, an impression of a strong, modern woman. "Not too badly. I have a bit of a headache from thinking about all I have to do before I leave. I thought a walk in the fresh air would help."

He came around to sit next to her.

She stiffened, keeping her gaze out over the creek. They sat in silence for a moment, her thoughts drifting to how many times she had sat in this very spot with Seth. And Thomas. Which reminded her that there was something she needed to ask him. A loose end to tie up. One thing she needed to know before she left, but was afraid to ask.

Plunging in before she changed her mind, she blurted, "What happened?" Her voice gave way, and she barely choked the words out. "You said in the telegram there was an accident, and he saved someone's life, but you never told me what happened."

He stared out over the creek and pushed his hair back from

his forehead. Her heart did something odd at that familiar gesture; he was thinking.

"There's not much more to it than that." He cleared his throat. "Somehow, one of the logs they were hauling to the ridge broke loose." He paused and his Adam's apple bobbed. When he spoke again his voice was rough. "Thomas pushed one man out of the way but got caught himself in some branches that hadn't been cleared. He couldn't get out of the way."

How like her brother, thinking of others first. Anger boiled up from some unknown fissure. "Why this time? Why couldn't he think of himself… or of me… just this once?"

"Becca… don't." He reached for her hand and squeezed it.

And where were you, Seth? Why couldn't you save my brother?

SETH WALKED through the kitchen intending to wash up, but stopped short in the doorway. There in the hall stood Becca, smiling up at Josh, looking happier than when she'd fled from her favorite rock earlier. Her laughter had caught his attention, but her hair dazzled him. Gilded by the nearly-setting sun pouring through the windows, it cascaded down her back. How would it feel trailing across his fingers? He closed his eyes to clear his mind and erase that image. Still off balance, he wasn't sure who this woman was who had replaced the girl he knew.

He must have hugged her a hundred times before, never thinking of her as anything more than his Li'l Sis. But yesterday after the funeral it had been different. The empty feeling in his arms when Maggie came on to the porch and led her away surprised him.

Seth frowned. A strange feeling clenched his heart. Ignoring it, he strode to the washbowl.

Maggie poked her head out from the dining room. "Supper's on the table."

"Be right there," Josh called. Out of the corner of his eye, Seth saw him offer Becca his arm with a smile.

Seth splashed water on his face and dried it quickly. He tossed the towel toward the hook but missed and had to grab it from the floor. Finally securing the towel on the hook, he entered the dining room in time to see Josh help Becca into her chair. Too late to sit next to her, Seth pulled out a chair across from them and sank into it.

Josh was turning on the charm. Apparently he didn't see her as Thomas's little sister anymore.

"Seth?" Maggie's voice found its way into his thoughts. Maggie's raised eyebrows told him she had repeated herself.

"I'm sorry. What were you saying?"

"Would you ask the blessing, please?"

"Certainly." He uttered a bland prayer he forgot the moment the words left his mouth. His gaze strayed throughout the meal to where Becca sat next to Josh, smiling and talking.

He forced his attention to his plate. Men would be flocking to Becca, so he'd best get used to it. Unless she had a beau back in Salem? The unsettled feeling gripped his stomach again. He supposed he better take some bicarbonate of soda after supper. Maggie's meals were usually enjoyable, but lately nothing sat right. Maybe he was coming down with something.

After supper, the stage passengers retired to their rooms while everyone else moved into the parlor. Seth and Josh lounged in their usual chairs flanking the fireplace, talking about the latest stage run and the logging camp. Maggie had shooed Becca out of the kitchen, and she sat on the sofa with some stitching, apparently ignoring them.

Becca dropped the fabric in her lap. "I'd like to go see the logging camp as soon as possible."

It took Seth a moment to realize what she had just said.

"No," he said in unison with Josh. He hadn't thought she'd even been listening to their conversation, her with her head bent over her needlework. He should have known better.

"Becca, a logging camp is no place for a lady," Josh explained. "We'll answer whatever questions you have, but you can't go up there."

"But surely there are some women up there. Don't some of the men have wives?"

"Very few." Seth recovered enough from his shock to answer her. What other nonsense had she come up with at that university? Would she continually surprise him this way? "And the women keep to themselves and don't go about unescorted. It's a dangerous place for a woman."

Becca's eyes hardened, and she set her jaw.

Seth suppressed a groan and wished he could take back his last comment. Why'd she have to get riled so easily? If having a simple conversation with her was going to be this difficult, he was almost glad she was going back to Willamette University. Almost.

"I want to see where he worked before I leave. I don't know when I'll return." Her jaw trembled a moment before tightening.

That implied she was leaving. His heart twisted. Before he formulated a question about it that wouldn't set her off, she continued.

"I understand you don't want me to go to the logging camp by myself, but what if one of you took me?" She gave them a deceptively sweet look.

Seth was shaking his head even before Becca finished. "No, Becca. I already told you—"

"Wait a minute, Seth," Josh interrupted. "She should see it if she wants to. If one of us goes with her, nothing will happen. If you don't want to take her, I will."

Seth shot Josh a look. The logging camp was *his* business, and if anyone was going to take Becca up there, it would be *him*. He sighed and pushed himself out of the chair, taking a step toward Becca. "I'll take you. But," he looked directly at her eyes, "you must stay with me at all times and do exactly as I say, without question. Do you understand?" He half expected her to say no.

But her face lit up with a smile. "Yes, I understand. I promise I'll do whatever you say."

The joy in her voice was so evident. A smile played on Seth's lips. He'd talk to her about leaving another time. He could talk her out of any notion she had of returning to Salem. At least he hoped so. "Good night, Becca."

"Good night, Seth. Thank you for helping me."

Josh stretched, his eyes twinkling. "I was just thinkin' about another cup of coffee."

"Suit yourself," Seth headed toward the door. He liked Becca being pleased with him.

"Well, if the party's breakin' up, I guess I'll head along home, too." Josh grunted, making a big effort to get out the chair. "I was just getting comfortable."

Seth ignored him, his mind already on how he was going to make sure Becca didn't run into Owen Taylor on her trip to the camp.

And how to make sure those chains stayed hidden.

Chapter Four

A virtual cloud of flour hung in Maggie's kitchen, reminding Becca of the dust on the stagecoach. Every available flat surface held something cooling from the oven.

When Josh let it be known the circuit preacher would be in town the following week, John McAlistar asked Annie Duncan to marry him. Though only seventeen, they had been sweet on each other for as long as anyone could remember. The town's women immediately went into action with a wedding dress to sew and food to prepare. It felt good to be useful in a very practical way, beyond shelving books or wiping down blackboards for her professors.

She worked alongside Maggie and her daughter, Sally. Sally Kincaid was a girl on the verge of womanhood. The little girl Becca remembered was practically grown. Changed, like everything else. Last night, Sally had shyly asked Becca about the university, and she had promised to help her. Maggie was a reasonable woman and would want all the best modern life offered for her daughter. But conversation this morning centered around town gossip in the midst of Maggie's instructions of what to mix, stir, or cut.

In the middle of this barely controlled chaos, Seth walked in.

Becca stopped kneading the dough. Though she wouldn't have acknowledged it out loud, Becca had wondered all morning if he would show up.

Maggie glanced up from rolling out a piecrust. "Coffee's still hot on the stove. Help yourself."

"Thanks." He strolled over and poured a cup.

Becca watched him out of the corner of her eye while she punched down the rising bread dough. He slowly sipped his coffee, eyeing the masses of freshly baked goods.

It wasn't unusual for Josh or James to step into the kitchen while taking a break. But both had been careful to avoid the whole area during the baking frenzy. Maggie was known to swipe at them with her dishtowel if they tried to filch a cookie. Yet Seth reached over and popped one into his mouth without consequence.

Becca shaped the bread dough into a loaf, laid it in a pan, and set it on the back of the stove, covered with a dishtowel for the second rising.

"I was thinking I could take you out to the logging camp today," Seth said around the cookie.

She whipped around from the stove to face him.

A twinkle lit his eye. "Would you be interested?"

"Oh, yes!" She tugged at her apron ties, and then looked around the kitchen. Empty pie pans, bowls of filling, and piles of ingredients accused her. It wasn't fair to leave it all for Maggie and Sally.

Her shoulders slumped as she dropped her hands away from the ties. "I can't. There's too much to do here."

"Nonsense," Maggie said. "We can manage just fine. You go on."

Becca hesitated for a second, but at Maggie's confirming nod, she yanked off her apron, wiped her hands on it, and then hung it on the pantry door. "Just let me get my hat," she called over her shoulder as she dashed out of the kitchen. In her room, she grabbed her straw hat off its peg and looked in the mirror to adjust it. Though she wasn't sure why it mattered. Neither the hat nor her dress had been fashionable in the last five years. Not that anyone here would know.

To her dismay, flour dusted her nose and cheek. She scrubbed it off with her sleeve.

"No wonder Seth was smiling," she muttered. "Laughing at me as usual." She jabbed the hatpin through the hat and into her knot of hair, taking one last look to make sure nothing else was amiss.

Seth waited for her at the foot of the stairs, just outside the kitchen, holding a milk pail with something inside wrapped in a dishtowel. She raised her eyebrows.

He lifted it up. "Maggie thought we might get hungry, so she sent a snack."

Becca laughed. "Maggie thinks a body might starve walking through town."

They left through the front door, avoiding the activity in the kitchen. She saw Seth had already hitched up Maggie's buggy. He set the pail behind the seat then lifted her in. The warmth of his hands seemed to surge to her face, and she only hoped her cheeks weren't bright red. *Please, Lord, don't let him notice.*

She feigned interest in a store across the street as he climbed in beside her. Slapping the reins, he clucked to the horses and headed down the road out of town. She risked a glance out of the corner of her eye and concluded he hadn't noticed her reaction.

"So, did I rescue you from the kitchen or were you enjoying all that baking?"

His teasing was more comfortable footing. She folded her hands in her lap. "I don't mind baking, but on a beautiful day like today, with no rain, the kitchen was a bit confining. And since I'm only staying through Annie and John's wedding, I have to make efficient use of my time."

"Yeah, it's been dry. Can't be good for the farmers. I'm not complaining, though. It's much easier to fell trees when we don't have to drag them through the mud."

She noted he skipped completely over her comments about leaving. Expecting at least some retort, she wasn't sure what to make of that. Maybe he couldn't wait for her to leave so she wouldn't create embarrassing situations for him. Fine with her. After today, she would only have to see him when he took his meals at Maggie's.

He leaned back and let the reins hang loosely in his hands. The soft thud of the horse's hooves and the swaying of the buggy surrounded them with a soft rhythm. For a moment, she could almost imagine they were going for a drive instead of to the place that killed her brother. A frisson of fear raced through her. Was she making a mistake? Did she really need to go to the logging camp? She wanted to, had felt almost compelled to go. But now that she was actually going, she was afraid of what she might find, of what she might feel.

She looked away from Seth and out of the buggy, desperately wishing the high lace collar of her dress could hide her attempt to swallow her tears. Tears in front of Seth. How unusual. He would be happy to put her on the stage at the end of the week.

Looking for a subject to get her mind off their destination, she let her mind wander over their growing-up years. Mostly she pictured the three of them together. Seth had experienced loss, too, she realized. Not only had he lost his best friend, he'd never known his mother. At least Becca had memories of hers.

"Do you remember your mother at all?"

He looked startled at her question. She wished she could take it back, but she didn't say anything. He glanced at the road before looking back at her. "I'm not sure what parts are actually memories and what are things I heard from my father. He talked about her so much while I was growing up. Told me how much she loved me, how happy she was when I was born. In many ways I feel like I know her."

What was it like growing up without a mother? Her heart

softened at the image of him as a little boy. She missed her parents, desperately, but she was old enough when they died to have many memories. Most included Thomas.

Seth shifted in his seat and stared out across the road. His voice was low and soft, almost like he was talking to himself more than her. "When I was little, I'd watch the ladies come into my dad's store and sometimes imagine one of them was my mother. I always felt odd being the only kid without one. For a while, I wanted my dad to marry someone—anyone—just so I could have a mother too. I'll never forget what he said: 'They had a love that comes once in a lifetime.' I still don't know what he meant by that."

Somewhere far above, the ring of an axe and a man's shout floated down to them, breaking the stillness. Becca leaned forward on the padded leather seat. The road rose steeply and narrowed, the canopy of trees closing in and casting shadows across the road.

They seemed to fall over her soul as well. Her heart beat in her throat. Anticipation or dread? How would it feel to actually stand in the last place Thomas stood before his death? Would she feel closer to him or would the pain be overwhelming? She was a little afraid of the answer.

Seth jolted her out of her thoughts. "Becca, while we're at the camp, I need you to stay right by me and do exactly as I say. This is a rough place. They aren't used to having women up here, and there aren't too many gentlemen. It's not Willamette University." The wistful little boy was gone, replaced by a bossy big brother.

Did he believe she didn't know the difference between a logging camp and a university? "I've managed to take care of myself." She straightened her back. "I know how to be careful." He still thought of her as an incompetent child. A particularly obtuse one at that, from his tone. What was he implying? That she'd grown used to city life and couldn't handle living on the edge of the wilderness? He, of all people, should know how well she could take care of herself. The very nerve!

"Because you've been surrounded by gentlemen who look out for ladies like you."

She swung around to stare at him. "And I had nothing to do with it?"

"Not if a man wanted to be ungentlemanly." Exasperation crept into his voice. "Now, Becca, I'll not belabor the point. If you don't agree to do as I say, I'll take you home."

"I'm not a little girl anymore, Seth Blake." If he was going to be annoyed with her, he could surely well know she was annoyed with him.

"No, you're definitely not. You're a grown woman and that's the problem."

Her cheeks burned. She said nothing else. But the faint glimmer of hope that he actually saw her as a woman instead of a little girl redeemed the moment, if only slightly.

THEY ROUNDED a final bend and came to a clearing. Wooden bunkhouses scattered in the distance. A large structure sat straight ahead, with a smaller one off to the side. All of the buildings were strictly functional boxes or rectangles; none had porches, trim, or even paint. Seth pulled the buggy up near the smaller building. He jumped down and was helping Becca out when a man came out of the building.

Though only slightly taller than Becca, he easily was twice her weight. His clothes barely contained his thick chest and thighs, and his rolled-up sleeves revealed deeply corded forearms. Full, red cheeks gave him a boyish look that contrasted with his perfectly bald head.

"Owen, this is Rebecca Wilson, Thomas's sister. Becca, this is Owen Taylor, my foreman."

"How do you do?"

"Miss, I'm surely sorry about your brother. He was a good man." Sorrow filtered in, creating lines in Mr. Taylor's boyish face. "I wasn't there that morning. I was in the tool barn sharpening axes." He looked past her, seeing something no one else could. "If I had been there, maybe…"

He cleared his throat and scratched his scalp with the tips of blunt fingers. "Now, I don't believe there's anything of Thomas's left up here."

"Actually, I came to show Miss Wilson around."

A puzzled look crossed his face. "You're going near that place?" He blinked and glanced at her before he looked at Seth. "A woman's bad luck around here. We have enough curses on this place as it is."

Seth shifted his weight. "That's just a bunch of superstitious old woman talk."

She turned to Seth. "What are they saying? Tell me."

He jammed his hand into his hip pocket. "The men won't go near the site. They say it's bad luck. Some even think it's haunted."

"That's the most ridiculous thing I've ever heard. Grown men—big burly lumberjacks—afraid of something that doesn't even exist." She shook her head. Men! She'd never figure them out as long as she lived.

Mr. Taylor opened his mouth, but Seth cut him off. "We'll stop back before we leave." He indicated a well-worn path to Becca with a sweep of his hand.

They started down the path, and out of earshot she turned to Seth. "Surely you don't believe that nonsense about bad luck and ghosts."

"No, but a lot of the men do, and if I want them to keep working for me I have to take that into consideration."

She shook her head. It was so illogical.

Fewer and fewer trees lined the path, and the way grew rougher. Becca stepped on a rock. It wiggled under her foot. She bobbled in a most unladylike fashion despite her sturdy boots. And lost her balance.

A strong hand grabbed her elbow, steadying her. She met Seth's gaze. Slowly he released his grip on her.

She should thank him for saving her dignity, but she couldn't get the words out. Pride lodged in her throat.

As they walked, Seth explained the various logging methods, using trees, stumps and cuts in the mountain as illustrations. Finally, they reached an old logging site. Countless stumps stretched out in every direction. The sounds of men working grew louder. The scent of wood chips, loamy earth, and something oily hung heavy around them.

"What are these?" Becca pointed to logs mostly buried in the dirt road.

"Those are skids. The men put axle grease on them so the oxen can pull the logs out easier."

A little farther on a few trees had been cleared but several lay scattered on the ground, forgotten.

Becca knew without being told where they were.

After a few minutes she took a deep breath. "Where did it happen?"

Seth looked down at the ground, then off into the distance. Finally, he turned and pointed toward the ridge.

The events replayed before her eyes. *The log tumbled down the hill. Thomas spotted it and pushed a man out of the way. The log careened toward him and*—Becca shut her eyes. Everything went blank.

Seth's arms wrapped around her. For a moment she struggled, wanting to break free, wanting to warn Thomas, wanting to stop the log and push him out of the way. Seth's arms grew tighter.

She rested against his chest and let her heart break.

Seth sat with his feet propped on a stool, nursing a cup of coffee. The only light in the room came from the glow of embers in the dying fire. He knew he shouldn't be drinking coffee so late. It would keep him up, no doubt, but he wouldn't be doing much sleeping tonight anyway.

The office had looked so different with Owen sitting behind the desk instead of Thomas. He had the strangest sense Thomas would come striding through the door any minute. Only when Seth walked in with Becca today did he realize how he avoided the office when Owen was there. After their trip to the woods, he'd shown her the books and worked out an arrangement for her to receive Thomas's share of the profits. Her share now. Will or no will, it's what Thomas would have wanted.

Not only had Thomas been his partner, he'd been his best friend for ten years. They'd formed a natural camaraderie—both not boys, but not quite men, either. Thomas was trying to be brother and parent to Becca while Seth, thirsty for adventure, had followed Maggie and her husband from Portland to help start their stagecoach line. Until he'd taken Becca up to the site today, he hadn't fully grasped the harsh reality that Thomas was gone.

And he was responsible.

The morning of the accident was a typical one. He checked the equipment, making sure the axles had sufficient grease, the harnesses had no tears, the horses were in good health. He was going over the chains when he noticed a couple of links didn't quite look right. He picked up the chain to inspect it more closely when Owen interrupted him with a question. He couldn't even remember his reply. All he remembered now was dropping that chain to respond. Owen looked unusually confused, so Seth walked him to where he needed to go. He never finished inspecting the chain.

Now Thomas was dead because of him. He exhaled slowly and dropped his head into his hands. Good thing Becca was leaving.

Chapter Five

Only three days left. Then she'd be back at Willamette University, buried beneath books and papers, trying to get caught up on her work so she could graduate. The university made her happy. This dogged sense of unease would leave once she was back where she belonged.

"Do you know where I can find Thomas's belongings?" Becca looked over her coffee cup to where Maggie sat across from her at the breakfast table.

"Seth packed up your brother's things at the logging camp and brought them here," Maggie replied. "Your old homestead is abandoned, so I had him put the box down in the cellar."

Becca twisted the napkin in her lap. Visiting the logging camp and going over its books with Seth hadn't given her the sense of completion she longed for. Maybe going through Thomas's papers would provide that. Maybe she'd find his will.

"I can bring it up if you'd like," Josh said.

"Oh, thank you. You can do it later. I know you have work to get to." She fiddled with the utensils, precisely lining them next to her plate before looking at him.

Josh held her gaze with his. "No, I'm finished eating, so I'll run down and get the box. Back in a jiffy." He stood up and shoved the rest of a biscuit in his mouth.

She gave up on eating anything more. She pushed her chair back as she stood and began to clear the table.

Maggie shooed her into the parlor. "Sally and I can manage the dishes."

She stepped into the parlor and sat on Maggie's prized rose moiré settee. Josh strode into the parlor with a wooden box in his hands.

"Here you go." He set the box at her feet with a flourish. "I hope you don't mind, but we gave his clothes away to some of the folk Maggie knew could use them."

"Oh, no. I don't mind at all. I am glad they could be put to good use."

He left the room, but Becca barely noticed. She stared at the box, afraid to open it. What would it tell her about the time she had spent apart from her brother? His life had been reduced to this. She raised the lid.

The box was about three-quarters full of papers, books, and a few other items she glanced over. On top, the photograph of herself she sent to Thomas three years ago stared back at her.

She picked it up, running her fingers over the frame, marveling at how young she looked. She remembered thinking Thomas would be surprised at how grown-up she was. The girl in the photo would have come back sooner if she'd known her brother was going to die.

Setting the frame aside, she stared at the rest of his belongings. She flipped through a stack of papers until she saw his will. Scanning it, she saw it matched the one he had sent her.

Next, she spotted the pocketknife she had bought him one Christmas. Picking it up, she hefted its solid weight in her hand. Nestled in the box beside it was the gold watch that had belonged to their father. Somehow, it survived the stagecoach accident that had killed their parents and Maggie's husband Stephen. It was one of Thomas's most cherished possessions. She held it to her cheek, seeking the warmth of his hand, but found only cool metal. Tears made her nose tingle and she sniffed.

Carefully she set the knife and watch in her lap and continued through the box. Near the bottom, another photograph caught her gaze: a tintype of a pretty woman with pale hair and delicate features, not much older than Becca. *I wonder who this is.* She lifted it out and stared at it for a moment before setting it aside to ask Maggie or Josh.

On the sofa next to her, she put her letters to him, the photographs, and other personal papers and belongings. A set of rolled-up papers caught her eye. Pulling them out, she unrolled them and found what appeared to be building plans. Must be for the logging camp. But they didn't seem to be for any of the buildings she saw yesterday.

She inspected the building more closely. It seemed so familiar. Wait! It was their house; the homestead she and Thomas had grown up in. Larger, with rooms added, it was their place just the same, she was certain. She traced the plans with her finger. Thomas must have worked on this a long time. Maggie had mentioned the homestead was a mess, so Thomas probably hadn't started working on it. She sighed. His dreams would only live on paper and in her mind. *Why hadn't anyone told her?*

She paused. *Would it have made a difference?*

Saddened, but knowing she needed to finish, she examined the rest of the papers, skimming most of them. She was in the middle of one letter before the words *purchase* and *offer* leapt out at her. She stopped, went back to the beginning and reread it, carefully this time. It was an offer to buy the logging company from a Mr. Jeremiah McCormick of San Francisco. Becca looked at the date. Barely a month ago. Why would someone all the way from San Francisco want to buy Thomas and Seth's logging company?

Neither Seth nor Thomas must have thought much of the offer, because neither had mentioned it. At least not to her.

Which, as she thought about it, didn't mean much. There were apparently a lot of things people hadn't mentioned to her.

She set the paper on top of the others. Maybe she should show it to Seth. She chewed her lip. Two more letters had the same San Francisco letterhead. She set them aside with the first one. Nothing else seemed important, so she re-stacked the papers and returned them to the box.

She closed her eyes and massaged the bridge of her nose. Weary of thinking, she decided to head to the kitchen to help Maggie and get her mind off of things.

But Maggie eased down onto the settee next to Becca.

"I just finished with the papers, so I thought I'd come see if you needed any help."

"And I came to see if you needed any." Maggie's smile was soft and sad. She fingered the lid of the box. "I remember having to make so many decisions after Stephen died. I was grieving, too overwrought to think. And yet between taking care of Sally and James—they were just little ones—and running a new stagecoach business, somehow I managed. Couldn't have done it without your brother and Seth."

Becca barely remembered that time, lost in the fog of losing her parents in the same accident that killed Maggie's husband. She had never thought to consider what Maggie had gone through. In her determination to prove her independence, and being used to being on her own, Becca had forgotten Maggie knew what Becca was going through and the decisions she would have to make.

"There is no hurry to decide anything now. It will amaze you how easily life goes on while you have a gaping hole in your chest. Surround yourself with the people who love you and who understand." She patted Becca's knee.

Becca blinked back tears. Maggie didn't understand. "I have to finish the term; I've missed enough coursework as it is. Then I have to find work. There's not much I can do to support myself in Reedsville." There weren't many options for women anywhere, even in this modern age.

Maggie kept smiling that soft smile and patted Becca's knee again. "Well, those are difficult decisions for anyone to make. Pray for God's direction."

Becca looked at her hands twisted in her lap. "God just seems very far away right now."

"Just because it feels that way doesn't mean it is. Now," Maggie pushed herself off the settee. "I'm completely out of baking powder for the biscuits. I don't know how I forgot it last time I went to Fulton's. Would you be a dear and run over and pick some up for me?"

Becca wanted to hug Maggie for not pressing the issue. "Certainly. The fresh air will be a nice change."

MINUTES LATER, Becca stepped off Maggie's porch and headed down the street. Wagons lifted the dust off the streets as they passed. Horses stood tied to hitching posts. The town was expanding at a fast clip. Near its edges sat fresh-hewn shanties with only tarpaper to hold them together. Some had false second stories propped up from behind with poles. Her eyes scanned the street, and she noticed a livery stable, two more saloons, a blacksmith, a tailor, and several buildings whose purposes she could not determine. Her cozy hometown had burgeoned into a boomtown while she'd been away.

As she entered Fulton's Mercantile, a little bell above the door rang. She stopped in the doorway for a moment and waited for her eyes to adjust to the darker shop after the bright sunlight. Familiar smells of peppermint, coffee, sawdust, oil, sizing, and kerosene swirled around her; she would have known this place with her eyes closed. Sam Fulton carried everything. It didn't seem possible that he could cram more into his store, but he had.

She walked around the store to browse while Mr. Fulton waited on a customer. After a few moments, she spotted the supply of fabric and ribbons and lace—a few bolts tossed in the corner of the store.

She picked through the lace. She had always thought Mr. Fulton carried a fairly good supply, but it was pitiful compared to what she could find in Salem. Snippets of a conversation floated over to her, but she didn't pay much attention until she heard Seth's name.

"Shoulda sold it while he had the chance."

"Yep. Now he's likely to go bust what with all that ghost business goin' on up there."

The hair on the back of her neck rose. That ghost business again! She had a mind to set them straight about their superstitions. It reminded her what she appreciated about the university: Logic and intellectual stimulation, not backwoods nonsense.

She couldn't identify the voices. She peeked around to the aisle next to her. Two men, one had his back to her and could have been just about any man in town. The second was small but wiry, with curly black hair. He held a greasy hat in one hand, occasionally knocking it against his thigh.

They didn't pay any attention to her. The two chuckled, then glanced toward the counter. She followed their gaze.

Her heart almost stopped.

Seth leaned against the far end. Mrs. Fulton pulled a stack of envelopes from a mail slot and handed it to him.

Becca dropped the lace she'd been fingering and strode toward the counter. She glanced back over her shoulder, but the men were gone.

"Good morning."

Seth turned at her words. She thought his eyes lit up momentarily. For some reason, that pleased her. "Morning, Becca."

"Sure is good to have you back, Becca," Mr. Fulton said,

ambled over, wiping his hands on his apron. "Don't know as I would have recognized you on the street."

"My, yes," Mrs. Fulton added. "You've certainly grown up."

What did one say to a remark like that? She certainly hoped so. Four years at the university should have made some difference. She shifted her weight, cheeks growing warm, and caught Seth's grin. "Uh, well, thank you." She felt like she was being examined and discussed like livestock. She pressed on with the business that brought her here. "Maggie sent me for some baking powder. Seems she forgot it on her last visit."

"Coming right up." Mr. Fulton turned back to his shelves to retrieve the small tin. The bell above the door sounded, and Mrs. Fulton hurried over to assist the customer.

Becca turned to Seth. "What brings you to town?"

He held up the stack of mail. "This for the camp and a few supplies."

She nodded and glanced around the store, suddenly at a loss for words. Stepping closer to the counter, she pretended to examine the shelves.

"So, are you ready to go back to Salem on Monday?"

She blinked. The only thing she was aware of was how close he stood to her. His breath brushed her ear when he spoke.

Mr. Fulton brought over the baking powder. "Leaving us so soon, Becca? My daughter Mary would love to have you stop by for a visit before you go. She's pretty well tied to home with her two little ones, but a visit from you would surely brighten her day."

"Of course. I'll try and see her as soon as I can. I'd enjoying catching up on all that's happened since we were in school together." She took a step to the side so she could turn around without bumping into Seth, but he reached for her arm as she backed away.

Their gazes met.

"Let me walk you back to Maggie's."

She opened her mouth to state she was perfectly capable of

walking back on her own then shut it. She needed to show him the letter she'd found. Combined with what she'd overheard at the store, and what Mr. Taylor had said about the ghosts, someone had to be purposely causing problems at the logging camp. Between the two of them, surely they could find out what was happening and set everything to rights. "Thank you. And I'm sure Maggie would love to have you stay for dinner. She's making her famous baking powder biscuits." She waved the tin at him. "That is, as soon as I get this to her."

BUMPING INTO BECCA was a pleasant surprise, and a midday meal at Maggie's an added bonus.

"How is everything up at the camp?"

Becca's question jolted Seth out of his thoughts. The meal they had just finished turned to lead. They were the only two left at the table. He took a sip of water and tried to gather his thoughts.

She looked at him expectantly.

He set his glass down. "No change from yesterday. We have more orders than we can keep up with."

She shifted in her chair and leaned forward, moving her plate to the side.

"No more accidents or reports of ghosts?"

His heart stopped again. "No. No goblins or witches, either." He hoped he accomplished the light tone he was going for. But she didn't bat an eyelash.

"Did it ever occur to you someone might be encouraging the men to believe in these rumors of—" she waved her hand dismissively—"of ghosts and such? Wouldn't there be someone who might gain from that?"

He frowned. "Why would anyone do that?" He had no idea what she was up to now.

Instead of answering, she got up from the table and left. She returned a moment later and handed him a piece of paper.

It was a letter. She hovered over him as he read. It was an offer to buy the logging company. He hadn't seen this before. It was only addressed to Thomas.

He scowled. *Why* hadn't he seen this before? The figure this McCormick was offering was fairly generous. Still, they weren't for sale; that's why Thomas hadn't shown him the letter. It wasn't worth the bother. He probably meant to throw it away. He handed the letter back to Becca.

"Well?" she asked.

"Well, what?" The hem of her skirt fluttered from her unseen tapping toe.

"Doesn't this explain it?"

"Explain what?"

"The whole ghost thing! I would wager this Mr. McCormick started that rumor to get you to sell to him. I've heard of such things."

"Because I might be afraid of ghosts?" Seth couldn't keep the humor out of his voice. She was too easy to bait.

"No." She gave an exasperated sigh. "Because your men might be. If you can't get men to work for you, you're out of business. Then you have to sell to him."

"So if he buys my company, what does he do about the ghosts? Or do they only haunt me?"

Becca shot a look to the ceiling, and he wondered if she was praying for patience.

"I'm sure he's already thought through how to handle that situation."

He grinned as he stood. "Thanks for thinking of me, Becca." He put his hand lightly on her arm. So small and delicate. "It's not that unusual for an investor to take an interest in a successful company. But we weren't selling. You can bet he's found another company to purchase by now." She shook her head, but he stepped around her and stuck his head through the kitchen doorway. "Thanks for the meal, Maggie. Delicious, as always."

Maggie stood at the dishpan. "You're welcome at my table anytime, Seth Blake."He turned back to the dining room. Becca stood with her arms crossed. "Good-bye, Becca."

"Just think about it, will you, Seth?"

"I will. I promise." How could he think of anything else?

Chapter Six

The wagon was hitched up in front of the boardinghouse where Maggie supervised its lading with blankets, jugs of water, and all the baking from the past week. When the last pie had been loaded, Becca returned to the kitchen to take off the apron that covered her good dress, an cuirass-cut, blue-and-cream striped linen with a cream peek-a-boo ruffle in the front below her knees.

She was startled to find Seth there.

"Oh, hello, Seth. I didn't see you ride up." Becca didn't look at him as she hung up her apron.

When he didn't say anything, she turned around. His intensely blue eyes met hers, almost with a bit of longing in them. He worked his jaw, opened it, then shut it. The silence stretched. Tingles popped up and down her spine, and she broke eye contact.

"I think everything's in the wagon. Josh will drive Maggie, but the rest of us are walking." It was an inane comment, but she didn't know what else to say. She glanced at him again.

He nodded. "Let's go," He motioned with his hat.

She hurried ahead, wondering if she'd imagined the longing in his eyes.

Of course she had.

Outside, Maggie issued last-minute orders as Josh handed her up into the wagon. Once she settled into the seat, she turned and spotted Becca and Seth. "Oh, Seth. Good, you and Becca can keep the younguns in line."

Becca suppressed a laugh at Maggie's description of James and Sally as "younguns."

"It's not too far, but I'm sure they'll find some mischief to get into." Maggie tugged at her hat, tucking up stray hairs and muttering about her younguns, while Josh clucked to the horses and the wagon pulled away.

Becca couldn't help but smile and sneaked a peak at Seth whose lips tilted in a grin. He turned and winked at her. The moment stretched out and that odd look returned to Seth's eyes.

She suddenly became preoccupied with adjusting her dress. She hoped it would survive the walk to the church along the rutted dirt road. "Do you think we should start out?"

"We have plenty of time. You know Maggie. Always has to be the first one there to make sure everything's done properly." Seth offered Becca his arm as they began walking through the town to the schoolhouse that served as the church.

Laying her hand on his arm, she felt the broadcloth of his suit under her fingers and his derby hat was a nice change from the Stetson he usually wore. She caught a whiff of bay water and starch. The scent reminded her of crying in his arms the day of the funeral.

Emotions she didn't want to identify pushed up her chest and suddenly her corset constricted her breathing more than usual. She pushed away the thought of the funeral and instead concentrated on today. They were going to a wedding. Like Maggie had said, life continued despite her grief. She firmly pushed from her mind the thought of leaving Monday.

The smell of fresh paint greeted them as they drew near to the sparkling white clapboard building. In honor of the wedding and the circuit preacher's arrival, the men of the town had given the schoolhouse a new coat.

In her element, Maggie bustled around and directed the placement of food, using the schoolhouse desks as tables. She looked up from her supervising long enough to smile at Becca and Seth before shooing everyone inside the makeshift church. "The bride will be here any minute, and it wouldn't do for half the town to still be standing outside."

Once inside, the clean scent of paint mingled with the fragrance of wildflowers. The warming room caused the jars of flowers on nearly every flat surface to fill the air with their heavy perfume. Dust motes danced on the sunbeams that flooded the room through glassless windows. All in all, it looked as if fairies had transformed the common schoolhouse into a magical place.

A moment after Seth had escorted Becca to their seats, the groom and his best man took their places at the front. She hadn't seen John McAlistar in years. He'd grown from a scrawny boy into a gangly young man. His pale face made his brown eyes look big and wide. He shifted his weight nervously from foot to foot and kept taking his hands in and out of his pockets.

She found herself smiling in sympathy and wondering—she barely allowed herself the thought—if Seth would be that nervous. Somehow she couldn't imagine that of him. She was careful to control her features and not look Seth's way, lest he be able, by some means, to read her mind.

Beth Paige came to the front, as she did for every Reedsville wedding, and sang "O Promise Me" as Annie Duncan and her father walked down the aisle.

The circuit preacher performed a simple but meaningful ceremony, and soon the two young people were a married couple. Annie's face went from being so pale her freckles stood out to beet red when the preacher said John could kiss his bride. A rumble of laughter rippled through the schoolhouse. After a quick kiss, John and Annie hurried outside, as if they couldn't wait to leave.

SETH'S MIND wandered during the ceremony, thinking over the logging business. No matter how he tried to it brush off to Becca, the ghost nonsense was a thorn in his side. He turned over in his mind how he could disabuse the men of their superstitions until the image of Becca as a bride brought him up short.

She was a beautiful woman; of course she'd be a beautiful bride. But for whom? That disturbed him. She was still bent on heading for Salem Monday, which would make his job keeping any inappropriate suitors away difficult, if not nigh impossible.

By the time he escorted Becca out of the schoolhouse, Maggie was directing people in lines along the makeshift tables laden with food. Blankets were scattered throughout the clearing. The newlyweds occupied a private table off to the side.

Seth and Josh retrieved the blankets from the wagon and spread them out, then got in line behind the others. As usual, there was too much food. Seth took small portions but still didn't get to sample half of what the table held. In between serving himself, he surreptitiously glanced at Becca while she chatted with townsfolk, catching up on their lives.

After all the boardinghouse folk settled on their blankets and Maggie found a free moment, Josh asked the blessing on the food. "Thank You, Lord, for this special occasion and for the opportunity to fellowship with our neighbors. We thank You for this food, and ask that You bless the hands that made it. Amen."

The low drone of voices floated over the picnic area with occasional snatches of conversation or laughter mixed in providing a relaxed ambiance for their picnic. With a contentedly full stomach, Seth watched Becca lean back on her hands and look up at the pine treetops swaying in the breeze. A small sigh escaped her lips. A moment later she lowered her eyes and caught him staring at her.

"What was that sigh about?" He resettled his hat on his head.

She took another deep breath and let it out. "I don't know. It just seems like such a beautiful day. At this moment, I'm perfectly content. It's been a long time since I've felt that way." She smiled up at him.

For a moment he thought the world had stopped. Did she realize how she was looking at him? Not as a big brother or her brother's friend, but as a man. Was that how she saw him?

She lowered her eyes, and he caught a glimpse of pink tingeing her cheeks.

He jumped to his feet and reached his hand out to her. "Let's stretch our legs. My eyelids are starting to feel awfully heavy."

She put her small hand in his and let him help her to her feet. He was certain he had held her hand before but it never felt like this. When he released her hand, he could still feel the warm imprint of it on his palm.

Josh stretched out on the blanket with his hat over his eyes. Sally and James had already wandered off with their friends, one of the few opportunities to be with them outside of church.

"Maggie, can we bring you anything?" Becca asked.

"Not a thing I can think of at the moment. I'm just going to sit here and enjoy the day."

Seth and Becca walked slowly toward the schoolhouse, his hand at the small of her back, guiding her. They hadn't gotten far before several townspeople came up to talk to Becca.

He inwardly groaned and saw what looked like a flash of regret in her eyes. He listened politely as she accepted condolences and answered questions about life at Willamette University and in Salem. Owen Taylor even wandered over.

"Hey, Seth!" A man from across the schoolyard hailed him. He waved back.

"Becca, would you excuse me for a moment?"

She nodded and continued her conversation.

He strode over to Michael Riley, and Josh soon joined them. As the talked turned to finding a sheriff for the town, Seth glanced over at Becca and caught her looking in his direction. He flashed her a smile that she returned.

Something he couldn't identify surged through him. He wasn't certain what it was, but he sure would enjoy it while it lasted.

When Becca finally disengaged herself from the well-meaning but trying townspeople, she was disappointed to see Seth still deep in conversation. Wanting to rinse the remnants of the picnic from her hands, she headed toward the creek behind the schoolhouse and picked her way through the denser brush, reeds, and flowers near the stream. She knelt by the water's edge and rinsed her hands in the icy water, then ran her damp palms over her face and neck.

Standing up, she wiped her face with her handkerchief. She looked around and saw James about 50 feet down the creek with Timmy, Mary's oldest, who had rolled up his pant legs and was wading in the creek. He was going to catch it from Mary, when she saw him, for wearing his best pants in the creek. James, too, for not stopping him.

On the way back, she saw Seth still conversing with Michael Riley, so she looked around for Maggie. Bessie Smith had joined her under the massive oak. Becca tried to spot Mary to visit with her instead like she'd promised Mr. Fulton.

As she scanned the crowd, she noticed a man standing off to the side. She blinked and looked more carefully. It was the wiry man from the store, whose conversation she had overheard. He stood close to another man talking, but she couldn't tell if it was the same man he'd been talking to in the store. They were too far away for her to hear their conversation.

Looking to see if it were possible to hear them better, she strolled a bit closer, hoping they wouldn't notice. She plucked a leaf from a nearby tree and noticed how close they stood to the schoolhouse. Casually, she headed toward the schoolhouse and slipped around the corner. She scooted as close to the far corner of the building as possible, straining to hear their voices.

"... still believe it's being caused by ghosts." Both men chuckled.

"Just let them keep on believing it and ..." She couldn't make out the rest of the sentence.

"Don't know how much longer I can keep at this."

"Shouldn't be too much longer. He can't keep going on like this."

"There's too many men that don't believe the stories. They like Blake and they like working for him."

"Well maybe they won't if they start thinking he runs an unsafe outfit."

"Seth Blake runs the safest camp around. The men know he cares more about them than his own profits."

"We'll just have to change their minds."

She heard raised voices and cheering. The men stopped their conversation. She risked a peek around the corner and saw them saunter away. She needed to learn who they were. Someone had to know. Who could she ask?

"Come on, ladies. It's time!" someone shouted.

She retraced her steps around the schoolhouse and almost collided with Maggie.

"Maggie! You're just the person I need."

"There you are, dear. Come on, it's time for Annie to throw her bouquet."

"Just a minute. I need you to do me a favor." She stepped back around the building and pulled Maggie with her. "Do you know who those men are?" She gestured with her head over her shoulder.

Maggie moved alongside her. "Who?"

Becca turned to point but the men were gone. She let out a groan. They might as well be the ghosts themselves the way they disappeared on her.

"You can show me later." Maggie turned her around by her shoulders. "We have to get you out front for the bouquet toss."

"Oh, I don't know…" She started to protest but Maggie propelled her around the structure.

"Nonsense. All unmarried ladies line up."

Becca stopped and turned to Maggie. "Then you have to, too."

"I've been married and to a good man. That's more than some women can say. Now you get on up there."

Becca stood at the back of the group of giggling young women as Annie stood from her seat in the wagon. She turned around and tossed her bouquet high over her shoulder. The girls crowded close, their arms flailing in the air.

Having been raised on a farm, Annie had strong arms and her throw carried the bouquet farther than any of the girls had expected. In a squeal of female voices, the bouquet landed squarely in Becca's unreceptive hands.

She blinked and gave a wavering smile, relieved that the cheering of the girls would surely keep anyone from hearing the thundering of her heart.

Chapter Seven

Monday morning rolled in with the fog. It fit Becca's mood perfectly. Her stomach in knots, she couldn't eat the going-away breakfast Maggie had made. Instead, she stood on the porch of the boardinghouse, sipping a hot cup of coffee, her hands wrapped around its warmth against the morning chill. Her valise sat at her feet.

She stared out over Main Street and felt a twinge of sadness. What would change while she was gone this time?

Seth had promised to come say good-bye. She wanted to speak with him yesterday about her growing suspicions. She was certain if they put their heads together they could come up with a plan, but there never seemed to be a good time.

The town had gathered again at the schoolhouse for a time of singing, Bible reading and prayer, as they usually did when no preacher was in town. The circuit preacher had headed up to a mining camp after the wedding but would be preaching in Reedsville next Sunday before leaving.

In contrast to Seth's solicitousness on Saturday, yesterday he seemed intent on ignoring her, and she couldn't get him alone for a moment. But she would today. She'd tell him what she overheard and make him promise to look into it and let her know what he discovered.

Becca couldn't stand to have Thomas die and Seth lose his business. His profits were her future, too, but she couldn't imagine Seth living in a town where he thought he had failed. For a brief moment, she wondered if he would consider coming to Salem if that happened. But she quickly pushed that thought aside. No, he'd go back to Portland and work in his father's dry goods business instead.

The rattle of wheels shook her out of her musings as Josh pulled the stagecoach around to the front of the boardinghouse.

He hopped down, nodded to her, and made a final examination of the horses and the coach. James ambled around from the barn to help him.

She looked down the road. No sign of Seth.

Maggie came out and silently put her arm around Becca's waist. Sally followed her mother on to the porch and stood on the other side of Becca.

A few passengers wandered up and handed their tickets to Josh. He stowed their luggage in the boot. Soon all the passengers and their luggage were loaded. Josh looked up to where Becca stood on the porch. "Are you ready?"

She forced back tears. How different her feelings were now compared to the last time she left this porch to board the stagecoach.

Maggie tightened her hold on Becca's waist. "You don't have to go. Stay for awhile and let things sort themselves out. School will still be there."

Becca shook her head, waiting until she was sure her voice was steady. "I wish I could. But I can't."

"You know you're like one of my own." Maggie blinked back the tears pooling in her eyes. "Don't take another four years to visit. This will always be your home." She dabbed at her eyes with the corner of her apron.

Becca nodded, unable to speak for the knot in her throat.

She picked up her valise and blindly headed down the stairs, taking one last look up the road. How could he do this to her? How could he not come say good-bye? Maybe he's afraid of a repeat of last time, a bitter thought. The image of how he looked at her last Saturday flashed through her mind but she pushed it away. Clearly, she misunderstood what she thought she saw.

Josh must have taken her valise because he was now handing her up into the coach. She settled in her seat and gave Maggie and Sally one final wave, but glanced away when their tears threatened to start her own. With a jolt, the stagecoach lurched forward and pulled away from the boardinghouse.

Don't cry. Don't cry. Don't cry. You can lock yourself in your room when you get to Salem and cry until there are no more tears.

The stage came to an abrupt stop. The other passengers were looking out the window, muttering to themselves. Probably a stray dog lying in the road. Becca tapped her foot impatiently, hoping whatever it was in the road would soon move so they could leave. All she wanted to do was leave Reedsville far behind.

"Becca."

She nearly jumped. Looking around the coach at the puzzled faces of the passengers, it took her a moment to realize the voice came from outside the coach. Turning to the coach window, she saw Seth's face perfectly framed. Unexpectedly, hope and relief surged through her, threatening to undo her tenuous control.

"What are you doing here?"

"I told you I'd come say good-bye."

"Don't you think you're cutting it a little close?" A bit of her anger seeped through; she preferred it to crying.

"I was detained. There was another accident at the camp." His eyes flitted around the passenger compartment where four people intently followed their conversation. He took off his hat and resettled it on his head. "Look, Becca—"

"Another accident? Seth, that's what I wanted to talk to you about!" His gaze shifted meaningfully around the coach, and he tilted his head slightly. Making her suspicions public would only make matters worse. She reached for the handle of the stage-coach door.

"What are you doing?"

"We have to talk."

"Uh, we need to go." Josh called down from the driver's seat. "I've got a schedule to keep."

She opened the door, and Seth helped her out. "Could you get my bag out of the boot?"

Chapter Eight

Seth slumped at his desk, realizing he'd been staring at the same invoice for at least five minutes. His mind wasn't on his paperwork; it was on Becca.

The office door opened, and Owen walked through. Seth welcomed the interruption.

"How's Michael Flaherty?" Seth asked.

"He'll be right as rain in a day or two. Nothing's broke. Just a nasty bruise on his leg where the horse got him. Lucky for him he can move quick."

"Did you ask Willie about the bridle?"

"Yep. Said he didn't know how that sliver of wood got in there. He checks all the leather every day after they come in. Must have flown off an axe and lodged in there this morning."

Seth stared out the window. "Still, it seems odd it would lodge in just the place to poke the horse when it started pulling. Too bad the horse didn't know Flaherty was just trying to help."

Owen eased his bulk into the chair Seth still thought of as Thomas's. "Did you see Miz Wilson off?"

Seth shoved the papers away from him. "It seems Miss Wilson has decided to stay."

"She's stayin'?" Owen's eyebrows shot up.

He nodded.

Owen splayed his hand on his desk, studying it intently. "Did she say why?"

Seth sighed, flipping through the papers on his desk. "She's concerned about the logging company. Between an offer to buy the company and some conversations she's overheard, she's convinced someone is trying to run us out of business."

"You don't believe that, do you?" Owen opened a desk drawer and began rummaging through it.

He leaned back in his chair and ran both hands through his hair. "I didn't think so at first, but some of the things she said make sense and can't really be explained away."

"Like what?"

"Twice she's overheard parts of conversations that seem to indicate someone is deliberately causing accidents here and blaming them on ghosts so men won't work for us. I hope that's not true, that time will show it just to be a string of bad luck, but I owe it to my men to look into it." He grinned. "Plus, Becca's as stubborn as the day is long, and even if I didn't believe her, I'd follow up on it just to please her."

"Ah, found it!" Owen pulled a pocketknife out of the drawer. He stood up and shoved it in his hip pocket. "I'm gonna check on things out at the north ridge."

Seth nodded. He almost followed Owen out the door to avoid the stack of papers on his desk. Gritting his teeth, he tried to focus on his paperwork, but he couldn't get the morning's events out of his mind.

After Becca had climbed out of the stage, they went inside to warm up with a cup of coffee. Sitting around Maggie's kitchen table, he questioned Becca about what she had heard. She, in turn, interrogated him about the latest accident.

He asked what her plans were.

"I haven't really thought it out, but I will stay as long as it takes." Her eyes took on a far away, dreamy look he hadn't seen on her since before she left the last time. "I'd love to fix up the old homestead, although I have no idea how to go about it. Have either of you seen Thomas's plans for it?"

Both he and Maggie shook their heads.

"I'll be right back." She darted up the stairs and returned shortly with the box of Thomas's papers. She pulled out a set of rolled-up papers and spread them on the table.

"I knew he was working on plans for the homestead—he'd stay up late drawing—but I've never seen them before." Thomas had always drawn up the plans for the logging company buildings, but they were simple and functional.

This was the perfect home. Becca's face glowed in a way he hadn't seen since she'd returned to Reedsville. Seth watched as she pointed out to Maggie the convenient design of the kitchen and pantry. He wanted to believe she was home to stay, but he was wary. This was a new Becca, unfamiliar and intriguing. Would she ingrain herself into their lives just to decide she was unhappy and leave again?

Seth stood up and paced around the kitchen. "Are you sure you've decided to stay? Because if you're worried about the logging company providing you money—"

"I'm staying."

He stopped pacing and met her eyes. She held his gaze. After a moment, he nodded slightly then sat back down, uncertain of what to make of the warmth spreading through his chest. He seemed to be having a lot of indigestion of late.

"You can help me with something, though." Becca slid a photo out of the box. "I found this in the box of Thomas's papers. Do either of you know who it is?"

"Let me see," he said.

She handed him the photograph. He looked at it for a moment and then nodded. "That's Emily."

"Emily?" Becca took the photo back. "Who is she?"

"Thomas didn't write to you about her?"

She seemed to think on it for a moment. "Maybe. If he did, I didn't pay too much attention to it. Who is she?"

He glanced at Maggie. "Well, we all knew her from when we lived in Portland. She taught one semester of school here before leaving on a family emergency. Her grandfather became ill, wasn't that it?" He looked at Maggie, who nodded in confirmation.

He stood and nodded at Maggie and then Becca. "Ladies, as much as I am enjoying your company, I have to get back to work. I've got paperwork on my desk a mile high." He ignored the surprised look on Becca's face. A smile tugged at his lips. He supposed, regarding Emily, her curiosity wasn't quite satisfied. But he did have work to do.

Now, sitting at his desk, his mind seemed to be on anything but work. Sitting up straight, he gritted his teeth, forcing himself to concentrate on the papers in front of him. "And I'm accomplishing *so* much today," he muttered to himself.

Chapter Nine

Jeremiah McCormick heard the knock on his Portland hotel room door. He pulled a gold pocket watch out of his silk waistcoat, checked the time, and replaced it before getting up to answer the door. A small, wiry man stood there, trail dust coating his boots and battered hat.

"You're three days late." McCormick strode away from the door and sat on the one chair in the room.

The man hesitated then stepped across the threshold. He pulled off his greasy hat and twisted it in his hands. "Yeah, I know. I got held up. But I got good news for you."

McCormick scowled and waved for the man to close the door.

"Oh, yeah. Sorry." He turned and closed the door with a strained snicker.

McCormick leaned back in the chair and crossed his ankle over his other knee. "What's this news you have for me?"

"I've been working up at the logging camp, just like you said. Keeping an eye on things for you. That girl hasn't left town yet. Sounds like she's planning on sticking around."

McCormick kept his eyes expressionless. "Is that all?" He

twitched his foot across his knee and drummed his fingers on the table next to him.

"Well, no, not exactly. There's one other thing. She was at the logging camp."

McCormick's foot stilled. "You saw her?"

"Well, no, not me, exactly. Your friend up there did. Was going on about how purty she was and her being Wilson's sister and all—"

McCormick sat up. "Why didn't he wire me?"

"He's got to be real careful with the telegraph being in the Oregon Express office and all. Someone might get suspicious." He paused a moment, and a grin slanted his thin lips. "But that ain't it. Wilson's sister thinks someone's making all these accidents happen and blaming ghosts to run Blake out of business." A satisfied look replaced his grin.

The silence lengthened. The satisfied look slowly disappeared. The man crumpled his hat some more, shifting from foot to foot.

Finally, McCormick got to his feet, walked over to the dresser and pulled some bills out of his wallet. Tossing them to the man he said, "I've got a job for you."

Chapter Ten

S*eth Blake better have some answers today.* Becca huffed as she got dressed for church. It had been a whole week, and she hadn't heard from him at all. Reaching back to do up her buttons, she felt a twinge between her shoulder blades. She and Maggie had been spring cleaning between stagecoach arrivals, and Becca's muscles were protesting. Her decision to stay in Reedsville hadn't quite turned out like she'd planned.

Yesterday she had tossed out the now-dead wildflower wedding bouquet sitting on the mantle from Annie's wedding. It was lovely to look at, but she wished she had gotten it some other way. Certainly not standing with a horde of unmarried women clamoring to catch it as if it were pure gold. But there had been no good way around the tradition.

No one was more surprised than she when it plunked her in the chest and she instinctively grabbed it. Everyone cheered and Becca felt the fire in her cheeks. Holding the bouquet more like a limp dishrag than a prized possession, she searched for an escape while everyone was sending off the newlyweds.

Spinning around, she ran directly into Seth. His hands came up around her arms to steady her, his blue eyes twinkling.

Even now, the memory heated her cheeks and she sighed.

There was no question about it. Being part of a small town again would take some getting used to.

Falling into bed exhausted each night had kept her from thinking of much of anything, which she suspected was Maggie's plan. The one thing Becca had done was sit at Maggie's writing desk in the parlor and write to her professors. She hoped they would understand, allowing her to finish her work on an independent-study basis.

But that did nothing to alleviate her desire to ride up to the logging camp to demand Seth tell her what he'd discovered. Somewhat mollified at Maggie's assurance that Seth always came for Sunday supper, she hoped he had news to share today.

She hurried downstairs for breakfast with the rest of the boardinghouse occupants, which included the circuit preacher this morning. Roy Adams, on a horse borrowed from the Oregon Express, had been visiting the mining and logging camps dotting the area for the past week. A stocky man with a square, angular face and hawk nose that looked like it had been broken more than once, Preacher Adams had a deep rich voice and seemed pleased to answer questions about his work. The conversation continued after breakfast while the group walked to the little schoolhouse.

Becca found she enjoyed his preaching as much as his conversation. He delivered a simple but powerful sermon. With raven black hair swept back from his face and smoky brown eyes that looked like they were lit from behind by a fire, he spoke honestly about sin and the need for salvation.

She couldn't help but compare him to the more polished orators that usually preached at the university's chapel. His words weren't as educated and refined, but no one could doubt the genuineness of his heart. She'd never met a preacher who spoke so directly, yet seemed so caring toward others.

Owen Taylor had accepted Seth's offer to come to church today, and she was glad. Seth said he felt Owen was seeking answers, that they'd had a few discussions lately of a spiritual nature. She silently prayed that the scales would fall from his eyes, and he would see the truth of God's love for him.

Sam Fulton's daughter, Mary, sat across the aisle with a baby asleep on her lap. Her husband sat next to her with a tow-headed toddler on his lap playing with a handkerchief doll.

Becca couldn't help but wonder what her life would have been like if she hadn't gone away to the university. Would she have married and had children by now if she had stayed? She had never felt ready to give up her independence and settle down to a home and family, but watching Mary it didn't seem so bad. Had going to the university cost her something?

As much as she liked Preacher Adams, she'd heard his message before. It wasn't for her. But it was good to have someone give the message of salvation from time to time for the men at the logging camp and others who needed it. Her mind wandered to the plans Thomas had drawn up for their house.

Hearing Preacher Adams ask Mrs. Paige to lead the closing hymn brought her mind back to the present. And she had forgotten about Owen Taylor until she heard Maggie invite him to Sunday dinner. During dinner, the preacher regaled them with stories from his other churches. Becca suppressed a smile, noticing that Mr. Taylor seemed intrigued by Preacher Adams's stories and comfortable enough to ask questions.

She hoped Seth wasn't getting too comfortable, though. Because he was talking to her after dinner whether he liked it or not.

SETH EXCUSED HIMSELF, leaving Owen, Josh, and James talking on Maggie's front porch after Sunday dinner, and strode inside. He found Becca in the kitchen cleaning up with Maggie and Sally. Becca turned at the sound of his footsteps and smiled.

"Have you had a chance to look at your old homestead yet?"

She wiped her hands on a dish towel and began removing

the apron that covered her Sunday dress. "No, I haven't. Maggie and I have been busy with spring cleaning."

"Why don't you grab those plans, and we'll take a walk out that way and see what kind of shape it's in."

"That's a wonderful idea. I wanted to talk to you anyway."

Seth waited in the kitchen while she dashed upstairs, returning empty-handed with a thoughtful look on her face. Her eyes suddenly lit up.

"Ah, there it is!" She reached under the kitchen table and pulled out Thomas's box. "I must have walked by this five times without it occurring to me to take it upstairs." She pulled out the plans. "Remind me to do that when we get back."

They headed out the kitchen door towards the stream at the far end of the yard. Once out of earshot of the boardinghouse, she peered at Seth. "What have you discovered?"

He glanced at her then stared ahead. "Not much. No one has seen anything suspicious. Every accident has a reasonable explanation." He didn't mention one of the explanations was poor maintenance and bad equipment. Heads flying off axes, handles coming apart on whipsaws. One night someone let all of the horses loose. Some grumblings had reached his ears that men thought he was cutting corners to save money. He knew it wasn't true, but he couldn't blame the men; all the evidence made him look guilty. He turned his gaze back to Becca. She was frowning.

"Someone had to see something. Unless…" She stopped suddenly, causing him to take two steps back to where she was.

"What?"

She bit her lip and looked up at him. "What if it's someone who works at the camp? He could be in it with McCormick, acting like he's working for you, but secretly causing these accidents."

He stood for a moment. The same thought had crossed his mind. Either someone was trying to make him look bad, or he was losing his mind. But who? While he personally didn't know every man who worked for him, by and large they were a good group of hardworking men, and he treated them well. Questioning them wasn't going to endear him to them.

He turned and started walking, forcing Becca to pick up her skirts and hurry after him.

"Well?" She was struggling to match his stride. He slowed his pace.

She had a point, and maybe if he conceded that to her, she'd leave the subject alone. "I'm still not convinced there is any connection with the offer to buy the company. It is possible someone might be holding a grudge against me. But I find it hard to believe someone is willing to risk the safety of their fellow workers." He ran his hand over his face. It could be that he was just too tired lately; maybe he was overlooking basic safety and maintenance. Who knows? It would be too easy to blame someone else to ease his conscience. He certainly had enough to be guilty about.

They came to a trail, not as wide as the main road out of town and unused for some time. They stepped onto parallel paths carved by wagon wheels and separated by grass sprinkled with wildflowers. Trees crowded the edge of the road, helping alleviate some of the warmth of the day.

She suddenly stopped, hands on her hips and brows raised, forcing him to turn and face her. Her gaze challenged him. He smiled, tucking a strand of honey-colored hair behind her ear. "I'll think about who it could be, okay?" He grasped her elbow to prod her along. "And pray about it, too."

As soon as they entered the clearing, Becca's pulse began to race, tears pricking her eyes. *Home!* She stopped, hand curled to her mouth, taking it all in. The last time she'd been here Thomas had been alive. She kept expecting him to walk out the door.

The side closest to them was flat, for about half the length of the clearing, then sloped up toward the craggy mountains. Along the edge of the clearing, the same pretty stream from the boardinghouse gurgled, sporting tufts of wildflowers here and there. In the midst of it all stood an unpainted homestead weathered to a silvery grey. From a distance, it seemed to still be in good shape, but as they drew closer, she noticed shingles missing from the roof, one of the porch supports tilted, and the front door gaping wide open.

All thoughts of the logging camp vanished from her mind. Dropping the plans in front of the porch, she slowly walked to the front door, hesitating at the threshold.

Seth grabbed her arm.

Surprise, anger, and relief all raced through her in succession, leaving confusion in their wake. He tugged her back, stepping in front of her. She gripped his arm and peered around him, gasping when she saw what used to be the Wilson family main living area.

Thick dust covered everything. Pine needles and other debris, probably blown in by the wind through the open door, piled against the walls. She released her hold on his arm and tentatively took a few steps into the room, marking the floor with her footprints. He remained in the doorway.

A rustling came from one of the rooms. She squealed and jumped back, running into Seth's chest. His hands came up on her shoulders. "Let's go outside," she said with a shaky voice.

He guided her out of the house. Grateful for his steadying presence, she took a deep breath. Deciding to examine the house from the outside, she strolled around to the side when she noticed the dirt looked odd, like it had been disturbed.

She bent closer to the ground, her fingers tracing long gouges that had been partially obliterated by rain. Becca straightened and saw Seth studying her. "Come see this." She pointed to the ground. "These must mark the layout of the rooms."

As he scrutinized the markings, she hurried over to where she had dropped the plans and retrieved them, unrolling them as she came back to Seth.

He reached for the plans, brushing his hand against hers.

Sparks raced up her arm, and she blinked. She forced herself to focus on the drawings he held in his hands, translating the lines on paper to the lines in the dirt.

"Here." He pointed to the drawings. "See these lines? They're exactly like the ones in the dirt."

She looked from the paper to the dirt and back again. Trying to envision his plans for the rest of the house, she wandered around to the back and saw Thomas had already begun framing. She shook her head and laughed. How like a man! Start adding on without even cleaning up the existing house. Running her hands down the framing timber, she touched the nails, noticing the impressions the hammer had made in the wood around the nail.

Becca closed her eyes and imagined Thomas hammering those same nails. He had built these walls with his own hands. In her mind, she could see him bending over to pick up another board, pull a nail from between his teeth, and hammer the new board into place, giving his dream substance and form.

Seth came over and stood next to her, leaning his arm against the lumber near her head and nudged his Stetson off his brow with his knuckle.

She caught a faint whiff of shaving soap, leather, and horses. Her stomach seemed to be doing flips. She clasped her hands in front of her, desperate for something to say. What was wrong with her lately? She raised her eyes to his, which she instantly realized was the wrong thing to do. She suddenly felt as if the two of them were sharing some secret, being drawn into some private world. Her heart beat in her throat. She willed her mind to think of something—anything—to break the spell.

"So what part of the house is this?" Her voice came out as a whisper, and she gestured a little too broadly at the skeleton frame surrounding them.

He dropped his arm down from the framing and settled his hands on her shoulders, turning her slightly toward an opening in the wall. She was so conscious of the warmth and weight of his arm—and how oddly protected she felt—she almost missed what he was saying. "Out that window, I bet you'll see some of the prettiest sunsets. And the room up above has an even better view."

She turned in surprise, forgetting how close he was, and found her face inches from his chest. Whatever she was going to say flew from her mind. "Oh," was all she could manage. She tilted her head up. Seth's eyes met hers. He slid his arm from her shoulders and took her hand.

A little shiver ran up her arm as her hand was enveloped in his large, calloused one. She tried to get some perspective on the situation. *I'm sure he's just trying to help me walk around the house, to make sure I don't trip. Am I so addled that the simple courtesies of a gentleman unnerve me?*

"Let me show you something else." He led her around the frame, occasionally referring to the plans, to show her how Thomas had placed each window specifically to catch the best view. Each room revealed something different. Despite the heat of Seth's hand around hers and the fog his presence seemed to cause in her brain, she managed to be amazed.

"I can't wait to see it all built up. It's going to be even better than I imagined." She looked around the house, seeing it anew.

"Becca." Seth was still holding her hand.

She turned toward him, once again aware of how close he was. All thoughts of the house fled her brain, replaced with the feeling that every nerve ending in her hand—the one he was holding—was alive.

His eyes darkened with emotion, and her breath caught in her throat. She blinked, watching him swallow hard.

After a moment, he simply said, "I'm glad you decided to stay."

She smiled up at him, her chest feeling open and light so she could breathe again.

His gaze held hers for a long moment, and she thought he

was going to say something more. When he didn't, she became self-conscious. "We should be getting back," she said, breaking eye contact. "Maggie will be wondering where I am."

He nodded, squeezing her hand before letting it go, as they started back to the boardinghouse.

Chapter Eleven

Rain hammering on the roof awakened Becca. So far it had been a warm, dry spring, and she looked forward to a break from the heat that she knew the rain would bring. After breakfast, she and Maggie tackled the remainder of the spring cleaning chores, such as blacking the stove and dusting the parlor.

"There's no purpose in scrubbing the floors or washing the windows today," Maggie declared. "It'd just be wasted effort."

Around dinnertime, the rain stopped and the sun broke through the clouds. Taking a break to enjoy the beauty of the outdoors after a rainstorm, Maggie rested on the front porch swing.

Becca decided to take a walk out to her house. It felt odd to think of it that way, as *her* house. She grabbed the plans and a pencil to make some notes and traipsed past Maggie's garden, over the footbridge that crossed the stream. The smell of damp earth hung heavy in the air. Wandering through the meadow, her mind drifted as aimlessly as her feet. The sunshine warmed her shoulders, and her muscles began to un-kink, sore from all of the scrubbing she'd done.

She stopped short of the clearing and looked at the house.

Her house. She slowly circled it. Finally choosing the "parlor," she sat down with her back against one of the framing timbers.

After thinking about it so often, she could imagine it completed, even more than on her first trip here. She leaned against the wood and closed her eyes, imagining solid walls painted the sunny color of daffodils, the floors lined with vivid rugs surrounded by the furniture she'd grown up with. A warm fire burned in the fireplace while she served coffee and dessert to friends. She tried to picture what Thomas had in mind, and could almost see it. She could almost see him. She could feel him. He was here.

With her eyes closed, feeling the soft breeze on her face and hearing it rush through the trees, she felt something else. A gentle peace—God's peace.

It startled her. She hadn't realized it was missing. Possibly because she'd been so busy trying to handle everything herself. What had gone wrong? When had it disappeared? It must have been a gradual thing. In fact, the few times she'd actually thought about it, she had attributed the loss to growing up and losing her childish innocence. An independence-minded pride had taken its place.

As she leaned against the post, her soul expressed things to God she couldn't form into words. She knew without a doubt God wanted her here. And for the first time in a long while, she listened for His voice.

She opened her eyes with a start, not knowing how long she'd been sitting there. Wondering what time it was, she glanced up at the sky. The sun hung lower than she expected. She picked up the plans, realizing she'd have to make notes later. She stood and began to head back to the boardinghouse, thinking she'd pick some wildflowers on her way back for the supper table.

As soon as she left the shade of trees and entered the meadow, the sun turned the rainwater on the grass and flowers into steam. Her dress became sticky and clung to her. The nearby trees looked inviting and Becca strolled toward them. Walking back in their shade would be much more comfortable even if it would make for a bit longer trip.

When she reached the trees, the coolness refreshed her warm face. She laid her flowers and plans on a fallen tree and removed her hat, using it to fan away the dampness from her face and neck.

SETH HAD SPENT most of the day torn between staying at the logging camp to keep an eye on things and heading to town. Finally, when he knew he'd have only enough time to get to Fulton's before it closed, he rode off. The chance that he might get a meal from Maggie was added incentive. The fact that Becca would be there cinched the deal.

The horse knew the way, so Seth pulled the worn catalog out of his saddlebag. He wasn't sure if he should be doing this. Was it too soon? Would she think it was too much? He wasn't sure if she still saw him as a big brother or as a man, and he certainly hadn't sorted out his feelings for her. Still, he figured Thomas would approve.

He glanced at the catalog again. Didn't every woman want glass windows in her house? These would be just the ticket. And as long as she was caught up with plans for the house, maybe she'd lose interest in the goings-on at the camp.

He stuffed the catalog back into his saddlebag before he got to the boardinghouse.

Seth was considering whether he had time to stable his horse in the barn or if he should just ride to Fulton's. A movement beyond the house caught his eye. In the distance, he could see a small figure in the meadow heading toward the trees. It was Becca, he could tell, even at this distance.

Should he follow her? Knowing her temper when she thought she was being coddled, he wasn't keen on upsetting her.

Plus, how would he explain his presence? And Fulton's would close before he could get there.

He kept on riding, eyes fixed on the woods. Not too many people would have any reason to be out there. As she'd repeatedly told him, she could take care of herself.

BECCA TOSSED her hat on the log next to the wildflowers and the plans. She was about to sit down next to them when she heard a twig snap and leaves crunch. She looked around, hoping to see some sort of wildlife. Its appearance had been scarce, probably due to the town's growth. She stilled, hoping to encourage the creature to show itself.

Instead, not ten feet away, stood two unshaven men with uncut, greasy hair and stained buckskins.

Becca's legs turned to rubber, and she began to tremble. Her eyes widened as she sucked in her breath. She shot up a prayer, not even forming words in her mind, just hoping God would protect her and show her what to do. She released her breath, lifted her chin, and drew herself up to her full height, hoping to conceal her fear. She was probably over-reacting, anyway. Surely they were just travelers who lost their way off the road.

"Well looky what we have here! A purty little thing all alone in the woods." The man on the left snickered and nudged his partner, who said, "Looks like we're gonna have some fun!"

They weren't lost travelers. Hope vanished. Cold fear slithered in her stomach.

"You are trespassing," she said in her best classroom voice. "Leave immediately."

The two men laughed even harder and ambled toward her.

Becca looked around wildly for an escape. She had to leave here. She took a step back, stumbled into the log and lost her balance. Her back hit hard and she sprawled on the ground.

One of the men loomed over her and grabbed her by the

shoulders. She screamed and kicked her heel between his legs, sending the man reeling with a grunt of pain. The second man grabbed her from behind, pinning her arms to her sides as he dragged her over the log, scraping the backs of her thighs. She screamed at the top of her lungs.

SETH STILL HADN'T FIGURED out what he would say to Becca to explain his presence as he headed across the footbridge into the meadow, his long powerful legs eating up the ground. He hadn't figured it out himself why he was here. He'd have to make it to Fulton's another day.

A scream shattered the air.

He broke into a run. He pulled his Colt revolver from its holster and cocked it. Logic told him a small animal or bug had frightened her. But there was an ugly knot in his stomach, one he never ignored.

Chapter Twelve

As she gasped for air, she almost choked on the stench of her attackers. Her legs lashed out, trying to make contact with the man holding her from behind. But this one avoided her kicks. He wrapped her in a bear hug and held her off the ground.

The first man had recovered from her kick and stalked toward where his partner held her, his eyes menacing. He slapped her hard, twice, with the back of his hand, and called her a filthy name.

Her face burned. Warm blood trickled from the corner of her mouth, and one eye felt like it was starting to swell shut. She fought back tears and stared at the man with pure hatred.

He began to unbutton his dungarees. The man holding Becca sniggered.

She felt the bile rise in her throat as she realized what was happening. She forced the panic away from her, knowing her mind was her only weapon. *Lord, what am I going to do?*

Her attacker pinned her arms, but she could just reach the drawing pencil in her pocket if she bent her wrist. She grabbed it with her fingers and worked it up into her palm.

The man who held her arms threw her to the ground. Before

she could get up, he forced her shoulders to the damp, musty soil.

Her hand loosened its grip on the pencil, and it almost flew out of her hand. She re-gripped it, tightening her hold, and lay still.

"All the fight gone outta you yet, missy? We'll teach you a lesson." As her attacker loomed over her, his partner loosened his grip on her arms. He leaned within inches of her face.

She whipped the pencil up and aimed for his eye.

He caught her movement and dodged at the last second, but not in time to avoid a bloody gouge in his cheek. He grabbed at his face. "You little—"

His scream was cut short.

As if by magic, he levitated in front of her and sailed through the air. The back of his legs snagged the same log they'd dragged Becca over, and he crashed to the ground on his back.

Seth loomed over Becca and her remaining attacker. The attacker's grip relaxed.

Relief flooded through her and threatened to weaken her. She forced herself not to give in. She sprang to a sitting position and rammed her elbow into his stomach. He doubled over, nearly on top of her. She scrambled out of the way just in time to see Seth's fist catch his jaw and send him sprawling.

Becca jumped up and gave his shin a hard kick before running over to Seth.

He put his left arm around her. His right one, she just now noticed, held his revolver. She turned her head into his chest.

"Which one hit you?" His voice was deceptively calm, his eyes and his revolver leveled at the two men.

"Th-the one on the left." Her tongue felt thick, and her lips were swollen. The world started to spin. Afraid she was going to faint, she slipped her arms around Seth's waist and held on. He tightened his grip on her shoulder, holding her up against his side. She noticed how clean he smelled, with a trace of horses and leather. The scent of Seth. The scent of safety.

"We didn't mean no harm. We were just havin' a little—" The man on the left struggled to sit up, not finishing his sentence as the bullet whizzed past his ear and lodged in the tree behind his head.

Seth's voice was low and menacing. "One more word out of either of your filthy mouths and my next shot will have better aim. I ought to kill you both, but the lady's already upset enough."

He fired three more shots into the air. He gripped the revolver until his knuckles whitened. Powerful anger surged through him. It took all of his self-control to keep from pounding the men to a pulp. He was sure he had arrived in time to keep Becca's virtue intact. But what if he hadn't been on his way to town or seen her walk toward the woods? His stomach turned at the thought. Encircled by his arm, he was aware of just how small she was.

And vulnerable.

The clatter of whipping branches and crunching underbrush preceded Josh a moment before he appeared at a full run, his revolver out. James ran close behind carrying the rifle they used on stage runs.

"What happened?" Josh pulled up next to Seth, slightly out of breath, and leveled his weapon at Becca's attackers. "I heard your shots."

James came to a stop behind Josh's shoulder.

"These two here were bothering Becca." Seth's voice was hoarse. He cleared it. Details would just upset Becca further.

Becca turned in his arms, and Seth knew the moment Josh and James saw her face. Josh swore under his breath, his face darkening. James's face paled like a sheet on Maggie's wash line.

"James." Seth turned to face the boy who couldn't take his eyes off Becca. "James!"

James dragged his gaze from Becca's face and met Seth's.

"I need you to go to the barn, and bring back enough rope to tie up their hands and legs. We'll wire for the sheriff."

James nodded and took off at a run.

"Why go to through the effort to tie them up, Seth?" Josh's voice was casual. "They don't deserve to live."

"I agree, but I don't want Becca upset any more than she already is."

Becca began to tremble. He tightened his arm around her shoulders, afraid she would collapse any minute. He motioned Josh closer and spoke low.

"Can you and James handle these two? I need to take her back to Maggie's."

"No problem. You take care of Becca. Make sure she's all right."

Seth holstered his weapon, lifted Becca into his arms and carried her away from the woods. She tucked her head into his shoulder, putting her arms around his neck while he held her tightly against his chest.

Something ached in his chest, and his eyes moistened. He blinked and swallowed, forcing his mind away from the men in the woods.

At the stream, he stopped and eased her down. She might want a few minutes to collect herself before they returned to the way station. Truth be told, he wasn't ready to relinquish her to Maggie's ministrations yet, and he could use a few minutes to collect himself.

Keeping one arm around her, he pulled his bandana out and dipped it in the cool water. His hand shook. He hoped she didn't see. Gently pushing her hair back, the vision of her battered face intensified the ache until he thought he couldn't draw a breath. He eased out a breath, and concentrated on Becca. Her lips were swollen and purple, her left eye had swelled shut and a bruise was forming on her cheek. He sponged the blood off her face.

"Are you hurt anywhere else?" His voice sounded funny even to him.

Becca gingerly shook her head, not looking at him. Tears spilled out of her eyes and she began sobbing.

Seth pulled her to his chest and let her cry, stroking her hair, not knowing what else to do. "Oh, Becca. I couldn't bear it if anything happened to you," he whispered into her hair. "I'll keep you safe. Don't worry." If he had anything to do with it, nothing would ever hurt her again.

Do you think you can protect her all the time? Only I can do that. I love her more than you do.

The voice spoke to his heart. But he had to do everything he could to protect her. He owed it to her brother.

When she stopped sobbing, Seth mopped up her tears with his bandana, but she kept her eyes downcast. Dusk had settled while they sat by the stream and now it was almost dark. He held her silently for a few more minutes; he didn't want to let her go. "Are you ready to go back to the boardinghouse?"

She nodded and struggled to her feet.

Seth lifted her up and carried her across the footbridge. When they reached the back door Maggie flung it open, her apron knotted in her hands.

"Oh, my dear! Josh told me what happened. How badly are you hurt? Did you—" Maggie caught his sharp look and broke off her sentence.

Becca kept her face turned toward Seth's chest.

"Well, let's just set you down here and get some hot tea in you, and then I'll tend to your face."

He carried her over to the kitchen table and sat her in a chair. Kneeling in front of her, he took her small hands in his, rubbing his thumb over them. When she still didn't look at him, he used his forefinger to lift her chin.

"Hey. You're safe here. Okay? I'm not going to let anything happen to you. Maggie's going to take care of you." He ran his thumb along her chin.

She raised her eyes to meet his.

"That's my girl." He slid his hand along her jaw and held her face gently for a moment before releasing her and straightening up. Her eyes followed him as he pulled out a chair next to hers and sat down.

Maggie poured Becca's tea and generously dosed it with sugar. She handed it to Becca, whose hands shook too much to hold the cup. Seth covered her hands with one of his to help her.

As Becca got some tea in her, Maggie ordered Sally to bring her bandages and supplies and then finish her chores. She told Seth to get a plate from the stove where they were keeping warm and to eat.

He shook his head. Eating was the last thing on his mind right now.

Once the tea was gone, Maggie made a poultice for Becca's eye. Becca winced as Maggie cleaned and bandaged her wounds. Seth squeezed her hand.

When she was done with Becca, Maggie insisted they both eat. She brought out two steaming plates. He ate mechanically, the food tasteless to him, while watching Becca pick at her supper. Seth saw her shudder and raised his eyebrows, but she wasn't looking at him. A few moments of silence passed.

"Could I have a bath?" Becca looked at Maggie.

"Certainly, my dear. It should help you sleep. Seth, could you take the tub to her room? I think she'll be more comfortable there."

Seth nodded and set the kettle to boil before retrieving the metal tub from its nail just outside the kitchen door. He carried it through the kitchen and up the stairs, not sure which guest room was Becca's. It happened to be the first door he opened, the faint scent of roses greeting him. He set the tub down in the middle of the floor and scanned her room for a moment, noticing her hat on the dresser, an open book on the bed. Things that made the room hers. He returned to the kitchen and spent the next few minutes carrying water to fill the tub, then topping it off with boiling water from the now-steaming kettle. It was good to be useful.

When the women disappeared into the room, and shut the door on him, he paced in the hall for a bit. Finally, he pulled up a chair outside the door. The sounds of water and low conversation reached his ears.

In what seemed a short time later, the door opened and Seth looked up. Maggie stared at him with a look of surprise, her mouth slightly open. But then she seemed to recover her composure and with a slight smile asked, "Could you remove the bath water?"

Seth nodded, offering no explanation for his presence. He stepped into the room and saw Becca tucked into bed, asleep. He was grateful she could get some rest. Nevertheless, her injuries tugged at his heart. He stepped closer to the bed and watched her sleep for a moment. Reaching out, he brushed her cheek with the back of his hand. "Sleep well," he whispered.

He stepped back and picked up the tub. When he turned to leave the room, he saw Maggie in the doorway holding a lamp. *Had she been standing there the whole time, or did she just arrive?* Mentally, he shrugged as he carried the tub past her. Did it matter what she thought? The thing was, he wasn't sure what *he* thought.

After tossing the bathwater on Maggie's garden and returning to the house, he found Maggie alone in the parlor, knitting. She stopped and looked at him expectantly. He sat down and stretched out his legs, gazing into the empty fireplace.

Maggie needed to know, and Becca shouldn't have to be the one to tell her. He rubbed his hands over his face. In a voice that sounded emotionless even to him, he told Maggie what happened to Becca.

Maggie remained silent until he was finished, then stood and crossed the room to lay a hand on his shoulder.

"You're hurting for her." It was a statement, not a question, in Maggie's direct and motherly way.

His throat tightened. He did hurt for her, more than he could ever imagine. And he hated how powerless he felt.

"Thomas's mind would be at ease knowing you were taking care of her." Maggie turned and started to leave the room, pausing at the door. "And loving her."

Before he could speak, Maggie had left the room.

THE EVENTS of the day had drained him, and conflicting emotions warred within. He'd always loved her as a little sister and had always felt protective of her. But now it went beyond a sense of duty. But was it the kind of love a man feels for a woman? Maggie's comment had surprised him.

It didn't matter. Becca couldn't be the woman for him, could she? He always imagined that he'd marry someone like his mother: gentle, quiet. Not that he remembered much about her. But the way his father talked about her, Seth knew he was still in love with her after all these years.

At the sound of approaching footsteps, Seth headed outside to the porch.

Josh and James were just climbing the steps.

"Go on inside, James," Seth said brusquely. "Your mother has supper keeping warm for you."

James started to protest, but when he looked at Seth's face he hurried inside and took Becca's hat and house plans with him.

Josh raised his eyebrow at Seth, but only said, "Is Becca okay?"

"She looks like she do-si-doed with a train, but nothing's broken. What did you do with those two?"

Josh grinned. "We locked them in the bank vault. Figured that was the most secure place in town. Wilkins looked pretty shocked when we asked him, but he hurried to open up the vault right away. Ben wired the sheriff. We got lucky and got a wire right back. He'll be here tomorrow."

"Did you find out anything about those two?"

Josh plopped into the porch swing with a sigh before

answering. "I don't know whether to believe those two scoundrels or not, but they're in deep enough as it is, so there is no reason for them to lie. They said a man approached them and paid them to scare Becca really bad."

"Scare Becca? Did they say why, or who the man was?"

"Not really. They said the man only wanted her to leave town. Their happening on her in the woods was just luck. They gave me a description of the man—small but strong, with a beat up, dirty hat, curly dark hair, dark eyes."

"Could be anybody." Seth leaned his elbows on the porch railing and dropped his head into his hands.

"Yep, but they all work at the logging camp."

Seth's head snapped up. "What?"

"It's Charley Tillman and George Atlee."

Seth ran his hands through his hair. The names sounded familiar. And now that Josh mentioned it, their faces did look vaguely familiar, although they were never that dirty when they worked for him. He wondered if it was supposed to be some sort of disguise.

Josh sighed. "There's one more thing."

Seth groaned. Could it get any worse?

"This was the picture he gave them." Josh pulled a tintype from his breast pocket and handed it to Seth.

It was of Becca. And it was the same one that used to sit on Thomas's desk.

Chapter Thirteen

Seth could feel every nerve in his body. The events of yesterday, the lack of sleep, the information Josh had given him all conspired to drive him into a foul mood. He poured himself a cup of coffee from Maggie's stove, hoping it would help.

He had just plunked himself into one of Maggie's kitchen chairs when she entered. She didn't seem surprised to see him there.

"Did you get any sleep?" she asked.

"A little."

Maggie nodded and began her work in the kitchen in silence. Seth was glad. He wasn't up to conversation.

The kitchen door opened, and James came in cradling eggs in his arm. Maggie hurried to take them from him. "Thank you, James. I hadn't gotten out there yet."

James grinned. "I was hungry and eggs sounded good."

Maggie took the eggs over to the stove, and he heard cracking. A moment later, James pulled out a chair and plopped down next to him. "Uh, how's Becca?"

He glanced over at James who was studying the kitchen table. "She's still sleeping."

James nodded.

Seth planted his elbows on the table, the coffee cup warming his hands. He should be getting back to the camp, but he felt compelled to stay. It was irrational; Maggie could take care of Becca just fine. But it was his fault Thomas was killed. He wasn't going to let anything else happen to Becca.

Thomas's death resulted from Seth's negligence. Now the "ghosts" at the logging camp had included Becca in their "accidents." It was bad enough seeing his men hurt; they knew they worked a dangerous job. But Becca....

They might try again. And not fail. That much had become clear during the long night. There was someone behind all of this. He should have listened to Becca. If he had, maybe she wouldn't have been hurt.

A plate of eggs slid next to him, interrupting his thoughts. He looked up and nodded his thanks to Maggie. She set plates down for James and herself before taking a seat and blessing the food.

His first bite filled his mouth with warm, buttery eggs. The cook at the camp was good as far as cooks went, but he had nothing on Maggie. He ate silently, forcing himself to listen while James and Maggie discussed the upcoming day.

"Josh is taking me with him on the run to Salem," James said in between bites. "He's going to let me drive part of the time."

"I'll pack some extra food," Maggie said. "I don't think that way station feeds you nearly well enough."

It took a moment for the full impact of James's words to hit Seth. "You and Josh are both going?"

"Yeah." James leaned back in his chair. "Josh says—"

Seth cut him off. "There will be no men around here for two days? Who's going to look after Becca?" Images of the scene he had come upon, Becca on the ground with the two men over her, flooded his mind.

He shoved the memory away and looked from James to

Maggie. She was supposed to be the mothering type. How could she allow this?

Maggie reached across the table and clasped Seth's hand. "We'll be fine."

He didn't want to worry them with his suspicions—and he knew Maggie would worry. But the fear that this unknown person could strike at any time just about undid him.

He pulled his hand away from Maggie's. "I don't want her going out alone." His throat tightened. "She's very lucky nothing more serious happened to her."

Maggie gave him a sympathetic look, which irked him. She should be more worried.

"God apparently had other plans for her. He was watching over her. You can't mean to make her a prisoner here. She's a grown woman. No one can watch her every minute of the day." She leaned forward but this time didn't try to take his hand. "Seth, you have to trust God with this."

"I'll talk to her and make her understand." Seth downed the rest of his coffee and set the mug down none too gently. Maggie didn't understand the danger.

She sighed and shook her head.

BECCA AWOKE in a dark room to the sounds of screams and found herself on one elbow. For a long moment she saw the woods instead of her room. One eye wouldn't open—it was stuck shut—and it took her a minute to remember the poultice. Perspiration soaked her nightgown. With a shuddering breath she sank back on the pillow, eyelids heavy.

A familiar presence calmed her, held her hand, and soothed her back to sleep. By morning, she almost believed the presence was real. The lock of hair that fell over his forehead was exactly like Seth's.

She awoke stiff and sore to a light-filled room. She managed to remove the poultice from her eye, wash her face, and get dressed.

Every movement reminded her of her injuries . . . and the actions that caused them. She could not bear to think of what might have happened if Seth had not been there. She shuddered, glad she didn't have to find out. She pushed every image out of her mind before it could unfold. Least remembered, soonest mended.

Leaving her room, she noticed a chair sat outside the door.

She remembered that comforting presence from last night. Had someone been there, or did she imagine it?

She entered the kitchen, pleasantly surprised to see Seth sitting at the table.

A rush of tenderness filled Becca's heart. Had Seth sat outside her room all night? Warm comfort spread over her as she remembered his words by the stream yesterday. She started to smile, but winced when the skin on her cut lip pulled.

He stood and took a step toward her. "Are you sure you're ready to get up? How are you feeling? You didn't seem to sleep well."

"You *were* outside my room. Were you there all night?"

"Most of it." Seth looked at her a moment before turning to the stove and picking up the coffee pot.

She didn't know what to say. His tenderness overwhelmed her, and she was a little embarrassed to know he had comforted her during the night.

She plucked at her skirt. "Where's Maggie?"

"Outside pulling weeds in the garden."

Seth poured a second cup and brought both back to the table. He motioned for her to sit before he took his own seat.

She picked up her cup and started to take a sip.

"I think you should go back to Salem. Josh and James are just about ready to leave on a run there and you should go with them."

Her cup stilled in mid-air at Seth's pronouncement. Her eye and lip began to throb. What was he saying? After all that tenderness yesterday and last night, he wanted her to leave? The coffee soured in her stomach.

She set her coffee cup on the table but kept her hands wrapped around it so they wouldn't shake. *I did it again, didn't I? I must have said something in my sleep, confessed my feelings for him like I did four years ago.* Becca stared at her cup. She didn't know if Seth was looking at her, but she couldn't look at him. *Do I have feelings for him? Could they have come out in my sleep without my even acknowledging them?*

She didn't know, didn't want to think about it right now, and certainly wasn't going to ask Seth. She willed herself to sound calm and collected then she lifted her eyes to meet his gaze. "I'm not going. This is where I'm supposed to be. I haven't always known the right thing to do these last several years, but this is one thing I am perfectly clear about: I know God wants me here, and I am staying." She continued to hold his gaze.

"There'll be no men around here for two days. I can't keep my eye on you every second; I've got a logging camp to run despite someone's best efforts to destroy it. I don't know if I'll be there to rescue you next time you get in trouble. So if you're not going to Salem, you'd better tell someone before you go anywhere outside this house. Better yet, stay inside."

She couldn't breathe, stunned by the vehemence of Seth's words. How dare he speak to her as if she hadn't a brain in her head! She stood up abruptly, and her chair teetered on two legs before finally righting itself.

"Does that also include using the outhouse?" Turning, she stormed out the back door. It took her a few steps before she spotted Maggie and Sally weeding the garden.

Maggie called out to her. "Becca! Come over here. We could use your help weeding this section."

She went over and plopped down with a groan in the soft

dirt. She started tugging weeds with a vengeance in the section Maggie indicated.

"This is the perfect day to do this, after the rain," Maggie commented. "It never ceases to amaze me how much weeding a garden needs. I could come out here every day and find a patch that needs to be weeded."

Becca worked vigorously in her patch, hurling the weeds into a pile. Her soreness from yesterday a faint memory, her anger so consumed her.

After they worked for a while in silence, Maggie called to Sally. "Why don't you go down by the stream and see if you can find some greens for a salad. This hot weather has just about ruined the lettuce. What hasn't wilted will soon bolt and turn bitter. Yesterday's rain didn't do anything to change that."

As soon as Sally was out of earshot, Becca spoke. "Do you know Seth thinks I should leave?" Not giving Maggie a chance to answer she continued. "Because I, apparently, cannot take care of myself and require someone to watch me every minute. He saw me taking care of myself just fine yesterday. I don't understand how he could be so caring and tender one day and then the next—"

She sat back on her haunches, her lips tight. "Did you know he stayed outside my room all night? How can he be like that—kind and protective one minute and then be so–so… oh, I don't know, so *mean* the next?" She snatched out a few more weeds.

Maggie didn't answer right away and for a moment, Becca wondered if Maggie would respond at all. "Sometimes a body gets scared by how intense his feelings are, and reacts by getting angry," Maggie gave a small laugh. "At least most menfolk do. I imagine that probably happened to Seth. Give him time to work it out."

"He can have all the time he wants. I'm not leaving."

Maggie laughed. "No, I didn't figure you would."

SETH STRODE INTO THE BARN, nodding at Josh and James readying the stagecoach. He had to get back to the camp. Heaving the saddle on top of his horse, he thought about what Maggie had said. *Okay, God, it's up to You. You have to take care of her now.* Yesterday's feelings of tenderness and protection surged up again, abating his anger.

When Becca's face paled at his suggestion, her black eye and swollen lip stood out even more. Her injuries tugged at his heart, and he wanted nothing more than to pull her into his lap and hold her until the bruises were better. But his first priority had to be her protection.

He looked up from cinching the saddle. Josh stood there. "Are you going to tell her who her attackers were?"

Seth straightened but didn't answer for a moment. "I don't think so. It would only worry her more. I told her not to leave the house."

Josh raised his eyebrows, and Seth expected him to disagree. But Josh merely asked, "Do you think the same thing happened to Thomas?"

Seth thought his heart would stop beating. It took him a moment to register what Josh was saying. Seth had never put the pieces together quite that way before by including Thomas's death in the string of accidents at the camp. "Are you saying you think it was a staged accident to scare Thomas, or me, and it went wrong?"

Josh nodded.

Seth swallowed hard, a cold chill seeping into his bones. But Josh didn't know about the cut chains—that Seth had inspected them, and his failure allowed the faulty chains to be used. No one knew. But if Josh thought Thomas's death was the first in the string of accidents, then maybe Becca would too. She wouldn't ever have to know.

It was the coward's way out, and it bothered Seth more than he cared to admit that he was seriously considering taking it.

Seth grabbed the reins, stepped up with his left foot in to the stirrup and swung into the saddle. “Tell Maggie I’ll be stopping in for supper.”

Chapter Fourteen

The clouds had rolled in again on a stiff breeze, and it began to rain. Maggie, Sally, and Becca hurried inside. Becca wandered around the house, tidying up a bit, but not finding much to do. Maggie refused to let her help with any chores. She tried to open her schoolbooks but couldn't concentrate on them.

She ended up in the parlor where she spied her hat and sketchbook. If it wasn't raining, that would give her something to do. She could finish …

Her thought trailed off as she saw the way her hat and sketchbook were laying. As she stared, the image of them lying on the log in the woods superimposed itself over the present. Visions of the attack flooded her mind.

Overpowered, she sat. She tried to force the memories away, but she couldn't. Wrapping her arms around herself, she sobbed uncontrollably.

Fear as dark and oppressive as the clouds outside settled over her. Image after image crashed over her again and again, until she felt battered and raw. She didn't believe she could ever summon strength and confidence again. She didn't have to disregard Seth's order. She didn't want to go outside at all.

She was still huddled on the sofa, dried tears on her cheeks, when Maggie came looking for her. She sat down and put her arms around Becca's shoulders.

"I was wondering when you would get around to crying it out. That's God's way of helping us release all those feelings tumbling around inside."

She looked up at Maggie, and her tears started flowing again. "But I'm so afraid. I don't ever want to leave the house. Maybe Seth was right. Maybe I should go back to Salem."

Maggie squeezed Becca's shoulders. "You know, he said those words out of fear for you, and now you're saying them out of fear as well." She reached over to the end table and picked up her Bible. "What does God tell us about fear?"

She knew the Bible said something about it, of course, but her head felt stuffed with cotton; she couldn't think. She shook her head.

Maggie flipped through her Bible. "It's only natural to be afraid. I know you can't imagine it now, but those feelings will fade in time. Nothing comes as a surprise to God. Not your attack in the woods, not your brother's death. I don't know how it all fits into God's plan, but we don't need to be afraid of what He has planned for us, because it'll ultimately be for good."

Becca wiped her nose with the handkerchief from her apron pocket.

Maggie opened her mouth as if to speak but was interrupted by a knock at the front door. She patted Becca's knee. "I'll go see who that is." She set her open Bible next to Becca. Becca let her eyes drift down the page until she saw the underlined verse: *For God hath not given us the spirit of fear; but of power, and of love, and of a sound mind.*

Footsteps echoed down the hallway. Becca heard a deep, male voice and then Maggie was escorting someone into the parlor.

"Becca," Maggie began, "this is Sheriff Carlisle from the

county seat. Sheriff, this is Miss Wilson. Please, make yourself comfortable. I'll go fetch some coffee."

The sheriff nodded in her direction at the introduction. When Maggie left, he seated himself in the chair opposite Becca, placing his hat on his knee.

He was older than she would have expected. A bit of a paunch hung over his gun belt, and he was gray at the temples. He smiled at Becca, his pale blue eyes wrinkling up in the corners as if he did a lot of laughing.

She watched as his eyes took in her bruises, now a purplish-green, and her swollen eye and lips. He leaned forward.

"Were you the one attacked, Miss?"

"Yes." She swallowed. Her heart raced at the thought of retelling her story, but she brought her mind back to the verse she had just read. *I can choose to trust God and not fear.*

"I know it might be kinda hard on you," the sheriff said, surprisingly gentle, "but you'd be helping me out if you could tell me what happened."

Becca clasped her hands in her lap and took a deep breath.

SETH FORCED himself to pay attention to the activity on the north ridge. Work here had been progressing slower than normal. The men were extra careful, almost too much so. He couldn't blame them.

The sound of pounding horse hooves caused him to turn. Not more bad news.

John McAlistar came into view and reined in just as he got to Seth. "Sheriff just came into town," he huffed, a little out of breath. "He stopped in at the telegraph office, and Ben sent me to tell you."

He released his pent-up breath. "Thanks, John. I'll be right there."

John nodded and wheeled his horse back toward town,

Moments later, Seth followed John's trail to town. Would Becca still be mad at him? Had he made the right decision in telling her to leave? Didn't matter, because she hadn't gotten on the stage. He wasn't sure if he was glad or mad.

So what do I do next, Lord?

A verse he had memorized came to mind. Proverbs three, verses five and six: "Trust in the Lord with all thine heart; and lean not unto thine own understanding. In all thy ways acknowledge him, and he shall direct thy paths."

Seth shifted in the saddle and blew out a breath. *I've been trying to figure it out on my own and rely on my own understanding of the situation. I haven't been trusting You to take care of Becca and everything else. I guess I need to remember You've already figured it all out. I just need to wait until You show me what to do.* Seth pushed the rim of his hat up just a notch. *But waiting's the hard part, Lord.* He sighed again, trying to relinquish it to God.

But how would Becca receive him?

He rode up just as the sheriff was descending Maggie's porch steps. Seth dismounted and threw the reins over the railing. "Thanks for getting here so soon, Sheriff."

"Your town's getting big enough to have its own deputy. That's something you all might want to consider.

Seth rubbed his chin. "Yeah, we'll have to look in to it."

The sheriff shifted his bulk to his other leg. "So, tell me about these men you caught. Miss Wilson's already told me her part."

He wondered how Becca had handled that. He relayed to the sheriff what he saw and what they had done with the men.

The sheriff listened, nodding occasionally. "Let's go see those men."

"There's one more thing." He reached into his pocket and pulled out the photograph of Becca he had found on her attackers. He handed it to the sheriff. "The men we caught had this on them."

"Do you have any idea how they got this?" The sheriff held Becca's photograph firmly between gloved fingers.

"Last I saw it, it was at the boardinghouse in a box of papers belonging to her brother."

"Could someone at the boardinghouse have taken it?"

"It's possible, I suppose. But I don't know who. Maggie doesn't have any boarders now, other than Becca, and way station passengers don't wander through the house."

"What about a break-in?"

"There's always someone there, except for Sunday services. Even if someone came into the house, how would they know where to look?" Seth took his hat off and ran his fingers through his hair. "I can't find any explanation for it, and it's eating me up."

The sheriff nodded and gave the photograph back to Seth. "Let's go get those men out of the bank vault."

BECCA SURVIVED RELATING the details of her attack to the sheriff. Some of the heaviness was gone, but it left in its wake a gnawing uncertainty. *Lord, I know You told me You wanted me to stay here. But if You want me to leave now, let me know. I'm too independent by half, always rushing to prove how self-sufficient I am without stopping to think about what You would have me do.*

She thought about Seth's words this morning. She had roamed the woods and meadows often as a child—they all had—and never given a thought to it. Certainly the stage line and the booming logging business brought more strangers through town, and some of those might be like the men who attacked her. So she would be more careful in the future. But return to Salem? That seemed a bit extreme.

There was no explanation for Seth's overreaction. So until he cared to explain himself, she was going to continue to figure out what really happened to Thomas, and what was going on at the logging camp. Seth could think what he liked.

Now what? Almost as if it were calling her, she deliberately turned to look at her sketchpad. By the time the sheriff had left, it had stopped raining, and the sun was out again and shining.

And part of her yearned to be outside. It would be a perfect way to confront her fears, to begin to replace bad memories with good ones. She held onto her verse, "For God hath not given us the spirit of fear..."

She picked up the sketchpad.

Stepping out the back door of the boardinghouse, she hesitated. Then she walked the opposite direction of the forest and went down to the stream behind the house. She was not going to give in to her fear, but she found being within sight of the house comforting. Despite her slight tremor of fear, she wondered what Seth would think about her being out here. Would he consider it defying his order?

She smiled at the thought.

Coming to her favorite rock, she settled herself comfortably on the boulder, still slightly damp, but warm. She'd have to change her skirt when she got back. Several kinds of wildflowers grew along the banks of the stream.

She sketched roughly at first and then, pleased with her efforts, went on to more detail. She had only been able to fit two drawing classes into her schedule at school, but found that little bit of training had made her natural gift more enjoyable.

Soon she was lost in the sketch she was creating, enjoying the warm sun on her back and the smell of damp earth and wet grass rising up in the heat of the afternoon sun.

SETH WALKED BACK to the boardinghouse after seeing the sheriff and his prisoners off. Maggie sat on the front porch swing with a bowl in her lap, snapping green beans.

"Where's Becca?" he asked.

"She was in the parlor, last I saw her. She may be resting."

"How did it go?"

Maggie smiled. "She did fine."

Seth strode into the house and stuck his head in the doorway of the parlor. She wasn't there. He stood at the foot of the stairs and called her name. Getting no response, he looked into each of the rooms downstairs. Empty.

He debated with himself briefly before dashing upstairs to Becca's room. Her door was open but she wasn't there. She was not anywhere in the house. He ran down the stairs two at a time, trying to push down his fear.

He ran out the kitchen door and strode across the meadow. All he could think was that she was in trouble again. He had images of the sheriff releasing Becca's attackers. Or that someone else had been sent to finish the job. And it was his fault for not protecting her. He had let Thomas down.

His thoughts were whirling so fast it took a moment for his mind to register that he had stopped in his tracks.

There was Becca, calm as you please, sitting by the river.

Slowly, he turned and walked back to the boardinghouse and lowered his frame to the back steps. As he watched Becca, Maggie's words came back to him. He never would be able to keep her safe all of the time. He guessed he'd better do some praying again.

BECCA HAD FILLED in her sketches with pastels, using her fingers to smudge the color to the right shade.

"That's really good. You have quite a talent for drawing." A familiar deep voice came from behind her.

She jumped nearly a foot, blood rushing through her veins. With a soft plop, her charcoal flew into the creek. "You scared me!" She was concentrating so intensely, she hadn't heard Seth come up behind her.

He didn't say anything, but walked around the rock, rolled up his sleeve, and reached into the water to retrieve it for her.

"Thank you," she whispered as he handed it back to her, her heart still pounding. She took a deep breath and looked at his face to see if he was angry, but his eyes were unreadable in the shadow of his Stetson.

What did she care? She was a grown woman. She was within sight of the boardinghouse. Never mind she about fell off the rock in fright a moment ago.

She attempted to turn back to her drawing, but remembered her charcoal was wet. She picked up a pastel, but found she'd lost her artistic perspective. She wanted to leave, but unless she crawled over the rock, Seth blocked her way.

She glared at him, not sure if she was angrier with herself for being too engrossed in her art, or at him for scaring her. "Did you come out here to guard me, or to tell me that I am exposing myself to danger? I suppose you tried to scare me on purpose to make a point."

He didn't reply, but sat down on the rock next to her.

She was too surprised to say anything. And now that she could see his face, she was puzzled. It had that same gentle look on it the night he rescued her.

"I deserved that." His voice was quiet. "I want to apologize for what I said this morning. I was concerned about your safety." He averted his gaze, staring out into the stream. "I guess I'm used to being in control. But I have to remember God's ultimately in control and He'll be looking after you even when I can't."

His Stetson was again shading his blue eyes, but Becca's heart still did a flip-flop at his profile.

It took her a moment to realize his gaze had shifted from the stream to her drawing. She quickly flipped the tablet over.

"Why'd you do that? I told you your work is good."

"I'm just not used to letting others view it. It's for my personal enjoyment only."

"You have nothing to be ashamed of." He took the tablet from her lap and began turning the pages, careful not to smudge the charcoal. "Really, these are good." He handed the tablet back to her. "But if you don't want me to tell anyone, I won't." He grinned.

She smiled back. Then she remembered their visitor. "The sheriff was here."

"I know. I saw him in town. He just left with … with his prisoners to the county jail. They admitted their crimes, so they'll be doing jail time. You don't have to worry, Becca. They won't be able to hurt you again."

She nodded and looked out over the stream. "That *is* good news." Still, talking about the sheriff and those men had ruined the mood she'd managed to capture by drawing.

"Are you all right?"

She nodded again.

Seth's hand cupped her chin and turned her head to face him. "Are you sure?"

His touch warmed her to her toes. "Yes," she said, smiling. And meant it.

He ran his thumb over her cheek before dropping his hand. "Do you want to head back in? It's not an order or anything. You can stay out here if you'd like. But I think supper will be ready shortly."

She folded up her sketchbook, noticing the light had begun to fade as the sun touched the tips of the trees. "I can't believe it's that late already. I should have been inside helping Maggie long ago."

Seth got to his feet and offered Becca his hand. "I think Maggie managed to make meals before you came to help her."

She felt a tingle run up her arm as she put her small hand in his large, calloused one. He held her hand firmly as he helped her to her feet. She was so aware of her hand in his that it took her a moment to realize that he hadn't released it after she stood up.

"Becca?"

"Yes?" she said, wanting to blush at how breathless she sounded.

"You still haven't accepted my apology."

She smiled up at him. "I forgive you, Seth."

He smiled back and squeezed her hand before releasing it. "Good," he muttered with a half-smile on his lips. "I'm hungry. Sure don't want anything ruining my appetite." The smile turned into a grin as he stepped back, allowing her to pass before he walked with her toward the boardinghouse.

Chapter Fifteen

Josh and James had just returned from Salem and were putting the coach away when Seth walked into the barn. They had unhitched the horses, and James turned them out to the corral.

"Need a hand?" Seth asked.

"From a greenhorn like you?" Josh teased. "Nah."

Seth ignored his jibe and started cleaning tack.

Josh grinned at him before turning back to the coach. "Anything happen while we were gone? Did the sheriff come by?"

"Yep and he took those scoundrels back. They told him what they told us, so they'll be sitting in jail for awhile." Seth paused. "The sheriff talked to Becca, too, and she told him what happened."

"She did? How'd she handle it?"

"I wasn't there, but she seemed all right. A little shook up, but not too upset."

Josh nodded. "She's got gumption. Most other women would have headed back to the big city by now."

Seth felt a little awkward. "That's just what I told her to do."

Josh looked up and then laughed. "I can just imagine what she said to that suggestion."

Seth nodded, giving Josh a half-grin.

Josh continued to stare at him. "You're smitten."

Seth stared back for a moment, then returned to cleaning. He'd only yet admitted his feelings to himself. He wasn't going to admit them to anyone else, even if it was Josh. A change of subject seemed the best course of action.

"The thing that I can't get my mind around is the photograph." Seth hung up the tack. "How did it get from that box to those two?"

"I'd forgotten about that. Did you ask Becca?"

"Not yet."

"Then I guess we should ask her tonight."

Becca wiped her hands on her apron after drying the last of the dishes. She moved into the dining room to see if she'd missed anything and was surprised to see Seth and Josh still sitting there, hunched over the table. Usually, with a run the next day, Josh went to bed early.

They both looked up at her.

Why didn't they go home? They looked tired. "I thought you would have retired by now, Josh. Too much of Maggie's coffee keeping you up?"

Josh didn't answer her question. "Becca, you know that photograph of you Thomas had in his box of papers? Could I see it?"

She furrowed her brow. What could he possibly want with it? "I'll go get it."

Upstairs in her room, she looked in the box of Thomas's papers. She lifted the lid, expecting to see the photograph on top.

Not seeing it, she dug around. "I thought for sure I had left it in here," she muttered. She rummaged through her dresser drawers. Maybe she put it in there. Not there, either. She surveyed the room with her hands on her hips. Where could it be? She knew she had left it in the box.

Wondering if it might have slipped down the side of the box, she slid her hands down the edges. *There* was *something there.*

She pulled out papers and stacked them on the floor and was rewarded by the sight of the edge of the frame. "Here it is. It must have slipped down." She pulled it from its hiding place.

It was empty.

Her face dropped. "Oh, no. What happened to the photograph?"

Then it dawned on her. *Those two!* They were playing a joke on her.

She started to stomp downstairs then realized a couple of treads down that, since passengers were sleeping, she should make the rest of her way more quietly. She stood in the doorway of the dining room brandishing the empty frame.

"Is this one of your practical jokes? Very funny. I give up. What have you done with my photograph?"

She looked from one to the other but neither was laughing. In fact, she thought they looked concerned. Becca was confused.

Seth stood up and took the frame from her hand. He pulled her picture out of his shirt pocket.

She sighed with relief. "So you did have it. I was afraid—"

Seth cut her off. "Becca, Josh found this on the men who attacked you. The sheriff and I are trying to figure out how they got it."

Her hands fell to her side. "What? How did they—"

Seth pulled out a chair and she sank into it. He sat down in his own chair and put the frame and photograph on the table.

"When did you see it last?" Josh asked.

She thought a moment. "I moved the box from the kitchen several days ago. I had brought it down when we looked at the house plans with Maggie and didn't realize it was still under the table."

"Did you see the picture then?" Seth asked.

"I don't remember. I know it was there when I showed you and Maggie the plans because it was sitting just below Emily's photograph."

Seth fitted the photograph back in its frame and handed it to Becca. "I don't want you to worry about this." He stood up. "Promise?"

She looked up at him and nodded.

Josh stood, too, and looked at Seth. "Want to bunk with me tonight? Save you a ride home."

"Thanks."

Seth reached over and squeezed her shoulder, his hand lingering.

She felt his warmth seep through the fabric of her shirtwaist, remaining even after he removed his hand.

"Good night."

Once they were outside the kitchen door and on the way to Josh's cabin, certain Becca couldn't hear them, Seth spoke. "That didn't help much."

"Nope." Josh's tone was light and his stride easy as they followed the path to his cabin, but he had known Josh too long to assume he wasn't doing some heavy thinking.

"I'm thinking Becca's right. There's been too many 'accidents' lately. We've never had people come through the woods like that," Seth continued. "And then there's that letter to Thomas offering to buy the logging company, but he never mentioned it."

"Are you thinking they're connected?"

"I don't know. Why would he make an offer to Thomas and not me? And what does Becca being attacked have to do with the logging company?" He lifted his hat and pushed his hair back from his forehead.

"I think we need to do two things."

"What's that?"

"Find out who at the logging camp knew those two scoundrels. See if anyone knows this fellow who hired them."

Seth nodded. He'd been thinking the same thing but hadn't had a moment to do anything about it. "And second?"

"We need to keep a close eye on Becca."

A chill raced through him at Josh's words.

They had reached the cabin, but neither made a move to go in.

"I'll leave James here instead of taking him with me to Portland," Josh continued. "You can't keep trying to be at the boardinghouse and your camp all at once, and if you don't get some rest soon, you'll be of no use to anyone."

Seth lightly shoved Josh's shoulder as they both went inside.

Chapter Sixteen

He most assuredly hoped his trip would be worth the journey. Stagecoaches were infernal contraptions. Despite his discomfort, his instincts from spending years on the streets forced him to allow the other passengers off first, giving him time to survey his surroundings. When at last he stepped off the coach, he deliberately pulled his pocket watch from his vest and glanced at it before snapping it shut. He noted grudgingly they were on time. His satchel was the only one left.

A buxom, redheaded woman was greeting the passengers ahead of him.

He waited until they were inside.

She smiled at him. "I'm Maggie Kincaid. Will you be staying with us?"

"No, I'll not have that pleasure. Would you be so kind as to point me in the direction of Parsons's Hotel?"

"Just follow Main Street, and it'll be about two blocks up on your left."

"Thank you." He tipped his hat to her, picked up his satchel, and started up the street.

A few minutes later he reached the hotel and entered the lobby. It was a small lobby, nothing like what he was used to in

San Francisco, and certainly not like Portland, but it was surprisingly well-appointed for this part of the country. One of the many things he'd learned from Mike was an appreciation for fine things.

He approached the desk. "I'd like to procure a room."

"Of course." A man with a bald pate and a thin mustache turned the register towards him. "Your name?"

"Jeremiah McCormick."

THE SUPPER in the hotel's dining room was surprisingly good. McCormick wiped his mouth, making sure no food remained in his mustache.

He had noticed the curious glances sent his way throughout his meal from what he assumed were local townspeople. With both a stage line and a logging camp, they must be accustomed to strangers in their town, so he calculated it was the fine cut of his clothes that made him stand out. He hadn't seen anyone as well dressed as he.

Lifting his coffee cup to his lips, he scanned the room over the rim. This could work to his advantage. Seeing Parsons hovering, he motioned him over. It was time to put his plan into action.

"Mr. McCormick, how was your meal? May I get you anything else?"

"Dessert and the pleasure of your company." McCormick smiled at the man, hoping to put him at ease.

When Parsons looked confused, McCormick gestured to the chair opposite him. "Please. Bring out two desserts and join me. I'd like to ask you a few questions."

"As you wish." He scurried back to the kitchen.

McCormick figured it wasn't everyday a guest requested Parsons's presence at their table.

A moment later he returned balancing two plates, a coffee

cup and pot. Parsons set McCormick's dessert in front of him and refilled his cup before sitting down.

McCormick took a bite of the chocolate confection in front of him and savored it a moment before swallowing. Parsons's cook was excellent. It rivaled anything he'd tasted in Portland.

Parsons watched him expectantly.

"The best I've ever tasted."

The man across from him visibly relaxed and tasted his own dessert. McCormick asked how long he'd lived in Reedsville and how long he'd run his hotel. Parsons became more open as the conversation went on.

"Tell me about the politics of this town." McCormick gave a small chuckle. "First of all, are there any? Do you even have a mayor or a constable?"

Parsons shook his head. "Neither of those, although there's been talk lately about getting a deputy sheriff."

McCormick nodded and stroked his chin. "I'd heard that as well. It can't be long before you'll be needing a mayor. Do the townsfolk appreciate what a fine establishment you have here? Why it compares favorably with many I've stayed at in San Francisco and even Portland." McCormick glanced around and leaned in. "If word got out about your hotel and dining room, with the natural beauty of this area and the soon-to-be easy access by train, this could be the next fashionable tourist destination."

Disbelief, curiosity, and pride flitted across his face. The man had never learned to hide his emotions. That would be useful.

"And," McCormick continued, "it would bring prosperity to the whole town. Each establishment would have more business."

Parsons nodded, his dessert forgotten. McCormick took a sip of his coffee. "But such an enterprise needs someone to champion it. Someone in an official capacity for the town. Like a mayor." He picked up his fork and proceeded to finish his dessert.

Parsons looked crestfallen. "I supposed that's true. I guess we'll just have to wait until somebody decides we should hold an election."

McCormick nodded and pursed his lips. "I have an idea. What if that person were you?"

"Me? I suppose I could suggest an election. I don't know anything about that sort of thing. Ben at the telegraph office knows everyone and could get the word out, but how do you go about holding an election?" Parson drifted off, looking into the distance.

"Actually, I was thinking you should be mayor."

"What!"

Diners glanced in their direction, and Parsons's face grew red. McCormick calmly dabbed at his mouth.

Parsons leaned forward. "What do you mean I should be mayor?"

McCormick shrugged. "It only makes sense. It's your hotel that would be bringing the prosperity to the town. You deserve it. I'm a businessman myself, and I can tell by the way you run your business that you would be perfect for the job."

Parsons straightened in his chair trying to suppress a smile but not succeeding entirely. "I don't like to boast, but I've always thought a few others—I won't name names—could learn a thing or two from me."

McCormick nodded.

Parsons seemed to remember his dessert and took a bite. "What sort of business are you in, if I may ask?"

"Investments would be the best way to describe it. I match up enterprises with investors who are looking for a good return on their money. In certain cases, when I find a particularly good business, I invest my own money."

Parsons nodded like he understood, but McCormick was certain he didn't. "So … is it business that brings you to Reedsville?"

McCormick detected the hopeful tone in Parsons's voice.

"Yes. I have found a business. It's not run quite so well as yours. In fact it's run so poorly people are getting hurt. Still, it has potential." McCormick picked up his coffee cup, studying Parsons over the rim. His every move telegraphed he was dying of curiosity, fingers flitting between his silverware and his coffee cup as if he couldn't quite decide which to pick up.

McCormick took a sip and decided to make Parsons ask.

Parsons finally decided on his coffee cup. He picked it up and took a quick sip. "People are getting hurt, eh? Well that's a shame." He put his cup down. "Anyone I know?"

McCormick used all his training to hide his smile. He'd love to play poker with this man.

He leaned in. "I normally don't divulge that information, as it could hurt me in the bargaining process if a competitor found out I was interested in a business and tried to out-bid me."

"Oh." Parsons's face started to reveal understanding, but disappointment crept across.

"But since you're a businessman like myself, and I don't believe I have any competitors around, I'll let you in on it if you promise to keep the information to yourself."

"Certainly. And I'm a man of my word. Just ask anybody."

McCormick nodded solemnly. "That is as I suspected." He pushed his plate aside to lean further over the table. "It's the logging company owned by Misters Seth Blake and Thomas Wilson."

Parsons's face went as white as the tablecloth. McCormick could almost see the information rolling around Parsons's head.

"Oh." He paused a moment. "You know Thomas Wilson is dead."

McCormick had to proceed carefully here. "Yes, I'd heard that. Logging accident, wasn't it?" At Parsons's nod he continued. "That's exactly the kind of carelessness I'm talking about. When one of the owners is killed, one must wonder how dangerous it is for the average working man."

Parsons nodded again. McCormick drained his coffee cup. Tonight went very well indeed.

Chapter Seventeen

I'm thinking about moving out to my old home," Becca announced.

Maggie had just finished praying after the family morning devotions. She closed her Bible before she looked at Becca.

"You're not a burden to me, Becca; you're like one of my own."

"I know, Maggie. And that's not why I want to leave." She stood and began gathering the breakfast dishes. "I can't really explain it. I suppose because the house has so many memories. After seeing Thomas's plans for it, I feel like I need to be there."

Maggie was silent as she followed Becca into the kitchen. They worked together, filling the dishpan with hot water from the reservoir on the stove and shaving in the soap.

"I understand why you're wanting to go," Maggie said with a sigh. "I can't imagine living anywhere else but in this house. There are memories in every corner, from the mantle in the parlor Stephen carved our first winter here…" Her voice trailed off. "As soon as the dishes are done, go get an old dress on, and we'll take some supplies out to your place in the wagon. Heaven only knows how much work it's going to take to make that place livable."

Becca threw her arms around Maggie, dripping sudsy water on the kitchen floor. "Thank you for understanding and helping. I don't know what I would have done without you."

Maggie gave her a squeeze and then set her a bit away. "You're a smart girl, Rebecca Wilson. You're capable and resourceful. Don't ever forget it."

BECCA HAD THOUGHT spring cleaning at the boardinghouse was hard. It was nothing compared to this. She straightened from where she was scrubbing the walls, putting her hand to her lower back. She was going to feel it tomorrow.

They'd made some progress, but at this rate it would take her forever to be able to move in. The homestead was in worse shape than she thought.

She looked around the room. Cobwebs hung from every corner. Piles of dirt, pine needles and leaves covered the main living area floor. Some creature had made a nest in the fireplace. She had laughed when Maggie had tossed a shovel in the back of the wagon, but now she was grateful for it. And there were three more rooms to clean, plus the attic and root cellar.

Tossing the scrub brush in the bucket of water, she ventured outside to catch a breeze on the front porch. She grabbed the jug Maggie had brought and lowered herself to the stairs, trying not to groan. While the breeze lifted her hair off her sweaty brow, she took a long drink of the cool water.

After a few minutes of rest, she decided all the work would be worth it. It would just take longer than she had originally thought.

Maggie stepped outside and Becca handed up the jug to her. She took a drink. "About ready to head back?"

"If we don't, I soon won't be able to move."

Maggie laughed. They gathered up their supplies, moving

slower than when they first arrived, and headed back to the boardinghouse.

As they neared Maggie's, Becca longed to wash in her room. She didn't need a bath, just warm water in her washbasin. She was certain she had time for that.

As they pulled around back to put the wagon in the barn, she caught sight of a man sitting on the front porch, apparently waiting for them. He tipped his derby hat as they continued out of sight.

"Maggie, do you know who that was?"

"I didn't get a good look, but I think he might have been one of the passengers on the stage Saturday. I directed him to Parsons's, so I'm not sure what he'd need with us. I suppose we'll find out shortly."

Becca glanced down at her faded and dirty work dress. She pulled the kerchief off her hair, but she still wasn't in any condition to receive visitors. And her wash up would have to wait.

James sauntered up and took care of the horses and wagon for Maggie while the women unloaded their supplies. Becca headed towards the kitchen door with her arms full.

"James, have you seen Seth today?" Maggie asked her son.

"Nope."

"When you're finished here, would you ride up to the camp and ask him to supper. He's been working himself too hard lately."

Becca couldn't see him, but she assumed James nodded. She'd never heard either of Maggie's children tell her no. Come to think of it, she'd never heard anyone tell Maggie no.

Before she could reach for the kitchen door, it flew open and Sally stood there with a look of panic. "I'm so glad you're back. There's a man here wanting to see you."

"Me?" She'd assumed he was here to see Maggie.

"He asked for you. I asked him to wait on the porch and brought him some lemonade and cookies that Mama had made. I hope I did right."

Becca smiled at her. "You did exactly right." She walked into the kitchen and put her things in the pantry. "I'm going to freshen up, and then I'll be right out."

She slipped upstairs into her room, splashing water on her face and hands, and quickly changed into a day dress. A quick glance in the mirror told her she was presentable, and she walked downstairs to the front door. She couldn't resist peeking out the window.

A mustached man dressed in a silk waistcoat with a gold watch chain peeking out of its pocket sat on the porch. A plate with crumbs on it sat on the chair next to him. He looked relaxed, as if he had all the time in the world to wait.

She took a deep breath and opened the door. "Hello. I'm Rebecca Wilson. Sally said you were looking for me?"

He looked startled or confused—she wasn't sure which—as he came to his feet and took a slow step toward her. "You're Miss Wilson?"

"Yes, I am."

He paused a moment, and she wondered if he really wanted to see Maggie.

Then he smiled. "It's a pleasure to meet you. I am Jeremiah McCormick."

Her heart dropped to her feet, and an instant later her pulse pounded in her throat. Fear surged through her, and she fought to keep her head above it. She swallowed. "How can I help you?"

"First, I have an apology to offer."

This was the last thing she expected him to say. Her mind couldn't make sense of the situation fast enough.

Mr. McCormick glanced around, looking up and down the street. "Is there a better place where we might talk, without so many … observers?"

She followed his eyes up the street and belatedly understood his meaning. "Of course. We can sit in the parlor. Forgive me for not offering sooner."

Manners. Being polite. Going through the routine of social niceties should help her regain her balance until she could figure out why Mr. McCormick was here. And what apology did he owe her? Anger began replacing her fear as she showed Mr. McCormick into the parlor. He was the one who should have been nervous over this meeting, not her. He had a lot of explaining to do.

She sat on Maggie's moiré settee and indicated a chair for Mr. McCormick.

He took his time placing his hat on a table, and straightening his jacket and waistcoat. He finally looked up at her.

"Miss Wilson. I don't—" He faltered and picked at some invisible speck on his trousers. He looked up at her again. "I don't know how to put this into words."

She waited, not eager to ease his apparent discomfort.

He took a deep breath and sat back. "Your injuries disturb me, and I feel responsible."

The air left her lungs. She knew the bruises on her face were still visible, although the swelling was gone. Of course he would notice, but was he saying he was responsible for her attack? Her brain seemed stuck on his words, and she didn't know how to respond.

"It embarrasses me to admit this," McCormick continued, "but my pain is nothing compared to what you must have felt. Let me assure you I never intended for you to come to physical harm." He leaned forward. "As you probably already know, I made an offer to your brother regarding the logging company. When I learned of his death, I had hoped to persuade you to sell his share to me."

He looked down and shook his head. "I consulted with a colleague of mine who knew I was interested in this business. He said he could persuade you to return to your studies and sell your brother's share of the business. I had no idea what he had planned." He looked up and met her gaze.

She saw his fist clench on his knee. "Believe me when I tell you I will never do business with this man again. I've already turned over information regarding his activities to the authorities."

Her neck and back were stiff from holding herself ramrod straight. Her head was spinning with information. She needed time to sort this out. "Why didn't you come to see me yourself?"

She thought Mr. McCormick had the grace to look abashed.

"I'm ashamed to say I couldn't be bothered. My conception of you was completely wrong." His voice softened. "You're nothing like I expected." He gave a small laugh. "You know, most women who get the notion to go off to college do so because spinsterhood is their only other option."

She closed her eyes against her rising anger at his cavalier assumption. He had such ridiculous, uninformed opinions. When she opened her eyes he was staring at her. She wanted this conversation to be over. "Was there anything else you wanted to discuss? I need to help with the supper preparations."

Mr. McCormick stood, picking up his hat from the table.

She stood as well, relieved this was coming to an end.

"Please accept my most humble apologies for your injuries. Is there anything I can do to make it up to you?"

Becca couldn't think of anything she'd want from him, yet she'd suffered injuries. While he seemed contrite, part of her wanted him to hurt as much as she had.

"Please. The best thing would be for you to leave now."

He nodded and took a step forward, his gaze seeming to search her face. Raising his hand, he reached out and touched under her eye.

She flinched and pulled away, taking a half-step back.

He slowly lowered his hand, turned on his heel and left.

Becca lifted her hand to cover the area he touched, feeling as if he had somehow marked her with his touch. The sound of the front door closing roused her. She took a deep breath and headed into the kitchen.

McCormick was careful to keep his features neutral as he walked back to Parsons's Hotel even though his mind was whirling.

The moment he'd seen Rebecca Wilson, his carefully laid plans had flown out of his mind. Approaching her first had seemed like a good idea. She would be the weak link, the one easily broken. He had no idea she was so beautiful, her golden hair, green eyes. A man could get lost in those eyes. Except hers held a wariness of him. He wished he could change that.

That would require some doing. He tapped his chin.

He thought he'd done a good job explaining his instigation of her attack. She was a woman of character and would appreciate his truthfulness. He smiled at that thought.

Opening the door to the hotel, he nodded at Parsons's behind the desk then climbed the stairs to his room. But she hadn't accepted his apology. He really hadn't expected her to.

Letting his nervousness show had been a good move. Counter to his instincts, as he always controlled what others saw about him. She had thrown him. That hadn't happened in a long time. Yet he felt it would go a long way in establishing him in some esteem in Rebecca's eyes.

Using his key, he opened the door to his room. Yes, he'd have to think of a plan to get close to her. He entered his room and closed the door behind him, leaning against it.

The game just got sweeter.

"What? He was here? He's in town?" Seth turned to face Becca next to him on the settee in Maggie's parlor. They and Josh had retired there after supper. Becca had something on her mind all evening and now he knew what it was. He ran his hand through his hair. "What did he want?"

"He apologized." Becca shook her head slightly. "I still can't figure it all out. He said he wanted to buy the logging company and had made Thomas the offer. When he found out Thomas was dead, a colleague of his offered to approach me and persuade me to sell my brother's interest and go back to Salem. He said he didn't know what his colleague had in mind and has turned him in to the authorities."

Becca still met Seth's eyes but her face had paled, making her yellow-green bruises stand out more than usual. His gut wrenched at the sight and his blood boiled. He wanted nothing more than to go over and have a "talk" with McCormick right now.

He pushed himself off the sofa and paced the room.

"What does McCormick look like?" Josh asked. His legs were stretched out and he looked relaxed, but Seth knew his mind was working through the information Becca had given them.

"Well-dressed, like a man of means. He had a silk waistcoat and pocket watch, so I think he must be fairly well off. He had good manners and speech."

Josh looked at Seth. "Doesn't sound like the description of the man that hired Becca's attackers."

"No. That must have been the *colleague* he spoke of." Seth didn't have a problem showing his disbelief in McCormick's version of the events.

"So he came all this way just to apologize?" Josh asked.

Becca looked from Josh to Seth. "I don't know. He didn't say anything else. But I was so surprised I really felt in a muddle, and I asked him to leave."

"I can't believe he wouldn't at least make you another offer for your brother's share of the company. If it mattered so much to him that he had you attacked—"

"He didn't have me attacked." Becca cut him off.

"I can't believe you're defending him," Seth shot back.

"I'm not defending him. You're jumping to conclusions. I

don't like the man, and I think money is his god, but that doesn't mean he had me attacked."

The image of what he saw when he came upon Becca in the woods would haunt Seth for the rest of his life. He held anyone who was connected in any sort of way responsible. "I don't trust him."

"You don't have to."

"Why don't we wait to see what he does next?" Josh suggested. "If he came to apologize, he's done that. He'll leave. If he wants something else, he'll stay. We'll know soon enough."

Josh was right. When did he get to be the level-headed one? Usually, he was the one raising mischief, and Seth was the one getting them out of it.

He sat back down next to Becca. "So McCormick just walked up to the front door and asked for you?"

"I don't know. Maggie and I were out at the homestead, and Sally was here. When we got back, he was sitting on the porch, and Sally said he wanted to see me."

"What were you doing out at the homestead?" He had gotten the windows ordered and wanted to surprise her. He mentally checked off what he had done the last time he was out there, hoping he hadn't left any clues to give his surprise away.

"Cleaning. I want to move back there."

He was hoping she would want to so she would stay. That was why he was getting the windows. But moving out to the homestead now wasn't safe, especially with McCormick around. He had to tread carefully; Becca didn't take orders well. But McCormick's visit had shaken him up. Her safety came above all else, whether she liked it or not. "I don't think that's such a good idea right now."

"Why not?"

"Because it isn't safe." He could feel the tension radiating from her. This wasn't going well. He wanted to just pull her into his arms and make her understand.

Becca let out a long sigh. "Mr. McCormick explained what

happened. It won't happen again." She stood up. "It's been a long day and I'm tired. Good night."

She left the room, leaving Seth with a sense of loss. He leaned his head back against the sofa. "That went well."

Chapter Eighteen

Seth strode up the steps to Parsons's Hotel. He'd gotten his crews started for the day and left Taylor in charge. Opening the hotel door, he saw Bill Parsons behind the desk.

Parsons looked up, surprised, when Seth walked in. Then his expression turned cautious.

"Morning." Seth approached the desk. "I have business with Mr. McCormick. Is he in his room?"

Parsons nodded and the corners of his mouth turned slightly upward. Seth had the uneasy feeling he'd been a topic of conversation. How much did Parsons know? Did he know who McCormick really was?

"Yes. He had breakfast sent up. He's in 104, our very best room."

"Thank you." He gave Parsons a quick nod and headed up the stairs, feeling the man's gaze boring holes in his back. He reached the top of the stairs and headed down the hall. Stopping in front of a door with 104 painted on it, he said a quick prayer, and knocked.

The door opened almost instantly.

"Mr. Blake, I presume." McCormick stood in the doorway

in shirtsleeves and a vest. A jacket was slung over a chair behind him.

Becca was right; the man exuded wealth. Seth disliked him immediately. Especially since McCormick seemed to be expecting him. "We have something to discuss."

"Yes, we do. I was just penning you a note, inviting you to dine with me tonight. It seems so much more civilized to discuss business over a meal."

"This isn't exactly Portland."

"No, but it certainly has its own charm and... attractions." McCormick's eyes held a challenge in them. He held Seth's gaze for a moment and then turned and walked into the room. "Come in and close the door."

Seth's hand clenched around his hat brim, and he forced himself to relax his grip. He really didn't like this man. It was like walking into the dragon's lair, but he stepped inside and closed the door behind him.

McCormick lowered himself into a chair and motioned toward the other one, but Seth ignored him. Glancing around the room, he noticed how grand it was. He'd never seen any of Parsons's hotel rooms before. A large four-poster bed took up a good portion of the room, but there was a small table with chairs, a large dresser and a washstand. Everything was covered in that silky stuff that was on Maggie's sofa.

"We don't have much to discuss. I came to tell you not to bother Miss Wilson anymore. You've hurt her enough, and I won't stand by and see it happen again."

"I have no intention of hurting Miss Wilson. I simply came to beg her forgiveness and to discuss business with you."

"We don't have any business to discuss."

"You haven't heard my offer."

"My company is not for sale."

McCormick toyed with a pen on the table. "I was thinking more along the lines of a partnership. I have more connections than you can imagine. I can get you government contracts. And in case you haven't heard, the twentieth century is nearly here, bringing with it the power of steam. The most prosperous logging outfits are moving to new technology. Yes, it costs money. But that's where I come in."

Seth eyed the man, sorting through and discarding various responses.

"That would mean more jobs for this town, more people coming into town, and everyone here would prosper. Surely you wouldn't want to deprive your fellow townsfolk of the opportunity for success?"

"I wouldn't have a man of your character as my partner," Seth said, loosening his jaw enough to get the words out evenly.

"What could you possibly know of my character?"

"You had Becca attacked. That's all I need to know."

McCormick jumped to his feet. "I resent that! I did not have Miss Wilson attacked. I explained that to her."

"You're responsible." He pointed his hat at McCormick. "Stay away from her or you'll deal with me." Seth turned on his heel and yanked open the door. He stepped into the hallway and started to pull the door shut with greater force than necessary. But then he paused and pushed the door back open, hearing it lightly bounce on the wall. Let McCormick shut his own door.

He stormed down the stairs, tossing a nod to Parsons on his way out the door. He stopped at Fulton's to pick up the mail for the camp, and then headed over to the Oregon Express office.

"Howdy, Seth." Ben greeted him as he walked through the door.

"Hey, Ben. I need to send a wire."

The older man's gnarled fingers managed to pick up a slip and push it along the counter to him.

Seth wondered how much longer the man would be able to work. The rain made Ben's rheumatism act up, but he always managed a cheerful smile and had the latest news for anyone who walked through the door.

He finished printing out his message and handed it over to Ben who looked it over.

"I'll get this out right now and let you know as soon as I hear something back."

"Appreciate it."

Seth strode toward the boardinghouse, but went around back to the barn to retrieve his horse instead of going inside. In his mood, he wouldn't be good company.

The cut-off to Becca's homestead caught his attention, and without thinking about it, he turned off. The grasses of the clearing muted his horse's hooves, and the surrounding trees seemed to create stillness. He felt the tension begin to leave his neck and shoulders. No wonder Becca wanted to stay here. Peace covered the area like a blanket.

Lord, I hate feeling like I can't control this situation. I'm afraid Becca's going to get hurt again, and I'm trying to prevent that. I don't trust McCormick, and I don't know what he's going to do next. He blew out a breath. *I guess that's the point, isn't it. I can't control any of this. I have to trust You to do it. I'm going to need Your help to do that.*

Seth sat a moment longer, letting the silence seep into him. Then he wheeled his horse back toward Maggie's.

McCormick turned the pen over in his hand, a slow grin spreading over his face. *So it's Becca, is it?* The stakes just rose higher, and there was now one more thing to take from Seth Blake.

McCormick didn't like to lose, and he didn't intend to this time. His time on the streets as a boy had taught him that to win was to survive another day. And when Mike had taken him in, he'd taught him how valuable winning could be.

This deal would be it. It would be the one that ensured he'd never have to work hard again, he'd never have to look over his shoulder and wonder if he was a day away from the back-breaking labor that killed his father and sent McCormick to the streets as a young boy. Never again. With this deal, he'd have security.

He tossed the pen aside and stood to put on his coat. Picking up the paper on the table next to him, he folded it and slipped it in his pocket. He scanned his room to make sure he'd left nothing out of importance then headed downstairs to the lobby.

Parsons sat behind the desk and looked up expectantly at him. "Did Seth Blake find your room?"

McCormick sighed. "Yes, he did." He straightened the cuffs on his jacket, taking his time.

"Did it, well, you know ..." Parsons looked around and lowered his voice. "Did your business go well with him?"

McCormick shook his head. "The only explanation I have for his behavior is that he is still grieving the loss of his friend. And when grief is combined with guilt..."

Parsons's brows furrowed. "Guilt?"

"Yes. It's obvious he feels some guilt over his friend's death. You know, when people don't want to admit their guilt, they'll blame anyone they can think of, regardless of how ridiculous the accusation."

Parsons tapped his mustache. "That surprises me. I've always thought of Seth Blake as an honest man."

"Oh, I'm sure he is. He just isn't in his right mind now. He deserves our sympathy." He brushed the last bit of lint from his sleeve and settled his hat on his head. "Tell your wife I cannot wait to taste the delicious meal she has planned for tonight."

He left the hotel and walked down the street to Fulton's. As he entered the store, he let his gaze wander around, wondering if he'd find anything suitable here. Unfortunately, there wasn't time to order anything to be delivered from Portland. He strolled up and down the aisles, his eyes on the shelves, but his ears were attuned to the conversations around him.

Finally, he picked out some chocolates and a small porcelain box. When the conversation turned to the latest accident at the logging camp, he carried his items to the counter. The two men lounging against the counter turned to look at McCormick.

He set his purchases on the counter and waited to be helped.

"You must be new in town," one of the men said, looking him up and down.

"Yes, I am."

"Just passing through?"

"It depends on how my business goes." McCormick casually looked around the room. The man he assumed was Mr. Fulton was cutting fabric off a bolt for an older lady. He felt the two men watching him. "I'm an investor, and I'm looking for a partnership in a logging company. I heard there were some good ones around here."

The men nodded, and the other one grinned. "If you like ghosts."

McCormick smiled with them. "Oh? Something haunted by the ghosts of loggers gone before?"

"There's been a few accidents at Seth Blake's outfit. Some folks think it's ghosts."

"I don't think it's ghosts," said the second man, "but something put Seth in a mood when he was in here earlier."

Fulton wrapped up the cloth and handed it to the lady then joined them at the counter. "Is this what you'd like to purchase?"

"Yes, thank you."

"Will there be anything else?"

"A bag of licorice whips. Would it be possible to have these delivered?"

"Certainly." Fulton began wrapping up McCormick's selections.

McCormick turned back to the men. "I had a meeting with Mr. Blake earlier today."

"Is that so?"

McCormick knew they wanted to ask but wouldn't pry into

another man's business. "Yes, as I told you, I'm looking for a logging camp to invest in. I have many business contacts up and down the Pacific Coast and could bring a great amount of business through government contracts and the like. There's opportunity just waiting to be seized. It would mean more jobs for any company I choose to invest in."

"Never heard of a place that had too many jobs."

"Nope," his friend agreed.

"So does that mean you'll be staying with us awhile?" Fulton asked, handing McCormick his candy.

"Not much longer, I'm afraid. Seth Blake turned down my offer. I plan on staying in your lovely town a bit longer, hoping he'll change his mind. But I do have pressing business back in San Francisco to get to, and I will be looking at other logging companies." McCormick pulled several bills from his pocket, along with the folded piece of paper and handed them to Fulton. "Here's where I'd like them delivered."

Fulton looked at the note and nodded. He tucked it under the string and handed McCormick his change.

McCormick tucked the coins in his pocket and turned to leave. "Good day, gentlemen. A pleasure talking to you." On his way out the door, he pulled one of the licorice whips from its bag and took a bite, a small reward for the victory about to drop into his lap.

Chapter Nineteen

A knock sounded. Becca was surprised to hear it come from the front door. Almost everyone they knew used the kitchen door. She wiped her hands on her apron and went to open the door, wary it might be Mr. McCormick again.

When she pulled open the door, she was surprised to see John Duncan.

"Good morning, Becca. I got a delivery here for you."

"Oh." She'd forgotten that John worked for Mr. Fulton. "Thank you." She took the brown paper package John thrust into her hands.

He turned to leave, saying, "Good day to you," over his shoulder.

"Good day," Becca mumbled, bringing the package inside and closing the door. What could it be? Who could it be from? Frowning, she carried it to the dining room table.

Maggie walked in from the kitchen. "A package for you?"

"Yes." She slid the note out from under the string and opened it.

Dear Miss Wilson,

Please accept these gifts as a small token of my regret. I offer my most sincere apologies and hope you can find it in your heart to forgive me.

Yours truly,
Jeremiah McCormick

Becca re-folded the note and set it aside. Was he trying to buy her forgiveness? Maybe she should make him try. She scolded herself for even thinking such a thought. But still, he hadn't paid at all for what he did to her, even if he didn't intend for it to happen.

And was it appropriate for her to be accepting gifts from him? They were tokens of remorse, not anything of a romantic nature. It felt odd, a bit too intimate. A small amount of guilt crept over her. Mr. McCormick only came to ask for her forgiveness. That was all.

She hadn't given it to him. She could try and rationalize it away as being disconcerted by his presence, but as she truly thought about forgiving him, she hesitated. He had hurt her badly—not only physically, but he had also left her with nightmares and a residue of fear.

"Going to open it?" Maggie asked.

Becca nodded and slipped the string off. She pulled back the stiff paper to reveal a tissue paper-wrapped package sitting on a flat box. Unwrapping the tissue paper, she revealed a delicate porcelain box. A small spray of roses was painted on the lid with gilt touching the edges.

"Oh, that's lovely," Maggie breathed. "I've seen that sitting at Fulton's for some time, wondering who would snatch it up."

Becca ran her finger around the edges, touching the smooth, cool surface before setting it aside. She easily recognized the box underneath as fine imported chocolates. She opened the lid and offered Maggie one. "Go ahead and spoil your appetite for lunch," she teased.

Maggie selected one, and Becca popped one in her mouth, too, before closing the box. The silky chocolate melted in her mouth to a creamy smoothness. "Hmm, that's good."

Maggie nodded in agreement.

She sighed and looked at Maggie. "I suppose I'd better write him a note thanking him." She tapped her finger on the table. "And telling him I've forgiven him." After all, it just meant she was making it God's business to deal with him, not hers.

"I'll leave you to it." Maggie squeezed Becca's shoulder as she left the room.

She retrieved pen, ink, and paper from the parlor and sat down at the dining room table. She truly appreciated the gifts. The box would be beautiful to look at on her dresser, and the chocolates were a special treat she hadn't had in a long time. And in her note, she could make it clear that she was accepting them as tokens of forgiveness, nothing more. She tapped the end of the pen to her chin, trying to think of the best way to begin the note.

Dear Mr. McCormick,

Thank you for the lovely gifts—

"What are you doing?"

She jumped, nearly knocking over the ink bottle. Spinning around, she saw Seth standing behind her chair. She put her hand to her chest. "I didn't hear you."

"Obviously. What are these?" He picked up the porcelain box.

His tone was neutral, but Becca wasn't sure how he'd take hearing the gifts came from Mr. McCormick. But the list of people who would send her gifts was short, and she was fairly certain he could see who she was writing to.

"Mr. McCormick sent a note asking for my forgiveness again. I think the gifts are his attempt to convince me of his sincerity. The chocolate is quite good. Would you like one?" She lifted the lid.

He carefully set the porcelain box down. "No thanks. So what are you going to tell him?"

"I'm sending him a note thanking him for the gifts and telling him I forgive him."

"You're keeping the gifts?"

"I believe he's sincere."

"So the fact that he almost had you—" Seth swallowed—"almost had you killed doesn't matter? What about next time? Will you let him take you to supper if he says he's sorry? Becca, you don't know who you're dealing with."

"Seth, I have to forgive him. God tells us to. I believe Mr. McCormick's explanation for what happened, but regardless, God knows his heart and will deal with him."

"That doesn't mean you have to associate with him."

"I'm not associating with him. I'm simply being polite."

"I don't think he'll take it that way. If you accept his gifts, he'll take that as an invitation."

She shook her head. He was so impossible sometimes. "Thank you for your opinion. I disagree."

"Fine. Disagree. Just don't expect me to be around to rescue you from him next time he gets it into his mind to *persuade* you of something."

Anger rose in her chest. She stood, shoving her chair away with the back of her legs. "Maybe *you* need to forgive him and let it go."

Seth opened his mouth as if he was going to say something but clamped his jaw firmly shut instead. He glared at her for a long second before he turned around and walked out.

Her legs turned to jelly as her anger receded. She pulled her chair back up to the table and sat down, realizing she still held the pen in her hand. Looking at the paper, she tried to finish her note, but the words swam before her eyes.

She dropped the pen and put her head in her hands.

She supposed she could understand why Seth disliked Mr. McCormick so much. They were so different. Seth would never forgive himself if someone got hurt because of something he said or did. But Mr. McCormick was sorry, and she must forgive him. She didn't care about the gifts. She'd rather they came from Seth.

She looked up as the thought struck her. Could Seth be jealous?

A scream shattered the air.

She startled, her head snapping up. It came from the direction of the kitchen, but it seemed farther away. It had to be Maggie. Becca's legs were shaking so badly, it took her two tries to push her chair back and stand. She approached the doorway to the kitchen, but she couldn't make her legs move any farther.

Should she go help Maggie? What kind of help could she be? Or go get someone? But should she leave Maggie alone?

She bit her lip and forced her wobbly legs to walk through the kitchen. The door to the cellar stood open. Rustling and footsteps came from the cellar.

Trembling, she edged toward the opening. The footsteps were coming up the stairs.

She froze.

Maggie appeared from the stairwell, her face beet red and her mouth set in a firm line Becca had never seen.

"Mice! In my cellar!" Maggie fumed. "They've gotten into just about everything. And we have a stagecoach coming in tonight." She stomped over to the stove, slammed the lid back on the water reservoir, and started ladling hot water into a bucket.

Becca sagged against the wall with relief. She took a couple of deep breaths and tried to slow her galloping heart. "How can I help, Maggie?"

Maggie shook her head as she pulled cleaning rags and a broom out of her pantry. "There's such a big mess down there, I hardly know where to begin." She propped a hand full of rags on her ample hip. "First things first. We have to have supper ready for the passengers tonight." She tapped her foot while she stared past Becca. "Here's what we'll do. Go ask one of the men to take the wagon to Fulton's. I'll give you a list of what we need. Then ask the other to come in here. I'll set him to patching up those mouse holes." Maggie gathered her supplies and headed down into the cellar.

Becca stood rooted to the floor. She hoped Seth had left already and wasn't out in the barn talking to James and Josh. But if she didn't hurry, Maggie wouldn't have time to get supper started.

She resolutely headed out to the barn.

SETH WAS LEADING his horse out of the barn when he saw Becca heading toward him. He frowned. Was she coming to continue their conversation? Or to apologize? No, she wasn't going to apologize. She didn't need to.

She was biting her lip and looking behind him to the barn.

She wasn't looking for him. Before he could register his disappointment, she was in front of him.

"Are James and Josh in the barn? Mice got into Maggie's cellar and the supplies for tonight's supper."

He stopped in his tracks and burst out in laughter. He wouldn't have imagined that's why Becca was out here. "I feel sorry for those poor mice. They don't stand a chance against Maggie when she's in a mood."

Becca smiled. "She's quite angry."

"I'll bet. Nobody musses up Maggie Kincaid's kitchen and lives to tell about it." Seth looked at her for a moment.

Her green eyes lit up and sparkled like a pool in the forest. He much preferred her smiling at him than mad at him. He thought about telling her what he had originally planned to say when he came upon her in the dining room.

No, it would wait.

Chapter Twenty

McCormick walked down Main Street with two pieces of paper in his pocket. One he had received from Miss Wilson—Rebecca, as he'd begun to think of her—yesterday thanking him for his gifts and giving him her forgiveness.

He hadn't expected it that quickly and had planned on sending a few more gifts. She must have readily believed the story about his unscrupulous business partner. He tried to concentrate on how he could exploit that weakness, but his mind kept drifting to the last time someone had forgiven him. Strange, he couldn't remember a time as an adult. The only memory was of his father.

A warm feeling had enveloped his heart ever since he received Rebecca's note. He found her intriguing. She was the type of woman that needed to be in silks and jewels attending society functions… on his arm.

The boardinghouse came into view, and he checked to make sure he had the second piece of paper in his pocket as well. He pulled it out and had it in his hand when he noticed someone sitting on the porch. When he drew nearer, he saw it was Rebecca. As his feet hit the porch steps, she looked up from what she was doing.

She was snapping beans in a bowl. He hadn't seen anyone do that in years.

A vague memory floated to the surface and tugged at his heart. His mother. His memory of her was faint. She had died before his father, but now he could clearly see her sitting in their one chair outside the cabin door snapping beans. He hadn't thought of her in a long time.

"Mr. McCormick? Are you ill?"

Rebecca's voice caused the vision to vanish. Confused for a moment, he tried to smile at her while he got his bearings. He didn't know if he was succeeding because concern lingered in her eyes. Yet being the center of her attention wasn't the worst thing that had happened to him lately. He rather liked it.

Sufficiently back in the present, he finally answered her. "I'm quite well, especially since I got your note." He removed his hat.

She gave him the first genuine smile he'd seen. He thought she was the most beautiful woman he'd ever seen.

"I'm glad. I thought perhaps you'd had bad news."

He frowned in puzzlement until she gestured to the paper in his hand.

"Oh, the telegram. No, it's not bad news. It's a business proposition that I must make a decision on."

"Please, have a seat."

"Thank you." He sat, placing his hat on the seat next to him, and tapped the telegram against his knee. "It poses a bit of a dilemma for me."

"Oh?"

"Yes. The gentlemen who sent me this telegram has been involved in, shall we say, not quite legitimate business activities. I have declined to do business with him in the past, but now he is making me an offer to partner in a legitimate business venture that could be quite profitable. However, he needs an answer by tomorrow. It was good fortune that I happened to be in my hotel room when the telegram was delivered."

Rebecca merely nodded and continued to snap beans.

"Miss Wilson, your conduct toward me has been very forgiving. You are a woman of the highest character. I importune you for your opinion on this matter."

"While I have attended the university in Salem, I studied literature and history, not business. I'm not sure how I could advise you."

"Ah, but it is not your business expertise I am asking for. It is your moral compass. If a close friend of yours found himself in the situation I am in, what would be your recommendation?"

"I cannot tell you, Mr. McCormick, what decision to make. However, I would certainly consider a person's character as least as important a factor in a partnership as business acumen. If he has no compunction in breaking the law, what is to keep him from taking advantage of you? Or, what if the venture is not as he has presented it?"

Mr. McCormick slowly nodded. "Yes, I see." He picked up the telegram and tore it into pieces.

Rebecca looked startled. "Why did you do that?"

McCormick tucked the pieces into his pocket. "I have no need to respond to him. I agree with you. It doesn't matter how much money is at stake."

He was pleased to see Rebecca looked surprised. "Now, for your good advice, may I repay you with supper at the hotel?"

She shifted in her seat, and he watched as indecision flickered across her face. She brushed at her skirt before answering him. "I'm afraid I must decline. But thank you for your offer."

Was there anything he could say to change her mind? Her gaze was steady, with none of the flirtatious coyness he'd seen in other women who just wanted to be begged.

He stood and put his hat on. "Well, then, thank you again for your wisdom. Good day." He touched the brim of his hat and left, hearing her soft "Good day" as he descended the steps.

"I only got her lumber," Seth muttered to himself as he rode into town. "And windows. Can't forget the windows."

He knew how much Becca's old homestead meant to her, and the lumber and windows would help make her dream a reality. But he wasn't sure how it compared to a china box and chocolates. Women were funny about gifts. He'd learned that while helping out at his father's dry goods store.

He resettled his hat on his head. He'd gotten Fulton's message the windows had been delivered to Becca's homestead. He had just stopped by there to make sure the lumber had arrived as well, so now there was nothing left but to go forward with his plan. If she was determined to stay at the homestead, the least he could do was to help fix it up a bit. Plus, it would give him a good excuse to keep an eye on her.

When he arrived at Maggie's, he put his horse in the barn and went inside. He caught Becca in the parlor, reading. "Let's go for a walk."

She put her book down. "Hello to you too." She smiled. "Is there any new information?"

It took Seth a minute to switch gears. The camp.

"There's a few things we can discuss."

Becca stood, and Seth let her lead the way through the kitchen and out the back door. They hadn't gotten but a few steps from the house when she asked, "What have you found out?"

He didn't reply right away. His investigation into the men who had attacked her had turned up nothing. Seems those men hadn't talked to hardly anyone at the logging camp, something that wasn't too unusual given there were many men who kept to themselves.

Owen Taylor had the most information on them. He had a form for new workers fill out listing their hometown and people that should be notified if an accident should happen. Both men had listed towns in California Seth had never heard of. But he couldn't share this with Becca. She didn't know of the connection of her attackers to the logging camp.

"Nothing new. As much as I hate to admit it, I think it's pretty much what McCormick said. Now I don't buy the part about his not knowing what his *associate* was doing, but I do think he designed your attack and the accidents at the camp to get one or both of us to sell to him. It didn't work, and he came here to make an offer in person. Since we've both turned him down—"

"When did you talk to him?"

"Yesterday I paid a visit to his hotel room. He changed his offer to a partnership, said he could bring in all sorts of contracts, more business."

"And you declined."

"Of course."

"Hmm."

Seth looked at her. "What?"

"Well, considering all the trouble he went to, he hasn't asked me about selling my brother's share."

"He hasn't?"

"No."

They walked in silence for a moment.

She gave a half-smile. "Maybe he assumed it would be rude to ask after admitting he played a part in my attack."

They'd never discussed Becca's ownership in the company. He'd never really thought about it, just assumed things would continue the way they were. "You don't want to sell your share, do you?"

"Oh no. I haven't heard back from my professors yet, but assuming they let me finish my work here, then the income from the logging company means I don't have to worry about looking for work when I finish college."

"Thomas never would have let you work anyway."

She looked at him. "He told you that?"

"A few times. He felt responsible for you. He wasn't going to let you try to support yourself." *And neither would I.* But she didn't need to know that yet.

She considered what Seth said. "He never tried to dissuade me."

"Because you would have argued with him about it."

She at least had the grace to grin. "True."

"I'm sure he didn't want to waste what little time he had with you arguing." They had taken the cutoff to her house and were almost at the clearing. "Close your eyes."

"Why? I can't see where I'm going."

He grinned at her. "I know." He reached for her hand. "I'll lead you."

She reluctantly closed her eyes, squeezing Seth's hand tight. He led her forward, watching their path to make sure she didn't trip. Her first few steps were tentative, but then she seemed to relax and trust him to lead her. Seth smiled at the thought of that.

As they came around the bend, her house came into view. They walked a few steps into the clearing where Seth was sure she'd be able to see everything. "Okay, open your eyes."

He watched her face as she looked at her house and then at the lumber and windows. Her eyes went wide and she turned to Seth.

"I didn't order that. How did that get here?"

He grinned. Surprising her was even better than he'd imagined. And the feeling that he wanted to do it again was so strong it almost took his breath away.

"Seth, you know about this? What's going on?" A smile tugged at the corners of her mouth.

"Since you're staying and determined to live out here, I thought I'd fix it up the way you wanted, the way Thomas planned."

Shock replaced the confusion in Becca's face, and a moment later she flung her arms around his neck.

Instinctively, he grabbed her waist and then slipped his hands behind her back to pull her closer.

She laid her cheek against his chest. "Thank you. Thank you so much," she whispered.

She felt so right in his arms. He'd do anything she asked if it got him this kind of reaction. He pressed a kiss to her forehead.

She lifted her head and looked up at him.

He reached up and cupped the back of her neck with his hand, rubbing his thumb over her cheek. Only a faint shadow remained of her bruise. She shouldn't be looking at him like that, all soft and trusting. He wanted to kiss her, hold her tight, make her his.

He leaned forward.

And stopped himself. If he kissed her, it would change everything.

She lowered her arms from his neck and looked away, pink tingeing her cheeks.

He slowly released her, but reached down to take her hand, not wanting to break contact with her. "Come on. I'll show you what I was thinking." Seth hoped his voice sounded normal, and she couldn't tell the breath he took was shaky. He kept her hand tightly in his as he showed her where he planned to start, and they talked about the process. But he was acutely aware that he didn't know how she felt about him. He planned on changing that.

He wasn't sure how he got Becca back to Maggie's. It was a bit of a blur. And now, as he walked into the Oregon Express office, he felt a strange sense of loss. Having Becca with him felt right.

"Seth, I was just about to send someone out to give this to you. It just came in." Ben waved a yellow piece of paper in Seth's direction.

"Thanks." Seth took it from Ben's hand and quickly scanned it. It was what he expected, but he read it again carefully to make sure.

He folded it and put it in his breast pocket and then paid Ben. *Looks like it's time to pay McCormick another visit.*

SHE THOUGHT he was going to kiss her.

That single thought had distracted her the whole time she and Seth looked at her homestead. But he had brought her back to Maggie's and left.

Now she was peeling potatoes and wondering what was going on. She felt a pinch on her thumb and looked down to see the skin turning red. She'd cut herself with the paring knife. Sticking her thumb in her mouth, she grabbed a rag. She pulled her thumb out and squeezed the rag against it.

That's what she got for thinking about Seth instead of what she was doing.

The way he'd looked at her… She had expected to feel his lips on hers any moment, and when he pulled back, the loss was almost palpable. Why didn't he? The image of her throwing her arms around his neck flashed in her mind, and she felt her cheeks grow hot. Maybe he thought her too forward. But he didn't seem to mind. He was the one who pulled her tight up against him. She could still feel the solid wall of his chest and his arms encircling her. When she realized what she had done, she pulled back.

She unwound the rag and looked at her thumb. It was only a nick and had already stopped bleeding. She picked up a potato and began peeling, paying more attention this time.

Something had changed about their relationship. She was certain he didn't see her as a little sister anymore.

PARSONS WASN'T at the front desk, but Seth knew which room to go to. He rapped the door with his knuckles, not sure if McCormick was in. If not, he'd go looking for him.

The door swung open, and McCormick stood in the doorway, dressed to go out. Seth's muscles tensed. He'd be glad when this joker was gone for good.

"Have you changed your mind about the partnership?" Satisfaction glinted in McCormick's eyes.

"No. I brought some news. I wired the sheriff, and he got back to me." He pulled the telegram out of his pocket. "Seems he hasn't had any information on the man who hired Miss Wilson's attackers." He paused, noting with satisfaction as the smug look faded on McCormick's face. "I guess you never gave him the information on your *associate* after all. Miss Wilson doesn't like liars." His conscious twinged, but he ignored it, telling himself the situation with McCormick was different.

"If you're on the stage to Portland tomorrow, she doesn't have to know about this." Seth shook the thin yellow paper. "If you're still around, I'll have to let her know the truth. Your choice."

McCormick leaned his forearm against the doorjamb, crowding Seth's space, but Seth didn't move. "I know a lot of people in the logging business. I'm sure a few of your competitors would love to see some extra contracts come in. A few words about how it's not—shall I say, healthy?—to do business with you, and those ghosts of yours won't have anything left to haunt."

Seth forced himself not to react, but his arm ached with the desire to flatten McCormick's nose.

McCormick pushed away from the doorframe. "I've got business to attend to in Portland. I was leaving anyway. Let me know your decision by tomorrow." He turned back into the room and then paused and turned back part way. "Your choice."

Chapter Twenty-One

McCormick shut the door to his room and sank heavily on the chair.

He tried to be nice, to offer a partnership, but it didn't work. It never did. He didn't know why he bothered. People just didn't seem to see what he offered them. They always had to be convinced. He smiled to himself. *But that's what I'm best at.* He had one more thing to take care of before he left.

Pulling out his pocket watch, he glanced at it. Almost time for supper. Good.

He headed downstairs and stopped at the front desk. Parsons appeared from the back a moment later.

"Mr. Parsons, could you join me for supper tonight, in say fifteen minutes?"

"It would be my pleasure."

"Good. I'll see you then." McCormick put on his hat and left the hotel. He took his time walking to the Oregon Express station, making sure he smiled and nodded at those who crossed his path.

He was glad to see Ben at his post behind the counter at the Oregon Express office.

"Good afternoon. A ticket on tomorrow's stage to Portland, and I'll need to send a telegram."

Ben pulled out the requisite forms. "Leaving our town?"

"Unfortunately, yes. I have business to attend to. But I hope to be back. This town has great potential with its natural beauty." McCormick scrawled across a form and handed over some bills. "I consider it a best-kept secret. But I imagine it won't be that way for long. With Parsons as mayor, it won't be long until there'll be so much business this town won't know how to manage it all."

Ben pushed across the ticket. "Parsons as mayor? Who told you that?"

"Why he'd be a natural. This town needs someone who will be able to bring in business. There are people who'd love to do business with the good folk of Reedsville if they only knew about it. I personally know of investors looking for logging and mining operations. It could be a boon for the whole town if someone could just head it up."

"Does Seth Blake know about these … investors?"

"Yes. We've talked." McCormick barely shook his head. "He wasn't interested. Refused to even discuss it."

Ben looked puzzled. "That doesn't sound like Seth. He's a fair man, willing to listen."

"I'm sure he is. I don't think he's been in a good frame of mind since his partner died. And now with all the talk about ghosts up there, well …" He tapped his ticket on the counter. "Thank you for this. I hope to return to your town soon." He smiled at Ben before leaving.

By the time he arrived at the hotel dining room, Parsons was ready for him. He led McCormick to a table set in the far back corner. They were barely seated when their supper arrived.

"Thank you," Parsons said to the waiter as soon as the plates were on the table. "Please make sure we're not disturbed."

The young man nodded and left.

McCormick took a bite of his food before speaking to

Parsons. He noticed Parsons giving him a sideways glance, trying to anticipate him.

"Delicious as always. Your wife is an amazing cook. Together you will be quite successful. In fact, the town is abuzz with the rumors of your being mayor." McCormick watched as the mix of pride and uncertainty crossed Parsons's face.

"A few people have mentioned it to me." Parsons fiddled with his silverware. "But I wouldn't want folks to get the wrong impression."

"I'm certain that a man of your upstanding reputation in this community has nothing to worry about. You simply reassure anyone when the subject comes up that you are doing it for the good of the city. There is business to be had out there, and you are the man to bring it to your town." He took another bite while he watched Parsons think.

After a moment, Parsons took a sip from his water glass. Setting it down, he said, "So how does a person go about becoming a mayor?"

McCormick hid his smile. "This is what you need to do." He proceeded to outline a plan for Parsons.

MAIN STREET WAS STILL in early morning shadows when Becca peeked out the window and saw Mr. McCormick walking up the street with his valise in hand.

Had he purposely arrived early to speak with her? She pulled back before he spotted her and busied herself serving the passengers breakfasting at Maggie's table. When they had finished and left the table, she cleared their dishes to the kitchen and stepped into the hall.

Mr. McCormick stood there. She looked past him, out the front door, to see the other passengers boarding the stage. She had hoped he would be one of the first on.

Apparently, he had other plans.

"May I speak with you, Miss Wilson?"

"Certainly."

He gestured down the hall. "Perhaps in the parlor?" He had a strange, almost intimate look in his eyes.

"I believe this is private enough."

He nodded. "Very well. I've enjoyed your company. It's rare to find such intelligence and beauty in the same woman. I wanted to ask your permission to write you."

Becca hesitated. It seemed like such a simple and innocent request. It would be easier to say yes and not disappoint him. She didn't have an obvious reason to turn him down, like an engagement. Her mind flashed to Seth, and she knew he would not be pleased to find out Mr. McCormick was sending her letters. Yet there was something more, something she couldn't quite define, that made her eager to end her association with him.

"I don't think that would be wise."

For an instant, his eyes narrowed, and Becca saw something flash quickly through them. She didn't know what it was, but a chill ran up her spine, and she hoped he would leave quickly.

After a long moment he nodded. "As the lady wishes." He turned to walk out the front door and then stopped. "Please take care of yourself, Miss Wilson. This is the edge of the wilderness, after all, and I'm sure Seth Blake can't always be around." He turned and left.

She started to tremble from head to toe and leaned against the wall for support. Slowly she let out her breath. At least he was leaving. She was still in the hall when she heard the stage pull out, and Maggie came inside.

"Are you feeling all right? You look a little pale." Maggie placed her hand against Becca's forehead.

"I'm fine. Just glad that Mr. McCormick is gone."

Maggie nodded. "I don't know what it is about that man. He was always very polite and well mannered. I've not said this about a passenger before, but I was never so glad to see a body leave as I was when he got on the stage."

Chapter Twenty-Two

It was Saturday, and Seth had secretly recruited everyone from Maggie's to work on Becca's homestead. Now that McCormick was gone, Seth hoped their lives could return to normal. Becca hadn't heard back from her professors yet, but Seth wanted to give her every reason to stay, no matter what the university said. And if that meant giving her back her family's homestead, that's what he was going to do. Besides, spending a day with her wasn't the worst thing.

He found Becca at the boardinghouse sweeping the kitchen floor.

"Morning. Where is everyone?" He was glad she was concentrating on what she was doing and not looking at him. He wasn't sure how well he could keep her from guessing what was going on.

"Maggie and Sally had errands to run. I suppose Josh and James are outside somewhere."

"Good. Then I can steal you away for a moment. I want to check on something out at the homestead."

She looked up at him and smiled. "Let's go."

Seth wasn't sure what they talked about as they walked to the homestead. He was straining to listen for sounds from the homestead, hoping she wouldn't notice.

They were almost at the clearing when a puzzled looked crossed her face. "Did you hear that?" He saw fear flicker for a moment and disappear. He hated to see that, even if the end result was going to please her.

He laid his hand on the small of her back. "It was probably an animal that's not used to someone coming this way." He noticed she leaned into his hand a bit.

A few more steps and they reached the clearing. He watched her face as she noticed the wagon out front. Then Maggie, Sally, James, and Josh came out onto the front porch.

She looked up at Seth. "What's going on?"

He grinned.

"Seth, you know about this?" A smile tugged at the corners of her mouth.

"We're helping you get your house ready so you can move in."

Astonishment filled her face and her eyes went wide. She looked from him to the group on the porch and back again. "Did you set this up?"

He cocked his head to the side. "I had something to do with it."

She reached out and squeezed his hand. "Thank you." But she didn't have to say it; he could see it in her eyes.

When they reached the porch, she gave Sally and Maggie a hug. "Thank you, all of you, so much."

"We wanted to help you settle in and feel at home," Maggie said. "Now, let's get this work done."

Maggie, Sally, and Becca worked on the inside, finishing the cleaning they had started last week. Josh, James, and Seth began framing the additions on the outside and hung the windows. Seth caught glimpses of her while he was working and remained acutely aware of her presence.

Maggie had managed to pack dinner for all of them without

Becca knowing. They sat in the shade of the porch to rest while they ate the noon meal. Afterward, Josh and James stretched out lengthwise under one of the trees in the front yard.

Seth held out his hand to Becca. "Come on, I'll show you what we've done." He helped her to her feet, but didn't let go of her hand as they walked around to the back of the house where they were adding on. The room was framed and the windows hung, but it was still open to the elements.

"See how we left the current wall intact? That'll be the last thing we cut through so you can still move in before we finish the addition."

Becca's face lit up, and Seth felt the warmth of it flood his body. It pleased him to no end to make her happy. He slipped his arm around her waist and pulled her up next to him. She leaned her head on his arm, and he felt her relax against him. It was a good feeling, one he didn't want to end.

"Hey, Seth, do you know where—" Josh appeared around the corner of the building but stopped when he saw them.

Seth immediately felt Becca stiffen and pull away from him, but he tightened his hand on her waist.

"Oh." Josh started to turn around.

"Uh, I need to go see Maggie." Becca broke free from him and hurriedly walked away without looking back.

Seth and Josh watched her leave.

"Did I interrupt something?" Josh had lowered his voice and took a couple of steps toward Seth.

"No. Not yet."

Josh didn't say anything else, but moved to where he had left off working.

Seth stood there a moment and then got back to work. He pounded out his frustration on the nail he was driving into the clapboard siding, annoyed with himself more than anything. He had no business touching Becca. But lately it was as if he couldn't help himself. Whenever she was near, his hands reached out to her almost before he realized it. But if his intentions toward her weren't serious, then he'd just have to restrain himself.

Seth pulled another nail from between his teeth, held it up to the siding and pounded it in. That was the question, wasn't it? What were his intentions with Becca? She was stubborn and didn't listen. But she didn't give up either. He thought about how she held her own against her attackers. Seth pounded in another nail. He didn't want to think about that day. She did seem to occupy his thoughts a great deal, despite his efforts to the contrary.

But what were her feelings towards him? He'd like to think she returned his feelings, but he could interpret nearly everything she had said and done to this point as brotherly affection. Even when she left to go to Willamette University…

He stopped hammering. He'd always thought she'd returned to say "I love you" because she thought of him as a big brother. But she hadn't done that to Thomas. He'd thought little of it at the time, but now, putting it with something he remembered Thomas saying…

"You should come with me, Seth. Becca needs to see you."

Seth had responded, "We both can't be gone from the logging camp. Who would run it? Besides, I'm sure Becca will be back to visit soon."

Thomas shook his head. "She won't come back unless she has to. Come see her."

Seth had been consumed with getting the logging company started. He hadn't really heard what Thomas was trying to say without revealing Becca's confidence.

He finished hammering in the nail. Maybe he *did* know how she felt about him. He knew for sure she had melted his heart. *Who am I kidding? She could form it into a locket and wear it around her neck.*

He picked up another board and let his mind dwell freely for once on Becca. He figured he ought to throw in a little prayer there too.

BECCA STOOD and surveyed her house, visualizing where she would put her things. It had been a long day, but the extra help was just what was needed. It was nearly finished, ready to move in. A deep sense of satisfaction filled her. It wasn't quite the same as when she had lived here with her family, but she could see the memories here, feel them resonating in the walls.

Her roommate in Salem had packed up her trunk, and it had arrived with Josh's last trip from there. Bittersweet feelings washed over her. Was she making the right decision or throwing away her future?

The front door opened and Seth walked in. He grinned at her. "So, what do you think?"

She smiled back and clasped her hands in front of her. "It's wonderful. I can't wait to move in. I'd do it tonight if it wasn't already so late."

"One thing left. We need to check out that fireplace."

James had cut and stacked some firewood and kindling earlier. Seth added it to the fireplace and began to light a fire. As he worked, the fabric of his shirt pulled across his back revealing thick muscles. She was still staring at him when he turned around. The fire had caught, and golden light danced across his sandy hair. He flipped a lock of hair back from his forehead and stood up, his eyes meeting Becca's.

She saw the corners of his mouth tilt up, and she knew he'd caught her staring. She shifted her eyes away. When he stood the room got smaller, he took up such a large part of it. She could hear the sounds of James and Josh finishing up outside, and Maggie and Sally had already headed home to start supper. But for Becca, her world had narrowed down to this one room.

Seth pulled up two chairs next to the fireplace. He motioned her to one and took the other, using the poker to check the small fire he'd made. She watched as he looked in the firebox and examined the chimney and mantle.

"Why did you never make it home to visit?" He concentrated on the fire.

The blood rushed to her face. How much should she tell him? "I, uh, had some opportunities to work on research projects with one of my professors. Then Thomas came to visit, so I didn't feel like I was missing too much." She brushed dust off her skirt.

Seth looked at her. "Didn't you miss home?" His voice was low.

Becca pressed her lips together and nodded. "I did." It came out as a whisper.

The front door opened, and Josh blew in with a gust of cool air. The day had been warm, but it still cooled off quite a bit at night. "Got the fireplace working, I see. Looks good from the outside. It's drawing well with no leaks."

After a few minutes, the small fire had died down to a pile of glowing embers. Seth looked at her one last time. "I'll bank it, and then we can head home."

Josh couldn't possibly know how grateful Becca was for the interruption. But she couldn't help but wonder what Seth had on his mind with his questions.

Becca enjoyed the worship services at the little church. There was no preacher this week, but Josh read from Matthew where Jesus says His burden is easy and His yoke is light. She was finding that to be more true every day. They closed with a few hymns and sharing prayer requests.

Dinner had been Maggie's cold fried chicken, and with a full stomach and thoughts of moving into her own house tomorrow, Becca couldn't remember when she felt more content.

Seth walked into the parlor and pulled the book she was holding out of her hand. "Let's take a walk."

She smiled up at him as she stood. The book wasn't holding

her interest anyway; she was dreaming about her house. It'd be better to see it in person.

They left the boardinghouse and crossed the footbridge over the stream. But instead of heading toward her house, Seth angled them farther back into the forest.

"My house is that way."

Seth gave her a lazy grin. "I know. It reminds me of all the work I did yesterday." He rotated his shoulder. "I'm still a little sore."

She remembered the sight of him working yesterday. There were no doubts at all he could protect her; she felt safe around him. Remembering what McCormick said to her the day he left, she shuddered.

Seth put his arm around her shoulders and squeezed. "You okay?"

She nodded. She didn't want to talk about McCormick today, didn't even want to think about him. He was gone and that was that.

They walked in comfortable silence until they came to the edge of the woods, where a small trail appeared only when she walked right up to it.

"I don't remember this being here," she said as they stepped into the cool shadow of the trees.

"We never showed you our secret fishing spot?"

She laughed. "I guess that's why it was a secret. So—" she stopped mid-sentence. The trees separated to reveal a perfect emerald pool surrounded by large boulders and fed by a small waterfall. The sound of splashing water surrounded them. It was beautiful and peaceful. "I can't believe I never discovered this."

He took her hand and led her over to one of the big boulders. It was large enough to stretch out on. She could just imagine Seth and Thomas sneaking off here with their fishing poles and lazing away an afternoon in the sun.

She settled on the boulder, and he sat next to her, staring out over the water. "I think this was the only secret we didn't let you in on." He nudged her shoulder. "We had to keep something from you."

Leaning back on her hands, she sighed. "It's beautiful. I'm glad you shared it with me now."

He gazed at her intently. "Not as beautiful as you."

She felt her pulse quicken and her cheeks grow warm.

"Now right about there—" he pointed to part of the pond where the sunlight glinted off the surface, "that's just about the color of your eyes." He turned back to her with a tender smile. "Come here." He slid his arm around her shoulders and pulled her up next to him. Taking one of her hands in his, he rubbed his thumb on the back of it.

Warmth flowed throughout her body, and she couldn't think of any place she'd rather be than here next to Seth. In fact, she couldn't think of much of anything other than how close he was to her.

"Becca Wilson, may I have your permission to court you?"

For a moment she felt as if she couldn't catch her breath. She sat stock still for a moment, certain she hadn't heard correctly, but not wanting to break the spell.

"Excuse me?" Her voice was barely a whisper.

His voice was nearly as low. "May I court you?"

He wants to court me? The pressure in her chest broke free, sending sparks all the way to her toes. She couldn't help but smile. Tilting her head, she looked up at him. "I'd like that very much."

His laugh rumbled deep from his chest. He squeezed her hand and brought it to his lips. Then lifting her chin with his finger, he leaned forward and softly kissed her lips. She thought her heart was going to pound right out of her chest.

He rubbed his thumb over her cheek one last time before easing back.

Why had she ever been afraid of coming home?

Chapter Twenty-Three

As the first fingers of dawn crept through his bedroom window, Josh rolled over in bed with a groan. Fighting the urge to go back to sleep, he got out of bed and pulled his clothes on. He stifled a yawn and scratched his head.

Did he smell smoke? Had he forgotten to put the stove out? He wandered into the kitchen. The smell was stronger out here, but the stove was cold. He opened the front door.

He definitely smelled a fire out here. The hairs on the back of his neck stood. He grabbed his boots by the door and shoved his feet inside. A plume of smoke rose to the east of him.

"Oh, no." He grabbed a shovel out of the lean-to and ran toward the smoke. Loud crackling and a wave of heat greeted him as he arrived at the clearing.

Becca's homestead and the pile of lumber were completely engulfed in flames. The shovel dropped from his hand. He wiped his hand over his eyes.

He couldn't save her house, but he still had work to do. Grabbing the shovel, he cut into the earth, throwing dirt on the pyre as he circled it to keep the flames from spreading to the surrounding meadow or trees. When Josh was halfway through, James ran up.

"We could smell the smoke at home, and I saw it from the road." James tried to catch his breath.

"Yeah, I smelled it, too. Doesn't look like it's going to spread, though."

James helped Josh build the firebreak, and they stayed until the house was just a pile of glowing embers.

Josh wiped a grimy arm across an equally dirty forehead. "I'm going to wash up. Tell your ma I'll be right up. I hope Seth gets here before I have to break the news to Becca."

WHEN SETH RODE up to the barn, Josh was waiting for him, looking like he'd put in a hard day already. He hoped Josh wasn't too tired to help them move Becca into her new house. He swung off his horse. "Didn't get much sleep last night?"

Josh ran his hand over his face. "Becca's homestead burned down this morning."

Seth didn't move. Had he'd heard correctly? "What happened?"

Josh told him what he'd found.

"The fireplace. It must have had a crack somewhere. I should have made sure it was completely out." His stomach felt like lead and shoulders sagged. She was never going to trust him again.

"Seth!"

He jerked up, realizing that Josh had been trying to get his attention.

"That's not what happened. We've both seen houses burn from fires that weren't put out right. This didn't look like that. It went down hot and fast. Plus the lumber pile was burning."

Seth shook his head. He didn't buy it. Josh was trying to make him feel better. "It could have started from a spark."

Josh grabbed Seth's shoulder and gave him a quick shake. "Knock it off. Becca needs you." He paused. "Seth, I smelled kerosene."

It took Seth a minute to sort out the implications of Josh's words. His momentary relief at not causing the fire was replaced by cold fear at the realization someone had come after Becca. "Let's talk while I put Red away." He picked up the reins and led the horse into the barn. "So it was set deliberately."

"Looks that way." Josh opened the door to an empty stall, and Seth led Red in. They tended to the horse together.

"McCormick's gone. I guess it could have been the same man that hired Becca's attackers. Is McCormick after revenge since we wouldn't sell to him? Or is he still trying to convince us to sell?"

"Whatever his motivation, the result's the same. Becca's in danger, and she needs to know. She's strong, Seth, she can handle it."

Seth put the currycomb back on the shelf. "You're right. I'll tell her everything today."

Almost everything.

BECCA KICKED at the cold ashes with the toe of her boot, glad Seth was with her. She had steeled herself for the sight of her dream reduced to cinders, but the reality of it hit her harder than she imagined. She'd hoped it wouldn't be true. Maybe her dreams wouldn't be shattered again.

Everything was gone.

Her last physical connection to her parents and her brother, gone.

The hard work of her friends to make it a home for her again, gone.

The smell of charred wood hung heavy in the air, nauseating her. She wasn't sure she could ever enjoy another roaring fire again. When she could no longer stand to look at the ash heap, she turned around to find Seth studying her.

He stepped toward her and held out his hand. She took it,

soothed by his hand warming her icy one. His gentleness breeched the dam keeping her feelings in check. She felt her lip tremble and tears sting her eyes.

Seth pulled her in to his arms, and with his chin on her head, stroked her hair. She took a shuddering breath, concentrating on how safe and protected she felt.

After holding her a moment, he took her hand and led her away from the homestead and into the meadow, finding a fallen log to sit on. From this distance, with Seth next to her, the charred ruins were a slightly more tolerable sight.

He reached up and pushed back a strand of hair that had escaped from her pins, letting his fingers linger on her face. He looked into her eyes. "What do you want to do?"

Her gaze never left his. "I want to rebuild my house."

"Seth." Josh walked toward them. "You'll want to see this. Hoof prints. A single rider. It wasn't one of our horses, and no one else would have any business down here. They weren't on the road, either. They came and left through the meadow, and I lost them where they circled back through the woods."

"Someone didn't want to be seen."

"What are you talking about?" She looked from Josh to Seth.

"Someone did this on purpose." Seth gestured toward the ashes.

She'd never gotten around to asking herself how her house burned down. She was still just trying to grasp the fact that it had. "What? Who?"

"Jeremiah McCormick. Or, more likely, someone he hired."

As she realized the implication of Seth's words, bile rose in her throat. Heat washed over her face, and for a moment she thought she was going to be sick. She leaned over the back of the log.

"Becca? Are you okay?" Seth had one hand on her shoulder. "You've gone all pale."

She nodded, not trusting herself to speak.

"Should we go back to Maggie's?"

She took a deep breath and sat up as the wave receded. "I'll be fine." She turned to face Seth. "He said to me, right before he left, that the wilderness was a dangerous place, that I should be careful because you couldn't protect me all the time. At the time, I thought he was making a comment about how he thought I should be in the city, because he was upset that I wouldn't let him write to me." She stared at where her house used to stand. "But now I wonder if he meant something different."

"He wanted to write to you?" Tension saturated his voice. "Why didn't you tell me?"

"It wasn't important."

"Look," Josh interjected, "it's obvious McCormick's not giving up. I don't know why he wants the logging camp so bad, but for whatever reason, he seems to think Becca is the way to get it. Maybe he thinks she'll sell her share to him, or convince you to sell as well. Or, knowing you for the gentleman you are —" Josh gave Seth a wry grin—"he thinks you'll sell to protect Becca."

She touched his arm. "Seth, I don't want you to do that."

Seth took off his hat and ran his hand through his hair. "I don't know. Sometimes it doesn't sound like a bad idea." He put his hat back on. "We need to figure out the connection to the logging camp. Becca, there's something else you need to know: McCormick lied about turning in the man who hired your attackers. I wired the sheriff to find out. McCormick never sent him any information about his so-called associate. And," he paused, "the two men who attacked you worked at the logging camp."

Her breath caught and wouldn't release. Her head was spinning and nothing made sense anymore. "And when were you and Josh planning to tell me of all this?" Her voice was tight and high-pitched and didn't sound like her at all. She tried swallowing, but it didn't alleviate the pressure. She stood, trying to get more air.

"Becca." Seth reached out for her, but she jerked away from

him. She knew she was being unreasonable, but the comfort and protection she had moments ago disappeared into ash like her house. She didn't feel like being rational. She wanted to crawl out of her skin. "I suppose it's because I'm just a woman."

"Becca—" Seth tried again to grab her hand, but she stepped away from him.

"Maybe if you'd let me in on your discussions I would still have my house." She stalked off, tears blurring her vision and obscuring the ruins of her house. She knew she was being unfair, but right now she didn't care.

Seth called after her, but she didn't turn around. Reaching the road, she kept walking toward the boardinghouse. The crunch of boots on gravel told her Seth was following her. She should have known he would.

This is ridiculous. I'm stomping off, and he's coming after me to make sure I get home safely. She kept going, not able to think of any way out of the situation that would salvage her pride.

Chapter Twenty-Four

This is ridiculous. Seth followed Becca by about twenty feet. She was not going to walk home by herself, but he didn't figure there was any point in trying to talk to her right now. Why was she so upset? Sure, Josh and he should have told her their suspicions from the beginning, he'd admit that. But they wanted to protect her and keep her from worrying needlessly. She obviously did not like the implication that she needed protecting. But what kind of relationship could they have if she couldn't respect his judgment on her safety?

She had shrunken into herself and seemed so small under the gray sky and darkly shadowed trees. So different from the usual confident Becca he knew that he couldn't help but feel protective of her. He knew how much that homestead meant to her. He had bought her the lumber—to show his commitment to her dream. How would its loss would affect their future? If they had one.

ELMER CHUCKLED, careful not to be too loud, as he watched Becca stomp off and Seth follow her. *It wasn't what I had*

planned, but it might work even better. He peered through the trees, moving only when he thought he wouldn't be heard. When Becca and Seth were out of sight, he circled back to where he'd left his horse tied up. A day or two more and he should have enough tidbits to give McCormick in his fancy hotel room. He laughed to himself again, pulling his greasy hat lower over his eyes.

BECCA STARTED TO HEAD HOME, but she had a strong desire to see her brother's grave. It was the last location that connected her to her family. She didn't spend much time thinking about why she wanted to be there. She just went.

Walking through the meadow behind the boardinghouse, her footsteps were muted. She couldn't hear Seth anymore, but didn't turn to see if he was still following her. She traced the stream's path off to the right for awhile until she reached a small knoll where a wooden cross emerged from the emerald grass. At the top, she noticed a small plaque had been carved and embedded in the ground. Someone had laid fresh wildflowers on it.

The plaque read THOMAS WILSON, OUR DEAR FRIEND AND BROTHER. 1857-1881. Becca ran her hand over the smooth wood, fingers tracing the carved words. She was touched by the time and thought put into it. She suspected it was Josh. He was a craftsman when it came to woodworking.

She thought back over the years she and Thomas had spent together, all of the things her brother had taught her. She laughed, remembering Thomas talking her into riding a horse wearing an old pair of his trousers.

"I don't understand how women can stand to wear those things," Thomas had said, pointing at her skirts and layers of petticoats. "They're always in the way, and you can't do anything, let alone ride a horse properly." Becca had agreed with him and had loved the freedom from her bulky skirt—until her mother had found out. She would have been mortified if anyone from town had seen them, although Becca suspected she sympathized with her daughter.

She looked at the plaque again. There were a lot of memories, and not just in the walls of her family home. She could rebuild the house according to Thomas's plans. No one could take away what she had tucked in her heart.

When she stood, her legs ached with the new position. She had forgotten about Seth and looked for him, but he was nowhere in sight. She needed to apologize.

The puffy, white clouds now piled up heavy and gray. The wind picked up, bringing the scent of rain and a chill with it. Becca hurried, not wanting to get caught in a thunderstorm.

She was so intent on getting home it took a moment before the noise behind her registered. She hesitated, and then attributed it to the wind. But when she heard it again, it sounded much more like something or someone coming through the woods. She tried to find the source of the sound, but it kept shifting.

Was it an animal? The town had grown enough that most of the large animals had fled to the mountains. She heard it again, this time directly to her left. There was a metallic clink and a grunt. It was no animal.

Seth was right. She should have listened to him. He was only trying to protect her. Why did she have to let her stupid pride get in the way? *God, forgive me for my pride and my stiff-necked ways.*

She walked quickly now. Wouldn't just be better to run? She gathered her skirts in her hands. What if it was just her imagination? Well, so what if it was? It sounded like her pride talking. An overwhelming sense of urgency pushed her to run.

She picked up her skirts and ran; she didn't stop until she could see the barn.

As she came to the footbridge, she heard a crash in the

bushes behind her. A horse whinnied. A man yelled. Becca kept running, but looked back over her shoulder. Not seeing anything, she turned back around. Seth was right in front of her, and she ran straight for his arms.

"What was that? Are you okay?" He pulled her close.

She panted for breath and pushed her hair out of her face that had come loose while she was running. "Back there—a noise—sounded like a man."

"I heard it. Go inside. I'll be right back." He turned her toward the boardinghouse. She stood there, a little stunned, holding her side and trying to catch her breath, thankful she hadn't laced her corset tighter this morning in her hurry to get out to her homestead.

Seth ran inside the barn and came out a moment later strapping on his gun belt. When he saw she hadn't moved, he pointed. "Go!"

Becca nodded and hurried inside. She stumbled into the kitchen where Maggie took one look at her, settled her in a chair near the kitchen stove, and poured her a cup of tea.

"What was that all about?" she asked.

"I heard something in the woods while I was coming back from Thomas's grave. I wasn't sure what it was, but when I got here, Seth was outside. He'd heard it, too. He went to investigate."

She took a sip of the steaming tea; its heat released the tension in her throat. She turned to Maggie. "Did Josh or Seth tell you they suspect Mr. McCormick burned down my house, and that Josh had found hoof prints coming and going from the woods to my homestead?"

"No, they didn't. But if Mr. McCormick's behind it, then that brings up a whole other set of questions. Do you think that's who was after you today?"

"Probably he hired men like the ones who attacked me."

Maggie's eyes went wide and her hand covered her open

mouth. "Oh, my." She squeezed Becca's hand. "The good Lord was looking after you today, I suspect."

Becca squeezed back. "I think so, too."

She wanted to leave it at that, but her new resolution to battle her pride caused her to admit the truth to Maggie. "It was my fault. Seth had warned me to be careful until we knew what Mr. McCormick was doing. I got angry at him, when all he and Josh were trying to do was protect me."

The kitchen door banged open, and Seth stormed in. Both women turned.

"I didn't find him, but there was someone there. The underbrush had been trampled down, and there were hoof prints. Josh is out looking at them to see if he thinks they're the same ones he saw out by your house." He paused. "Are you okay?"

She nodded. "I'm sorry, Seth." She looked at his blue eyes filled with concern. "I should have listened to you. I know you and Josh were looking out for me. My pride got the better of me. Will you forgive me?"

Maggie slid out of her chair. "I think I have something to do elsewhere."

Seth tossed his hat on the table, unbuckled his gun belt and set it next to his hat, and then sat in the chair Maggie had just vacated, his eyes never leaving Becca's face.

Her breathing quickened.

He took one of her hands in both of his. "Of course I forgive you. And I need you to forgive me for making decisions about things involving you without consulting you. Josh and I never should have kept our suspicions to ourselves."

The tension drained from her, and she smiled. "I forgive you."

He swiped his hair back from his forehead. "I guess it takes a bit of getting used to, thinking of someone else when you're used to looking after yourself. So what shall *we* do about McCormick and the logging camp? I'm wondering if we should just sell it before something else happens." He tucked a strand of hair behind her ear then fanned his thumb across her cheek.

His light touch sent shivers up her back that piled up in her stomach.

"What do you want to do?" His voice was low and soft.

For a moment she had no idea what he was asking. All she could think of was his touch on her face. Oh, Mr. McCormick. She definitely didn't want to think about him right now. "I don't know."

"I forgot something." He slid his hand to the back of her head. He leaned in, and his warm lips touched hers before the kitchen door banged open.

ELMER CURSED his horse and his bad luck. Fool thing had been spooked by a thunderclap nowhere near them. The way the horse sidled and shied through the brush it's a wonder the whole town didn't hear 'em. The girl sure enough did. And Blake almost followed him back to town. He jammed his greasy hat down on his head. He wasn't too smart, but he knew enough to know folks were on to him. How was he supposed to "convince" the girl if she was never alone? He hoped McCormick didn't hear about this.

SETH AND JOSH made their way slowly through the underbrush in the forest, concentrating on their surroundings.

When Seth spotted the broken branches and trampled plants, he stopped and pointed. "There. See how this is broken off? I saw one group of hoof prints over here, and then followed them along towards town."

Josh watched where he stepped and bent closer to the ground where Seth was pointing. Squatting down, he examined the ground. After a minute he said, "They look the same, but I couldn't tell you if they were exactly the same." He pushed his finger in the ground next to a small indention on the side of the horseshoe print. "This looks like a mark from a calk here, just like the ones from near Becca's place. Only logging horses use those shoes for grip. Still, like with Becca's place, what business would anyone have here, going through the trees instead of the road?"

Seth nodded.

They followed the trail toward town until the hoofprints mingled with others and the trail disappeared.

"He could have gone anywhere from here." Seth studied the surrounding area.

Josh nodded. "We know someone's out there. We just don't know who."

"It's another connection to the logging camp," Seth surmised. "How could someone be hiding right under my nose?"

Chapter Twenty-Five

Owen Taylor walked into the logging company office and plopped into his chair. "Five more men quit."

Seth didn't look up from the piece of paper he was reading. His desk was stacked with papers, not typical of its usual orderliness. "I suppose it's just as well. We lost another contract. We won't have enough work to keep the men busy through the summer."

He slapped the letter down and rubbed his hand over his face. "The only contracts we have left are Benning and Ashton. Benning's fair, but we'd never do business with Ashton under other circumstances. His terms are outrageous. But what choice do I have?"

When would McCormick quit? *When I'm ruined.*

The accidents had started again too. He and Owen had been trying to figure out a pattern and were watching a few men, but neither could catch on to who was behind the accidents.

He watched Owen mark something on some papers. Nothing seemed to rattle that man. Seth supposed it was his boyish face.

Owen looked up. "Did you say something?"

"Oh, I was just muttering about what contracts we have left."

Owen put his papers away and stood. He clasped Seth's shoulder and squeezed. "Something will turn up. It always does." He strode out the door.

Seth sighed and put his head in his hands. Discouragement weighed on him like a skid of logs. He wished he shared Owen's optimism. *Lord, what am I missing? What's right before my eyes that I can't see?*

In the silence he felt the Lord speak to his heart. *Trust me. Lean not on your own understanding. Acknowledge me in all your ways and I will direct your paths.* That was the problem. He'd been trying to figure it out on his own. He closed his eyes and spent more time in prayer.

BECCA STOOD at the counter at Fulton's waiting for Mr. Fulton to fill her list.

Mrs. Fulton brought over the mail from the slots. "This is for the boardinghouse folk." She set it on the counter in front of Becca. "I'm so sorry to hear about your homestead burning down. I guess it was a blessing you weren't living there yet."

Becca put the mail into her basket, buying herself a minute. Mrs. Fulton was trying to be kind, and Becca knew she didn't intend to tread on a sore spot. "Yes, it was a blessing."

"We never used to have such strange goings-on here. But lately…" She shook her head. "I suppose that's what comes of being a growing town. And if Mr. Parsons has his way, we'll be growing ever larger."

Becca tilted her head. "What does Mr. Parsons have planned?"

One of the other store customers sauntered to the counter before Mrs. Fulton could answer. Becca recognized his face, but couldn't recall his name. She thought he owned one of the saloons. "Parsons is gonna be our new mayor. A few of us have been talking. It seems that there are people out there who'd like to do business with our town. Parsons is going to be the man who brings their business to us. It'll mean more jobs, and more money, for everyone."

Mr. Fulton had begun to stack her purchases on the counter, and she turned to put them in her basket. "I see. I wish Mr. Parsons well in his endeavor."

"Yeah, we'll he'll do a far sight better than Seth Blake's doing."

Anger welled up and Becca spun to look at him. "What do you mean?"

The man leaned against the counter and regarded her, his eyes darting down and up the length of her. "Seems Blake's been turning down business opportunities. Opportunities that could bring us more jobs, which means more business for the whole town. Instead, Blake's losing business, and men are quitting on him right and left."

How dare he? She pulled herself to her full height and glared at the man. "Seth Blake is an honorable man who treats his workers well. He would never do business with someone of questionable character."

His eyes darted over her again. "You're Wilson's sister, right? The one that went off to that fancy college?"

She suppressed the shivers running through her. "I'm Rebecca Wilson, yes."

"Figures. Don't you ever wonder why that place has been falling apart since your brother's *accident*?" He gave a tight grin. "Then again, you're probably sweet on Blake."

Shaking, she whirled back to the counter. "Mr. Fulton, I'll get the rest of my order later." She grabbed her basket and left, but the man's chuckle followed her out the door.

SETH WAS out at the equipment barn double-checking all the equipment himself, not trusting anyone. He rubbed his eyes with the back of his hand. He'd been putting in late nights, poring over the books, trying to make the numbers work. They wouldn't for long if he didn't get more work.

Running the links through his hands, he studied the chain. He had moved on past the link before his brain registered what he'd seen. He stopped and went back through the links, thinking his mind was playing tricks on him. It was eerily like the morning Thomas died. Was he seeing a memory rather than reality?

There it was! The chain hung oddly because several links in a row had been cut and pulled apart. With the weight of the logs on this chain, it would break for sure.

Just like what happened to Thomas.

Seth set the chain aside to take it to the blacksmith. He examined the rest of the equipment while he loaded it in the wagon. After taking everything to the logging site, and making sure the men knew where they were working for the day, he drove back to the office.

He tugged the chain out from under the wagon seat and carried it into the office with him. He found the damaged links and set that section on his desk. He picked up the other chain heaped behind his desk. Finding those broken links, he laid them next to the others on his desk. Both had the same number of links cut in the same way.

Seth sagged in his chair and stared at the two chains on his desk. Now he knew for sure Thomas's death was the first accident.

The chains had clearly been cut; he could see that now looking at them side by side. So someone wanted to cause an accident the day Thomas died. But how did he know Thomas would be the one hurt? He probably didn't. Thomas had been pushing a new man out of the way. If the log broke free and everyone had seen it in time, no one would have been hurt.

Seth rubbed his stubbly chin. He hadn't taken the time to shave this morning. He needed to do that before he saw Becca at Maggie's for supper tonight. He tipped his chair back on two legs, bracing his knees against the desk to keep from falling backward.

McCormick knew about Thomas's death before he came to Reedsville. How? From the same *associate* that hired Becca's attackers? It had to be someone in town, though not necessarily someone at the logging camp. A person didn't have to be at the logging camp to know Thomas had died.

Still, McCormick had had Becca attacked. The man was callous and cruel, which meant there wasn't much, if anything, that would stop him. Thomas's death hadn't been intentional, but that didn't mean the next one wouldn't be. He and Becca would be the targets. If McCormick had Seth killed, Becca couldn't run the camp. She would have to sell it.

But Becca was a target because threatening her safety was a good way to get Seth to comply with McCormick's wishes. Seth moved his knees, and his chair came down on all four legs with a thump. The question was, should he tell her what he'd found?

SETH SAT in Maggie's parlor, head back against the chair. Josh sat in the chair flanking his. A comfortable silence surrounded them. Seth knew, though, he didn't have much time to bring up the subject that had been bothering him all through supper. The women would be done with the dishes soon. Seth told Josh about the two chains.

"It has to be costing him a fortune to be buying out my logging contracts. He could get any of several logging companies for that amount of money. Why does he want this one so badly?" Seth stretched out his legs in front of him. "I don't want to keep putting my men, Becca, and maybe you all in danger. It's not worth it."

Josh stared into the empty fireplace before looking at Seth. "Let's say you decide to sell. Then what? He becomes part of this town, and this town won't be the same. Instead of being a farming town with a small, well-run logging camp nearby, it'll be like every other logging town with more saloons, loose women, and gambling. He won't run the camp the way you do. He might even shut it down and put everyone out of work. We don't know. But we do know his character, and because of that we have to keep fighting him."

Seth nodded. Josh made sense, but Seth was tired of fighting. "It's going to come down to the money. I don't know how long mine's going to last." He and Thomas had put in several more buildings last spring and bought some equipment. He had been paying extra to the families of the men who were injured. The money wasn't going to last. If he weren't so tired, he'd be frustrated and angry.

"We'll do what we have to. We'll keep praying and seeking the Lord's direction on this."

He'd wanted Josh's opinion without having to watch his words in front of Becca. He didn't want to worry her, but she'd be upset if she knew he was withholding information from her. Right now, he wanted it to all go away. He wanted to spend time with her and enjoy her company without worrying about McCormick and his minions.

BECCA AND MAGGIE had finished the dishes, and Becca was looking forward to visiting with Seth. That was the nice thing about courting. She didn't have to guess as to when she would see him. Maggie had issued him a standing invitation to supper each night, and Becca found comfort in knowing he would come every chance he could possibly get.

When Becca entered the parlor, Seth stood. Her heart

dropped. Dark circles smudged his eyes and fine lines etched around his mouth.

"Let's go for a walk." He strode across the room and, coming even with her, bent his head and lowered his voice. "There's a full moon tonight."

The idea of the walk lightened her concern for him. "That sounds nice."

Outside, he took her hand, pulling it through his arm as they descended the porch steps. The evening still held the warmth of the day. The full moon shone down Main Street, lighting a path for them as they walked toward the center of town. Everyone had closed up for the night, although she knew the saloons were open on the far side of town, and light spilled out of Parsons's dining room several blocks ahead.

The silence was comforting. She leaned her head against Seth's arm a moment and sighed.

His lips brushed her hair. "What was that for?" His voice was low and intimate, and she loved how it made her tingle.

"Nothing in particular. It's just a nice night." She grinned. "The company's nice too."

He winked.

They'd almost reached Parsons's Hotel. Becca knew they'd turn around at that point. "Oh, I almost forgot to tell you. I heard from my professors."

"You did?"

"Yes." The letter had been in the stack Jane Fulton had given her this morning. She decided against telling him about what had happened at the store. He didn't need to worry about rumors. He had enough to deal with. Mr. Fulton had brought over the rest of her order himself a little later and told Becca not to worry about what a few rabble rousers said. Most of the town liked Seth and thought he did right by his workers.

"What did they say?" Seth squeezed her hand.

"Oh, they gave me my assignments to finish up and said, when I mailed them in, I would graduate. Isn't that wonderful?"

"That is good news. Do you feel now like you made the right decision in staying? Even though—" He hesitated. They had reached Parsons's Hotel, and Seth turned them around.

He opened his mouth to speak again, but she got the distinct impression he changed his mind about what he was going to say. She wanted to press him on it, but didn't want to add to his burden. "Yes, I do feel I made the right decision. I have peace here, despite the circumstances. You know, that peace that surpasses all understanding? I know this is where God wants me." She giggled. "But I'm quite happy I'll still get to graduate."

He smiled with her, but it didn't reach his eyes. She didn't ask about the logging camp. He would talk about it if he wanted to. She hoped to sit next to him on Maggie's porch swing, but he still had to ride home.

She wasn't surprised when they reached Maggie's and he took both of her hands in his. He rubbed his thumbs over the backs of her hands before gazing into her eyes. "I'd better say good night out here."

He kissed her, long enough for Becca to tighten her hold on his hands to keep her knees from melting. He looked at her a moment before opening the front door and ushering her inside.

She took a few steps toward the stairs and turned around. "Good night, Seth."

He winked, and she hurried up the stairs, feeling his gaze on her back.

Chapter Twenty-Six

Seth had already put in a good morning's work before the bank opened. He dismounted his horse and threw the reins over the hitching rail just as the window shades on the bank slid up and the door lock clicked open. He walked in and asked the man behind the counter for Mr. Wilkins. The clerk excused himself and returned a moment later to usher him into Mr. Wilkins's office.

"Mr. Blake." The older gentleman rose from behind his desk. His trimmed white beard and mustache matched his white hair. His white shirt and collar were starched so stiffly and his black suit pressed so crisply that Seth wondered how he could sit. "What can I do for you today?"

Seth shook Wilkins's extended hand and then took the seat indicated. Setting his hat on his knee, Seth said, "I'll get straight to the point. I need a loan on the logging company."

Wilkins clasped his hands on the blotter on his desk. "I'd like you help you. But I don't see how I can. What with the recent injuries and the loss of your contracts—"

"How did you know about the contracts?"

Wilkins met Seth's gaze steadily. The man didn't even have the good conscience to look abashed. "I make it my business to know what goes on in this town. Like I was saying, with what's been happening at your camp, I can't justify risking the bank's money on an enterprise that looks, quite frankly, ready to fail."

Seth worked his jaw and stood up. "Thank you for your time." He strode out of the office.

He had almost passed Maggie's when he decided to stop. He needed to see Becca. Josh was keeping an eye on her, but he'd rest easier if he checked on her himself.

WITH THE LAST sheet on the line, Becca bent over to pick up the basket when she spotted Seth leading his horse into the barn, his stride longer than usual. She frowned. Was it her imagination or did he seem upset? She tossed the remaining clothespins in the basket, propped it on her hip, and headed inside. As she hung the basket on its peg, Seth entered the kitchen.

She smiled. "You're just in time. Maggie and I made cookies this morning. We changed the recipe a little so you can test them for us. You know, to see if they are still up to Maggie's standards."

He grinned. "I'd be glad to be your taste tester anytime. I'm surprised James hasn't jumped at it."

"Oh, he doesn't know. He's been avoiding the kitchen. You know how Maggie takes after anyone who tries to sample her cooking without permission."

He sat at the kitchen table while she poured two cups of coffee. When she handed him his cup, their hands touched, and she was certain she saw sparks. It was a miracle the coffee didn't end up in his lap.

She grabbed the plate of cookies from where they'd been cooling in the pantry and brought them to the table. He picked up a cookie as she sat down. The image of being married to him and sharing cookies and coffee in their own kitchen flashed through her mind. She hoped she didn't blush, but the vision was very appealing.

"Hmm. Cinnamon. This is good. Definitely an improvement. But you know," he lowered his head conspiratorially toward her, "I think I'll have to eat a few more to make sure."

She laughed. "You do that. I wouldn't want to ruin the boardinghouse's reputation for good food."

As he selected another cookie, she picked at her apron. She enjoyed having him here, but for some reason she was completely at a loss for words. "What brings you out here?" She watched the coffee swirl around in her mug.

"A pretty lady."

Her head snapped up. His eyes were twinkling, and her cheeks grew warm. She gave him a half-smile and shook her head.

"What? You don't think I stopped by just to see the woman I'm courting?" He leaned forward and took one of her hands in his. She felt the calluses on his palms as his hand engulfed hers.

"I know you have a lot of work to do. Other work, that is, besides tasting cookies."

His eyes grew distant for a moment. "Well, I did have some business to take care of at the bank. But, I'd much rather spend time with you." He released her hand and leaned back. "You are right, though. I do have to get back." He stood and leaned over and kissed her cheek. "I'll see you at supper tonight. Maybe we can take another walk in the moonlight."

She smiled up at him, and he snatched another cookie before heading out the door.

BECCA WAS DISHING up their food from the stove when Josh came in for dinner a little before noon.

"Have you seen Seth today?" Josh pulled out his chair and slid into it.

Becca set the steaming food on the table. "He was here earlier this morning for a bit."

Josh stared at her, his expression a mixture of concern and uncertainty. It wasn't like him. James came in from washing up, and Maggie set the other two plates down on the table.

"Let's ask the blessing," Maggie said.

Josh gave a quick but heartfelt blessing but didn't start in on his food right away.

"What's wrong?" Becca asked. Something had to be wrong to keep Josh from his food.

"Ben told me Wilkins is letting it be known around town that Seth approached him for a loan for the logging camp and that he turned him down."

"Oh no." The look she saw on Seth's face earlier now made sense. She closed her eyes and put her hand to her forehead. It must be worse than he'd let on if he went to Wilkins for a loan. And now the whole town would know. She wanted to put her arms around him and tell him that no matter what happened she loved him and nothing would change that.

She looked around the table. Josh had started eating again, and no one was paying attention to her. She took a bite of her food but didn't taste it. *I love him.* She let the thought roll around her head for a moment. It shouldn't have surprised her. She suspected it had been true for some time now. Who was she fooling? It had always been true. She had never stopped loving him. But instead of a childish, schoolgirl infatuation, she now loved Seth with the full heart of a grown woman.

"I don't know what concern of his Mr. Wilkins thinks it is to go talking about other people's business." Maggie shook her head. "I have a good mind to go tell him so."

"I wonder why Wilkins did it," Josh mused. "I've never heard him talk about anyone else's business before."

"Do you think Mr. Wilkins is involved somehow with Mr. McCormick or the man who hired my attackers?" Becca asked.

Josh chuckled. That wasn't the response she expected. "Sorry,

Becca. I wasn't laughing at you. I was remembering the look on Wilkins's face when we demanded he lock up those outlaws in the vault. If he was involved with McCormick, he must have been surprised."

She paused, her fork in midair. "He must not be Mr. McCormick's associate, however. He's too well-known, and my attackers would have identified him. Besides, he doesn't look anything like the man they described."

"And, I can't imagine Wilkins sullying himself by associating with loggers." Josh rubbed his chin. "Not only do we need a sheriff, it looks like we also need a new banker."

Maggie had been quiet through the exchange. She looked around the table. "I have an idea, but Josh—and you, too, James—have to agree completely with me or we won't do it."

THE NEXT MORNING, the moment the bank opened, doors Josh walked through them. Looking around the lobby, he spied Mr. Wilkins talking to a clerk behind the counter. He strode over and rapped his knuckles on the counter. Mr. Wilkins stopped mid-sentence and looked up.

"Mr. Benson. Good morning. How can I help you?"

"I need to talk to you in private."

"Certainly."

They went back to Wilkins's office. Wilkins started to sit down, gesturing to Josh to do the same.

Josh shook his head. "Seth Blake needs a loan. You won't give it to him. I want to put up the Oregon Express as collateral for his loan."

Wilkins stared at him for a moment. "I understand the two of you are close friends, but don't let your emotions cloud your judgment. The logging company is a losing business. Don't let it destroy your business too."

"Will you do it or not?"

"Of course I will. The receipts from the Oregon Express are far more than what Blake wants. If you're going to be so foolish, who am I to stop you? You and Blake come back in an hour. I'll have the papers drawn up to sign then. Mrs. Kincaid will need to sign them too."

THE DOOR to Seth's office opened and he looked up, surprised to see Josh step inside. He hadn't said anything about coming up last night at supper.

"What brings you here this morning?" Fear ran through his chest. "It's not Becca, is it?" He started to stand. "She's okay, isn't she?"

Josh waved him back down. "She's fine. James is keeping an eye on them, but I told them it'd be best if they could find something to do inside the boardinghouse until I got back."

The tension drained from him.

Josh straddled the chair across from Seth's desk. Seth got the impression he was biding his time, but knew better than to rush him. "Owen going to be out a while?"

"Yeah. He's out on the north ridge."

"Wilkins wants you to come sign loan papers."

Seth clenched his jaw. "Wilkins turned me down for a loan."

"He changed his mind."

Seth stared at him. "What did you do?" He almost didn't want to know.

Josh met his gaze. "Just had a chat with him."

Seth crossed his arms and shook his head. He wasn't buying it. "You didn't hurt him, did you?" He half-hoped Josh had.

"No. I put up the stagecoach line as collateral."

He didn't know what to say; he was stunned. "You can't do that."

"I already did. Look, Maggie and I want to do this for you. You helped her and Stephen get the stagecoach line and boardinghouse off the ground. She loves you like one of her own. You know if it was the other way around you'd do it for her."

Seth's throat tightened.

Josh stood up and slapped him on the shoulder. "Come on. Let's go sign those papers."

Seth got up and followed him, feeling like a drowning man who'd just been thrown a rope.

They stopped by the boardinghouse and picked up Maggie. She handed Josh a small valise, and the three of them walked to the bank. Within a few minutes, they had all signed the papers.

Mr. Wilkins was escorting them out of his office and into the lobby, when Josh turned around. "There's one more thing."

Seth would have sworn Wilkins suppressed a sigh. "What is that?"

"You can close out the Oregon Express account."

"Excuse me?" Mr. Wilkins looked bewildered.

"You can close out our account."

"B-but why? Surely—" he stammered.

Josh leaned over the counter, his voice low but threaded with iron. "Because we don't do business with men who can't keep other's business private."

Mr. Wilkins paled. "I don't know what you mean."

"I think you do."

Mr. Wilkins said nothing further, but soon he had a stack of cash on the counter and shoved a form in front of Josh to sign.

"The loan money too," Seth added.

Wilkins glared at him as he shoved another form across the counter and another stack of bills joined the first.

Josh took their copies of the forms and the money and piled it into the valise he carried. He tipped his hat to Wilkins, and they all left the bank.

They had gone just a bit down Main Street when Seth leaned near Josh and said in a low voice, "We're crazy to have this much cash. I wouldn't put it past Wilkins to advertise the fact."

Josh gave him a wicked smile. "That's why I put a safe in the barn floor."

"Wise man."

Twenty minutes later, Josh swept off a section of the barn floor near the tack room. Seth had to look carefully to see the trapdoor set in the floor. Josh bent down and lifted it up, using a knot hole in the board, to reveal a shiny black safe. He looked up at Seth and grinned.

"How did you manage this?"

"I was saving it for a special occasion. Today seemed like a good day."

"Whatever made you think you needed a safe in your barn?"

"The station master in Salem was selling it, getting a bigger one. I figured we could use it, the way the town is growing and more strangers coming in. Never knew it would be so handy."

Seth grinned. Josh had always been resourceful. Josh dialed the combination, swung open the door, and placed the money inside. He closed the door, put the trapdoor in place, and used his foot to push dirt and straw over the floor. Even knowing what to look for, the trapdoor was hard to find.

"Ride with me back to the camp?" Seth asked as Josh straightened up. "I wanted to show you those cut chains."

"Sure."

SETH AND JOSH DISMOUNTED, tied their horses to the hitching post in front of the logging camp office and walked in. Seth stepped behind his desk to pull out the chains to show Josh. It took him a second to realize he was seeing bare wood floor instead of the pile of chains.

Seth looked around the office for a moment, trying to remember if he'd put them somewhere else, or if for some reason Owen had moved them out of the way. "They aren't here. I told

Owen not to touch them. Maybe he stuck them out in the tool barn. I hope no one's using them."

Josh followed silently as they walked over to the tool barn. Seth racked his brain trying to remember when he saw the chains last. He couldn't remember if they were in the office this morning or not. He was so tired the days were starting to run together.

He yanked open the door to the tool barn. It was mostly empty since almost all the equipment was in use. the chains weren't there.

He jerked off his hat and raked his hair. Slamming the door shut, he turned to Josh. "I don't know what to tell you. I wanted to show you those chains and get your opinion." Over Josh's shoulder, Seth spotted Owen Taylor. He resettled his hat on his head. "Hey, Owen, come here a minute."

Owen changed direction and headed toward them. "Hey, Josh."

Josh nodded. "Hey."

"You know those chains I had behind my desk?" Seth asked. "Do you know where they went?"

Owen scratched his bald head. "They aren't there?"

"No."

"I thought they were there. I haven't seen them." He shifted his weight. "I got to go get more axle grease. Need anything else?"

"No, that's it. Thanks."

Seth kicked his boot into the ground. "I just hope someone doesn't use them before I can find them." He looked up at Josh, who nodded him back towards the office.

Inside, Josh said, "Maybe you should be thinking of those chains as proof. And someone took them to keep you from having that proof."

Seth slowly nodded. "Whoever's causing the accidents."

"Yep."

Mr. Wilkins sat back down at his desk and thought for a moment. Then, with decision, he picked up his pen, dipped it in the inkwell, and wrote a note. After blotting it, he folded the paper and sealed it. When he was finished, he called to his clerk.

"Robertson!"

The man appeared quickly in the doorway.

Wilkins held out the sealed envelope. "Take this to Fulton's to be mailed."

"Yes, sir." Robertson took the letter and left.

Mr. Wilkins reflected at his desk for a moment before returning to the papers he was working on.

Chapter Twenty-Seven

Becca wiped the back of her hand across her forehead. It was still morning and already hot. Even the usually cool dirt of the garden felt warm. Kneeling, she leaned forward to pluck out a few weeds and pull up the last of the lettuce. There were a few tomatoes ripening so she added those to her basket.

She stood and shook the dirt off her skirt while she surveyed the garden to see if anything else needed doing. If this heat kept up without rain, they'd have to start watering the garden with buckets from the stream. At least it was close. Maybe they could just dig a ditch between the garden and the stream. Hmm. Josh was good with things like that. She'd ask him.

Once in the kitchen, she set the basket on the dry sink. The kitchen was hotter than the back yard. Maybe Josh could build them a summer kitchen too.

Maggie came up from the basement, her arms full of jars. "I declare I'm going to put my chair down there. It's the only place that's tolerably cool." She set her load down on the table and turned to Becca. "Do you remember how to hitch up the buggy?"

"I think so."

"Good. The boys are out at your homestead and you can bring them dinner and make sure they're doing things the way you'd like them."

She blinked. She had no idea.

"By the time you're done, I should be finished packing their dinner. It's too heavy to carry over there."

"Don't you want to come along?"

Maggie shook her head. "I'm planning on sitting on the front porch with some ginger tea and the latest *Godey's Lady's Book* that Josh brought back yesterday from his trip to Salem."

She hitched up the buggy and pulled it up to the backdoor. She and Maggie loaded it and soon Becca was on her way. The buggy made it a quick trip and soon the sounds of hammers on nails and men's voices drifted to her on the breeze.

As she rounded the bend and her homestead became visible in the clearing, the reins went slack in her hands. The old mare plodded along until Becca remembered to rein her in.

Tears filled her eyes and she couldn't catch her breath. Boards gleamed golden in the sunlight and the smell of freshly cut lumber filled the air. The skeleton of her house rose from the clearing.

One of the men looked up and caught sight of her. He tossed his hammer on the ground and walked over. Although his hat shadowed his face, Becca knew from his stride and his build it was Seth. He covered the distance between them in a few steps, grinning at her.

Speechless, she looked between Seth and the house several times before finally blurting, "When— how did this happen?"

He took the reins from her hands and laid them on the dash. "Since things are a little slow at the logging camp, I thought I could put a couple of my best men to work down here." He reached up and, putting his hands on her waist, lifted her from the buggy. His voice was pitched low. "They have families to feed. You needed a house built. We wanted to surprise you."

He hadn't let go of her yet. She looked behind him at her house as if she were dreaming. All of the rooms had been framed, and the second story was in process. When the house finally seemed to be real, and not some dream, the shock wore off and her chest filled with love and gratitude. She turned back to Seth. The grey flecks his blue eyes reflected silver in the sun. "You did this for me?"

Seth's gaze grew tender as he nodded slowly.

She threw her arms around his neck. His hands tightened around her waist, and he pulled her close. Tears welled in her eyes, and she squeezed them shut. Not only had he done it for her, he'd found a way to take care of his best workers without making them feel they were getting charity. She wished the townsfolk could know about this instead of all the problems at the camp. "Thank you," she whispered into his shirt.

"You're welcome." His voice was husky. "I know how much this place means to you." He planted a kiss on her brow and took her hand. "Come on. I'll show you what we've done."

Footsteps crunched on the dirt and someone was whistling. She shifted her eyes around Seth and saw Josh coming toward them. Four other men were with him. She felt herself blushing. The skeleton of the house hadn't hid them from the men's view.

She wiped her eyes with the back of her other hand. Seth gave her a wry look as he let go of her hand and turned to greet the men.

"So you found out our surprise, huh?" Josh asked, grinning broadly.

She included all of the men with her smile. "Thank you all so much. I can't believe it. You couldn't possibly know how much this means to me."

Seth gestured to the men as he introduced them, one hand settled protectively on the small of her back. "Becca, this is Tim Donnelly, Andrew Paige, Charlie Lee, and Bill Johnson. Gentlemen, this is Rebecca Wilson, Thomas's sister."

"How do, Miss?"

"Awfully sorry to hear about your brother."

"He was a good man. We miss him."

She nodded at the comments, appreciating their sentiments. She struggled to remember their names, while her every nerve focused on Seth's warm hand on her back.

"Come on. I'll show you the inside. And," he paused, "If I know Maggie, I bet she had you bring the buggy because those baskets are full of food." He winked at her. "Josh, you think you can handle unloading the food?"

Josh just grinned.

"Save some for us."

"Don't be too long then, or I can't guarantee it."

The men started in on the food, and Seth led Becca to the spot where the door would soon be. It was about two feet off the ground; the men had not yet built the steps.

"I'll show you what we've done inside. Here, let me help you up." He put his hands around her waist and lifted her inside. He had no problem getting in himself with his long legs. She could still feel the warmth on her waist where his hands had been.

As they walked around the house, she continued to be amazed. She didn't have to imagine how her house would look. It would soon be a reality. All thanks to this man here, holding her hand. She couldn't ever remember someone doing something more loving for her than this.

"So how do you like it?" Seth's low voice interrupted her imagining.

She looked up at him. Words couldn't express what she was feeling. "It's perfect."

A low chuckle rumbled from his chest. "It's not halfway done yet."

"I don't care. I still think it's perfect."

Seth guided her over to the far end of the house and then turned her so his body blocked her from the view of the other men. He looked intently at her face. "Does it hurt anymore?" He ran his thumb where her bruise used to be.

Her breath caught. For a moment she could think of nothing but the gentle roughness of his thumb on her face. Then she remembered what he had asked her.

"Not really." She licked her lips. Her throat felt parched.

There was a scrape of boots on the floor as someone else came into the house. Seth slowly lowered his hand.

"So, what do you think of our craftsmanship?" Josh's voice sounded from the doorway. Seth shifted and Josh came into view strolling toward them. Seth tossed Josh an annoyed look.

"I'm amazed at how you've gotten so far so quickly."

Josh looked back over his shoulder where the men were still eating. He lowered his voice and angled his head toward Seth. "How many men know about you and Becca courting?"

Seth followed his glance toward the men. "It's not a secret, but we haven't told anyone outside of you and Maggie. Why?"

Josh shifted his weight and stuck his heel out. "Until we know who at the camp is a danger, maybe you don't want to make it too well known."

Her cheeks grew warm. The men had seen her throw her arms around Seth. But most of the town knew he was like a big brother to her. Maybe they would still think that. Not that she thought of him that way anymore.

He was turned slightly away from her so she risked a quick look at him from head to toe. No, definitely not a big brother.

Seth considered it a moment. "You're right. We'd best be on the safe side." The two men exchanged a look she didn't understand. There was something they weren't telling her. She started to ask, but then, remembering the other men around, decided against it. He'd tell he later. He had promised not to keep information from her.

"I need to head back to the boardinghouse to help Maggie anyway."

They walked to the doorway, and Seth jumped down. "Put your hands on my shoulders."

She felt the heat of his skin and the tightness of his muscles under her hands as he grasped her waist and set her gently down. Josh jumped down behind her. Seth held her for a moment longer than necessary, looking into her eyes. She met his gaze, heart pounding, thinking he wanted to say something. But in the next moment he released her.

She took a deep breath and pretended that Seth was still a brother figure to her before she walked over and thanked the men again for the work on her house. Bill and Andrew shifted uncomfortably under the praise.

Josh rummaged through what was left in the baskets, and stuffed a biscuit in his mouth. "Thanks for bringing the food, Becca."

"Yeah, we sure do appreciate that," Charlie added. "Tell Miss Maggie hey for us."

Seth walked over to his tools and pulled out something. He helped her into the buggy before he handed it to her. It was a furniture catalog. "Start picking things out." His eyes were soft and intense at the same time.

Her heart leaped into her throat at what she thought she saw in his gaze. But she couldn't ask him here what he meant.

He squeezed her hand before giving her the reins.

The sounds of hammers and saws began as she left the clearing and headed to the boardinghouse. She returned the buggy to the barn, unhitched it, and took care of the mare. When she was finished, she found Maggie just where she had said she would be. She smiled when Becca when stepped on to the porch.

"You knew about this, didn't you?" Becca demanded in a mock accusatory tone.

Maggie laughed. "I knew something about it. And by the look on your face I presume it meets with your approval."

Becca clutched the catalogue to her chest. "Oh my, yes!"

Maggie gestured to the catalogue. "What's that?"

She lifted it, having forgotten about it for the moment. "Oh, it's a furniture catalogue." She blushed and looked down. "Seth said I should start picking things out."

"I see." Maggie didn't hide her smile before she went back to her magazine, and Becca headed upstairs to put the catalog in her room before fixing supper.

He wanted to tell her he loved her, but he couldn't. He hammered the nail in with more force than necessary. Seth didn't know what he had to offer her. A failing logging company and enemy who had no qualms about harming her. He'd managed to risk his friends' business too. *And, oh, by the by, your brother was McCormick's first victim, but my negligence allowed it to happen.* Sounded like a proposal any woman would want. He finished nailing up the board and tossed his hammer down.

Should he tell her about her brother? He had told her he wouldn't keep information from her that involved her. But he didn't see how it would help her, and it would only hurt him. She had trusted him to protect her brother, and he had let her down. He didn't know if she would get over it. She'd probably forgive him, eventually, because God required it, and it was in her nature to do so. But would she love him?

"Hey, Seth, give me a hand with this." Josh held one end of a beam that would support the second floor. Seth picked up the other end and, straining a bit under its weight, they lifted it in place while Charlie and Andrew braced the ends and nailed it all in place. The men worked in silence except for a request to hand someone something or move a board a bit to the right or left.

He hoped Josh knew what he was doing in putting up the Oregon Express as collateral. He was afraid he was creating disaster in Becca's life. He didn't want to do that to Josh and Maggie too. *Lord, can You help me out here? I don't know what*

McCormick's after. At this point, I'd probably just give it to him. Help me know what to do. Help me protect these people who are like family to me.

Help me to know when to quit.

JEREMIAH MCCORMICK STARED at the letter in front of him. He didn't have to look at the ledgers open underneath the letter to know this was particularly bad news. Why was it so difficult to find people to do a job correctly?

Wilkins, whose letter McCormick held, was so eager for the chance to gain control of the Oregon Express that he couldn't see he had damaged his chances for bigger profits. People just couldn't see the big picture.

McCormick crumpled the letter and tossed it on the floor, revealing his ledgers. He ran his hand over his face. If Wilkins had ruined his chances ....

McCormick needed Seth Blake to give in soon. He had used up all of his funds and leveraged all of his assets to raise enough cash to buy out Blake's contracts and pay a few "incentives." But payments were coming due soon, and he was just about out of cash. Those he owed payments to were friends of Mike's, but that wouldn't keep them from doing what they did best: collecting debts. And if he couldn't pay—well, he would pay ... one way or another.

He stood and paced the length of his Portland hotel room. He had stayed because he hadn't wanted to be too far from the action. Besides, it made it a little harder for Mike's friends to find him. He had to have a plan. A way to speed things up. He had never lost and didn't plan to now. Especially now that he was so close to getting the security that would set him for life. Security that would ensure he'd never have the remotest chance of having to stoop to doing the kind of back-breaking labor that killed his father.

Security that would allow him to marry someone like Becca Wilson.

He stopped pacing. Plans were going to have to be moved up. He sat down and began a letter. He needed the man who had been his eyes and ears to pick up the action. And there would be nothing Seth Blake could do about this.

Chapter Twenty-Eight

W*hy couldn't it have been on the other side of the road?*

Josh groaned as he lay on his back in the dirt. A rock dug into his ribs, and his right arm twisted underneath him. If only the snake had been on the other side of the road. It was long gone, having slithered into the brush after doing its damage.

Snakes terrified his wheel horse, so of course that's the side the snake had to be on. His lead horse didn't like snakes either, but he wouldn't have done much more than sidle a bit to the middle. Jake, the wheel horse, however … well if a horse could pitch a fit, Jake just did. Josh figured his sailing over the horses' heads had startled Jake enough to make him forget whatever had bothered him to begin with.

If only the landing hadn't been so rough. He gritted his teeth and rolled over to his stomach. Taking the pressure off his arm caused pain to shoot through it, and a hiss escaped his lips. But at least he knew his ribs weren't broken. It hurt a little to take a deep breath, but that was probably a bruise caused by the rock. He'd love to see what that would look like in the morning.

He was easing his knees under him, using his good arm to

brace his weight, when he heard one of the passengers come up next to him.

"You all right, Mister?"

"Yeah. Think my arm's broke, though."

"Let's get you up." The man reached around Josh's waist and helped him stand. Jostling his arm shot out shards of pain. Josh grabbed the man's arm and waited for his vision to clear.

"Thanks." Josh looked at his horses standing perfectly still, except for twitching ears and a few shuffling hooves. They were good horses. Mostly. They hadn't trampled him.

Josh stumbled over to the stage and looked inside. "Everybody okay?"

He got a few nods, and the man beside him said, "Just shook up a bit. A few bumped heads. You took the worst of it."

If he didn't move his arm or breathe too deeply, he was only in moderate pain. Now he just had to figure out how to get them back to Reedsville. They weren't too far out—*Thank You, Lord*—so that was the best option. But there was no way he could drive with a busted arm, and it was too far to ask the passengers to walk back.

He looked at the man standing next to him. He was the biggest of the passengers. Not a tall man, but big through the shoulders and thighs. "Ever drive a stage before?"

"Can't say that I have. I've driven oxen, mules, horses. Just not six of them at once."

"What's your name?"

"Will Emerson."

"I'm Josh Benson. You're my new driver. Now, I need you to help me make a sling."

They went to the boot, and Josh showed Will which was his bag and had him pull out a shirt. They gently tucked it under his arm and looped the sleeves over his neck and tied them together.

With his arm secure, Josh pulled himself up into the driver's seat with one arm. He then explained to Will how to pick up the reins from where they'd scattered, making sure the lines didn't tangle. Josh leaned over to take them from him and wrapped them around the brake. "Climb on up."

He pulled his gloves off, wincing as it moved his right arm. He couldn't grip with his right hand to pull the left one off.

"Let me help." Will eased the glove off of Josh.

Josh handed him the other glove. "Put these on and unwrap the lines from the brake handle. Think of it as three pairs of horses. Use your fingers to separate the teams." Josh showed him and was glad Will seemed to understand. "They're good horses; they know the route well. The problem will be getting them to turn around up here so we can go back."

The horses were hesitant at first, sensing someone else at the lines. But with Will's firm hand and Josh's familiar voice encouraging them, they got moving, turned around, and headed for Reedsville.

JOSH RESTED in his favorite chair in Maggie's parlor, but Seth thought he still looked pale and could see fine lines around his mouth.

Becca handed Josh a cup of Maggie's special tea. It had willow bark in it to ease his pain.

"Thanks." He smiled at her, but it didn't quite reach his eyes.

Seth watched her as she left the room. He had come the moment James had fetched him, giving him a brief account of what had happened. The passengers were in the dining room, being taken care of by Maggie, but he could tell she was shaken. It had to remind Maggie of when Stephen had died.

He settled in the chair opposite Josh. "I'll take the stage run to Portland tomorrow."

Josh started to say something and then just nodded. He leaned his head back and closed his eyes. "Thanks. The thought of making that run again, even with James driving.... I believe I felt every rock on the way back."

"James isn't ready to take the runs by himself yet."

Josh opened his eyes. "No. He's still a bit afraid, and the horses know that. And, after Stephen getting shot and killed in a robbery attempt, I don't think Maggie's ready to let James go by himself yet."

"It's slow at the logging camp, and it's hot and dry enough now that the men have to quit working shortly after dinner. Owen can do what needs to be done while I take the runs for you."

Josh moved in the chair, trying to get more comfortable, and grimaced. "I was thinking of sending James with you, but we should probably hold off. At least until I'm more proficient with my left hand."

Seth glanced toward the open parlor door and lowered his voice. "I think that's wise after what's been going on. I'll leave him here until you're able to handle a gun again." He stood up. "Need anything? I'm going to get some things from my place. Looks like we're bunking together again for awhile."

Josh grinned. "Do you still snore?"

"I'd throw something at you, but you're an injured man."

He had reached the doorway when Josh called him back. "Hey, Seth?"

Seth paused and turned his head.

"Thanks."

He nodded slowly. "It can't compare to what you did for me." He turned and left the room.

It was odd to Becca, having Seth in the kitchen for breakfast. He'd come in, kissed her good morning, and poured himself a cup of coffee. He tugged a kitchen chair out with his foot and sat down, studying her.

She set a slab of bacon on the cutting board and sliced it, feeling his eyes on her. It took all her concentration not to cut herself. She set the skillet on the stove and fried up the bacon. Glancing over at him, she found he was still watching her.

"Stop. You're making me nervous."

"I like watching you. And I'm not going to be able to for a couple of days."

"You made me cut up too much bacon."

"I like bacon."

She shook her head. He was impossible. But she couldn't completely bury her smile.

Maggie came in the back door, apron full of eggs. Becca cooked them while Maggie saw to the passengers who were beginning to wander into the dining room. The morning work began, and she was too busy to notice Seth anymore. At some point he left the kitchen and ate breakfast with the passengers.

She hadn't had a chance to eat breakfast herself before she realized the stage was boarding. Hurrying up to her room, she grabbed a letter and stuck it in her apron pocket. Back downstairs, she found Seth on the front porch, sipping his coffee.

"Oh good. I didn't miss you," she said, a bit breathless.

"I wouldn't leave without saying good-bye." His gaze sought hers and held it. She was acutely aware of the passengers around them. "Be careful while I'm gone. Josh and James will be here, but I don't want you going out to the homestead without one of them."

"I'll be careful. I promise."

"Good." She saw some of the concern ease from his eyes.

She reached into her apron pocket. "Here. This is for you." She handed him a letter with his name on the front. He raised his eyebrows. "Read it tonight." She smiled at him, wishing he could take her in his arms, but knowing he couldn't.

He tucked the letter in his breast pocket and reached to squeeze her hand. "Good-bye, Becca."

"Good-bye, Seth."

Handing her his coffee cup, he winked at her. He stepped off the porch and climbed up to the driver's seat, tipping his hat to her as he drove off.

Two days later, coming around the bend back into Reedsville, Seth couldn't remember when Maggie's place looked so good. He supposed Becca had something to do with it. He didn't know he would miss her so much. The letter she had written him had helped, however. He treasured it. She had told him how much it meant that he believed in her dreams and showed it by rebuilding her house. She trusted him to protect her and wrote that together they would get through this situation. She didn't name McCormick specifically, but he knew. He only wished he was worthy of that trust.

As he pulled up in front of the boardinghouse, he was a little disappointed she wasn't on the porch to meet him. He'd hoped she'd be out there, but maybe she was putting finishing touches on supper. He tamped down the fear that something had happened to her.

Josh opened the stage door and helped the passengers out with his good hand, and Maggie stood on the porch greeting them. Seth climbed down as the last of the passengers went inside. James scrambled up to take his place and drive the stage around to the barn.

As he mounted the porch steps, the front door opened and Becca came out. In two steps he was in front of her.

"I missed you." He kept his voice low. "How've you been?"

"I missed you, too."

He put his hand on her shoulder and guided her into the house. Most of the guests were in the dining room, so he propelled her into the parlor out of their sight.

She looked up at him, eyebrows raised and a smile tugging at her mouth.

Once they were in the parlor, he pulled her in to his arms and hugged her tightly. He was pleased she squeezed him back just as much. He eased her away and lifted her chin with his finger, looking into her eyes for a minute before brushing her lips lightly with his own. "Now that's a more proper welcome home."

"WHAT'D YOU DO, Seth? You managed to put all the passengers to sleep."

"What can I say? I gave them a smooth ride."

Josh and Seth entered the parlor devoid of passengers, all of whom had elected to turn in early. Seth wasn't sure if it was a compliment to his driving or not. He wasn't going to dwell on it; he was too tired. "How'd it go while I was gone?"

"No problems. Actually—" Josh broke off when Becca walked in the room carrying a tray with cups and passed them to the men.

When she turned to leave the room, Seth caught her hand and tugged her down on the settee next to him. "Sit with me."

"I should help Maggie." She wasn't protesting too much though.

"Maggie won't mind." He let go of her hand and draped his arm across the back of the settee.

Josh gulped his coffee. "Becca and I were talking—"

He heard her soft sigh as she leaned back. She straightened for a moment when she felt his arm against her shoulders.

"On your next run, bring your books and paperwork down here."

He dropped his hand on her shoulder and squeezed lightly, pleased when she relaxed against his arm. He took a sip of his coffee.

"I'll know what the paperwork means, and Becca can do the entries and writing."

He started paying attention to what Josh was saying. "Thanks. That'd help me a lot. I know Owen can run the crews, but he doesn't do much paperwork. I'm dreading what I'm going to have waiting for me."

"How was your trip?" Becca asked.

"I saw my father and had a good visit with him." He had told his father all about the situation with McCormick and about Becca and appreciated the insight his father had given him. His father wanted to meet Becca now that she was all grown up. "What'd I miss while I was gone?"

Josh chuckled. "Parsons has started a campaign to elect himself mayor. Bill Benchly, owner of the Golden Tree Saloon, is running against him."

Seth raised an eyebrow.

"Their main campaign issue seems to be bringing more business to Reedsville. Of course each of them seems to have a different idea on what that means." Josh shifted in his chair, pain flashing across his face. "The only thing they seem to agree upon is you." Josh looked directly at him. "You might as well know. Both of them are saying you have cost this town business and jobs by turning down investors in the logging company."

Seth tightened his hand on Becca's shoulder. "McCormick."

"Yep. That's pretty much what I thought. I asked Ben when he started hearing this talk, and it was right around the time McCormick was here. When he came in to send a telegram, he told Ben himself that Parsons ought to be mayor."

His gut tightened. McCormick was chipping away at every aspect of his life. Becca's safety. The logging camp. His hometown.

Becca looked up at him. "Seth, not everyone thinks that way. There are many people who know the good you've done for the town and the men who work for you."

He nodded and tightened his jaw. "How's the arm?"

"It hurts. I must be getting old. The pain's wearing me out."

He swallowed the last of the coffee from his cup. "So, I think I'll say good night."

"I'm ready to turn in, too." Seth stretched his arms over head.

"Take your time. I can find the cabin by myself even with a busted arm." He eased himself out of the chair and left.

Seth leaned back against the sofa and smiled. "He wasn't too subtle about leaving us alone."

SETH STARED at the pile of paperwork on his desk. He'd be glad to take Becca and Josh up on their offer to handle it for him on the next stage run. He ran his hand over his face and picked up the first sheet.

The office door opened, and Owen stepped through. "You're back."

"Yep. How were things while I was gone?"

"Fine. No problems." Owen eased his bulk between the desks and sat in his chair. "Actually, since it's been so slow I was thinking of taking some time off to go see my mother."

Seth looked at Owen. "She's not sick, is she?"

"Oh, no. I just haven't seen her in a while and thought now might be a good time to go, it being so slow and all."

"The stage isn't making another run to Portland for almost another week."

"I was just going to ride on up."

"How much time do you need?"

Owen tapped his fingers on his desk. "About a week should be fine."

"When did you want to leave?"

"I thought if you had everything under control, I'd go this morning."

Seth nodded. "I'll give you your pay early."

"Thanks, Boss. I appreciate it." Owen practically jumped up and ran out the door.

Seth rubbed his eyes and looked at the stack of paperwork. It would have to wait. He stood up, stretched, and headed out to the site where the crew was working.

Chapter Twenty-Nine

Becca hadn't seen Seth in two days, and he was leaving tomorrow for a stage run to Salem. Without Owen, Seth spent the days on the site and evenings doing paperwork. He'd hadn't been able to get away to come to supper at Maggie's, taking his meals in the dining hall with his men instead. If she didn't see him tonight, she wouldn't for another three days as he'd stay in Salem over Sunday.

But she had a plan. If Seth couldn't come to supper, she'd bring supper to him. Knowing he would not approve of her coming up by herself, she asked James to take her. He brought the buggy around, helped her load it, and drove her to the camp.

Last time she came up to the camp, her feelings were a mix of anticipation and dread. Today she felt pure excitement.

James pulled the buggy up to the logging company office, and she hopped out before he could help her. She wanted to hurry in and surprise Seth before he came out and saw her. She hoped he was in the office.

She pushed open the door to the office. Seth was sitting at his desk and looked up when the door opened. Surprise crossed his face, and she smiled at him.

Then he frowned. "What are you doing here?" He stood up

and came around his desk. "You're not supposed to leave Maggie's alone, let alone come up here."

She took a step toward him, still smiling. "I didn't come alone. James brought me."

He was still frowning.

She took another step and put her hand on his arm. "I brought you something."

He raised his eyebrows.

She turned away from him and stepped back out the door. He followed her.

James had tied the buggy to the hitching rail and was untying his horse from the back of the buggy. "Hey, Seth. I'm leaving the buggy here. Becca said you'd drive her back."

Seth gave her pointed look, but she pretended to be busy fussing with the baskets in the buggy. "Help me with these."

"Becca, what's going on?

"I brought you supper."

James mounted his horse. "See you back at Maggie's."

"Thank you, James."

James nodded and wheeled his horse around to head back down the road.

Seth picked up both baskets and carried them into the office, setting them on Owen's empty desk. She followed him inside and began unpacking the baskets, setting out plates and food. A savory aroma filled the room.

He leaned against his desk and crossed his arms. "You really did bring me supper."

"Yes. Should we sit at Owen's desk to eat?"

He nodded and brought his chair over and held it while she seated herself. He sat down and blessed the food. "Is this what you were having at Maggie's tonight?"

"Yes. When we started supper, I was thinking about how much you liked everything we were making. And I started feeling sorry for myself because I hadn't seen you and probably wouldn't before you left for Salem. So, I thought I'd bring supper up here and kill two birds with one stone." Happy she had surprised and pleased him, she smiled.

He smiled back. "It's a far sight better than what I would have gotten in the dining hall. Thank you." He reached across their makeshift table and squeezed her hand.

She caught him up on the happenings at Maggie's during the past few days while they ate. But when she asked him about the logging camp, she saw the tight lines reappear around his mouth and eyes. She reached over and touched his hand. "You're working too hard. I'm concerned about you."

He covered her hand with his, rubbing the back of her hand lightly. "There's not much I can do about that."

She bit her lip, considering her words. "Is it possible to not make stage runs, or make fewer of them, until Josh is better?"

He was silent for a moment. What he was thinking? "In other circumstances, probably. But now…" He looked at their hands. Was he going to finish his sentence?

"Becca." He met her gaze. "Josh put the Oregon Express up as collateral so I could get a loan to keep the logging camp running." Pain deepened the lines fatigue had already carved in his face, and his shoulders visibly slumped. He told her about what Josh and Maggie did.

Her heart hurt for him. He now had the responsibility of keeping two companies afloat, and it weighed heavily on him.

She slipped her hand from under his. Standing, she came around the desk. His gaze followed her.

"Could you stand up a minute?"

His brow furrowed, but he came to his feet. The moment he straightened, she slipped her arms around his waist and held him tight. His arms went around her a second later, pulling her closer.

She laid her cheek against his chest, feeling his heartbeat and faintly smelling washing soap in his shirt. "I wish there were an easier way. Sometimes I just want to go somewhere else and start over and forget I've ever heard of Jeremiah McCormick."

He rested his chin on the top of her head. "I have to try to save it, Becca. It's not just a matter of letting him win. It's for us. It's for our future. Without the logging company, I don't have anything to offer you."

She pulled back and looked up at him. She couldn't believe she was going to be so bold, but somehow she had to make him see. "You have yourself. I don't want this—" she gestured around the room—"if it means I can't have you. You are my future." She laid her head back against his chest. "I need you," she whispered.

His arms tightened around her.

SETH LET himself into Josh's cabin, being careful not to let the door slam shut in case Josh was already asleep. He wasted no time getting ready for bed and slipping under the sheets, nearly groaning as his muscles unwound. Stretching out, he stacked his hands behind his head. He was still pleasantly surprised Becca'd brought him supper. It wasn't a picnic; she'd laid out a full meal. Dishes had been wrapped in towels to keep warm. No wonder he loved her. He'd been missing her too.

He wanted to take her away from here, someplace where they could forget their problems for a few days and just spend time together.

Maybe she was right. Maybe they should go somewhere and start over. He knew his father would be more than happy to have him work in his dry goods business. He let out a breath. He couldn't do that to Josh and Maggie. And Seth knew he wouldn't be happy spending his days cooped up in a store, living in a big city. Still, for Becca…

He rolled over and punched his pillow under his head, trying to get it into a comfortable shape.

He might not want to live there, but Portland was a great city to visit. He'd check the stage schedule tomorrow, but he was pretty sure as soon as Owen got back, he'd be able to take Becca to Portland for a few days. He smiled, liking the idea more and more. His father could meet her. He could show her the sights, take her someplace fancy for supper. And maybe do a little digging on McCormick while he was there. Yep, this was a good idea.

"We need to move things along more quickly." McCormick was dining at the Hotel Columbia, the best hotel in Portland. Across the table, his companion, Owen Taylor, had proven a useful source of information and had taken care of a few small matters. But his cooperation in this matter would be key. "I expected the logging camp to be out of business by now, or Seth Blake begging to take me up on my offer."

Taylor drummed his fingers on the tablecloth. "Blake has a lot of men who are still loyal to him. Townsfolk too."

McCormick looked at him pointedly. "But not you. That goes without saying or else you wouldn't be here."

Taylor avoided his gaze, and McCormick suspected he felt guilty. He couldn't let him do that. If he felt guilty, he wouldn't do what needed to be done. "Those who are loyal to Blake are glad to have a job and a roof over their heads. They don't care who provides it. They're destined to a life of menial labor. You're a more intelligent man than that, and Blake is a fool not to realize it."

Taylor nodded and briefly met McCormick's gaze. He took a bite of his food.

McCormick leaned back in his chair and sipped his coffee. People were so transparent. He could nearly see the thoughts forming in Taylor's brain. "You've been working in logging longer than him or Wilson. They were fools not to make you a partner." He watched Taylor's jaw harden.

"I thought after Wilson died, Blake would want me to be his partner. But he's too content bossing me around."

"Well, I see the advantage of having you as a partner, which is why I offered you the position once the logging company is mine. But we need to speed things along. My associates are eager for a return on their investments, and they are getting impatient." McCormick had already received one warning letter. It had been routed to him from his San Francisco office; they hadn't found him here in Portland, yet, but they would. It was only a matter of time.

He patted his mustache with his napkin. He could simply tell Taylor what he wanted done, but in the last few instances, the "hired help" had taken matters into their own hands and ruined the job. Taylor needed to be persuaded to his way of thinking. He would feel like he was part of the decision-making process—clearly something important to him—and be more likely to do the job the way McCormick himself would do it.

He set his napkin in his lap. "What's the most important asset to a logging company?"

"Timber, of course. No trees, no business."

"So if we remove the assets—the trees—then there is no more business."

Taylor frowned. "How are we going to do that? We can't hardly sell the timber we're cutting now. And it takes a long time to fell trees. That's not going to speed things up."

McCormick smiled. "Yes. The lack of sales? That's my doing." He was pleased by the shocked look on Taylor's face. "No, I wasn't thinking of cutting them. What do loggers fear the most, especially in the summer?"

Taylor answered easily. "A fire."

McCormick's smile turned into a full-fledged grin.

Chapter Thirty

"Come watch the sunset with me," Seth whispered over Becca's shoulder as she wiped the last of the dishes. His breath brushed her ear, sending tingles down her spine.

She hung up the dishrag, took off her apron, and followed him out to the front porch. The sun had set, but the sky looked like molten gold and the puffy clouds were on fire.

They sat on the porch swing and watched the sky in silence. Seth's long legs stretched out in front of him and bent slightly with the motion of the swing. "Thanks for doing the books and paperwork for me while I was gone this last time."

"My pleasure. I can actually understand some of it now without Josh's interpretation." She nudged his shoulder. "And I think I have a better appreciation of what you do."

"Well, I had far less work waiting for me when I got back, and I appreciated that. Although, if working late causes you to bring me supper again…" He grinned.

She blushed at the thought of their private supper. With some effort, she pulled her thoughts away from that scene. "I'm glad you're having an easier time of it."

"Yeah. Owen's back from visiting his mother. There's been no accidents lately. Josh's arm is mending." He paused. "So, is it over, or are we just waiting for the next thing to happen?" Seth stretched his arm along the back of the swing and let his fingers lightly brush her shoulder. "As much as McCormick's done already he's not going to stop now. We know he'll try something else." He looked up at the porch ceiling. "I wish we knew more about why he wants the logging camp. What's so special about my company? Or is it the land?"

She looked out at the darkening sky. "Can you imagine what it would be like if we did sell to him? He'd be a part of this town, and we'd have to interact with him. I couldn't do that, knowing all that he's done."

They rocked silently for a moment more before he said, "I think you should get away from here for a while."

Becca's first instinct was to protest, but she stopped herself and decided to hear out his reasoning for this particular idea. "What did you have in mind? I'm not going to let him scare me off."

"I know. But I was thinking that if we went somewhere like, say, Portland, he might be forced to show his hand more. It might be more obvious if someone's following you. There'll be a lot more people around, so you'd be safer. And on a positive side, you could do some shopping, and I could take you someplace fancy for supper." He paused. "And we could visit with my father."

She was with him right up to the point where he mentioned his father. Spending time with Seth doing enjoyable things like shopping and going to supper sounded wonderful. She longed to forget about Mr. McCormick for a few days. But the thought of meeting his father sent a whole group of butterflies flapping in her stomach. She'd only met Josiah Blake once a long time ago when he'd come to Reedsville to visit Seth.

He had continued to talk while her mind was racing. "Plus I can poke around the land office a bit, do a little research, see we can't figure out what's going on with McCormick. The sheriff in Portland is a friend of my father's, so I'll see if he knows anything helpful." He stopped the swing and looked at her. "What are you thinking?"

She put aside all of her swirling thoughts and followed her heart. "I'll go."

A slow grin spread across his face.

Becca couldn't help but think how different her life was now compared to the last time she was on this stage. She was wearing her blue traveling suit, but that was about the only thing the same. While she was hugging everyone good-bye, Josh loaded her valise in the boot, and Seth climbed up to the driver's seat.

Josh helped her into the stage with his good arm. "Have a good time, Becca."

"I will. Thank you." She sat back in the seat and sighed, trying to calm the butterflies in her stomach.

After all the passengers had boarded, Becca heard Seth tell Josh thanks and good-bye when one more passenger joined them. A wiry man with a greasy hat squeezed in next to the man in the brocade waistcoat across from Becca.

He half-hoped he'd miss the stage. He dreaded giving McCormick his report, but he had no place else to go since that Owen Taylor thought he was so smart and could do the job better. He'd practically kicked him out of the logging camp. The money McCormick had given him was gone, and he couldn't get up the courage to wire him for more. He knew McCormick wasn't going to be happy with the way things had been going. Elmer would like to blame bad luck, but that didn't hold water with McCormick.

Passengers were already boarding the stage when he walked

into the office to buy his ticket. A moment later he was back outside. He walked down to the boardinghouse that served as a way station and handed his grip to the man to throw in the boot. The driver turned around to say something to the man loading the luggage, and the wiry man pushed his greasy hat further down on his head. So Blake was driving this one. Elmer felt Blake's eyes on him, but knew Blake couldn't possibly know who he was.

He climbed in the stage and squeezed next to a guy all duded up. He sat back in his seat and nudged his hat up on his brow a bit, looking at the other passengers. When he saw the pretty little thing in a dress the color of a summer sky he froze and stared at her until she frowned a bit and looked out the window. His shoulders relaxed, and he grinned to himself. Suddenly his report was looking much better.

ONE THING that hadn't changed on the stagecoach was the bumping and jostling. Becca was glad she was sitting next to a woman because she bumped her constantly. Even more uncomfortable than the jostling were the stares of the man sitting across from her. With his greasy hat pushed back on his head, he gave her a slight leer. She kept her gaze out the window as much as possible.

"So, are you headed to Portland?"

She risked a sideways glance back inside the stagecoach. The greasy hat man was talking to her. She could think of no way to avoid talking to him.

"Yes," she said evenly. "I believe that's where this stage goes." Maybe he would get the hint and leave her alone.

"Me too."

She looked back out the window. Something about this man, other than his lack of manners, was nagging at her.

"You have family up there?"

Suppressing a sigh, she turned her eyes, but not her head, back inside the coach. "No. Friends." He looked familiar, but she couldn't place him. Maybe he was a logger.

"Me, I'm on business. Got me a business meetin' in Portland."

It took all of Becca's good breeding to keep her from rolling her eyes. *You're very important, I can tell.* If she couldn't say it out loud, maybe she could entertain herself by thinking it. She dared not give any hint of a smile, knowing that it would only encourage him.

"Been to Portland before?"

Would he ever give up? She wished Maggie were here to rap him across the knuckles. "Once."

Then it hit her. It was the hat. He was the man she'd seen at Fulton's and then at Annie and John's wedding talking about the accidents at the logging camp. She looked at him a second too long, and he took it as encouragement.

"Well I've been there lots. I could show you all the sights. Where're you stayin'?"

She glanced at the other two men in her section, hoping they'd come to her defense. Apparently they were engrossed in the scenery. "Sir, we have not been properly introduced. Your suggestion is impertinent. Now, if you please, I'd like to rest." She leaned her head back against the seat cushion and closed her eyes. Her heart pounded. She would tell Seth when they stopped. But what could they do? Demand to know what he was talking about and with whom?

"Well, now, don't get all uppity. I didn't mean nothin' by it. Just trying to be friendly."

She kept her eyes closed and ignored him, even when he sighed loudly and muttered under his breath. She replayed in her mind the conversations she had overheard, turning them over in her mind to find some sort of clue.

After what seemed like an eternity, they arrived at their stop for dinner. She purposely let the other passengers go ahead of her, except Mr. Greasy Hat was having none of it.

"No, miss, I insist that you go first. It's the gentlemanly thing to do."

"I'd prefer to be the last off, if you don't mind."

Seth looked in at their exchange, raising his eyebrows.

She scooted across the seat and grabbed Seth's hand. He squeezed hers back and helped her down before releasing her hand and turning his back on the last passenger.

Taking her arm, he guided her to the side. "What was that all about?"

"Oh, he's been annoying me the whole trip. I had to pretend to be asleep to get him to stop talking to me. He actually wanted to know where I was staying and offered to 'show me the sights.' Hmmph. But Seth," she gripped his arm tightly, "I think he was the man I overheard at Fulton's and Annie and John's wedding talking about the accidents at the camp."

Seth's hand tightened on Becca's elbow as he helped her to her chair. "I'll talk to him," he said for her ears alone as he pushed in her chair.

"No," she whispered over her shoulder. "We can't prove anything."

Seth was particularly attentive to her during the meal. She appreciated his attention and was grateful he was such a gentleman. After the wiry man's behavior, the comparison came easily.

She didn't miss Seth's eyes roaming the table during dinner, resting on each man for a moment before moving on. When they reached the wiry man, they stopped and narrowed. The man met his eyes only for a moment before returning to his food.

The dinner stop was too short. As soon as everyone had eaten and taken care of their personal needs, Seth told the passengers it was time to board. He helped Becca on first. She scooted to the far corner but watched the door.

When the wiry man stepped up to the stagecoach door,

Seth's arm shot out and held him back. "I believe these people were boarding next."

He allowed the husband and wife to climb on. The wiry man glowered at him but said nothing. Seth continued to hold him back until he was the last to board.

Grabbing the man by the upper arm he said, "I don't put up with ungentlemanly behavior on my stage. If you try anything else, I'll put you off." Seth stared at the man hard before releasing his arm.

The wiry man gave Seth a surly look and climbed into the second section of the stage.

Seth glanced at Becca before he closed the door behind him, climbed up to the driver's seat and they were off.

She gave him a grateful smile.

The wiry man pulled his greasy hat down over his eyes and pretended to sleep. Becca suspected he was quite angry by the tight lines around his mouth and the rigid way he held himself. But she wasn't afraid of him. Seth was looking after her, and she curled that feeling around her heart for the rest of the trip.

Chapter Thirty-One

When they pulled into Portland for the night, the stagecoach was full and the sun was setting. The sole employee of the Oregon Express's Portland office stood by to open the door and help the passengers out. By the time Becca got to the door, Seth had climbed down to help her out, and his employee had begun unloading the baggage from the boot of the stagecoach. Seth took her arm and led her over to where a man was waiting that she would recognize anywhere as Seth's father.

He stood the same way she had seen Seth stand a hundred times, legs slightly apart, hands jammed in his hip pockets. He looked just like an older version of Seth, tall and lean with hair that had turned mostly silver, but was still full.

"Becca, you remember my father, Josiah Blake."

"Becca, it is my great pleasure to see you again. I don't know how you managed to get off that contraption looking so fresh and beautiful. The time I rode it to Reedsville it took me days to recover. I don't know how my son stands it." His broad smile was contagious, and she couldn't help but smile back. Evidence of life had begun to show in lines on his face and in crinkles around his eyes, which were a paler blue than Seth's. Now that she stood next to him, she could see he was slightly shorter than Seth.

"I need to take the stage into the livery and see to the horses. Becca, can I leave you in my father's capable hands for a few minutes?"

She smiled at the two men. "Absolutely."

Josiah took her arm from Seth's and placed it on his own. "Don't worry about us. I'll take good care of her, and we can get acquainted."

Seth touched his hat to her and sauntered off to the coach.

Josiah turned to her. "Would you care to sit inside, or do you feel the need to stretch your legs after all that sitting?"

"I would love to stretch my legs."

"Good, then we'll just take a turn around the block until my son joins us."

She felt the kinks ease out of her muscles as they strolled along the wooden sidewalk while Josiah told her a little bit about Portland and the things she might want to see while she was here.

After their second turn, she spotted Seth loading their bags into a wagon pulled up alongside the sidewalk with "Blake's Dry Goods" painted on the side in green.

"I apologize I don't have anything fancier, but I don't really have need of a buggy. I mostly just use this for my deliveries and to pick up shipments." Josiah climbed agilely into the wagon seat and picked up the reins."

As Seth lifted her up, Josiah gave her a hand. When she was seated, Seth climbed up next to her. "It's not a long ride from here, seven or eight blocks. Your hotel is right across the street from my store, and I know the owner."

"Yep," Seth added. "You should feel privileged, Becca. When I come into town, I usually have to walk to Dad's."

"You're a strong, young man," Josiah rejoined. "You can handle it. But Becca's a lady, and it wouldn't do to make her tromp through the streets."

She smiled at their banter. Sitting between the two men, she let out her breath and let the tension fall from her shoulders. Josiah told her a little bit about Portland and the things she might want to see while she was here. Though tired from the journey, she was more at ease than she had been in a long time.

When they reached the hotel, Josiah wrapped the reins around the brake and handed her down to Seth. The sign hanging above the sidewalk said HOTEL PACIFIC. Seth grabbed her bag out of the wagon and all three went inside.

The young clerk looked up from the desk. "Hello, Mr. Blake. My father's been saving a table for you in the dining room."

"Thanks, Matthew. This is Miss Wilson. She'll be staying here while she's visiting Portland. And of course, you know my son, Seth."

Seth nodded. "Good to see you again, Matthew."

"Miss Wilson," Matthew extended a key. "You're in room 202, just up the stairs to your right. You can leave your bag here, and we'll take it up to your room while you're having supper. Just sign right here." He extended a pen as he swiveled the register around on its wooden turntable.

She took the key and signed her name while Seth handed over her valise.

"Thank you." Matthew gestured towards the dining room. "Your table's waiting for you."

Her stomach rumbled at the mention of food, and the most appetizing smells wafted from the dining room, reminding her of how long it had been since she'd eaten.

Mr. Hanson, the hotel proprietor, greeted them warmly as they entered the dining room and sat them at a table by the window. Their suppers were brought promptly, but as hungry as she was, tiredness was settling on her like a blanket.

As they finished eating, Josiah reminded her to come over in the morning as soon as she was up to it. "If the store's not open yet, just knock and I'll let you in."

They passed on dessert and coffee, and the men walked with

her to the lobby. Seth looked at her, his eyes dark in the gaslights. "Good night," he said softly. "I'll see you in the morning."

"Good night."

She headed up to her room, each step reminding her of the soreness in her legs that she hadn't worked out yet. She turned the key in the lock and opened the door to her room. The lamp was lit, and her valise was on the chair. She quickly undressed, climbed into bed and turned out the lamp, still pondering what connection Mr. Greasy Hat had to it all.

ELMER HAD FOLLOWED the wagon to the hotel and watched from across the street, nearly in front of Blake's Dry Goods, as the trio ate, framed perfectly by the window. As they left the table, he hurried down the street to darker shadows. The men had come out of the hotel, crossed the street, and entered the dry goods store. He moved back to his position across from the hotel, not certain if he would be able to determine which room was hers. But his patience was rewarded a moment later when the light in a room facing the street went out.

Elmer pulled the greasy hat further over his eyes as he stepped out of the shadows and started down the street. He chuckled. *Just you wait, Blake. Just you wait.*

Chapter Thirty-Two

Becca had just finished pinning up her hair when someone knocked on her room door. She turned the knob and then hesitated. She should have asked who it was. What if that man had found her? It was too late. If the person had evil intentions, he only needed to shove the door open.

"Miss Wilson?" She recognized Matthew's voice on the other side of the door and let her breath out. She opened the door.

He stood there with a tray. "My father thought you might enjoy having breakfast in your room rather than in the dining room."

She stepped aside and let him come in the room. "Thank you. That was very considerate."

Matthew set the tray on the dresser.

She grabbed her reticule, retrieved a coin, and handed it to him. "Thank your father for me as well."

"Thank you, Miss Wilson. I will." Matthew closed the door behind him as he left her room.

Mr. Hanson had sent up a pot of tea, biscuits with jam, and a bowl of sliced fruit. Becca sampled a biscuit. They weren't as light and flakey as Maggie's, but they were still quite good.

Putting the food on a plate and fixing herself a cup of tea, Becca settled back on her bed to eat her breakfast and read her Bible.

After breakfast, Becca put her best hat on, skewering it with a long hatpin through her hair, pinned up at the back of her head. She wouldn't have been able to afford such a fancy hat, but she had purchased it plain in Salem and added the lace and ribbons herself.

It matched her dress, one of her two best dresses she had brought with her. She enjoyed the freedom of the simple shirtwaists and skirts she wore in Reedsville as opposed to the confining corsets and bodices of her day dresses. Yet she had to admit that it was fun to dress up in such beautiful gowns once in awhile.

This one had a long-waisted curiass bodice in blue that fitted tightly through her thighs, then the skirt gathered in the back and fell in ruffles to the floor. The two-tiered underskirt was white with a blue pin stripe and matched the short jacket she wore. The jacket had a high lace collar held together at the neck with her mother's cameo. It had taken her weeks of sewing over the Christmas holidays last year to complete the dress, copying the design from *Godey's Lady's Book*.

Looking in the mirror turning from side to side, she was satisfied with her reflection. She pulled on gloves, slipped her matching reticule over her wrist and left her room, locking the door, and dropping the key into her bag. She headed downstairs, and crossed the street to the dry goods store.

The store was Italianate in style, with two stories of a flat brick facade and a recessed central entry. Portland had such a hodgepodge of architectural styles. An OPEN sign hung in the door's window. She turned the knob and walked down the aisles of goods to the counter at the back of the store. A young man, about James' age but rail thin with pale skin, stood behind the counter. His dark eyes and hair served to only accentuate his paleness.

She smiled at him. "Good morning. Is Mr. Blake in?"

"He's in the stockroom. You must be Miss Wilson." At her nod he said, "He's expecting you."

Josiah came around the corner from the stockroom. "I thought I heard your voice. Good morning, Becca. Did you sleep well last night?"

"Good morning. I slept well. Mr. Hanson runs a very nice hotel."

"Glad to hear it. Seth left early to check on things at the Oregon Express, but he asked if you would wait for him. He should be back shortly. In the meantime, would you care to have a cup of coffee with me and one of Mrs. Hanson's world-famous cinnamon rolls?"

"I'd love to." She removed her gloves as she followed Josiah.

Josiah led her to the corner of the store where a pot-bellied stove sat. A coffee pot bubbled, and an array of mugs sat on a shelf above the stove. Several wooden chairs sat near the stove, and an old pickle barrel had been converted to a checkerboard.

Josiah poured a cup of coffee and handed it to her. "I'll be right back."

The bell above the store's door rang as someone entered. She glanced idly over. A man entered and glanced around, walking slowly up the aisles.

"May I help you find something?" she heard Jake ask. The man mumbled something in return.

Her attention turned back to Josiah who carried two plates containing large, gooey cinnamon rolls. He handed her one with a fork and napkin and sat down opposite her.

She cut into her roll with a fork and took a bite. Sweet with just enough cinnamon, the yeasty roll melted in her mouth, still warm from the oven.

"These are delicious."

Josiah nodded, chewing. "One of the few indulgences I allow myself."

A moment later, she saw him looking over her shoulder and

she turned around. Seth stood there wearing his dark suit. She smiled at him.

"Becca, my father must be truly taken with you if he's sharing his cinnamon rolls." He reached over her shoulder and pinched a piece off her cinnamon roll and popped it in his mouth, grinning at her.

"Like father, like son," Josiah said dryly as he forked another bite of cinnamon roll into his mouth.

Her cheeks heated, but Seth kept grinning at her. "I was wondering if you wanted to make a dent in the shopping list you and Maggie put together." He pulled up a chair next to her.

"Where are you planning on going?" Josiah asked.

Becca pulled out Maggie's list from her reticule and handed it to Josiah. "These are the stores Maggie recommended."

Josiah nodded as he read the list. "Maggie's a wise woman. These are all the shops I'd send you to. Just leave your purchases at the stores, and tell them I'll send Jake over for them later with the wagon."

He handed the list back to her and gathered up the plates and mugs. "When you return, you can look through my catalogs, if you'd like."

"Are you ready to go?" Seth asked her.

"Yes!" She slid on her gloves. "I'd forgotten how much I enjoy this."

"You two have a good time," Josiah said, waving them off.

"We will. Thank you," she answered.

Seth took her arm and slipped it through his as they left the store. "Enjoy what?"

"Dressing up, shopping, looking at store windows. I can't imagine doing chores in this," she ran a hand down her skirt, laughing. "But it's fun to wear on occasion."

"It is a very pretty dress. And the hat doesn't hide your face nearly as much as your straw hat does." He walked next to the street, putting her on his arm to the inside, as they headed down the wooden sidewalk, walking over a block to the streetcar.

They boarded the Portland Street Railway Company's horse-drawn streetcar and rode it to the end of the line. She thought Josiah was right; it did almost feel like flying. She was glad the car was enclosed. What amazed her most was how smooth the ride was. A far cry from the jostling of the stagecoach.

"May we ride it back when we've finished?" she asked.

"Absolutely."

Their first stop was a dress and millinery store. As they approached the store, she sensed Seth hesitate. Biting her lip, she was chagrined for not thinking that he might not be comfortable here.

"I think I'm going to be a while here. Is there any place you need to go, and we can meet up later?"

He smiled. "I don't suppose I'd be much help to you in there. I do need to go to the bank and the land office to see if I can find out anything on McCormick."

She looked at her list and then up the street. "The next shop is just up there, Olsen's Shoes. If I finish here before you return, I'll be there."

"All right." He looked her directly in the eyes. "Please don't go anywhere else. Wait for me until I come back."

She smiled up at him. "I promise."

He smiled back, squeezed her hand as he let go of her arm, and walked across the street. She watched him for a moment before turning into the dress shop. Even in a suit he moved powerfully and with grace.

ELMER PUSHED AWAY from the side of the building he'd been leaning on when Wilson's sister came out of the dress shop. He'd been following her since she left the hotel this morning, afraid that Blake would recognize him from the stage, but it'd been easier than he thought. Blake was too smitten by her pretty smile to pay attention to his surroundings, let alone picking him out among all the people on the busy streets.

He pulled his hat lower on his head and ignored the upturned noses and condescending looks of people who passed him on the sidewalk. He had barely passed the dress shop when Becca turned into another store. He kept looking up and down the street, figuring Blake would be back any minute. He had half a mind to follow Blake. Whatever he was up to had to be more interesting than watching a girl shop.

But he was sure McCormick would want the information on Miss Wilson, and he planned to have something to give him when he met with him today. He was in luck. She came out of the store a few minutes later.

Casually, so as not to attract attention, he pretended to stop and look at a store window. Out of the corner of his eye, he watched as she paused on the sidewalk. Her eyes turned his way. They stopped for a brief minute before moving on, and he didn't think she'd noticed him. Then she turned and entered the store again. Puzzled, he took a few steps closer to the store.

SETH CROSSED the street and walked two blocks over to the bank where he deposited the Oregon Express's receipts. Then he went a couple of doors down to the county district land office. The only person in the office was the man behind the desk.

"Can I help you?" He looked at Seth over the top of his glasses.

Seth studied the map on the wall. "I want to find out about a piece of land." His eyes followed the Willamette River to Reedsville, and then up to the logging camp. He poked his index finger at that part of the map. "I know about this property here. I'm curious about this property here." His finger traced to the north and west of the logging camp.

The man peered at the map, jotted down the township,

range, and section numbers and went to his books. After a moment he looked up at the map and back down at his book. "Both those areas are owned by a Mr. Jeremiah McCormick. Looks like he's got a mining claim on them, too."

So, did McCormick want the logging company to expand his current holdings, or did it have something to do with the mine? "I see," he said slowly. "Thank you for your time."

"Any time."

Seth walked outside and headed to the assay office.

BECCA'S HEART hammered in her chest. She was glad she had forgotten her reticule on the counter in the shoe store. It gave her an excuse to go back inside and figure out what to do.

She hadn't been imagining things. The man from the stage was outside the shoe store. He had been following her all morning, starting at Josiah's shop. She picked up her reticule from the counter and thanked the clerk for watching it.

Seth wasn't here yet, and she knew he'd want her to wait for him. She decided to walk back to the dress shop. There were a few things there she wouldn't mind taking a closer look at.

Stepping out of the shoe store again, she let her gaze slide to the right before turning left down the street. He was still there, closer than the last time.

She tried to take a deep breath to calm herself, but her corset was laced too tight. Drat those things! No wonder women were always swooning. She couldn't wait to go back to wearing just her chemise. Her heeled shoes and narrow-skirted dress kept her strides small as well. She focused on the dress shop, just a little ways ahead. Glancing around the street, there was no sign of Seth yet. *Please hurry.*

The dress shop was closed. She stared at the sign in disbelief. *No, I was just here!* It was a small shop; the proprietress must have closed up for dinner. Yes, a small sign under the larger one said *Will return at 1 o'clock.*

Now what, Lord? She scanned the streets. Still no sign of Seth.

The man was slowly closing the gap between them.

Seth had headed across the street and back north. She'd walk that way and hopefully meet up with him. Abruptly turning, hoping to catch her follower off-guard, she crossed the street.

A different set of stores lined this side of the street, and Becca pretended to be looking at their displays, although she knew she was walking too fast to be window shopping. She couldn't get her feet to slow down. In the window's reflection, she saw she was still being followed.

She looked ahead. Still no Seth.

What would she do if she got to the next block and he wasn't there? She had no idea which direction he had gone after he had crossed the street. He'd be looking for her here, so she really couldn't go anywhere else.

"Excuse me, Miss?"

Without thinking, Becca slowed her steps and turned around. Only to discover it was her pursuer. She spun around and walked as quickly as she could. *Seth, where are you?*

"Miss, please."

She was at the end of the block. Panic filled her chest and she darted into the street.

The streetcar barreled down the street directly at her.

She froze, unable to get her legs to move. She tried but between her slick heels and her tight dress she couldn't seem to get her body working in the same direction.

Her leg jerked forward and stopped. Her heel wedged between the track and the street. She yanked, nearly knocking herself off her feet. Without a buttonhook, she couldn't even get her foot out of the boot.

The streetcar was only feet away.

Chapter Thirty-Three

Seth turned the corner and started looking down the street, wondering if Becca was at the dress shop or the shoe store. The streetcar blocked his line of sight. As soon as it passed, he would be able to see across the street.

Movement in the corner of his eye caught his attention. He turned to see Becca dash in front of the streetcar and halt.

His heart stopped, filled with anguish.

"Becca! No!"

He started running, even though he knew there was no way for him to get there in time. *God, please…*

Someone gripped her arm and yanked her backward, loosening her heel and knocking her feet out from under her. The man dragged her to the sidewalk and shoved her up next to a building before he released his grip on her arm. Her legs shook, and she didn't think they'd hold her for long. She put her hand on the building.

"You all right?" It was Greasy Hat Man from the stagecoach.

The one who had been following her. The one she'd been running from.

Her throat closed and she nodded. He looked over her shoulder and then spun around and ran off.

She turned and saw Seth running toward her.

"Stay here!" Seth ordered and took off after the man.

A few people looked in their direction, but most passed by while she leaned against the building. She felt the rough bricks pull at her dress and hoped she didn't snag the fabric, but she didn't have the strength to move away.

Seth came back a minute later, breathing hard. He looked at her for a moment then pulled her roughly into his arms. "I thought I'd lost you." He held her for a moment more then eased her back. "Are you okay?"

She nodded, not trusting herself to speak.

"I didn't catch him. But I recognized him as the man from the stage."

"He was following me, and I was trying to get away." Her voice shook. "He pulled me back. He saved my life."

Seth kept his arm firmly under her elbow as he hailed them a cab back to the dry goods store. She was thankful for his thoughtfulness. There was no way her shaky legs would carry her back to the store, and she had no desire to get on the contraption that just nearly killed her.

Josiah had their noon meal waiting for them when they returned. Leaving the store to Jake, he led the way up a set of stairs in the storeroom that led to the living quarters upstairs. Josiah took one look at her and wanted to know what happened.

Seth rubbed her shoulders as she told the story. A few times Josiah looked over her head at Seth.

"The good Lord was watching out for you today," Josiah remarked. "I'm glad you're okay. Do you feel up to eating?"

"Yes. I think it might help." Maybe it would stop the shaking. She tried to help Josiah get the food to the table but he shooed her away.

Once they were into their meal, Seth began telling them what he found out at the land office. "McCormick owns most of the land to the north and east of the logging camps," Seth said between bites. "And he's taken out mining claims."

"Mining claims?" Josiah raised his eyebrows. "What kind?"

"That's what I wanted to know, so I went to the assay office. I asked if he'd seen anyone bring in anything from a mine near Reedsville. He told me that about six months ago a man brought in some gold from that area. He wasn't specific about where the gold was from, but then a lot of miners aren't, for fear of getting their claim jumped. But when I asked what the man looked like, the assayer remembered him real well because he didn't look like a miner. He was well-dressed, and his hands were soft. He thought that was real strange."

"So you think Mr. McCormick is mining gold from the land that he owns near the logging camp, and that he thinks there is or might be gold in the logging camp land?" she asked.

"I can't say for sure that's what he's doing, but it sure looks that way. It would certainly explain why he wants the logging camp so bad."

Becca picked at the rest of her food. She'd lost her appetite. If there was gold involved, Mr. McCormick would never quit. Gold did that to people.

Seth laid his hand on hers. "I didn't mean to upset you. But I knew you'd want to know."

She gave him a weak smile. "I know. Thank you. So what did that man want with me?"

"There could be any number of answers to that question, but the way things are going, I'd say he's reporting to McCormick about you."

"You think Mr. McCormick is here in Portland?" Josiah asked. "Following you?"

"It's a good guess."

McCormick opened the door to his hotel room and let Elmer in. He had less dust on him than before, but he still twisted his greasy hat in his hands. McCormick shut the door behind the man and again took the only chair in the room.

"Well? What do you have to report? It had better be good."

The man shifted from foot to foot. "Oh, you'll like this. I sat on the same stage with her, and she's here in Portland."

McCormick sat forward in his chair. "She's here?"

"Yes, sir. I tried to ask her on the stage what her plans were, you know, real friendly like, but she was too uppity for me. She did say she was visiting friends. I followed her around today, and all she did was shop."

McCormick sat back and tapped his mustache. "What friends would she have here?" he mused. "You followed her. Do you know where she's staying?"

"Hotel Pacific."

"Did you see these friends of hers?"

"Well..." He shifted his weight again. "I don't rightly know what friends she was talkin' about. The only person I've seen her with is Blake and another man that looks like he could be Blake's pa."

"Blake! She's here with Blake? Why didn't you say so?"

"She said she was visiting friends. I didn't think she meant Blake."

McCormick scowled and stared at nothing. After a moment he looked up at the man. "Is there anything else?"

"Uh, no, not that I can think of..."

He was ready to dismiss the man, but the way he kept looking off to the side raised McCormick's suspicions.

"Why do I have the feeling there's something you're not telling me?"

"I don't know. I think I've told you about all there is." Elmer stared at the expensive carpet.

He decided to try another tactic. "It must have been a pleasant afternoon. Miss Wilson is quite lovely."

Elmer looked up and grinned at that. "Yeah, she sure is, but she doesn't give a fella like me the time of day. But someone like Blake, she'll hang on his arm and bat her eyelashes at him. She even complained to him..." He let the sentence trail off.

McCormick nonchalantly got up and went to his wallet on the dresser, counting out bills. "Complained about what?" he said with his back to the man.

"Oh, I don't know what she said, but he threatened to throw me off the stage if I bothered her."

"Hmm. Bet you'd like to pound him."

"Oh yeah, I almost did—"

McCormick turned around slowly. "You almost did what?"

"Well, I was following them, you see, like I figured you'd want, when she started across the street and almost walked in front of the streetcar. I yanked her back and made sure she was okay. Blake showed up then and started running toward me. I didn't want him to start askin' me questions so I just took off. I thought about waitin' for him around the alley when he followed me, but decided I'd better just come here and tell you what I seen." He had creased his hat brim completely around.

McCormick's blood boiled. "You idiot! You couldn't have said you rescued a lady in distress and then excused yourself? You had to take off like a scared rabbit so he knew you'd been following them. Here." He tossed the man some bills. "Get out of my sight."

The man fumbled for the bills and grabbed them, hurriedly stuffing them into his pockets. He dropped his hat in the process and had to bend over and pick it up.

McCormick turned his back on the man until the door had opened and shut. He slammed his fist on the dresser, causing the mirror to jump with a clank.

"Taylor better come through for me," he whispered.

Chapter Thirty-Four

Becca went about her morning routine mindlessly humming a little song. Seth would be meeting her downstairs in the hotel restaurant for breakfast, and they had planned a day together, seeing the sights in Portland. She was looking forward to having him to herself for the whole day.

She knew she loved him, although she wasn't sure how he felt about her. He had to have some feelings to court her, but did he love her and think she could be his wife? She knew her independent streak had to give him pause. But what kind of marriage could they have if she had to be someone other than who she was?

She bit her lip. She didn't think Seth would be unreasonable in asking her to obey him. She had to admit he had been concerned about her safety and not trying to assert authority over her. In her opinion, however, he underestimated her ability to take care of herself. Becca sighed. He must be at least thinking about marriage if he was courting her. But was it out of an overzealous sense of duty to take care of her because Thomas had been his best friend? Or did he truly love her?

She slipped her reticule over her arm and checked her reflection one last time. Only time would tell. But under no uncertain terms, no matter how much she loved him, would she let him marry her out of a sense of obligation to her brother.

Seth was sitting in the lobby and stood when he spotted her coming downstairs. As he took her arm, he leaned over and whispered, “You look beautiful again.” Today her dress was dark pink with jetted buttons down the bodice. She felt herself blush and hoped her cheeks weren’t as pink as the dress.

After breakfast in the dining room, Seth helped her into the buggy he had rented from the livery to show her the sights of Portland. Leaving the hotel, they headed north on Second Avenue several blocks until they came to Chinatown. The tree-lined streets had quite a bit of traffic but she didn’t mind. It gave her plenty of time to look around at the oriental architecture of rounded windows, awnings, and covered sidewalks that characterized the area. Even the iron grille work had an oriental flair.

Chinese men with straw hats like large, flattened cones hurried up and down the street carrying laundry, produce, and wood in two tall, cylindrical baskets suspended from ropes attached to the ends of a wooden pole that they balanced across their shoulders. The lilting, sing-song sound of their language and the smell of unusual foods cooking buffeted her senses. She leaned forward and sat on the edge of the buggy seat to take it all in and it was all she could do not to say, “Look!” and point every minute or so.

Seth noticed Becca’s enthusiasm and smiled to himself. It pleased him to make her happy, and he was pleasantly surprised at how enchanting she found Portland. He sat back against the buggy seat, reins resting loosely in his hands, and enjoyed watching her wide eyes take everything in.

It was a far cry from yesterday. When he saw her step in front of the streetcar and knew he was too far away to do anything, he thought part of him would die with her. He was so thankful God had spared her. It was all he could do not to whisk her off to Pastor Kendall tonight to marry him. He didn't want to let her out of his sight.

A few blocks after they left Chinatown, he hitched the buggy to a rail and helped Becca out. She slipped her arm in his and they walked to Ankeny's New Market and Theater. Although he'd been here several times, he still thought it was an amazing place.

It looked like a Renaissance palace with its centralized arcade lined with marbleized columns and arches supporting a high ceiling. Vendors manned stalls that ran down both sides of the arcade for as far as the eye could see. Each stall had its own counter with marble tops and carved wood fronts and was lit by a small gas chandelier. Next to the arcade, a theater marquee announced the next performance.

He felt as if he was seeing it all for the first time through Becca's eyes. He watched as she looked from the architecture to the variety of food presented by the vendors. An exotic blend of aromas filled the air including fresh fruit, coffee, fresh bread, spices, and fish, while music played somewhere in the background. Grocers displayed their wares in elegant displays: shiny piles of apples and oranges and plums, warm brown bins of nuts, baskets of fresh herbs.

She turned to him as they strolled along the arcade. "How do you ever decide what to buy?"

He smiled at her. "The secret is to come early and bring a wagon."

She laughed with him. "Then that's what we'll have to do. I can't imagine leaving here without bringing some of this back."

After encouraging her to buy something and nearly laughing at how difficult the decision was for her, they walked back to the buggy. He took them up Ash Street and turned left down Sixth Avenue. After several blocks he pointed to a two-story brick building, with a four-story tower in the center.

"That's Central School. I went there. Across the street's the courthouse."

He turned back to see her smiling, with a mischievous glint in her eyes.

"And what are you smiling about?" he teased.

"I was just imagining you as a little boy. Did you like school?"

"Most of the time. I always like learning about new things. But a few times Josh made fishing sound mighty tempting."

A couple more blocks and they turned up Salmon Street, leaving the business district and heading toward the residential area. The farther away they went from the city, the more ornate the houses became. Most were Victorian with a lot of wooden gingerbread decoration and painted with elaborate color schemes. But a few Italianate homes sat among them.

After several blocks they came to a section where grass covered the whole block, one block wide, and stretched almost as far as they could see. "These are the Park Blocks," he explained, pulling the buggy over. "I thought we'd have a picnic here."

Her eyes widened as he pulled out a basket he had hidden behind the seat. He just grinned back at her, pleased that he'd been able to surprise her. He helped her out of the buggy then grabbed a blanket he had hidden too.

Spreading out the blanket, she asked, "When did you do all this?"

"This morning. Or last night, I suppose. I asked Mrs. Hanson if she could make us a picnic basket. Then I asked Matthew at the hotel to hide it in the buggy while we were having breakfast."

She sat down on the blanket. Leaning back on her hands, she raised her eyebrows. "You're quite resourceful, Mr. Blake."

He looked steadily at her. "When it's important." He held her gaze for a moment longer. "Should I ask the blessing?"

She nodded. He blessed the food, and she fixed their plates from the wonderful food Mrs. Hanson had prepared.

While they were eating, and she was no longer being amazed by new sights and sounds, Seth watched her features cloud as she became quiet. She was trying to decide whether or not to bring something up. He wished she trusted him enough to say what was on her mind, but he didn't force the issue. She'd talk about it when she was ready.

"Do you think there's gold under the logging camp?" she asked.

He leaned back on his hands, wanting to be careful with how he answered her, but wanted to tell her the truth. "I don't know. But McCormick seems to think so. That's what has me worried."

"What do you think we should do?" she asked quietly.

Seth's heart warmed. As near as he could remember, it was the first time she'd asked him what to do. To Seth, that indicated that she trusted him. "Gold does funny things to a man. Most will stop at nothing to get their hands on it. McCormick's like that. We've seen what he's willing to do." He scanned the park for a moment before studying her. "I know we've talked about this a little before, that you don't want McCormick to be part of the town, or to get away with what he's done. But now we know he already owns land in the area. And—" He looked away, swallowing. Turning back, he leaned forward. "I don't want anything else to happen to you."

He started to reach for her hand, but she broke eye contact and picked at the blanket she was sitting on. "I suppose one of the reasons I've felt so strongly about holding on to the logging camp is because of Thomas. Particularly after seeing where he lived and worked ... I know it's silly, but it almost seemed like he could have come walking around the corner at any moment."

This time he reached out and lifted her chin with his finger. "It makes perfect sense. I feel that way often. If there were any other way to protect you, and anyone else that might get in his way, I'd do it. But I just can't think of another way to stop the danger." He ran his thumb across her jaw before lowering his hand.

She gave him a sad smile, and he wasn't sure what she was thinking.

"Tell you what. Josh and I will poke around the logging camp and McCormick's land when we get back. Maybe we'll find out something useful. Then I'll talk to McCormick if you want. Maybe he'll make a deal and only buy part of the land. In the meantime, we can pray about it."

Her face lit up. He'd do anything to make her happy, but he had to keep her safe first. Even if it meant sacrificing everything he'd worked for up to this point in his life. Maybe Josh and Maggie would let him be a part owner in the Oregon Express. They'd offered it to him before. But could he stand living in the same town as McCormick, seeing him everyday and remembering what he'd lost?

Seth shoved the thoughts from his head. He didn't want to ruin this day. "Would you like to head back so you can rest tonight before supper? I know I'm about ready for a nap with this warm sun and my full stomach."

"That sounds like a good plan."

THE GENTLE SWAYING of the buggy, along with the sunlight filtering through the trees that lined the street, put Becca in a sleepy mood. Seth saw her into the hotel lobby with a promise to call for her at six, and suggested that she could come over to the store if she didn't feel like staying in her hotel room.

In her room, Becca took off her hat, kicked off her shoes, and lay down for a nap. Instead of falling asleep, she thought about her conversation with Seth in the park. She hadn't wanted to ruin their day by bringing up Mr. McCormick, but she also knew it wasn't a burden she could continue to carry alone. She had promised the Lord she would stop trying to do it all alone and start trusting Him. And Seth.

She was glad she brought it up. His concern for her touched her deeply. Yet she also felt a great sense of loss over the thought of selling the logging camp. Not only was it letting Mr. McCormick win, since her house had burned down, it was the last tangible thing that tied her to Thomas.

Holding on to the logging camp wouldn't bring back Thomas. What would Seth think if she refused to agree with him on this point? Did she really want to risk her future with him because of a tenuous tie to Thomas? And could she let God settle the score for Thomas's death?

Becca sighed. She was trying to control things again and not give them to God. Here was an opportunity to step out in faith and believe God could make everything right. *Please God, I want to trust You. It's just so hard. Help me to do the right thing.*

She must have fallen asleep because she awoke refreshed about an hour later. Not wanting to go over to Josiah's store for a short period of time before coming back to get ready, she looked around her room for something to do. Spying the catalog Josiah had given her, she spent the rest of the afternoon selecting furniture for her house.

On impulse, she had put her one evening dress in her valise. She had made it for a formal function at school and had only worn it once. She changed into the gown of amethyst silk. It had short sleeves covered with lace that draped across the bodice. The overskirt was gathered around the hem to reveal an underskirt of a slightly darker shade.

She knew she made the right decision when she saw Seth's face as she came downstairs. He was waiting for her in the lobby. The moment he saw her, an appreciative look filled his eyes. He didn't take his gaze off her. A frisson of pleasure ran through her.

As he took her arm, he said for her ears alone, "You look beautiful. I don't suppose you'd ever have an opportunity to wear that dress in Reedsville?"

She smiled, feeling a little coquettish at his attention. "No, I don't think so."

"Then we'll just have to come up to Portland more often."

Outside the streetlights had come on, some of them electric, casting a warm glow over the street. They walked the few blocks to the Hotel Columbia, the fanciest hotel in the city.

Between her dress, Seth's attention, and the elegant dining room, she felt like a princess. She couldn't remember the last time she'd used real china or silver. The tablecloth was snowy white with a small flower arrangement in the middle.

They were lingering over coffee. The way he was looking at her.... She didn't want the evening to end. Was he going to propose? She fiddled with her coffee cup, hoping her thoughts didn't show on her face. Why hadn't she thought of that before? She clutched her hands in her lap. *Stop it! You are borrowing trouble. You don't even know if he wants to marry you.*

"Good evening, Mr. McCormick," she heard the maitre d' say.

She bobbled her cup and sloshed coffee over its rim. Her heart pounded so fiercely she was certain it could be seen through her dress. Surely she was imagining things. But Seth's face had hardened as he stared past her. Her heart plummeted to her toes. She would have slumped if her corset would let her.

Unable to stand the suspense, she shifted in her chair and followed Seth's gaze. Mr. McCormick stood staring at her, his forehead furrowed and eyes glittering strangely.

"Let's go," Seth said in a low voice.

He slid out of his chair and moved to help Becca from hers. They had to pass Mr. McCormick's table but Seth put himself in between.

"Miss Wilson, Mr. Blake." She could hear Mr. McCormick's voice, but Seth's broad shoulders blocked her view. "What a surprise."

She felt Seth hesitate the briefest of seconds. "McCormick.

Good evening." Then they were past him. As they left the dining room, she felt Mr. McCormick's eyes boring into her back.

Once outside, she started trembling. Seth held her tightly against his side until they reached the next block.

"Are you all right?"

She nodded.

"I'm sorry he ruined our evening."

Becca turned a forced smile on Seth. "I'm not letting him ruin this evening. He's ruined enough already." She released her breath. "Let's talk about something pleasant. How about my house? I've been thinking of ordering furniture, but I don't want it delivered before the house is finished. When do you think that will be?"

Seth gazed at her for a moment before a soft smile lifted the corners of his mouth.

"Well, Mr. Blake? What do you think?" She lifted her eyebrows, pleased that she had surprised him a second time tonight.

"I think you're amazing."

When they reached the dry goods store, he insisted she come up to his father's apartment for some tea rather than head straight to her room and be alone. "I don't want *him* to be the last thing on your mind before you go to sleep. Besides, it's early yet and my father would enjoy visiting with you."

"I think that would be a wonderful way to end the evening."

While Becca sipped her tea, she told Josiah all about their supper.

"Never been there myself," Josiah said. "Then again, I don't have anyone as pretty as you to take."

She blushed slightly, but she was getting used to the way Josiah complimented her often.

She and Seth told his father about their adventures of the

day. Josiah's eyes sparkled in merriment over her enthusiastic descriptions. But when she caught herself stifling a yawn, she declared she was ready to turn in.

Seth walked her down the stairs. They stood in the stockroom, which led to the back door. He paused before opening the door.

"I'm glad you enjoyed our day today, but I'm eager to get back home." His voice was low and husky.

Only the streetlight pouring through the window lit the stockroom. She couldn't see his eyes well enough to read what was in them. What he was leaving unsaid. "Why?"

He cupped her cheek in his hand. "Because I haven't gotten to do this." He bent down and kissed her softly on the lips. She felt her stomach turn to liquid. Too soon he pulled away and planted a quick kiss on her brow. "And now I have to take you to your hotel."

He walked her to the hotel lobby and said good night. She climbed the stairs and turned around at the top to find him still watching her. She gave him a small wave and a smile before turning and heading to her room.

Chapter Thirty-Five

Seth knew it was early, but he knocked anyway. He heard someone stir inside, then a gruff, "I'm coming," before the door opened.

He had obviously roused McCormick, who was barefoot with his shirttails hanging out over his waistband. A flash of surprise crossed McCormick's face. "Mr. Blake. Did you and Miss Wilson enjoy your supper last night?"

Anger surged through Seth, but he schooled his features to reveal nothing. "I'm not interested in partnering with you, nor in selling the logging company. However, I might be willing to deal on some of the land we're not using."

McCormick's eyes narrowed, and he looked Seth up and down before replying.

Seth coolly met his eyes and said nothing.

"I don't deal. You have my offer, and it's not good indefinitely." He gave a harsh laugh. "I hear your company is having trouble getting enough business. Even though it's not worth as much, I'm still willing to maintain my original offer."

"I'm only offering some land. Nothing more." Seth didn't think McCormick would want just the land, but he had to try.

McCormick leaned on the doorframe. "Things can happen

to make even the land values go down. Your land might not be worth as much in the near future." His lips twisted. "It would be a shame for your friends to lose their stage line. And Miss Wilson, would she really make time for man who has nothing to offer her?" He gave a low laugh. "It's my original offer or nothing." He shut the door in Seth's face.

Seth clenched his jaw and balled his fists, tempted to pound on the door. Thinking the better of it, he strode down the stairs, his feet heavy on the treads. The few blocks to the dry goods store weren't enough to calm his anger.

He had hoped to somehow keep part of the logging company to please Becca. Lead filled his stomach at the thought of disappointing her. He decided not to mention his visit to McCormick. Not yet, anyway. Maybe there was something that could still be done. He prayed it would be so.

He replayed the conversation in his mind. What did McCormick mean by the land values going down? Something else was going to happen. He just hoped it didn't involve Becca.

Once again he thought of asking their old family friend, Pastor Kendall, to marry them while they were here. Then he could make sure Becca was safe all the time.

McCormick's words echoed in Seth's head. *Would she really make time for man who has nothing to offer her?* He'd had the same thought himself. Would Becca marry him if he had nothing to offer her? Did he even have the right to ask her?

He went up to his room and opened his Bible, trying to get his mind prepared for church that morning. It was a long time before the words on the page actually registered in his mind.

Becca knew she didn't have much time. Making sure to be ready early, she headed downstairs and spotted Matthew at the front desk.

"Good morning." She smiled at him.

"Good morning, Miss Wilson. May I do something for you?"

"I was wondering if your mother was around. I'd like to ask her something."

"I think she's in the kitchen. I'll go find her."

Becca tapped her fingers on the desk as she waited and looked out the hotel's front windows, hoping Seth and Josiah didn't arrive too soon.

A moment later Mrs. Hanson came out from the back, wiping her hands on her apron. "Miss Wilson? Matthew says you wanted to see me?"

"Mrs. Hanson, yes, I wanted to ask you about your cinnamon rolls. They are absolutely delicious. I was wondering if you would be willing to share your recipe with me."

Mrs. Hanson flushed slightly. "Thank you. I'm so glad you enjoyed them. I don't have a recipe written down, but I suppose I could make a stab at putting something on paper for you. Would that be okay?"

"That would be wonderful."

"I'll have Matthew give it to you when I've finished it."

"Thank you so much, Mrs. Hanson."

The lady nodded and headed back to the kitchen just as Seth and Josiah came in through the front door. Becca greeted them both with a bright smile, and picked up her reticule and Bible from the lobby settee. They left for church.

In the short time before the service began, Becca met a few of Josiah's friends. Becca was warmly welcomed and surprised at the number of people who had known Thomas. Once Becca had gone to the university, it wasn't unusual for him to ride up to Portland with Seth or Josh on stage runs. He usually went if they were going to stay over on Sunday since the circuit preacher didn't get to Reedsville very often. People gave their regards to Maggie and Josh, and the trio found their seats just as the first notes of the first hymn began.

SETH NOTED the appraising glances of the congregation between him and Becca. He had practically grown up in this church before moving to Reedsville, and after his mother died, a few of the ladies had taken to mothering him. He was pleased at how warmly they greeted and accepted Becca. They were good Christian people; he had expected nothing less. Still, it was gratifying.

He sang the hymn from memory, his mind not really on the words. Instead, he was aware of how the side of his hand touched Becca's as they shared a hymnal, how her shoulder occasionally bumped his arm, and how her sweet, soft alto sang out next to him. Contentment and peace washed over him, obliterating the memory of his encounter with McCormick earlier that morning.

He sat with the rest of the congregation after the singing, but the pastor was well into his sermon before Seth began paying attention.

After the service, the pastor made a point to meet Becca. "Josiah, Seth, good to see you this morning."

"Good morning. It's good to be here. This is Rebecca Wilson, Thomas' sister. Becca, this is Bill Kendall, our pastor."

"Glad to meet you. Your brother was a good man. I was truly sorry to hear of his accident. I am grateful I was able to get to know him some when he came up here with Seth and Josh."

"Thank you" Becca's voice was soft.

"How long will you be staying?"

"We're returning to Reedsville first thing in the morning."

Pastor Kendall turned to Seth. "Well, you bring her back for a visit real soon."

Seth looked at the pastor directly in the eyes. "I plan on doing just that."

Pastor Kendall held his gaze for a moment then nodded shortly in understanding. "Good."

As Josiah moved to introduce Becca to someone else, Pastor Kendall bent towards Seth's ear and whispered. "You did good, son."

Seth grinned and said quietly, "I know. I'm very lucky."

"Luck had nothing to do with it." He clapped Seth on the shoulder and moved on.

After church, the three of them returned to Josiah's for dinner. Becca insisted on doing the dishes, and Seth helped her by drying and putting them away. The rest of the afternoon, she sat with Josiah at the table pouring over the catalog and showing him her selections. Then he helped her compile a list of things for Jake to pick up at Ankeny's New Market first thing in the morning so they could take the purchases with them on the stage. They had an early supper, and Seth walked her to the hotel so she could pack and retire.

When Seth returned to his father's apartments, he poured two cups of coffee and carried them into the living room. Handing his father a cup, he sat down across from him and stretched out his legs.

Josiah took a sip. "I really like her, Seth."

"I'm glad. I thought you would."

"You're going to marry her." It was a statement of fact, not a question.

Seth ran a hand through his hair. "If this thing with McCormick was over and done with. As it is, I'm not sure I have a future to offer her."

"Becca doesn't strike me as the type of woman who cares much for material things. But I do see in her eyes how much she cares about you."

"Really?"

Josiah laughed. "Since you can't keep your eyes off her, I thought you'd have noticed that by now."

Seth leaned back in his chair and was quiet for a moment. Did Becca love him? "I always thought I'd marry someone like

Mama. But Becca's got a real stubborn streak and a way of stepping on my nerves."

Josiah chuckled. "That sounds just like your mama."

Were they talking about the same woman? He couldn't recall seeing his parents argue. His mother had always exuded a calm strength.

"She may have not seemed that way to you, but seeing you and Becca is like seeing your mother and me twenty-five years ago. She never would have contradicted me in front of you, or anyone else. She always gave me that respect. But once we were alone, I often got an earful. Over time we learned to trust each other. But there's no getting around the fact we saw life differently.

"And that's a good thing. God designed us to be different so our strengths and weaknesses complemented each other." Josiah chuckled again. "Of course those are going to be the things that irritate you the most. But the Bible says as iron sharpens iron, so one man—or woman, in this case—sharpens another. Marriage will help you grow in ways you otherwise could never grow."

Seth was silent for a moment, absorbing his father's words. "I always wanted the kind of marriage you and Mama had."

"You will. It doesn't happen overnight. It takes work and the result of that work is what you remember."

Josiah set his cup down and leaned forward, elbows on his knees. "Seth, I don't usually meddle in your business. You're a hard worker and an honorable man. I'm proud of what you've become. Since Becca's been here, I've seen a light in your eyes and a spring in your step. Do you realize that the last time you were up here you were as restless as a caged animal? You couldn't wait to get back to Reedsville."

Seth couldn't deny it.

"She looks at you the way your mama looked at me. Can you even imagine life without her?"

"No." He couldn't bear to think of Becca returning to Salem and Willamette University.

Josiah got up and put his cup in the kitchen before disappearing down the hall.

Was their conversation over? Seth rubbed his chin. It took some mental adjustment for him to picture his mama the way his father had described her. He was still pondering this when his father came back in the room.

Josiah stood in front of Seth, fingering something in his hand. "Here."

Seth reached out and Josiah dropped a ring into Seth's hand. It was his mother's wedding ring. The delicate gold filigree band supported three small garnets across the top. A memory flashed through his mind of that ring on her finger while she was going about her day. Pressure built in his chest.

Josiah's voice thickened with emotion. "Give it to Becca. If she's the woman I think she is, she'll treasure it."

Seth couldn't speak for the knot in his throat. He nodded and swallowed before he could say, "Thanks, Dad. I know she will."

Josiah said good night and retired to his room. Seth sat up for a while longer, turning the ring over in his fingers, comforted by the blessing he knew his father had just given.

THE SUN WAS JUST CREEPING over the Cascades when Becca, Seth, and Josiah left the dry goods store for the interurban stop, the wagon piled high in the back with Becca's purchases, and the result of Jake's foray into Ankeny's New Market that morning.

"Josh was right when he said you'd bring back half of Portland," Seth teased her. "When we get on the stagecoach I might have to bump some passengers so we have room for all this."

She tapped his arm playfully and rolled her eyes then turned and gave Josiah a hug. "Thank you for everything."

"I didn't do much. You take care of yourself and keep this son of mine in line."

She smiled.

Seth shook his father's hand as Josiah reached out and clasped Seth's shoulder. "Drive carefully." Father and son held each other's gaze for a moment.

"I will."

Seth helped Becca into the stagecoach and shut the door behind her. She was the last one in and seated by the window, so she looked out and waved at Josiah. He waved back. As they pulled away, she leaned into the cushions, grateful for her time in Portland but eager to get home.

Home. She was surprised at how naturally it seemed to her to call Reedsville home once again. She hadn't noticed that before. She leaned her head back and closed her eyes. It was definitely good to be going home.

Chapter Thirty-Six

"Found out something interesting about McCormick in Portland," Seth said to Josh as they cleaned the stage the next morning. Josh could move his arm now, but couldn't lift anything with it. He'd gotten quite proficient with his left hand.

Josh glanced over at him before continuing to wipe down the body of the coach. "What's that?"

Seth filled him in on what he'd found at the land and assayer's offices, including running into McCormick at supper and his reaction to Seth's offer. His gut clenched at the thought of that conversation. Should he tell Becca about it? She had been so happy this morning he was reluctant to take that away from her.

Josh stopped. "Gold." He waited while Seth walked back with the bucket of axle grease. "That explains a lot. Maybe we should go have a look around there tomorrow, see if we can find anything out."

"That's just what I was thinking. I probably should warn Owen to be on the lookout for anything strange as well."

Josh wiped his brow with his forearm. "Men kill for gold."

"He already has." Seth threw the brush in the bucket of grease. "This isn't going to end well." He put his hand on Josh's shoulder. "Just keep praying."

Seth found Becca and Maggie giggling over something in the parlor.

"What did I miss?"

That just sent them into another round of giggles. He was glad to see Becca enjoying herself. The time could soon come when she wouldn't have much to smile about.

"Just girl talk," Maggie said, wiping at the corner of her eyes with her apron.

He turned to Becca, noticing her heightened color. She was beautiful. "Josh and I are finished with the stage, and I thought we could go check out your homestead before I head up to the logging camp. We could take the buggy, but I suspect you'd rather walk after being in the stagecoach all day yesterday."

"A good walk is just what I need."

Outside, he took her hand, intertwining their fingers. All the different information about McCormick and their future swirled in his head. He wasn't sure where to begin. *Lord, help me say the right words. Help Becca understand.*

"When we were in Portland, that morning before church I went to see McCormick." He watched Becca for her reaction. He wasn't sure what he was expecting, but he saw peace on her face when she looked up at him. And trust.

"What did he say?"

He told her about their conversation.

"So making a deal with him isn't an option," Becca stated.

"No. Josh and I are going to look at his land and see if we can get any other information." He hesitated, wondering if his next words would remove that look of trust from her face. "Gold makes men crazy. McCormick's offer letter to Thomas was dated shortly after he bought the land next to ours." Seth looked ahead. They were nearly at her homestead. He stopped and faced her, taking both of her hands in his. "Thomas's death was the result of the first accident McCormick staged. I'm sure of it. I don't think he targeted Thomas specifically because he had no way of knowing Thomas would push the other man out of the way. But I think it was his first attempt to try and get us to sell."

Becca paled and gripped his hands tighter. He felt a niggling in his heart that he should tell her the rest, tell her about the cut chains, but he pushed it aside. He'd tell her later. He didn't want to add to her distress. But if she asked how he knew, he would tell her.

"I don't know why we didn't see it sooner."

He released one of her hands and slid his arm around her shoulders, pulling her closer to him. "We weren't supposed to. It looked like an accident, and there was no reason to think otherwise."

Except for those chains.

They walked the rest of the way to her homestead in silence. Was finishing it a futile effort? Right now, it looked like McCormick was going to win, and Seth would have to take Becca away from here to somewhere they could start over. But as he watched her look at her almost-finished house, he knew he couldn't ask her to do that. He couldn't ask her to give up one more dream, one more thing that tied her to her family. He'd do whatever he could to keep McCormick from taking that from them too.

"Have you seen Josh swing a hammer with his left hand?" he asked.

She turned to him with a smile. "No. Is it something to see?"

He grinned. "If I get the nail started, he's pretty good at finishing it up. Shouldn't be too much longer before your house is done. Have you finished picking out furniture?"

"I ordered a few things from your father, but I haven't picked out furniture."

"Order what you need from the catalog I gave you. By the time it gets here, your house will be finished."

BECCA HURRIED out to the springhouse before breakfast to retrieve her dough. She didn't have an icebox like Mrs. Hanson, and had despaired of ever making her cinnamon rolls until she'd thought of the springhouse. Mrs. Hanson's recipe had called for letting the dough rise slowly overnight in an icebox. She wasn't sure if this was the key to her cinnamon rolls, but she didn't want to take any chances. Back in the kitchen she finished the rolls while Maggie was getting breakfast. After breakfast, she fixed a plate of the warm rolls and took them out to the barn.

Seth and Josh were pulling down gear for their horses. Seth turned when he heard footsteps, and smiled when he saw her.

"Good morning."

"Good morning. I've brought you something." She took the towel off the plate and extended it to Seth. He smiled as he took one of the rolls. She held out the plate to Josh but kept glancing back to Seth.

"Well I could get used to service like this." Josh grinned around a big bite.

She watched Seth's reaction as he took a bite. "These sure taste like Mrs. Hanson's cinnamon rolls." He stopped for a moment. "Did you bring some of them back? How'd you manage to keep them fresh?"

She laughed. "I made them. Mrs. Hanson was kind enough to give me her recipe. I wanted to surprise you."

"Mrs. Hanson gave you her recipe for her famous cinnamon rolls?" Josh raised his eyebrows. "She must think mighty highly of you. I know a few women in Portland who've been trying to get that recipe for years."

Seth's eyes softened as he looked at her. "You did surprise me. Thank you."

Josh popped the rest of the cinnamon roll in his mouth and headed toward a stall.

Seth stepped forward and took her hand. "Josh and I are going up to the logging camp to look around. We're going to look at where our land adjoins McCormick's and see what we can discover. I don't know what McCormick's up to, but while we're gone, I want you to be careful. Stay near Maggie's and don't go down to the homestead."

Surprisingly, she had no desire to bristle at his directive. She could see the concern in his eyes and smiled at him. "I won't leave Maggie's. I promise." Then the thought of what they were about to do overshadowed her contentment and filled her heart with dread. "You be careful, too. I'll be worried about you the whole time you're gone."

He gave her a lopsided grin. "Aw, Miss Wilson, it's nice to know you care."

His grin tugged at her heart, but she didn't let him put her off. "I'm serious, Seth. Promise me you'll be careful and not take any unnecessary risks."

His eyes grew intense as he looked at her. "I promise." He squeezed her hand and leaned forward, capturing her mouth with his for a brief moment. The next moment he had turned and walked down to the stalls.

Becca stood there, stunned, for a moment.

Josh led his horse down the aisle and passed her as he was heading out the barn. "Thanks for the cinnamon rolls, Becca. They were really good. I couldn't tell them apart from Mrs. Hanson's."

"I'm glad you liked them," she answered distractedly, barely noticing Josh. It took her a moment to realize he was looking at her, waiting.

"It'll be okay, Becca. Seth knows how to take care of himself."

"Here." She dumped the rest of the cinnamon rolls into the towel and quickly wrapped them and handed them to Josh. "Take these with you in case you get hungry."

Josh took the bundle and stowed it in his saddlebag, as Seth came down the aisle leading his horse.

She walked out of the barn with them. "You two be careful. I mean it."

"We will," Seth tipped his hat to her, watching her until he had to turn around.

She stared until they were out of sight then walked back inside. She helped Maggie with the breakfast dishes and then filled the big kettle with water and put it on to boil. Being washing day, there was plenty of hard labor to keep her hands busy. But occupying her mind was something else.

She knew the men were in God's care. The verse from First Peter, *casting all your care upon Him for He careth for you,* played through her mind as well as the verse in Philippians: *Be careful for nothing but in everything by prayer and supplication, with thanksgiving, let your requests be made known unto God. And the peace of God that passeth all understanding shall keep your hearts and minds in Christ Jesus.*

That's what she needed to do. She needed to be praying. She spent the rest of the morning lifting the men up to prayer as she did the wash. She prayed about the situation with McCormick, and her relationship with Seth. As she hung up the wash, she remembered the part of the verse about thanksgiving.

Here she'd been telling God everything she wanted and hadn't thought to thank Him for all that He'd already given her. Humbled, she thanked the Lord for all of the good things He had brought to her life. Her anxiety began to melt away as it was replaced with peace and gratefulness. God had been so good to her, and she knew He would continue to be in the future.

Even if their definitions of "good" were different.

Her back hurt from bending over the washtub and lifting the wet sheets and clothes on to the clothesline. While the clothes dried on the line, she went upstairs to read that verse in Philippians again while trying to rest her back. Sitting on her bed, she ended up reading all of chapter four.

She had just closed her Bible when she noticed the furniture catalog on her dresser. She picked it up, remembering what Seth had said. Was he going to ask her to marry him? Or was he just saying her house was empty and needed furniture? She giggled at the thought for some strange reason. Well of course it was empty! She shook her head at herself. It wouldn't hurt to look through the catalog, regardless of what Seth had meant. One way or another, she would need furniture.

The choices were overwhelming. She never knew there were so many different kinds of davenports, sofas, chairs, and tables. She would have to furnish the house completely since nothing was salvageable from the fire.

She was mentally making a list of the things she'd need, trying not to be overwhelmed, when she came to the bedroom furniture. "A dressing table would be nice," she mused. "Probably need a highboy more, though. And definitely a bed."

Her hands stilled on the page as she thought about that. What she would get for herself and what she would get if she were married to Seth were two entirely different things. Seth was a tall man and would need a much bigger bed than Becca would. She blushed at the thought.

"I can't do this," she muttered as she stared at the page. "If I order a bed for myself, what will he think? And if I order a big bed, what will he think?" Becca sighed, tossed the catalog on her bed, and headed downstairs.

Chapter Thirty-Seven

Leaving their horses tied at the bottom of the hill, Seth and Josh crawled up the ridgeline that separated the logging company property from McCormick's. They carefully peered over the ridge. An arrasta had been set up to grind ore. The huge stone basin was fitted with a matching heavy stone on top. A mule would be harnessed to this stone and pull it around in a circle, grinding up any ore between the two stones. At the moment it was still.

They scanned the area, noting a couple of small buildings, before Josh pointed. "Look at that," he whispered.

What looked like an entrance to a mine had been dug in the side of the mountain. If the tunnel went straight back, it would hit logging company property in about 100 feet.

"Doesn't look like he was going to wait for us to sell," Seth whispered back. He could only see several men, and it didn't look like there was too much activity. He shifted to get a better look. As he shifted, his gun belt poked him in the thigh and he jerked back. His boot dislodged a rock that rattled noisily down the mountain toward the men below. He and Josh ducked down below the crest, but not before shouts from the other side of the ridge reached them.

"We'd better go," Josh said. "I think we've seen enough."

Seth nodded as bark exploded from the tree near his head. Gunshots rang out in succession.

The men headed down the hill in a crouch. Josh broke to the left as Seth moved to the right. He concentrated on using the trees as cover. A splinter of wood stung Seth's cheek as a bullet hit a nearby tree. He could hear more gunshots as the bullets whipped back branches and splintered the tree trunks near him. The shots were so frequent they blended together in a hail.

He fought to keep his footing under the loose rocks and pine needles. Sweat plastered his shirt to his back and he was breathing hard. Relief surged through him as he glimpsed their horses through the trees. He realized there were fewer gunshots now and could hear each one distinctly again.

He reached his horse and swung up just as Josh broke through the trees to the left. The shots had stopped. Seth waited for Josh to mount up and then spurred his horse. They rode hard toward the logging camp, not taking any chances. As they neared the camp, and they'd heard no other shots, they slowed their horses to a walk to cool them down. Seth was glad for a chance to catch his breath.

"Must have been spotted by a lookout we didn't see." Josh gingerly moved his bad arm.

"That's the only logical explanation. There's no way those men could have climbed up the hill that fast and gotten off that many shots."

They rode the rest of the way to the office in silence. Owen walked out as they were sliding off their horses.

"Josh! Good to see you. How's your arm?"

"It's mending."

"Let's go in the office to talk." Seth opened the door and motioned the men inside. He followed them and eased himself behind his desk, ignoring the paperwork stacked there. Josh grabbed the chair across from him while Owen sat at his desk.

Seth turned to Owen. "Everything was fine while I was gone,

right? No more accidents?"

"No, it was pretty quiet around here. Why?"

Seth gave him a brief rundown of what he'd found out about McCormick in Portland and what they'd seen today.

"They shot at you?" Owen's eyes widened and his whole body stilled. "Not just a warning shot or two?"

Seth didn't think he'd ever seen that reaction in Owen before. Usually, nothing bothered the man and he never stopped fidgeting. "No, it was a volley of bullets."

"Better not tell Becca that," Josh cautioned Seth.

No, he wouldn't tell Becca that part. He looked back at Owen who seemed a bit pale. "We were just over the north ridge, so the men up there need to be particularly careful. I don't want any of them accidentally stumbling onto what we saw today."

"I'll keep them away." Owen wiped his hand over his face. Perspiration beaded his forehead.

"You feeling okay?" Seth leaned towards his foreman. "Do you need to go lay down?"

Taylor shook his head. "I'm fine. What are you going to do next?"

Seth sat back. "I'll wire the sheriff and tell him we think McCormick may be mining on our land. He can check it out." He hoped it would be the break they needed to stop McCormick.

"What about posting some guards?" Josh asked. "Particularly around the tool barn and horses."

Owen rubbed his forehead. "That's a good idea. I've got a few men I could trust with that. I'll take care of it now." He hurried out of the office.

"Unless you need to do something else in town, I'll wire the sheriff," Josh said.

Seth nodded and looked at the pile of paperwork on his desk. "Thanks."

Josh leaned back in his chair and crossed his ankles, a grin pulling at the corners of his mouth. "Speaking of Becca..."

Seth raised his eyebrows. "We were?"

"Yeah, you're not going to tell her about getting shot at. Anyhow, I'm kind of surprised you didn't come back from Portland hitched, or at least engaged. When are you going to ask that woman?"

Seth shook his head. "I didn't know that broken arm had turned you into a meddling old woman."

Josh grinned fully now. "Her house will be finished soon. You going to let her live there by herself?"

Seth frowned. He hadn't thought of that. He wanted to resolve this issue with McCormick and have a future to offer her before he asked Becca to marry him, but that might not happen anytime soon. He thought about what she said the night she brought him supper. She loved him no matter the circumstances. He was sure of that. Just thinking about it brought a sense of *rightness* to his soul. Was there any other reason he was waiting? He thought of his mother's ring sitting on his dresser at home and smiled. Nope, none at all.

He returned Josh's grin with one of his own.

Owen Taylor began packing his bag. Might as well save Blake the trouble of firing him. He regretted the day he met Jeremiah McCormick. Causing a few accidents when nobody got hurt to force Blake to treat him as an equal was one thing. Trying to kill people was another.

He broke out in a cold sweat. Until Blake had mentioned it, he didn't know Wilson's death wasn't an accident. Now Owen knew McCormick was behind it. Elmer had cut those chains, but when Owen showed them to Blake, it was only to scare him, just like the other accidents. He had no idea they'd been the ones that caused Thomas's death.

But he'd never be able to prove he was innocent. Not if

McCormick and Elmer spoke against him.

Finished gathering his few things, he opened his door a crack and peered out. No one was around. Slipping out, he pulled the door shut behind him. *Just walk casually.* He crossed the yard and walked out of the camp without anyone noticing.

JOSH HAD TURNED IN EARLY, but Seth stayed and talked to Becca on the porch swing after supper. They watched the stars come out and enjoyed the cool evening after the heat of the day. The weather had been fierce lately and the farmers were complaining about the lack of rain. His loggers still had to stop work early because the risk of a spark setting a fire was too high with everything so dry. And while he didn't like the idea of driving the coach through mud, he sure would have appreciated a rain shower to keep the dust down.

He reached over to take her hand. It felt so small and soft in his.

She leaned her head into his shoulder. "I'm so glad you're all right."

He looked down at her. "I told you I would be." Josh had told Becca everything was fine when he'd returned, but Seth knew she hadn't felt completely at ease until she saw him for herself.

"What did you find out?"

He told her briefly, leaving out the part about the gunfire. Bending down, he kissed the top of her head. She snuggled a bit closer to him.

They rocked in silence. He knew he needed to leave soon to go back to his cabin. It was getting harder to leave her, and harder for him to keep his thoughts from going where they shouldn't. All afternoon he'd thought about the best way to propose to her. Right now she looked so sweet next to him, he considered throwing his plans out the window and asking her right there on that porch swing. But he wanted to make it special, something that would really please her. He had thought up and discarded several ideas before settling on the final one.

Remembering how pleasantly surprised she had been at their picnic in Portland, he had decided that's what he'd do. He'd ask Maggie to make up a basket, and Sunday after church they'd go sit out in the meadow by her house.

Just thinking about it made him grin. He tucked her head under his chin so he wouldn't have to explain his grin to her.

"Hey, Becca, want to go with me up to the logging camp?" Josh stepped in through the kitchen door. "Seth has a pile of paperwork on his desk I thought we could help him out with."

"I'd love to. Let me get what we've already finished." Becca took off her apron and headed for the parlor.

Josh grinned, and it wasn't until she stepped off the kitchen porch that she understood why. He'd already hitched up the buggy.

"You must have figured I would agree to go."

Josh laughed. "I can't imagine what would keep you away."

At least he was kind enough not to tease her about the blush that heated her cheeks.

When they arrived at the logging camp office it was empty. They looked around inside but didn't see anything that indicated either Seth or Owen would be coming back soon.

"Stay here. I'm going next door to see if the cook knows where they are. He always knows what's going on."

She nodded and sat at Seth's desk. Sitting in his chair made her feel close to him, even though he wasn't in the room. She smiled and put the paperwork she and Josh had completed in one pile then began to sort through what was on his desk. She had done enough of it now to know what to look for. By the time Josh came back, she had created several piles.

"The cook thinks Seth is up by the north ridge. He hasn't seen Owen in a couple of days, but Seth mentioned he thought Owen was sick. He didn't look too well when I was here the other day."

"Has anyone checked on him?"

"I don't know."

"Well someone should. What if he's too ill to get up?"

Josh rubbed the back of his neck. "I'm not taking you to the north ridge where Seth's at, and I'm not leaving you here while I go up there." He tucked his good hand into his hip pocket. "Taylor's bunk isn't far from here. I'll go check on him, and you can come with me."

They walked across the camp until they came to a group of cabins. Two small ones sat to the front of the others.

"That's Seth's cabin there." Josh pointed. "Not that he's there much anymore. This is Owen's."

He knocked on the door while she stood back. "Owen? You in there?" He listened at the door for a moment before turning the knob and stepping in. A moment later he stuck his head out. "Becca, you can come on in. He's not here."

She stepped through the open door.

Josh scanned the room. "It's empty. His clothes and his bedroll are gone." Josh lifted the straw tick and looked under it. "What's this?" He dropped the tick and reached under the bed. She heard clanking and scratching as Josh drug out a handful of heavy, rust-flecked chains. "I wonder if these were the ones Seth wanted to show me."

She had no idea what he was talking about, but waited patiently as he ran the chains through his hands. If she wasn't going to see Seth, and Owen wasn't here, then she wanted to get back to Maggie's.

"Hmm. Here it is." Josh carefully laid one chain on the dresser. "I bet…" He examined the other one more carefully. "Yep. This one too." He put the second chain on the dresser next to the first. She hoped he was finished so they could leave.

"Becca, look at this." Josh stepped back from the dresser so she could see, but he was pointing at something.

She stepped closer. "What am I supposed to be seeing? It looks like several old chains."

"But see how they're cut? Both of them, the same way."

She peered at the chains specifically where Josh was pointing. She could see where new metal gleamed on the cut surfaces. "Why would someone want… Oh, were these involved in one of the accidents?"

Josh stared at her. "This one—" he pointed to the first chain —"is from Thomas's accident. There's still bark in a few links from where it wrapped around the logs. The one next to it Seth found one morning as he was inspecting the chains and pulled it."

She felt the blood drain from her face. She was staring at the chain that caused her brother's death. Hesitantly, she reached out to touch it. Surprisingly, it felt cold and rough beneath her fingers. She shook her head slightly, not knowing what she had expected. The second chain… If someone cut *both* chains….

She grabbed Josh's sleeve. "We know someone at the logging camp was involved. And these chains are in Owen's room."

He nodded and drew his lips into a firm line. "Seth was looking for them to show me the cuts. He couldn't find them. Unless there's another explanation, it looks like Owen was McCormick's man up here."

She pulled her hand back. She felt sick. Owen was so nice. She'd always liked him. It hurt to think he'd abused Seth's trust and played a part in trying to ruin him.

She stared at the second chain. "That chain didn't cause an accident, did it? Just the first one?"

"No. Seth caught it during his morning inspection."

Feeling cold suddenly, she wrapped her arms around herself. Pieces of a puzzle were floating around in her brain, and the answer seemed just out of reach. "Yes, you said that, didn't you?" Distractedly, her gazed wandered the room, not really seeing it.

She looked back at Josh. He was still staring at her. He knew the answer. And, suddenly so did she.

"Who checked the chains the morning of Thomas's accident?"

Josh shifted his weight. "Becca—"

"Who?"

"Let Seth talk to you about it."

"He's not here. You are."

She caught Josh's gaze shift over her shoulder and heard boots scrape the floor. She spun around to see Seth in the doorway.

"It was me, Becca. I checked the chains the morning Thomas died." She heard the tightness in Seth's voice but the light behind him kept his face in shadow.

As the pieces clicked into place, her world crumbled. Tears stung her eyes. "Why didn't you tell me?"

He took a step toward her. "Let me explain."

She backed away and let the hurt and anger pour out unchecked. "Did you ever trust me? Did you ever consider me your equal, your partner? I'm not a little girl anymore. I don't need protecting from the truth. You said you weren't going to keep information from me anymore."

"I know I should have—"

"Yes, you should have." She strode to the door. When Seth wouldn't move, she pushed past him. He grasped her arm but she shook it off. "Don't touch me."

He let go, and she continued across the camp.

"Becca, wait. We need to talk."

The pain she heard in his voice almost made her stop, but she kept going until she got to the buggy. She climbed in without looking back and headed down the hill. Safely away from the camp, she brushed the tears from her face with the back of her hands. She supposed Josh would find his own way home.

Chapter Thirty-Eight

Seth leaned his forearm against the doorjamb and rested his head on it. "I deserve everything she said. She's right. I should have told her sooner." His voice sounded raspy even to his own ears. He cleared his throat, but it didn't help.

Looking up, he saw Josh leaning against the dresser, steadily returning his gaze. There was no pity in his eyes.

Good. He couldn't stand that.

"Looks like Owen's gone." Josh straightened. "None of his stuff is left."

It took a moment for Seth's thoughts to catch up with Josh. Finally, he nodded. "He was probably working with McCormick." He felt like he'd been punched in the gut. He'd trusted Owen. "Can you go find out about him? Ask around. See if anyone knew what he was planning or where he went."

"Sure." Josh briefly squeezed Seth's shoulder as he passed him in the doorway.

"I'm going to my office. I need to write a letter."

BECCA HEARD a knock at her bedroom door. "Come in." She expected Maggie to come check on her since she'd missed supper.

The door opened and Josh stepped in.

"Josh." She sat up straighter on her bed.

He hesitated and then walked over to her bed and handed her an envelope. "Seth asked me to give this to you."

Her name was on the front in Seth's handwriting. "Is he here?"

Josh shook his head. "He stayed up at the camp to work." He crossed back to the door, but turned before leaving. Blowing out a breath he said, "I feel like a brother to both of you so I'm going to stick my nose where it doesn't belong. Seth loves you. Maybe he hasn't always handled everything right, but it was only because he didn't want what happened to Thomas to happen to you. Not because he thought any less of you."

She knew Seth's intentions had always been good. It made his actions only slightly less hurtful.

Josh turned to leave, pulling the door with him.

"Josh?"

He looked around the door, eyebrows raised.

"Thanks."

He gave her a small smile and left.

Becca leaned back against the headboard and sighed. She'd come to the same conclusion herself. But finding out Seth had inspected the chains that morning, and then knowing he had kept all of it from her after he told her he wouldn't was too much to take in rationally.

She looked at the envelope a moment more before she slid her finger under the flap, breaking the seal. She tugged the paper out and unfolded it, letting her eyes slowly move down the page, almost seeing him pen the words.

MY DEAREST BECCA,

I regret more than I can say that I never told you everything regarding your brother's death. I had planned on telling you the day I told you I suspected your brother's death was the first of McCormick's accidents. It just seemed like too much of a burden to place on you to tell you I was partly responsible.

The day you arrived in Reedsville, Owen Taylor had found the chains and showed them to me. I realized then that they were the cause of Thomas's death and that I was partly responsible. I was inspecting the chains that morning and had seen that one link was wrong. But before I could look further to see what else was damaged, I was interrupted and never got back to the chains. I didn't even remember them until Owen showed them to me. Someone had assumed I was finished inspecting them. They used them and the chain broke the way McCormick or his associate intended it to, and Thomas died.

While I know in my head that McCormick is guilty of causing Thomas's death, I can't help but blame myself for not preventing his death. If only I hadn't let myself get distracted. If only I had gone back to the chains, or taken them with me to make sure no one would use them. It pains me to admit it, but I couldn't stand to see that same accusation in your eyes that I see in my own when I look in the mirror. It does not excuse the fact that you had a right to know, and I should have told you much sooner.

I do love you, Becca, with all my heart. Forgive me. I realize that you may feel that you can never trust me again, and I regret that more than words can say.

Yours forever,

Seth

BECCA MOVED THE LETTER AWAY, careful not to let her tears fall on it and smudge the ink. She cried for Seth bearing the burden of guilt all alone. She cried for herself for not trusting him enough to let him explain.

McCormick slogged through the woods toward the logging camp, cursing under his breath. The crumpled telegram in his pocket only served to stoke his anger. This was supposed to be Taylor's job. Taylor knew McCormick couldn't trust Elmer with it.

Taylor was a fool, and he'd proved it with that telegram. McCormick expected the telegram to tell him the logging camp had burned down. Instead, Taylor informed him he'd quit. He'd run scared when they were so close! Taylor didn't want anyone to get hurt. He didn't seem to understand that if one wanted to be successful, he had to eliminate any obstacles in his path. What did he think had happened to Wilson this whole time? That one had worked out better than McCormick had planned.

And so would this, even if it meant doing the job himself while hating every minute of it. He wore ugly work clothes instead of his usual well-cut suit, but it didn't make this job any easier. The pine branches had torn at his hands and face, and he had blisters from his new work boots.

By the time he climbed up the ridge from his property and down the other side to the logging camp, dragging his supplies, he was panting. He swore this was the last time he would ever do physical labor. Staying out of sight behind a group of pine trees, he caught his breath and looked around the camp.

Sunday was the perfect day for this. Wilson and Blake were weak progressives who believed in giving men a day off, which meant most of the men were in their bunks sleeping off the effects of their Saturday-night carousing. A few, especially those with families, had wandered down to the schoolhouse where the townsfolk met on Sundays. He chuckled. For once, religion was going to serve a purpose in his life. With everyone out of the way, it should be easy to get this job done.

After seeing no movement for several minutes, he started to come out from the cover of the trees when he saw Seth Blake leave his office. As McCormick ducked back behind the trees, he noticed Blake was wearing a suit, of all things. If he was headed to church, he was late. Everyone else had already left for the service. McCormick watched Blake mount his horse and ride off. He waited until he was certain Blake wouldn't be coming back.

BECCA TAPPED her fan on the knee of the blue visiting dress she had worn in Portland. She had worn it, and the matching hat, specifically to bring back good memories and hoped Seth would notice. Where was he? He and Josh had spent yesterday trying to figure out where Owen went and how he was involved with McCormick. Seth hadn't made it to breakfast. She had stalled leaving for church as long as she dared without being left behind.

On the pretext of greeting her neighbors, she turned in her seat and scanned the room for Seth. There seemed to be more people in church than usual. Or maybe the room just felt crowded. No breeze drifted through the open windows. The air felt thick and stifling.

She waved to Mary and her husband. She spotted Andrew Paige and Charlie Lee from the camp. If Seth wasn't going to come, he would have sent word with one of them. Something must have held him up. She hoped it wasn't another accident.

Unless he was avoiding her.

Her heart sank at the thought. But she knew it was possible.

Beth Paige, who had sung at Annie and John's wedding, came to the front at that moment to lead the singing. As Becca stood to sing, she searched the room one last time. Seth's broad shoulders appeared in the doorway before he disappeared from view as the congregation stood.

She moved to make room for him, only to realize she was in the middle of the pew, between Maggie and Sally. The only space was at the end of the pew next to the aisle. She began singing while watching for him out of the corner of her eye.

He slid into the pew next to Josh, but kept his eyes to the front. He didn't look her direction at all. He was avoiding her. She stared at him, tears pricking her eyes.

McCormick moved toward the tool barn, forcing himself not to hurry. He hoped anyone who happened to see him would be fooled by his work clothes into thinking he belonged there.

As he neared the tool barn and stable area, he noticed a man walking around toting a shotgun. He cursed again. He hadn't planned on guards. Had Taylor warned Blake? Ducking behind the nearest building, he pressed his back against the wall. No, Taylor couldn't do that without cooking his own goose.

Most likely Blake was reacting to their conversation in Portland. McCormick had overplayed his hand when he threatened Blake, but he had hated seeing him in that restaurant with Becca. She looked especially beautiful that night. She should have been with *him*, not Blake. He jerked his mind away from the memory.

McCormick checked around the corner. He could see the guard strolling between buildings, gun slung over his shoulder, obviously not expecting trouble this sleepy Sunday morning. As the man started in the other direction, McCormick strode to the tool barn and tugged on the door. He almost laughed at his good fortune. A gun-toting guard but no lock on the door. He pulled the door open and slipped inside.

He removed the can from the sack and unscrewed the lid. The fumes made his eyes water, and he moved his head back to avoid breathing them. He made his way around the room, sloshing kerosene over the tools and walls. Satisfied everything burnable was soaked, he screwed the lid back on the can and returned it to his bag.

Moving to the door, he opened it a crack and looked out. The guard had apparently completed his circuit and was ambling away. McCormick waited another few seconds then pulled the matches from his pocket. He lit one after another, tossing them next to the walls and among tools. He watched as the fire caught. Peeking out the door one last time to make sure it was clear, he grabbed his bag and dashed off to the cover of the woods.

He only moved several trees deep before finding one he could hide behind and still watch the camp. He watched with pleasure as smoke began to curl out of the tool barn. The presence of the guard had ruined his plans to set the stables on fire. Without the mules and horses they wouldn't be able to pull logs out of the forest. Just burning the tools wouldn't be enough to put them out of business; those were too easy to replace. He needed to hurt them in some other way.

The guard spotted the smoke, and like a fool, pulled open the door to find its source. The sudden rush of air fed the flames, and they billowed out the door. The guard leaped back, but McCormick was willing to bet he'd lost his eyebrows. The guard wasted no time running to the dinner bell, clanging it fiercely to alert others. Men poured out of the bunkhouses, some staggering a bit, no doubt from their previous night's activities. Fire engulfed the tool shack now.

The confusion gave him an idea. He slipped out from the trees and over to the office and dining hall, which were completely deserted. Opening the can once again, he splashed more kerosene along the far side dining hall wall and tossed a couple of matches into the fuel. Flames quickly began licking the walls. He poured a trail of kerosene around the side to the office. Poking his head around the corner and seeing no one, he continued his trail into the office. He immediately guessed which desk was Seth's and had to repress a laugh as he drizzled kerosene over the papers.

Turning to splash fuel on the other desk, he saw flames

already jumping up the office doorposts. He hadn't counted on the flames following his trail so quickly. For a moment, panic rose in his throat. He pushed it down; he'd survived worse things than this working for Mike. The flames weren't that high. He grabbed his kerosene can and sack, leaped over the flames in the doorway, and ran for the trees.

He had almost reached the edge of the woods when he smelled burnt flesh, and a flash later felt his back sting. He dropped the can and sack, trying to rip his burning shirt off. The fabric came away in shreds, still burning as it fell to the ground. The searing pain on his back consumed him. Then his hands burned as well.

He stumbled up the hill toward the ridge, only thinking of how he could numb his pain. Belatedly, he remembered he had left his can and sack. He had wanted to use up all the kerosene, and there was still some left. Plus, he didn't want to leave anything that could be connected to him. He turned around and took a step back the way he came just as the can exploded, blowing flames high up into the surrounding trees.

He spun around and tried to scramble up the hill. His new boots could find no purchase on the pine needle-covered soil. He threw his hands out to break his fall and immediately regretted it as the raw flesh came in contact with the soil. Frenzied with pain in his back and hands, he kept at the hill, letting his knees take the brunt of his falls. Reaching the ridge, he didn't even stop to catch his breath. He slid down the other side on his backside and forgot to look at the inferno he had created.

Chapter Thirty-Nine

Becca tried to catch Seth's eye as they sat from singing but only managed to make Maggie look at her. She smothered a sigh and leaned back as Bill Johnson came to the front.

She couldn't pay attention to what Bill was saying. Instead, she thought about how she was going to be able to talk to Seth and what she would say to him. If he was avoiding her, he probably wouldn't go to Maggie's for dinner. Would Josh or James take her up to the logging camp? Then—

Familiar words penetrated Becca's thoughts. Bill was reading from Philippians chapter four. She listened intently, as he read the words she had covered herself just days ago. That was an interesting coincidence. Or maybe not. If God meant for Bill to read those verses, what did that mean? *God, am I supposed to trust You for this situation with Seth?*

Be anxious for nothing flitted through her mind.

She was still pondering this when she heard a horse gallop up outside. A murmur ran through the congregation, and people had already started to turn around before the door was thrown open.

One of the loggers stood in the doorway, breathing hard.

"Fire's broken out at the logging camp, and it's headed toward town!" He ran back out as the congregation came alive.

She turned toward Seth. He and Josh were already on their feet. He met her gaze and stretched over Maggie until his face was inches from Becca's. She could see the tension clouding his eyes and etching fine lines around his mouth. "Go to Maggie's and stay there. I'll be back when I can." He kissed her quickly and turned to leave.

"Seth!" She had to say something before he left.

He stopped and turned back.

She wanted to say *I love you*, but the words caught in her throat. The moment stretched, and she knew he was anxious to leave. "Be careful."

He nodded and followed Josh and the other men out the door.

She watched him leave, her feelings a mixture of relief and regret. She turned to Maggie, heaviness falling on her like a blanket.

Maggie reached over and patted her hand. "Let's pray. That's the best thing we can do right now."

The other women, many looking as lost as she felt, gathered around them as they knelt in prayer. She didn't know how long they were there, but they didn't leave until each woman who wanted to had lifted her heart to God and a soft peace flowed through the room.

"You're all welcome to come to the boardinghouse if you don't care to wait alone," Maggie told the women as they rose to leave. A few nodded, but she could tell most wanted desperately to see how close the fire was to their homes.

When she stepped outside, a dark black column was rising from the mountains. Her stomach churned. Jeremiah McCormick was surely behind this. If his battle with Seth and her cost the town, people uninvolved in the fight would pay the price. The price would be too high.

She and Maggie didn't speak as they walked back to the

boardinghouse. Sally was with them, but James had gone with the men. Becca couldn't keep her eyes off the column of smoke or repress the tinge of guilt in her heart. Unexpectedly, anger welled up. Mr. McCormick, had ruined too many things for her. This would be the end. He had already done too much damage. She'd have no trouble shooting the man if he showed his face to her at this moment.

They went inside and changed out of their Sunday clothes into work clothes. They laid dinner on the table, but none of them did much more than pick at their food.

"Maybe we should walk toward your homestead and see how far the fire's progressed." Maggie picked up the untouched food from the table.

That sounded just like the antidote to her restlessness. "I *would* like to see if my home is threatened—" She broke off, remembering what Seth had asked her to do. While she was certain she could get to and from her house with no danger, and he would probably never even know, she knew how angry and hurt he'd be if he found out. It wasn't a matter of obedience—he wasn't her husband yet so she didn't necessarily owe him that—but one of respect. If she was choosing a future with Seth, she had to respect his judgment about certain things, realizing that he was only doing it to protect her. If she wanted Seth to know she trusted him, she had to do what he asked.

"I can't. Seth asked me to stay here."

Maggie nodded and gave Becca a look she couldn't quite interpret. "I think that's probably best anyway."

They put away the rest of the food and tried to relax in the parlor, but one of them was looking out the windows every few minutes. She thought her nerves would be worn to a nub if she didn't hear some news soon.

The parlor darkened. Both women moved to look out the window but couldn't see what it was.

"Maybe it's a rain cloud," Maggie suggested hopefully. "That would sure be an answer to prayer."

She went out through the kitchen and stood on the back porch steps. The sky to the west was clear, but the smoke cloud had spread out across the sky in the east and overhead and blocked out the sun. She couldn't tell if the clouds that had hung over the mountains that morning were still there.

Staring at the smoke-filled sky, it took her a moment to realize that the wind wasn't coming around the house anymore but was blowing in her face. It lifted the damp tendrils off her temples. She closed her eyes and enjoyed the cooling sensation for a moment.

When she opened them, she thought she saw something along the ridge. The smoke was now blowing toward them, stinging her eyes and carrying the scent of burning wood towards her. She saw it again. Light flickered along the ridge and a moment later, the rim glowed red.

He is not going to win. He is not! She clinched her fists until her nails dug into her palms. McCormick was trying to take everything from her. He took her brother and her house. Now Seth was in danger because of him and so was Maggie's house. She wasn't going let him have it. She rubbed at the tears on her face. It stopped here.

She turned and ran back inside. "Maggie!" She ran into Maggie as she was coming into the kitchen. "The wind's shifted. The fire's crested the ridge and is heading this way."

Maggie stepped around Becca and onto the back porch. When she turned around, her mouth was set in a tight line. "Becca, I'm going over to the Johnsons' to see if we can borrow their plow and mule for a fire break. Sally," The girl was immediately at Maggie's side. "Gather up all the gunny sacks and blankets you can find. Look in the barn, too. Take them down to the creek and soak them. Becca, fill every bucket we have with water and set them around the house."

Ash was falling heavily by the time Becca headed to the creek with her first load of buckets. The smoke had blotted out the sky. It looked more like dusk than midday. She couldn't even see the fire on the mountain for the thickness of the smoke in that direction.

Back and forth from the boardinghouse to the creek, she and Sally hurried with their buckets and blankets.

Something stung her cheek. Becca set down her buckets and brushed at her face. Then she saw a glowing ember floating through the air. A few had landed on the ground ahead of her but were burning out as they landed. Where was Maggie? Shouldn't she be back yet? Several glowing embers drifted towards the roof.

Her stomach plummeted to her feet. She couldn't do this. The fire was too much. Her efforts were futile; their few buckets couldn't stop a forest fire. She wanted to be back in Salem, pouring over books, doing research. If she had stayed there, none of this would have happened.

She tried to take a deep breath and coughed on the smoke. But she wasn't in Salem, she was here. It might be too much, but she at least had to try. This—these people—were all she had left, and she needed to fight for them. She pushed the panic aside and prayed for help. *I can do all things through Christ which strengtheneth me.*

"Sally, take one of those gunny sacks and try to get any of the embers that land in the dry grass." The girl nodded and quickly began keeping a lookout in the yard.

Becca ran into the house, lifted her skirts, and took the stairs two at a time. Grabbing several handkerchiefs from her drawer, she ran back downstairs. Outside, she soaked them in the water.

"Here." She wrung one out and handed it to Sally. "Tie it over your nose and mouth."

Becca went into the barn and heard the horses whinny and nicker at her. They were restless in their stalls. As much as she would have liked to soothe each of them, she didn't have time.

She grabbed the ladder, wrestled it out the door and carried it back to the house. She leaned it up against the porch then hurried around back to grab a wet gunnysack. Back out at the ladder, she hiked up her skirts, tucked them into her waistband, and climbed to the porch roof.

Gingerly, she crawled up the roof and to the ridge until she could straddle it. The rough shakes tore her stockings and scratched her skin. She was thankful the embers weren't falling too fast. Mostly it was ash, but there were a few burn marks on the roof. She scooted along the ridge with her gunnysack, using it to smack glowing embers as they landed.

Seth would have a fit if he saw her up there, but she saw no other choice. She was mindful that, if she fell, they would lose an able-bodied person. Maggie and Sally couldn't fight the fire alone.

After a few minutes, she saw Maggie coming up the road from the Johnsons'.

"Be careful!" she yelled to Becca.

"I am!" Becca shouted back down. She noticed Maggie had tied her handkerchief around her nose and mouth as well. From her position, she watched Maggie hitch the Johnsons' mule to the plow and start making furrows behind the boardinghouse. The first were a little crooked but after a couple turns, they looked as good as any farmer's. Where Maggie had learned to plow like that? It didn't seem easy.

She alternately watched Maggie and slapped out glowing embers. Ash fell like rain, and after being burned by embers landing on her clothes, Becca slapped her shirtwaist and skirt with the gunnysack until they were thoroughly damp.

Maggie had turned over a wide swath of dirt from the sides and back of the house to the creek. Becca saw her standing at the edge of the creek, looking toward the mountain before calling up to Becca.

"Can you come down and help me get this plow across the creek?"

Becca nodded and gingerly retraced her steps off the roof. A moment later, the two of them lifted the plow over the creek while Sally led the mule across by its bridle.

"Just to be on the safe side, I'm going to plow a firebreak here too. This creek isn't big enough to stop a fire that size."

A gust of wind blew an opening in the heavy smoke. Becca caught a glimpse of the wall of fire eating its way down the mountain. It was halfway down. Nothing stood between it and them except trees and grass.

Her breath caught. Tears welled up and she swallowed hard. Their pitiful buckets of water and gunny sacks would do nothing against that blaze. Her hands shook as she scanned the area for the best escape route.

Her gaze was drawn to Maggie as she turned over a fresh ribbon of dirt. This was Becca's home now, for better or worse. This was her family. They needed her. She had to keep fighting until she couldn't fight anymore. *God, I can't do this without You. Help me!*

Owen Taylor sat on a rock overlooking Reedsville. He took a swig of water from his canteen. It was sweet and cold from the stream, but it wasn't coffee. The day was already hot, so the cool water felt good going down, but somehow the day didn't seem to start right without coffee. But it was too dry to start a fire, so he would do without. He hadn't needed a fire to keep him warm last night; his bedroll had been fine for the warm night. But he sure wished he had a fresh pot of coffee.

At first he thought he was imagining it, that the thought of coffee had made him think he smelled something. But a moment later the smell grew stronger. He looked around, scooting out farther on the rock to see both ends of the small valley that nestled Reedsville. Then he saw it to the east: a column of smoke rising from the mountain. Right above the logging camp.

Just what they'd feared most this summer. The logger in him responded. He jumped to his feet, trying to think of how he could help save whatever could be saved, knowing, even as he was thinking about it, there was no way he could get there in time to be any use.

So McCormick had done it without him. Either he had done it himself or he had Elmer do it.

He slapped his hat on his knee. "How could I have been so stupid? I thought if I told him I wouldn't do it that it would be the end of it." He should have known McCormick would find a way to get what he wanted.

He packed up his bedroll and gathered his things into his bag, not knowing where he was going, but needing to do something anyway. He wasn't going to sit here on this rock and watch his town burn.

BECCA CLIMBED BACK on the roof. An equal mixture of ash and embers fell from the sky now. The dirt behind the boardinghouse didn't provide fuel for the embers falling there, so Sally had moved closer to the barn to put out embers.

Becca looked up at the barn roof. It was covered with the same shake shingles as the boardinghouse, but there was no way for her to reach it. It was already pock-marked with burns.

If the roof caught fire they'd never get all the horses out in time, let alone the stage. They could replace the wagon and buggy, but the horses were the livelihood of this group of people. If they lost the stage, they lost the collateral on the loan. Both the Oregon Express and the logging company would be gone. Seth would never forgive himself.

"Sally!" She scooted near the edge of the porch roof. "Hand me those buckets of water. I'm going to try to soak this roof."

Sally climbed up several rungs and handed the buckets up to Becca. She leaned over the edge of the porch roof to grab them. By the time they had emptied every bucket over the roof,

Maggie had finished plowing and had begun refilling the buckets.

Becca climbed down. Her arms shook from hauling up the heavy buckets and tossing them onto the roof, but she couldn't rest. A sense of urgency crackled through her like lightning. "We've got to get the horses and stage out of the barn."

Maggie nodded. "Let's get the mule and plow back here, then we can take the animals down the creek a ways."

Sally dashed around fighting the embers that now fell fast and furious all around. Most died out from lack of fuel, but occasionally one would ignite. Sally would pounce with a damp gunnysack and put an end to it.

Becca and Maggie wrestled the plow into the back of the wagon and tied the mule to the back, then moved to the barn. They got bridles on the horses as quickly as they could; the animals were upset. After pulling her handkerchief down, Becca whispered to them as she put on the tack.

"What are we going to do with them once they're outside?"

Maggie shook her head. "The creek's not wide enough to give them any protection. The best we can do is give them a chance to run for their safety."

This couldn't be their only option. There had to be a better solution. She thought for a minute. Where would the creek be wide enough to offer protection?

An image of Seth comparing her eyes to the deepest part of his fishing pond flashed in her mind. "Have you seen Seth and Thomas's secret fishing pond? It's to the north a bit, between here and my place. It's not very deep, but it should be far enough from the fire to keep the animals safe."

Maggie smiled. "So that's where those boys would sneak off to."

"What about the stage?"

Maggie sighed. "I don't know that we can do anything about it."

Anger surged through Becca. McCormick was not going to

win. "We have to save it. There's no Oregon Express without the stage." Desperation laced her words. She had to do this for Seth. Taking a breath, she consciously lowered her voice and met Maggie's gaze. "And without the stage, there's no logging company."

"He told you about the loan."

"Yes."

Becca held Maggie's gaze until she slowly nodded. "All right. Here's what we'll do." Maggie outlined her plan while they got bridles on the rest of the horses.

Becca led a horse outside the barn to the waiting wagon. She tied it to the back, next to the mule. She went back inside the barn where Maggie was hitching up the buggy. After pulling it outside, they tied two more horses to the back.

Maggie stared at the stage inside the barn. "I've never hitched up the stage before."

Becca came and stood beside her.

"Well," Maggie started toward the stage. "It shouldn't be too different than the wagon, especially since we're only using two horses instead of six." Between the two of them, they managed to get the stage hitched up and outside the barn.

Sally ran around the yard smacking embers with an unflagging spirit.

"That's my girl. Keep it up." Maggie dropped her hands to her hips and surveyed the barn behind her. "We should grab what tools we can, and some feed, and throw it in the stage."

They grabbed what they could, wrestling the huge feed bags between the two of them. Hurry! Hurry! Hurry! But Becca's body wouldn't move any faster. Maggie's arms were shaking as badly as her own, and they both panted heavily. They leaned against the outside of the coach to catch their breath.

A clock ticked inside her. Time was running out; it moved faster than she could. They weren't going to make it, so why even bother? Just quit.

She shoved those thoughts aside. She had to try.

With shaky arms, she pushed away from the stage.

Maggie did, too. “I'll have Sally drive the buggy. You take the wagon; I've got the gentlest team hitched to it. I'll drive the stage. Let's take some supplies with us just in case.”

Becca knew what Maggie was thinking. *Just in case the fire gets here before we get back.*

SETH YANKED a whipsaw back and forth with one of his men. The loggers were trying to creating more open space by felling trees. The farmers and other men from town came behind them, plowing up the open land to create a firebreak between the burning logging camp and the outskirts of the town.

Wiping his sleeve across his forehead, he stepped back to watch the tree fall precisely where they had planned. With his bandana tied around his face, he couldn't use it to mop his brow. He hadn't worked a saw in a while, but he hadn't lost his touch. His shoulders ached from the strain, but he couldn't stop now. There would be no rest for anyone.

Josh—his broken arm keeping him from swinging an axe or handling a saw—directed the movements of the men, sending teams with shovels to where the embers fell the fastest and assigning townsmen to help the loggers. Since the wind had shifted, the flames approached at an angle rather than rushing head on. It was the only break they'd gotten all day. He was surprised they'd even gotten that.

Hauling the whipsaw back and forth in a familiar rhythm, Seth kept up a stream of prayers. He hadn't stopped praying, but lately it seemed his prayers disappeared like smoke up a chimney. Was God deliberately trying to pull everything he valued out of his life? His best friend. His company. Becca.

His gaze momentarily left the sawcut and tracked to the fire a moment, while he tried to predict where it would go next. He couldn't blame God for Becca. That was his own fault; he should have come clean with her. He had been afraid of losing her, but he'd lost her now. At least if he had told her himself, he would have had a chance.

Another quick glance showed a finger of the fire looked like it was edging around the far end of their break. He released the saw handle and started toward Josh, but he'd already seen it and was directing men to get on it.

So far, it looked like they were going to save the town. Seth was glad, but the fire had already swept through and completely destroyed his logging camp. That left a bottomless ache in his chest.

Bending over and feeling his back ache, he picked up his canteen from the ground where he'd tossed it. Pulling down his bandana, he took a long drink, not caring that it tasted faintly of ashes. He recapped the canteen and scanned the area the fire had already been through. *God, where are You? Haven't I always served You? What kind of punishment is this? I thought You wanted to bless me, to give me an abundant life.* He kicked at the ground. Tears stung his eyes. Yeah, it was just the smoke.

Chapter Forty

The smoke hung heavy but was blowing away from Owen toward the south. He'd cut across the ridge, thinking he knew where McCormick might be. The words of that circuit preacher, Preacher Adams, had rung through his head during his trek across the mountain. Up until today, he did think he was a good person. Well, he'd felt a bit guilty about what he was doing to Seth Blake, which was why he repeatedly declined his invitations to church and Sunday dinner.

But he didn't gamble, drink, or carouse with women. He'd never killed anybody. A chill ran up his spine. Unless his involvement with McCormick ended up killing someone today. Then Owen didn't think he could live with himself. Regardless, he realized he was a sorry excuse for a man. Or in Preacher Adams's words, a sinner. God surely wouldn't let Owen Taylor in to His heaven.

He came up on McCormick's goldmine. He was careful with his steps, even though he was certain the distant roar of the fire and the shouts of men floating up would cover any noise he made. But he also knew McCormick didn't leave anything to chance.

He stood in the woods and watched the buildings—shacks

really—for any sign of movement. They'd all probably fled at the first sign of the fire.

But where could McCormick go? Surely even he wasn't bold enough to stay in Parsons's Hotel while the fire he set burned the town down. Of course, McCormick probably figured no one would know he set the fire.

A low moan rose above the other sounds. Owen looked to see if the wind was blowing open any doors. No, they were all shut. He heard it again. Could it be an animal? He carefully moved toward the sound. It was coming from the bunkhouse. Sneaking closer, he pressed himself against the side of the building. The sound was coming from inside, and it was definitely human. He peered in the window and saw a man lying face down on a bunk. He strode over to the door and opened it. The smell of burnt flesh filled his nostrils.

THEIR LITTLE CARAVAN started off down the road toward Becca's homestead, Maggie leading the way and Becca bringing up the rear. She hadn't thought about her house until this moment and wondered if it would burn again. It couldn't be helped. They had to save the boardinghouse first. She could always rebuild her house again.

They pulled off the road before they reached the cutoff to her house and started the trek across the meadow. The wagon jostled and lurched. She risked a glance over her shoulder. they couldn't afford to lose any of their supplies.

The stagecoach swayed widely as it crossed the meadow, but it was built for rough terrain, and the horses were used to pulling it. Sally's buggy, having very little weight, was no problem for her horse to pull, but the buggy bounced over every rut and hill. Becca feared Sally would be tossed out.

The wagon had the most difficult time, being the heaviest. Several times Becca had to yell to the team and slap the reins across their backs to encourage them to pull the wagon out of a hole.

It was none too soon for her when they reached the pond. Maggie slowed as she came up to it, spoke to the team and then took the stagecoach into the pond. The horses seemed to take the water in stride and pulled steadily. The water rose past the bottom of the stagecoach but not much higher. In a moment, Maggie was urging the horses out the far side of the pond, water pouring off the stagecoach. She climbed down from the driver's seat and unhitched the horses.

Sally and Becca pulled up at the edge of the pond and unhitched their animals. Then they untied the animals at the back and slapped their rumps, trying to drive them into the pond. They might not stay there, but at least the women had given them the best chance they had to survive the fire.

The trio trudged back to Maggie's in silence. Becca's every step was a monumental effort of muscles and bones too tired to go on. Maggie and Sally had to be exhausted, too, though neither said anything.

As they drew closer to the spot where they'd be able to see the boardinghouse, Becca's stomach fluttered. No one spoke, but every eye strained to see. The air crackled with the tension of whether the next bend would reveal if their world as they had known it had been destroyed or still stood.

The boardinghouse still stood. The weight on Becca's shoulders evaporated like sun burning off morning dew. Renewed by hope, the group picked up their pace.

They were back into the thick ash and falling embers. Pulling their handkerchiefs back over their faces, they all slapped at their clothes more frequently. Too bad they hadn't thought to take a dip in the pond themselves.

Hurrying to get to the wet gunnysacks, Becca noticed small fires beginning to burn from the embers. Stomping on them to put them out, she was looking at the ground and didn't look up until she heard Maggie's gasp. She turned, saw Maggie's wide eyes, and spun around to see what she was looking at: a small fire on the barn roof.

Becca picked up her skirts and ran the remaining distance to the barn, with Sally close behind her. In seconds, the three of them grabbed the buckets of water they had left and ran to the barn.

Becca tossed the water from her bucket toward the roof, but the water only splashed halfway up and ran down the walls. Grunting, she tried again with the same results. She dropped the bucket and ran for the ladder still leaning against the porch, passing Sally who was back at work with her gunnysack putting out the little fires that were springing up.

Maggie carried two buckets to the barn as Becca leaned the ladder against it. "Becca, don't! It won't work."

She climbed the ladder. "I know I can't reach the roof, but maybe I can get the water closer from here."

Reluctantly, Maggie handed her a bucket and then held the ladder steady. Becca got her balance. She tried to toss the water in an arc over her head. Most of it got on the roof before it came cascading down on her head. But her aim was off and the water had missed the flames. They were growing by the minute.

"Let's move the ladder closer."

"No. I'm not going to let you do that. Any closer and you could get burned."

Becca relented and took the next bucket Maggie handed up to her. Adjusting her aim, this time she was rewarded with the hiss as the water hit the fire. A grin spread across her face, hoping bubbling up.

But it was short lived as the flames sprang back to life.

"Sally! Bring more water!" Maggie tossed two buckets in Sally's direction.

Sally grabbed them and ran to the stream. Maggie handed the last bucket to Becca and held on to the ladder.

She slung the water over the roof again. The flames retreated slightly. She craned her neck to see how far the flames had spread where the water hadn't reached. They were creeping down the far side of the barn roof. She willed Sally to hurry with the water.

The girl lugged a bucket in each hand. Her quick steps caused the water to slosh out the top and on her dress. Sally worked hard, not letting the fear Becca saw on her face immobilize her. Becca watched her with admiration. She didn't know many adults, let along young women, who could work so relentlessly in the face of such danger.

Sally dropped the buckets at her mother's feet and hurried off to fill others. Maggie handed one to Becca.

She looked over the roof again, trying to catch the spreading edge of the flames. She needed to be a bit father over. Jamming her leg against the ladder to counterbalance her weight, she arced the bucket over her head, reaching out beyond the ladder to throw water at the growing flames. Her momentum carried her away from the ladder. She dropped the bucket and scrambled to catch the ladder. She missed.

Falling, she couldn't catch herself. The ground slammed her hip. Her ankle caught in the ladder rung and pulled the ladder on top of her. Her ankle twisted with a sickening pop and pain shot through her whole leg.

Maggie immediately knelt at Becca's side. "Here, lay still and let me get this ladder off you." Maggie eased the ladder off Becca until her foot was free.

Her leg burned, but a quick glance told her it was her injury, not burning embers, causing the pain. Still, if she could manage at all. . . She tried to sit up. "We've got to get back up there, Maggie. We've got to save the barn."

"Hush. Let me look at your ankle." Becca grimaced as Maggie unlaced her boot and tugged it off, taking her stocking off next. Becca's foot was swelling and turning purple. Maggie probed Becca's ankle with her finger. "Can you move it at all?"

She gingerly flexed and pointed her foot slightly. "I can, but it hurts."

Maggie glanced up. Becca followed her gaze. Flames totally engulfed the barn roof. Her stomach turned leaden. Tears filled her eyes. She fell back on the ground. They couldn't do it. They couldn't save the barn. It would be a total loss. Why, God? All that hard work for nothing.

"We did the best we could, Becca. We saved the animals and the stage. Now, let's get you out of here."

Sally came over. Between her and Maggie, they lifted Becca up, and helped her hobble to the back porch. They settled her on the steps.

"Sally, get a wet cloth for Becca's ankle and some towels to prop up her foot." Maggie met Becca's gaze. "I don't suppose I can convince you to go inside?"

Becca shook her head.

"I didn't think so." Maggie stood up and hurried over to the burning barn. She pulled the ladder away from the flames.

Sally returned and sat on the steps near Becca's foot. She wrapped it with a wet cloth and then propped it up on the towels.

Becca watched Maggie carry the ladder across the yard.

"Is that okay?" Sally glanced up at Becca, patting her foot.

She nodded.

Maggie leaned the ladder against the porch. With a wet gunnysack, she took up Becca's former position on the roof.

A loud pop came from the barn, and they all watched as it swayed with a groan and then collapsed with an enormous crash and a shower of sparks.

Becca pulled off the handkerchief covering her face, just now noticing her hands stung. There were a few minor burns and abrasions across them. Tears poured down her cheeks. Her leg hurt, her hands hurt, the barn was gone How many more losses would they endure today? The men? The town? She didn't even try to stop the tears .

Chapter Forty-One

Seth was conferring with Josh where best to fight the fire next when he heard a horse gallop up behind him. He turned to see Andrew Paige ride up.

"Blake! Benson! Thought you might want to know the wind's shift caused the fire to crest the ridge behind the logging camp. A lot of embers are blowing toward the east side of town." He shifted in the saddle. "I heard someone say they think the boardinghouse is on fire."

Seth ran for his horse, Josh on his heels.

"James!" Seth gestured for him to come with them.

They swung up on their horses and headed down the hill. Seth wanted to ride hard, but it was impossible to see more than a few hundred feet in front of them due to the heavy smoke and ash. His muscles tightened and he leaned forward in his saddle.

He had told Becca to stay at Maggie's. He hoped, for once, she hadn't listened to him. *God, please. Don't let anything happen to her!* He hoped she, Maggie and Sally had gotten away. But he had a hard time imagining any of them leaving the house to burn without trying to fight to save it.

A glow seemed to beckon them from a distance. It took a

few seconds before Seth realized it was fire. His gut wrenched and a sick feeling washed over him. He prayed it wasn't the boardinghouse. Looking over at Josh, he saw his mouth pulled into a tight line.

He touched his heels to the flanks of his shying and sidling horse, urging her forward. A moment later, flames appeared out of the smoke, farther back from the road than if the boardinghouse were on fire. Relief washed through him.

But if the boardinghouse was safe, that meant the fire came from the barn. A sick feeling filled his mouth. The stagecoach, the horses, all gone. And if the women had tried to fight it…

His shoulders dropped, the reins fell slack. There was nothing left. His horse, no longer being pushed forward, stopped in the road.

Josh rode up next to him. They sat in silence, watching the flames consume both their futures. McCormick had won. He'd beaten Seth and dragged down Josh and Maggie with him.

"We can't do anything about the barn." The words tasted like the ash that fell around them. Seth couldn't look at Josh. Couldn't handle seeing the accusation or disappointment in his best friend's eyes.

"Let's go see if the women are still at the boardinghouse." Through the smoke, they could see that it still stood and didn't appear to be burning anywhere yet.

They had just nudged their horses forward when they were stopped by a yell. "Hey, boys!"

Josh pointed to the roof of the boardinghouse. Maggie was straddling the roof ridge with a wet gunnysack.

Seth couldn't get any words past the knot in his throat.

"Maggie! Are you okay?" Josh shouted.

"We're fine, but we could use your help."

The tightness loosened in Seth's chest. He caught Maggie's *we*. She had to be including Becca; the alternative was unthinkable. He nudged his horse again, scanning the area until he spotted Becca on the back porch steps. Her foot was propped up on towels with a cloth over it. Except for clean streaks down each of her cheeks, her face was nearly black with soot.

The desire to slide off his horse, run over to her, and take her in his arms made his legs quake.

But he couldn't. It wouldn't be fair to either of them. He'd disappointed her too many times, and even though she was alive, his actions had taken everything else from her.

Josh could handle things here. Seth would try to make some small amends for the disaster he had created. He tugged on the reins and wheeled his horse away.

Owen Taylor watched as the loggers' families set up camp near the schoolhouse. He didn't know if anyone knew he was missing, but he didn't want to take any chances. He couldn't let anything get in the way of the job he had to do. When he was sure no one was looking, he walked toward the center of town, avoiding Main Street by sticking to the alleys behind the buildings.

When he reached the Oregon Express office, he ducked inside. As he expected, Ben was behind the counter. "Hey Owen. Glad to see you're safe. How's the fight going up there?"

He didn't want to waste time explaining anything, but he knew it'd be faster to give Ben some sort of an answer. "Uh, it's going pretty good. Hey, has that sheriff Josh wired for come into town yet?"

"Yep. Rode in this morning. He was helping put out burning embers earlier, but last I heard he was over at the bank talking to Wilkins."

"Thanks, Ben. I'll try to track him down there."

Owen left the stage office and crossed the street to the bank. He walked in to find the sheriff talking to Wilkins. The sheriff watched Owen as he came toward them.

"Sheriff? My name's Owen Taylor. I hear you're looking for Jeremiah McCormick. I know where he is."

Wilkins's face paled. He began fiddling with papers on the counter. The sheriff studied Wilkins for a moment then turned back to Owen.

"You do? Where?"

"He's up at a goldmine he has north of the logging camp."

"Can we get past the fire to get up there?"

"I came across the ridge and down through the west of town. But the fire's pretty well burned out through the logging camp, so we could cut through there. It'll save us some time."

"Let's go. Wilkins, don't go anywhere. I want to ask you some questions when I get back."

If Becca had any emotions left, her heart would have broken. Now, she was just numb. Her heart had lightened when Seth rode up, knowing he was safe. She was certain he was going to dismount, come over, and pull her into his arms. Then she could tell him what she hadn't been able to at the church: she loved him.

Instead, he had looked at her with hollow eyes and a clenched jaw, and ridden away.

She wiped the tears from her face with the back of her hand and noticed the soot. She pulled the wet cloth off her ankle and used it to scrub her face. The cloth was black in no time, and she had a hard time finding a clean spot on it to finish wiping the soot off her face.

She pulled the towel away to see Josh standing in front of her.

"They've set up a camp for the loggers and their families at the school. I bet you could find Seth there."

She looked at him for a moment, trying to decide what to

do. It didn't take long. She was going after Seth, even if her pride took a beating. She regretted not telling him she loved him at the church. She wasn't going to live with any more regrets.

"If you can figure out how to get me there, I'll go."

"Okay." He left and reappeared a moment later leading his horse next to the steps she sat on. "It's not going to be real lady-like, but it'll get the job done."

"I think ladylike left a long time ago."

Josh laughed. "Can you put weight on your good leg?"

"I think so."

He shortened the stirrups on the saddle before climbing the steps. He slid his arm under her shoulders and lifted her up to stand on her good foot. "I'm going to pick you up. Put your good foot in the stirrup, and I'll help you swing over the horse."

In two seconds Becca sat astride Josh's horse. She gingerly rested her sore foot in the stirrup. It throbbed now that it was no longer elevated. Josh had made the stirrup on that side shorter so her skirts hid her foot. She took a deep breath. She could do this. She *had* to do this.

Josh smiled at her. "Godspeed, Becca." He turned to go inside, but as he did she heard him mutter, "I *am* turning into a meddling old woman."

SETH WAS HAMMERING a tent peg in the ground when, out of the corner of his eye, he saw someone ride up. He turned to look. Becca? His heart lifted for a moment before he tamped it back down. He dropped the hammer and strode over to her. What did she think she was doing riding a horse?

He grabbed the horse's bridle. It was Josh's mare. How had she talked him into being part of this? "What are you doing out here? You're hurt. You need to be at Maggie's resting."

Her face was pale and perspiration beaded her upper lip. She must be in a lot of pain. He took the reins from her and tied them around the hitching rail in front of the schoolhouse. Reaching up, he pulled her out of the saddle into his arms. He held her against him a moment, savoring the feel of her in his arms, before starting up the stairs into the schoolhouse. She laid her head on his shoulder and closed her eyes.

Inside, he lowered her to one of the benches, turning her so her legs would stretch out the length of the bench. He looked at her foot. It was swollen, streaked with red and purple. His chest twinged at the sight of it.

He pulled over the teacher's chair from the front of the room and sat close to her, not taking his eyes off her face.

She took a deep breath and opened her eyes. He saw them well up with tears. "I'm so sorry we couldn't save the barn. We tried, but I fell and—" Her voice broke, and she swallowed.

Seth took her hand and rubbed it between his. "Shh. It's okay. I'm just glad you're safe. I was hoping you'd left Maggie's when it started getting dangerous."

Her voice was soft. "You told me not to leave, so I didn't."

He closed his eyes as his chest tightened. "Becca—"

"Maggie plowed a fire break, and we used water and wet gunny sacks to put out the burning embers. I tried to get water to the roof of the barn, but I fell off the ladder."

He clenched his jaw at the picture of her climbing a ladder leaning against the burning barn and balancing a bucket of water. She risked herself for horses? Didn't she know she meant more to him than that?

"Maggie and I worked on saving the horses and coach first. We knew those had to be saved. They were more important than the barn."

Realization dawned on him. She hadn't done it for the horses. She had done it for him.

He brought her soot-covered, blistered hand up to his lips and pressed a kiss on it. "Thank you." He'd lost everything. But that would be bearable with her in his life. She believed in him, and that was all he needed.

"I supposed we should have stayed with the horses, since we couldn't save the barn. At least this wouldn't be hurting." She gestured to her foot.

Seth furrowed his brow. "What are you talking about? You couldn't have stayed in a burning barn. You did the best you could."

Becca looked at Seth blankly for a moment. He started to reassure her again—although the thought of those animals suffering just about did him in—when she stopped him.

"I didn't tell you, yet, did I?"

"Tell me what?"

She smiled at him, eyes dancing. "Your secret fishing spot isn't a secret anymore. The horses are there."

Seth blinked, thinking he was hearing things. "The horses are in the pond?"

"The stagecoach and wagon and buggy, too."

As her words sunk in, his muscles got watery, and he about fell off the bench. The tightness in his chest broke free. He loved this woman! He leaned over and held her head with both hands before pulling her to him, kissing her solidly on the lips. He pulled away for a moment and then kissed her again.

"You're wonderful."

Becca looked at him and traced his jaw with her finger. "I'm glad we could save the horses and stagecoach. But that's not what I came to tell you."

His eyes searched her face. "It's not?"

She shook her head and bit her lip. "I wanted to tell you that I don't blame you in any way for Thomas's death."

He started to speak, but she put her finger over his lips. "Just listen. I do wish you had told me sooner so you didn't have to carry that burden all alone for so long." She laid her hand on his cheek. "I love you. I want you to always be a part of my life."

He placed his hand over hers and turned his face to press a

kiss into her palm. Then he pulled her into his arms and held her tightly. Tears pricked his eyes. She was amazing; he didn't deserve her. But he was grateful. *Thank You, Lord.*

He stroked her hair until he was certain he could speak without his voice cracking. "I love you too, Becca. You have no idea how much."

Chapter Forty-Two

Later that evening, with the threat of the fire behind them due to the successful firebreak and a wind shift that blew the fire back on itself, Becca sat in the kitchen combing out her wet hair. The women had bathed while the men went to fetch the animals from the pond. Maggie had ordered them to dunk themselves while they were at it or she'd never get the soot out of the sheets.

Becca heard a knock on the front door and then voices and footsteps. A moment later, Seth walked into the kitchen. His hair was still wet, too, and he had changed into clean clothes. "The sheriff's here. He wants to tell us what he found."

Seth bent over Becca and scooped her into his arms. He smelled like soap. "What are you doing?" She couldn't keep the smile out of her voice. She didn't really care why he was picking her up.

He brushed his lips over hers. "Taking you to the parlor so you can hear everything he has to say." He carried her into the parlor and set her down on the sofa. He found a footstool for her ankle and then sat next to her.

Josh brought in extra chairs as the sheriff and Owen Taylor came in.

Becca's breath hitched. Where had Owen come from? She glanced at Seth, but he just shrugged and shook his head slightly.

"Sheriff, Owen, can I get you something cool to drink?" Maggie asked.

"Ma'am, that'd be mighty fine."

Maggie went into the kitchen. The men seated themselves.

"Sorry I didn't get here sooner. I was out of town on a case when your wire came in. I got in last night and was headed out here this morning when I heard about the fire. Owen here found me in town and said he knew where McCormick was."

Becca felt Seth sit up straighter. She figured he was wondering, like she was, what Owen's relationship with McCormick was. She hoped they were about to get some answers.

Maggie came out with a pitcher of water and glasses. She handed them out.

"Thank you, ma'am." He took a long drink. "McCormick was holed up in the bunkhouse at his mining camp. He set the fire at the logging camp and in the process burned himself pretty badly. We brought him down and got some salve from Bessie Smith to put on his burns. He's at Parsons's Hotel now. I don't think he'll be going anywhere, but I asked Ben Masters to sit outside his door with a shotgun."

Relief flooded through Becca. It was over. McCormick couldn't hurt them again. Seth reached for her hand and squeezed it.

"Wilkins and Taylor here have given me enough evidence to put him in jail for a long time."

"What kind of evidence?" Josh asked.

"Seems McCormick convinced Wilkins that he could bring money to this town, which would bring more business to Wilkins. He promised he would do all his banking and possibly loans with him, if he helped bring you—" he nodded toward Seth—"down. The faster the better. Wilkins didn't do anything illegal as far as I can tell, but he knows the town won't be too happy with him. He's anxious to make amends and wanted you to know that he'd do whatever you needed to help get the logging company going again."

Becca felt Seth's shoulders relax as he leaned back into the sofa.

"Can I get you something to eat, Sheriff? Owen?" Maggie asked.

Owen shook his head. He hadn't said anything this evening but kept his gaze mostly on the floor, shifting in his chair from time to time.

"No thank you, ma'am." He got to his feet and Owen did the same. "I'm headed back to town to get some shuteye. Looks like you folks are about ready to do the same. You must all be worn out from the fight you took on today."

"True. Thank you, Sheriff." Seth said as he and Josh stood and shook hands with the man.

Owen twisted his hat in his hand. "I'd like to come by and talk to you tomorrow, if I could."

"Sure. We'll be here." Seth closed the door behind their visitors.

THE MEN LEFT EARLY in the morning to look at the damage to the town and logging camp. The lack of rain that summer had made the underbrush dry and contributed to the rapid spread of the fire. The logging camp was destroyed; not a building was left standing. Fortunately, other than a few minor burns, no one from the logging camp was harmed. All of the men and families got out safely, and even the horses and mules were saved.

Josh and Seth led the sheriff up the blackened hill to the ridge where they had spotted McCormick's mine. The wind had shifted yesterday to come from the west as it did most afternoons. It blew the fire back on itself in most places, but here it crested the ridge and burned through his camp before moving on to the wilderness. It had been close when the sheriff and Owen had come for McCormick. They had probably saved his life.

It took a minute for the men to spot the mine. Rocks, dirt, and charred beams covered the entrance.

"Well, that was his mine," Josh pointed out to the sheriff. "You can see how, if it's deep at all, it'll go right back to the logging camp land."

"I'm surprised it collapsed like that," Seth commented. "I wouldn't think a fire would collapse a mine."

"I suspect he didn't shore it up too well," Josh said. "When those outer beams burned, the whole thing just came tumbling down."

"Doesn't look like he'll be doing any mining soon, what with his burns and this collapse." The sheriff looked around a few minutes more and asked a couple of questions about property lines. "All right. I've seen enough."

They headed back to town. Seth couldn't believe that, thanks to the townspeople's efforts and the sheer grace of God, only Maggie's barn and Charlie Lee's shed had burned in town. Next Sunday was sure to be a day of thanksgiving and praise for the Lord's protection.

"Have you thought about my suggestion of finding your own lawman out here?" The sheriff's words interrupted Seth's thoughts. He looked over at Josh.

"We were thinking about Michael Riley. We talked to him about it and he seemed interested." The men told the sheriff about Riley's qualifications and why they thought he'd be a good sheriff.

"It's your town. If this is the man you think you want, I'll go see him after we go back to the hotel. I can make him my deputy while he learns the ropes. Then you folks can hold an election and vote him sheriff if you want."

Josh laughed. "Maybe we can tie it in with Parsons and Benchly's election for mayor."

The sheriff left them at Maggie's. They were putting the horses on pickets when Owen Taylor walked up.

"You want to go in the house to talk?" Seth asked. "Maggie can get us something to eat."

"No, I'd prefer out here, if you don't mind."

Seth nodded and waited for Owen to begin.

"I, uh, I don't rightly know where to start, so I'll just jump in. Last spring, after Thomas turned down McCormick's offer, McCormick sent a letter asking to meet me. Elmer Laughlin was one of McCormick's men. He had been working at the camp and been reporting back to McCormick and had given him my name. McCormick said he needed someone to be his eyes and ears up there, just to let him know what was going on, the morale of the men, and so on. He said he was setting up to do a partnership with you, but if you knew about my involvement, you'd run up the price. McCormick promised me a partnership with him when it was over."

Owen looked at the ground and scuffed his feet in the dirt. "I was jealous of you and Thomas. I had been in logging longer than either of you and wanted to be a partner in the business. I guess Elmer must have told McCormick. He knew just how to get to me."

Seth didn't say anything. The pieces were coming together. He'd been forgiven himself; he couldn't do any less than hear the man out.

"Elmer was the one who set up all the accidents. They both promised me no one would be hurt. I was just supposed to keep you from finding out what was going on. I didn't know Thomas's death was one of their accidents until you told me. That's why I took off. I kept thinking about what that circuit preacher said. I'd always thought I was a good person, but now I'd made a real mess of my life. I tried to make it right as best I could by finding McCormick and telling the sheriff where he was. That's why I'm here. I hope you can forgive me."

Seth stuck out his hand. "Yes."

It took Owen a minute to look up and see Seth's hand. Owen looked from Seth's hand to his face and back to his hand again before grasping it. Seth smiled at him.

"I have a question for you," Josh said. "Do you know how the men that attacked Becca got a photograph of her?"

Owen shoved his hands in his pockets. "I got it for them. I shouldn't have. But when I was at the boardinghouse for Sunday dinner, I saw it in the box of Thomas's things. I didn't think anyone would miss it." He looked up at Seth. "I felt so guilty about it later I couldn't accept any of your invitations to church or dinner. But I know I need to figure out how to make things right with God. I'd like to know more about what Preacher Adams was talking about."

Seth clasped him on the shoulder. "We'll talk."

Becca hadn't been much help to Maggie in cleaning up the ashes and soot that covered every surface of the boardinghouse. Her ankle kept her confined to the sofa in the parlor. She felt guilty not being able to help and was restless at being confined. She was curious about how the town and logging camp had fared and hoped Seth and Josh would return soon with news.

A few minutes later, she heard the men come into the kitchen and she put down her book. As she hoped, Seth came into the parlor.

He lowered himself in the chair across from her. "How's your ankle?"

"Sore. As tired as I was last night, I had a hard time sleeping because it throbbed so much. And you'd think I'd be tired today, but I'm restless and sick of being on this sofa."

He grinned at her. "I think I have just the thing. How'd you like to go out and see your house?"

Hope rose in her. "Could we? I've been wondering about it

all morning." Even though she'd told God that whatever happened, she would accept it, she still couldn't wait to see it.

As the words left her mouth, he bent over and lifted her into his arms.

She laughed and threw her arms around his neck. She loved how he held her close to his chest. With a little sigh, she laid her head on his shoulder as he carried her through the parlor and out the front door. He already had the buggy hitched up and had placed a folded up blanket on the floor to prop up her foot. In a moment, he had her settled in the buggy. And then, slowly so as to not overly jostle her foot, they headed down the road to the homestead.

"What did you find out while you were in town?"

He told her about the mine and what Owen Taylor had told him.

"What about the logging camp?"

"No one was hurt. Even the animals were saved. But everything else is gone. We'll lose some men, but mostly drifters. The good men will stay on, and we'll need them to rebuild the camp." He looked over at her. "You do want to rebuild the camp, don't you?"

She nodded, pleased he was asking her opinion. "Yes. I was willing to let it go if we needed to. Now it looks like we have to start planning for the future."

He told her about the work that needed to be done. The burned logs would have to be culled. Some could be salvaged. They would have to rebuild, but they could be back in operation soon. He gave her the rest of the good news about the town, and soon they were taking the cutoff to her house.

Seth looked over at her. "There's something I've been meaning to ask you about. Remember the day you left for the university? You came back and told me you loved me before you got on the stage."

Becca's cheeks burned. "I'd hoped you'd forgotten about it."

"Forgot about it? Becca, I treasured that. I was so happy to have someone love me like a part of the family. It pleased me that you thought of me like another brother."

She glanced at him sideways. "That wasn't how I meant it."

"I figured that out now. It's why you never came back, isn't it?"

She nodded. "I was too embarrassed. And then it just got easier to stay away, especially since Thomas came to visit me."

Transferring the reins to one hand, he reached over and took her hand. "What you didn't hear was that I said, 'I love you, too, Lil Sis,' in return."

Astonished, Becca looked over at him.

"I missed you. Thomas tried to get me to come see you, but I was too busy with the logging company, and I always assumed you'd be coming home again eventually. If Thomas hadn't died, would you have come home?"

She sighed. "I don't know. I'd like to think I'd be grown up enough to come home. I now know what I would have missed."

He squeezed her hand. The trees edging her clearing stood in front of them. They both fell silent as they waited to see what would appear. As the horse drew them closer, a bit of framing came into view between the trees. Then a bit more. Soon they could see the whole house.

Becca let out a breath she hadn't even been aware she was holding. "It's still there! Can you believe it? It's still there. It looks just fine. Oh, thank You, Lord."

He pulled the buggy to a stop in front of the house. Turning to her, he said, "Should I go look around?"

She nodded, wishing she could go too.

He squeezed her hand again before getting out of the buggy. Her eyes never left him as she watched him tour the house. His boots kicked up soot and ashes as his eyes scanned the wood. Finally, he turned to Becca and grinned. "I don't even see any burn marks from embers."

She clapped her hands and laughed out loud. She felt as if

her future—their future—the thing that had looked so bleak such a short time ago, had been handed back to her.

He got back in the buggy. Taking her hand in his, he gently stroked it with his thumb. He was careful to avoid her burns. She met his gaze. The love she saw in his eyes took her breath away.

"This is going to be a beautiful house," he said softly.

She nodded. Why was he talking about her house when he was looking at her like that? She tried to say something but couldn't find the words. Finally, she choked out, "You built most of it."

"True. But what makes it so beautiful is the woman who will live in it." He lifted his other hand to lightly trail his fingers along her cheek.

She swallowed the lump in her throat and tried to catch her breath.

"I can just picture this house finished. And I can't help but picture myself living here too." He dropped his hand from her cheek and took both of hers in his.

Her thoughts were whirling. What was he saying? He wanted to live in her house? Did he mean—?

"Becca, I love you. I can't imagine my life without you. Will you let me live here with you? Will you marry me?"

So many things rushed into her head she couldn't form a coherent thought. She thought she was going to burst into tears. She couldn't do anything but throw her arms around his neck.

His arms went around her, and he pulled her close. He held her tightly for a moment before pulling back and smiling at her. "You haven't given me an answer yet. And you can't just sit there looking like that and not expect me to kiss you."

She slipped her arm from around his neck and stroked his jaw. "Seth Blake, I love you more than I could ever imagine. And I want to marry you and live in this house you built for me."

He lowered his head and touched his lips to hers, gently at first and then with greater intensity. She threaded her fingers through the hair at the back of his neck. He groaned and pulled her closer to him. After a long moment, he ended the kiss and eased her away from him.

He brushed a curl back from her face—she'd worn her hair down today—and combed his fingers through her hair. He cupped the back of her head and smiled slightly at her before he slanted his lips across hers, thoroughly kissing her again.

She kissed him back with passion and her senses went hazy before he pulled back and loosened his hold on her. It took her a moment to come to her senses. She took her hands down from his neck but left them resting lightly on his chest.

"I have something for you." He picked up her left hand and reached into his breast pocket. Pulling out the gold and garnet ring, he slipped it on her third finger.

Her breath caught as she felt the cool metal encircle her finger. She looked at her hand with awe.

"Oh, Seth, it's beautiful. When—how—?" She wasn't even sure what she was asking.

He held her hand and ran his thumb over the ring. Putting that ring on her finger sealed something between them. "It was my mother's. My father gave it to me when we were in Portland. He figured I'd be asking you soon."

She felt her jaw slacken. She had no idea.

He chuckled at her reaction. Tugging her hand up to his mouth, he kissed her palm.

Epilogue

The stagecoach had never been full of such a group of happy people. James was driving with Josh next to him. Inside, Becca and Seth sat with Maggie and Sally. Seth usually sat up with Josh, but he wasn't complaining. This way he could hold Becca's hand all the way to Portland.

In the two weeks since he'd asked her to marry him, he'd worked like a madman to finish her house. *Their* house, he amended. Two weeks wasn't a lot of time, but he didn't want to wait. Hew new partner, Owen Taylor, had promised to handle things at the camp.

He had surprised Becca with this fact while they were sitting on the porch swing the night they were engaged.

"We need to set a date," he had told her. "And I don't want to wait for the circuit preacher. That could be another month or two."

Her eyes widened a bit, but she didn't object. "What did you have in mind?"

"We could go to Portland and get married in my father's church by Pastor Kendall."

She smiled at the idea. "I'd like that." However, a moment

later, a frown creased her brow. "But what about Maggie and Josh and everyone else?"

"We can load everyone up in the stagecoach." Seth put his arms around her and smiled as she settled back into them.

"When were you thinking we would do this?" she asked.

"Two weeks should be enough time."

BECCA SETTLED back against the stagecoach seat and rolled her eyes as she thought about the previous two weeks. Men had no idea what went into a wedding. Maggie had taken it all in stride. Her house had been a flurry of activity since the day Becca and Seth had announced their engagement.

Some of the townspeople were disappointed to miss the wedding, but most understood. Quite a few of them dropped by to give Becca and Seth their good wishes and leave them gifts to help start their new life together.

Becca wasn't much help the first week with her injured ankle. By the second week, the swelling was going down and the pain had lessened. She concluded it was just a bad sprain and not broken.

Right now it didn't hurt at all. Sitting in the stagecoach next to this wonderful man who loved her, on the way to her own wedding, she didn't feel anything but joy. The last two weeks had been so busy she could hardly think, but now that she was sitting still, it almost didn't seem believable.

Once they arrived in Portland, last-minute details were taken care of. Seth's father, Josiah, worked with Maggie from the second she got off the stagecoach. The two of them—and whomever they could recruit for their plans—worked magic to pull everything off.

The next afternoon, Becca found herself standing in the same hotel room as on her previous trip. She wore the white lawn dress she had bought on that trip and held a bouquet of flowers Maggie and Sally had picked out for her at Ankeny's New Market that morning.

A knock sounded at the door. Becca turned and opened it, thinking it was Josh telling her it was time. Instead, Maggie slipped in, holding something behind her back and smiling.

"I have something for you." She produced a white frothy confection of lace and white silk ribbon.

"Oh, Maggie." Becca willed herself not to cry. She wanted to look beautiful for Seth, not red and blotchy. "It's beautiful. Whenever did you find time to make it?"

"Here and there." Maggie brushed the question off as she lifted the veil over Becca's head and arranged the beautiful lace around her face. Regardless of Maggie's answer, Becca knew the only time Maggie would have had free was late at night. Tears threatened again.

Another knock at the door interrupted her thoughts. She was grateful when Josh came through the door and saved her from tears.

Maggie slipped out, whispering, "I'll see you at the church." Her eyes glistened with unshed tears.

Josh smiled at her and took both of her hands in his. "You look beautiful. Seth's a lucky man." He kissed her softly on the cheek.

She squeezed his hands and smiled back. "I'm pretty lucky too."

He offered her his arm. "Shall we go? The man's almost wearing a hole in the floor waiting for you."

Josh led her downstairs to a carriage waiting to take them to the church. In no time at all, they were standing at the back of the church. She saw more people seated in the pews than she expected. Pastor Kendall stood up front.

But once she saw Seth, she only had eyes for him. She saw the appreciation and love in his eyes, and she couldn't help but return his gentle smile. And before she could think of how she got there, she was at the front of the church. Seth took over from

Josh as her escort, and the two of them were standing in front of the pastor. Was this really happening?

For as long as she lived, Becca would never forget the look in Seth's eyes as he promised to love, honor, and cherish her. In seemingly a brief moment, Pastor Kendall was pronouncing them husband and wife.

Seth lifted her veil. He held her gaze for a moment before cupping her jaw in his hand and kissing her gently.

Two weeks later, the first night in their own home, Seth came in to find their new table was set and candles lit, but Becca was nowhere to be found. He started to head upstairs to look for her when he heard her footsteps on the stairs.

She wore the same amethyst silk dress as when they went to supper on their first visit to Portland. She had piled her hair at the back of her neck, and a few soft ringlets cascaded around her ears. She smiled when she saw him waiting for her at the bottom of the stairs. He took her hands and pulled her to him.

"You look absolutely beautiful. To what do I owe this pleasure?"

She looked up at him. "It's our first night in our new home, and I thought it should be special."

He leaned over and kissed her neck. He meant to stop there, but her skin was so silky and, as the scent of her rose bath oil floated around him, he trailed kisses up her jaw and along her lips.

When he pulled away, he recognized the bemused look in her eyes he had come to know on their honeymoon. He took her hand and led her to their table, holding out her chair for her.

After they finished supper, he pushed his chair back and held out his hand to her. She went to him, and he pulled her into his lap. "Thank you so much, Becca. I'm glad you did this."

She smiled at him, putting her arms around his neck. "I am,

too." She looked away and then looked back at him with a mischievous smile. "Of course, I have to take this dress off before I wash the dishes." She pulled at the skirt of her dress.

He started kissing her collarbone. "I can help you with that," he murmured against her.

She threaded her fingers through his hair. "The dishes?"

He looked up at her. "The dress."

What's next?

Are you curious about what happens to Josh?

And who was the woman in photograph in Thomas's box?

What other adventures await the folks of Reedsville?

Find out by signing up for my latest news and updates at www.JenniferCrosswhite.com/beminefree and you'll get the prequel novella, *Be Mine.*

My bimonthly updates include upcoming books written by me and other authors you will enjoy, information on all my latest releases, sneak peeks of yet-to-be-released chapters, and exclusive giveaways. Your email address will never be shared, and you can unsubscribe at any time.

If you enjoyed this book, please consider leaving a review. Reviews can be as simple as "I couldn't put it down. I can't wait for the next one" and help raise the author's visibility and lets other readers find her.

Keep reading for a sneak peak of book 2 in The Route Home series: *The Road Home.*

Are you curious about what happens to Josh?

AND WHO WAS the woman in photograph in Thomas's box?

WHAT OTHER ADVENTURES await the folks of Reedsville?

FIND out by signing up for my latest news and updates at www.JenniferCrosswhite.com and you'll get the prequel novella, *Be Mine*.

My bimonthly updates include upcoming books written by me and other authors you will enjoy, information on all my latest releases, sneak peeks of yet-to-be-released chapters, and exclusive giveaways. Your email address will never be shared, and you can unsubscribe at any time.

IF YOU ENJOYED THIS BOOK, please consider leaving a review. Reviews can be as simple as "I couldn't put it down. I can't wait for the next one" and help raise the author's visibility and lets other readers find her. Click here to be taken directly to Amazon's review page for this book.

KEEP READING for a sneak peak of book 2 in The Route Home series: *The Road Home*.

Acknowledgments

This book would not be possible without the patience and willingness to read many, many drafts by Diana Brandmeyer, Malia Spencer, and Jenny Cary. Special thanks to Sara Benner for her expert proofreading and Pamela Martinez for her eagle eye! Many thanks to my beta readers!

Much thanks and love to my children, Caitlyn Elizabeth and Joshua Alexander, for supporting my dream for many years and giving me time to write. And to my Lord Jesus Christ for giving me the ability to live out my dreams and directing my paths.

Author's Note

The 1880s was a fascinating time in American history. The country was recovering from its greatest wounding, the Civil War. People were moving West to make new lives for themselves. Progress, in the form of trains, telegraphs, gas, and electricity were making life easier, and new inventions were just around the corner. Out West in particular, women were becoming more independent and taking charge of their own lives, including careers and schooling.

I chose to set this story in Oregon, because I visited there on a trip in high school and fell in love with its beauty. The very kernel of this story started as an AP English project that year. The characters never left me alone and over the years the story grew, morphed, and changed as my writing skills developed. Reedsville is inspired by the real town of Molalla, Oregon, which was the end of the trail and the beginning of a new life for many pioneers of the time.

I hope you have enjoyed this trip back in time as much as I have. Keep reading for a sneak peak of the next book in the series, *The Road Home.*

About the Author

My favorite thing is discovering how much there is to love about America the Beautiful and the great outdoors. I'm an Amazon bestselling author, a mom to two navigating the young adult years while battling my daughter's juvenile arthritis, exploring the delights of my son's autism, and keeping gluten free.

A California native who's spent significant time in the Midwest, I'm thrilled to be back in the Golden State. Follow me on social media to see all my adventures and how I get inspired for my books!

www.JLCrosswhite.com

Twitter: @jenlcross

Facebook: Author Jennifer Crosswhite

Instagram: jencrosswhite
Pinterest: Tandem Services

facebook.com/authorjennifercrosswhite
twitter.com/jenlcross
instagram.com/jencrosswhite
pinterest.com/tandemservices

Preview of *The Road Home*, book two in the Route Home series.

Portland, Oregon ~ October 5, 1881

The wind pushed up white-tipped waves on the water and bent the limbs of the trees lining the Columbia River shoreline. Dark clouds piled up to the south, directly in the path of the ferry Emily Stanton rode on. She paced along the railing of the ferry, tapping her gloved fingers on the top rail, glancing up at the ominous clouds. Up the Columbia, down the Willamette, and soon she'd be in Portland. The rhythmic slapping of the sternwheeler's paddles on the water seemed to echo her restlessness. She turned to pace again—her long strides hampered by her narrow-heeled boots—as if her movement would hurry the boat, when she nearly collided into a man sporting a shiny mustache that matched the coal black of his eyes.

He grabbed her arm to steady her, his fingers grasping her arm a little too tightly through her wool sleeve.

His cologne nearly overwhelmed her. Pulling her head back slightly, she took shallow breaths through parted lips. "Excuse me. I didn't see you."

"That's quite all right." He still held her arm. His eyes gleamed darkly.

A shiver ran up her spine. While he was dressed like a gentlemen, her instincts convinced her he wasn't what he seemed. Considering those instincts had saved her more times than she could count, she pulled away.

He tightened his hold.

"Where are you goin' in such a hurry?" His mouth twisted in an overly-friendly smile.

She pressed her lips into a firm line. "I said, excuse me." She tugged her arm harder, managing to free it from his grasp. She tried to brush past him, but he blocked her way.

"No need to get uppity. Just tryin' to be friendly. No harm in that, right?"

Emily spun and walked the other way, the man's low chuckle following her. Leaving the promenade, she strolled inside the enclosed area of the superstructure. She spotted a seat near an older couple, but she wanted to be left alone and not forced to make polite conversation. There was too much on her mind.

Threading her way through passengers and cargo, she reached her valise. Tucked into a corner, it sat nearly hidden next to a few other bags. She snapped open the faded carpetbag to retrieve a book, but her fingers touched a smooth, hard edge. Sliding it out, she gazed at the eyes in the tintype. Thomas. Lightly tracing the face she whispered, "Soon. I'll be home soon." She looked at the photograph a moment longer before pushing it further back into the bag. Snatching the book she originally came for, she closed her bag.

Making her way back to the couple, she sat next to them on the leather bench and, after a polite nod in their direction, buried herself in the book. Secure behind her book, her thoughts wanted to wander, but she reined them in, forcing herself to concentrate on the words on the page, knowing it was the fastest way to make the time pass.

Emily soon lost herself in the book. The steam whistle blew a seemingly few moments later, startling her. She was here. Her stomach quivered.

The crew called to the passengers to gather their belongings. Closing her book, she retrieved her valise. The catch was open, so she stuffed her book back inside and carefully latched it. It wouldn't do to have her bag come flying open when it got tossed onto the stagecoach.

A slight bump signaled the ferry had moored at the Alder Street wharf, and passengers lined up to cross the lowered bow ramp. After standing in one spot for several minutes, swaying with the movement of the ferry, Emily wondered why no one was moving. She was tired, her valise felt like it was filled with lead, and she was anxious to get off the boat. She switched the bag to her other hand.

Looking around, Emily smiled. This was one time her height gave her an advantage, allowing her to spot the cause of the delay. At the end of the bow ramp, a man questioned each person as they disembarked. She watched as he stopped the men and asked to look through their bags. When he shifted, the sun glinted off his badge.

Emily heard some murmurings among the passengers. Finally, one stopped a crew member hurrying by. "What's going on?"

The burly man stopped mid-stride. "A payroll delivery got held up a few days back, and the sheriff seems to think the robber might be on this ferry."

Passengers' voices grew louder. A man several people in front of Emily wondered aloud who the robber was and if he'd conversed with him on the trip. Emily's heart beat a little faster. She studied the sheriff. Another man wearing a different type of badge stood near him. Portland's marshal, she assumed. The two men would occasionally look at a piece of paper the sheriff held as each man passed by.

Slowly Emily inched her way down to the bow ramp with the rest of the passengers. Ahead she noticed the man she'd run into earlier. He was fingering his collar and shifting his weight from foot to foot. No doubt thinking he had somewhere important to be. As if the rest of them could just stand there all day.

It was the man's turn, and the sheriff and marshal looked repeatedly at the paper they held while questioning him. Their voices were low, and the wind coming off the river caught their words before Emily could hear the them. They examined the man's bag more thoroughly than anyone else's and reluctantly, it seemed to her, sent him on his way. She smirked at his obvious relief and hoped he was late to wherever he needed to be.

The officers moved quickly through the rest of the line. In no time, she found herself walking down muddy Front Street to the horse-drawn streetcar. It would make quick work of the ten blocks to the Oregon Express stage line office, the last leg of her journey home.

Emily hurried down the boardwalk in Portland toward Josh Benson. The last light of the day danced off his brown curls as he strode out of the barn behind the stagecoach office.

Recognition flickered in his eyes. "Emily!" He closed the last few steps between them. "How are you?" His grin caused the dimples she remembered so well to appear in his cheeks.

Pleasure warmed her throughout, surprising her in its intensity. Dropping her valise at her feet, she smiled at him. He was tall. So much so she actually had to tilt her head a bit to meet his gaze. Usually she was at eye-level or above most men. "I'm well. It's good to see you again."

"So has your grandfather recovered?"

Emily's chest constricted at the word grandfather. Ever since she'd known the truth, she couldn't bring herself to call the man that, but she couldn't tell anyone else.

"Uh, yes, he's better. He had the grippe and it took him awhile to recover. But he's back on his feet." Doing what he did best.

"Are you coming back to Reedsville to teach?" Josh asked.

She hesitated. "Yes, for now."

He nodded. "That's great. The town has really missed you."

Her pulse quickened. Had Thomas missed her too? She was so close. "When's the next stage to Reedsville?" She tried to keep her voice calm, but she was sure Josh heard it crack.

He crossed his arms over his chest. "It normally would be tomorrow, but those clouds—" he motioned behind him toward the mountains with a jerk of his head—"have been dark and threatening since yesterday. I suspect it's been raining there pretty steadily today. I'm not sure the roads are in good condition. We had a big fire last summer and the roads are washing out with any amount of rain. Since I don't have any passengers here, I was thinking of waiting a couple of days. It'll probably be the last run for the winter anyhow."

"Oh." She swallowed. "I was hoping you could take me to Reedsville tomorrow."

He was silent for so long, disappointment welled up. She worked to keep her lips tilted up as they wanted to slip down. She'd been gone six months. A few more days wouldn't matter. Still, she'd hoped…

He shifted his weight. "Okay. We'll leave in the morning. But be prepared to be cold and wet."

She wasn't sure she'd heard him correctly. Then her despair turned to elation. "What? Oh, yes. Thank you so much. I really appreciate it, and I know how much of an inconvenience this is for you."

Josh grinned. "I doubt it. But I'd like to get home too. Staying in the city too long makes me antsy."

Twirling a loose curl at her neck, she said, "What time should I be ready to leave in the morning?"

Emily hefted her valise onto the bed. It still felt heavy to her, but maybe she was just tired. A good night's rest should be the cure.

She unpacked her nightgown. Thomas. What would he say when he saw her again? Had his feelings changed? Would he be angry with her? There was no way to know before she got there.

Unless she asked Josh.

No. She discarded that idea immediately. She'd worry about it when she got there. No purpose in stewing about it now.

She sighed and reached in her bag for her book. Maybe reading would get her mind off things and help her settle down to sleep. She dug around, trying to find her book, when her fingers brushed soft leather.

"Oh no," she groaned, "not my work boots." Expecting to pull out a pair of boots ruined by the damp, she grasped the leather and yanked. She gasped and her jaw dropped. It wasn't her boots. It was a soft leather pouch, bulky and fairly heavy.

Confusion swirled through Emily's brain as her fingers fumbled with the leather thong, and she opened the bag. What was it, and how did it get in her bag? Peering inside, she saw what looked like paper. She withdraw a bundle and blinked, not believing what she was seeing: bank notes, issued by the National Bank of Walla Walla.

Her hands shook as her mind put the pieces together. She flipped through the bundles of tens, fifties, and even some hundreds, quickly totaling several thousand dollars. She was going to be sick. Silas, how could you? He'd promised he'd changed!

She sank on the bed, the money quivering in her hands. He must have slipped it in her bag before she left Seattle. Why did he do this? But she knew why. He was trying to take care of her. He never believed her when she told him she didn't need his help.

Silas was going to ruin everything, everything she'd worked so hard for. If the townsfolk found out, if Thomas found out …

Angry tears welled as she clapped her hand over her mouth to stifle a sob. Her shoulders shook as she rocked on the bed, tears streaming down her face.

She took a deep breath, and another, trying to get her emotions under control. When the tears stopped, she wiped her eyes with the backs of her hands and forced the painful thoughts from her mind. Pushing herself off the bed, she moved to the washstand and splashed water on her face. She glanced back. The leather pouch on the bed seemed to accuse her, mock her, tell her she hadn't changed.

"I have changed," she whispered through gritted teeth, fists clenched at her side. "I know I have, even if Silas doesn't." But to prove it meant one thing. Despite the awful dread in her stomach, she knew she had to get the money back to its owner.

She plopped back on the bed. Now what? She should go back to Seattle and confront Silas. Make him give the money back. But how would she explain that to Josh. "Oh, sorry, I've changed my mind" wouldn't be enough after she practically begged him to take her to Reedsville. It was likely his last run. If she went to Seattle now, she wouldn't be able to return to Reedsville until the roads dried out.

She slapped her hand on the bed. Silas, why do you keep ruining my life?

What if she took the money to the marshal's office in the morning? The marshal probably wouldn't believe she'd happened to find the money in her valise. She would have to explain about Silas. There'd be a lot of questions, and she'd delay Josh. Assuming the marshal would even let her go. Silas would most likely end up in jail. While he continued to make her life miserable, he had raised and provided for her for many years. Such as it was. Still, she owed him something. At least the chance to make things right himself.

She shook her head. She wasn't going to let him derail her plans any longer. She was going to see Thomas. Then she'd write Silas and get the money back to its rightful owner.

Somewhat satisfied by her decision, Emily quickly changed into her nightgown and crawled under the covers. She tried to read, but she couldn't seem to concentrate on the words. And sleep wouldn't come, either. Had she made the right decision?

Books by Jennifer Crosswhite

Contemporary Romance

The Inn at Cherry Blossom Lane

Can the summer magic of Lake Michigan bring first loves back together? Or will the secret they discover threaten everything they love?

Historical Romance

The Route Home Series

Be Mine

A woman searching for independence. A man searching for education. Can a simple thank you note turn into something more?

Coming Home

He was why she left. Now she's falling for him. Can a woman who turned her back on her hometown come home to find justice for her brother without falling in love with his best friend?

The Road Home

He is a stagecoach driver just trying to do his job. She is returning to her suitor only to find he has died. When a stack of stolen money shows up in her bag, she thinks the past she has desperately tried to hide has come back to haunt her.

Finally Home

The son of a wealthy banker, Hank Paulson poses as a lumberjack to carve out his own identity. But in a stagecoach robbery gone wrong, he meets Amelia Martin, a a soon-to-be schoolteacher with a vivid imagination, a gift for making things grow, and an obsession with dime novels. As the town is threatened by a past enemy, Hank might just be the hero they all need. Can he help without revealing who he is? And will Amelia love him when she learns the truth?

Books by JL Crosswhite

Romantic Suspense

The Hometown Heroes Series

Promise Me

Cait can't catch a break. What she witnessed could cost her job and her beloved farmhouse. Will Greyson help her or only make things worse?

Protective Custody

She's a key witness in a crime shaking the roots of the town's power brokers. He's protecting a woman he'll risk everything for. Doing the right thing may cost her everything. Including her life.

Flash Point

She's a directionally-challenged architect who stumbled on a crime that could destroy her life's work. He's a firefighter protecting his hometown… and the woman he loves.

Special Assignment

A brain-injured Navy pilot must work with the woman in charge of the program he blames for his injury. As they both grasp to save their careers, will their growing attraction hinder them as they attempt solve the mystery of who's really at fault before someone else dies?

In the Shadow Series

Off the Map

For her, it's a road trip adventure. For him, it's his best shot to win her back. But for the stalker after her, it's revenge.

Out of Range

It's her chance to prove she's good enough. It's his chance to prove he's more than just a fun guy. Is it their time to find love, or is her secret admirer his deadly competition?

Over Her Head

On a church singles' camping trip that no one wants to be on, a weekend away to renew and refresh becomes anything but. A group of friends trying to find their footing do a good deed and get much more than they bargained for.

Made in the USA
Monee, IL
08 January 2023

24784257R00215